2016

W9-DAX-376

AN
EYE FOR
AN EYE

AN EYE FOR AN EYE

L.D. BEYER

OLD STONE MILL
Publishing

This is a work of fiction. The events that unfold within these pages as well as the characters depicted are products of the author's imagination. Any connection to specific people, living or dead, is purely coincidental.

Copyright © 2016 by L.D. Beyer
All rights reserved. No part of this publication may be reproduced or transmitted in any form or by any means, electronic or mechanical, without written permission.

Cover and interior design by Lindsey Andrews

ISBN: 978-0-9963857-2-5

OLD STONE MILL
Publishing
Battle Creek, MI
http://www.ldbeyer.com

For Kaitlyn, Kyle and Matthew

DO NOT TAKE REVENGE, MY DEAR FRIENDS,
BUT LEAVE ROOM FOR GOD'S WRATH,
FOR IT IS WRITTEN: "IT IS MINE TO AVENGE;
I WILL REPAY," SAYS THE LORD

Romans 12:19

PROLOGUE

As he made his way through the cantina, Pablo Guerrero could hear the cries of the crowd, calling for blood. He tugged at the cap, pulling it low over his face. Dressed as he was in a laborer's clothes, and not the designer fashions he'd grown accustomed to, he wasn't recognized.

Stepping out the back door, he threaded his way through the crowd to the side of the ring. He caught the eye of the boy standing in the middle. The boy, no more than thirteen, nodded briefly then held the black rooster up for the judge to inspect. After checking for injuries, the judge held out his hand and the boy handed him the one-inch curved blade. The judge inspected this, first looking then sniffing for the tell-tale signs of poison. Although he didn't detect any, he wiped the blade with a lemon—a long-standing practice to guard against cheating. Satisfied, the judge tied the blade onto the rooster's leg then stepped back.

The boy moved to the center of the ring, thrusting the bird in front of him, letting him see his opponent. Across from him, an old man holding a white rooster did the same. Guerrero watched as his rooster twisted and writhed in the boy's hands, clucking and hissing, anxious to fight. A slight grin crossed his face then disappeared. The judge signaled; the boy and the old man retreated to opposite sides of the pit.

The judge eyed the crowd and called out once more, "Apuestas!" *Bets.*

Guerrero signaled and handed the judge one hundred pesos, nodding in the boy's direction.

"El negro." *The black one.*

The judge nodded, held the hundred pesos in the air and called out to the crowd again. When all bets were placed, he signaled to the boy and the old man. They stepped forward again, thrusting their roosters at each other several times as the noise grew. The spectators, those wagering and those just watching, began to shout and chant, excited by the imminent battle. The judge called out again, and the roosters were placed on the ground. Like prize fighters, they danced around each other for a second or two before the black rooster charged. Wings flapping, the birds pecked at each other, clawing and fighting as they'd been trained.

The black rooster jumped, fluttered a foot above the ground for a moment, and then dove at his opponent. The white rooster turned, swung his right claw out. As the chants and calls rose to a din, the black rooster crumpled to the ground.

For a second, Guerrero didn't move. Then he glanced at the old man holding the white rooster aloft, smiling, triumphant. He looked at his own bird lying in the dirt, the dark stains of blood appearing almost as black as the feathers. Guerrero stared at the old man again; his eyes dark. As he turned to leave, he caught the boy's eyes once more and nodded.

The old man would be found three days later, the dismembered white rooster sitting on top of his brutally beaten body.

CHAPTER ONE

Matthew Richter adjusted his radio wand and headset then glanced back at his team: eight heavily armed men, all wearing helmets and Kevlar vests and dressed in black tactical gear. He held up a thumb and nodded, receiving eight thumbs-up in reply. Opening the back door of the armored truck, he jumped to the ground and ran across the dark alley and then down the steep steps to the basement. When the last agent's head disappeared, a tenth agent, dressed in the uniform of an armored delivery guard, closed the cellar hatch in the sidewalk then climbed back in the rear of the truck. Seconds later, the truck pulled out of the alley. The insertion had taken less than twenty seconds.

Richter switched on his flashlight and made his way through the maze of pipes, past the furnace and up the stairway, his rubber-soled boots silent on the metal steps. At the top, he stopped and glanced back at his men, counting heads. Satisfied, he tapped his knuckles on the door once and it was opened immediately by another agent, dressed in the overalls of a janitor. The janitor led them down the hall to a door on the other side of the building where they stopped.

"We're just getting the audio feed online," the janitor whispered.

Richter nodded then glanced back at his team again, noting the hard eyes behind the tactical goggles, the tight muscles stretched across clenched jaws. They were ready. He switched his radio to the command net and his earbud hissed slightly. He cupped his hand over his ear to catch the conversation.

"...one million dollars. But we have some conditions."

Richter heard a grunt then: "There are always conditions."

There was a pause and then some scraping noises. "It has to be on December Twenty-fifth. He'll be in New York that day."

"How do you know that?"

Richter heard a sigh, then, "Please. We have our sources."

There was another pause, more scraping noises. "It has to be public?"

"Yes."

"That increases the risk significantly."

More scraping, another sigh. "How much?"

"Two million."

Richter heard some whispering, some words in Spanish that he didn't understand.

"Okay. Two million."

"What about the family?"

"They're unimportant. But if they get in the way, so be it."

"Okay. I think we have a deal. But just to be clear...you try to fuck me over, you know I'll hunt you down."

A second later, there was a click, and then Richter heard a much clearer voice in his earbud.

"Green Light! Green Light! Green Light!"

As the janitor opened the door to the alley, Richter switched his radio back to the assault net. Then he stuck his head out, glanced once in each direction before dashing across the alley. Crouched in the darkness behind the dumpster, he did another headcount then held up three fingers and pointed to his right. In a half crouch, three men moved down the alley along the brick wall to the back of the building. He held three fingers up again then pointed to his left. Another three agents moved silently toward the front. Two men remained with him.

When the teams were in position, he turned and nodded to the three men crouched at the back corner of the building. He got a nod in reply. A second later, he got another from the three men in front.

"Go! Go! Go!" he hissed as he jumped up and ran to the side

door, stepping out of the way of the agent on his heels. The man behind stepped up to the door, holding the Stinger ready. A second later there was a bright flash from the rear of the building followed by a loud bang. The agent swung the thirty-five pound steel battering ram at the metal door. It only took two strikes and the door flew open.

"Police!" Richter shouted as he sprang across the threshold, his gun in both hands. He darted to the left. A second agent followed, darting to the right. The third agent came last, a gun in his hand now, the battering ram discarded outside.

There were shouts from the front and the rear of the building. After a quick glance around the room—empty except for shelves of ingredients and supplies for the bakery in front—Richter and the two agents ran to the door that led to the hallway. Two shots rang out as they burst into the hall. Seconds later, he and his team converged on the back room where three men were lying on the floor.

"Clear!" several agents called out simultaneously.

Richter's eyes darted around the smoke-filled room then down to the men lying at his feet. Two dark-skinned men were writhing on the floor, hands cupped over their ears. He noticed blood seeping through one of the men's fingers, the tell-tale signs of a burst eardrum, courtesy of the flash-bang grenade. His eyes moved to the third man, a tall sandy-haired thug with a chiseled jaw—the Russian. The Russian's shirt was stained with blood, with more seeping onto the floor; his face was contorted in pain. One agent secured the Russian's gun while another knelt down to check his wounds. The Russian glared at the agent and then up at Richter. A second later, the hint of a smile crossed his face. Richter felt the hairs on the back of his neck stand up and reached for his web belt.

The Russian was quick. Despite his wounds, he sprang off the floor, knocking one agent over then lunging at another. Richter chopped once with his tactical baton, catching the Russian behind the ear. He crumpled to the ground.

Richter and one of his men exchanged a look. The agent nodded then placed his foot on the Russian's head, holding him down, while another agent cuffed him. Richter glanced around the room, did a quick headcount again. All of his men were accounted for, all uninjured; all except, he noticed, for the pride of the agent who had been knocked over.

Richter pulled the microphone wand closer to his mouth.

"Three tangos secure. Two with minor injuries, one wounded and unconscious. Request an ambulance."

"Copy Blue Lead. Three tangos secure. Ambulance on its way."

———

President David Kendall sat on the couch in the Oval Office across from FBI Director Patrick Monahan and National Security Advisor Brett Watson.

"Early this morning," Monahan began, "we arrested three men in New Jersey on charges of planning to assassinate the chief of operations for the DEA.

"Joe Delia?" The president frowned. "Go on."

"They were only in the planning stages, sir, but the attack was scheduled to take place in New York on Christmas Day."

Monahan handed three photos to the president. Kendall glanced at them briefly before passing them to Watson.

Monahan continued: "Two are Mexican nationals and one is a Russian immigrant. The Mexicans offered two million dollars to the Russian to arrange the killing."

President Kendall scowled; Watson remained tight-lipped as Monahan continued.

"The Mexicans work for a group known as *Los Alacránes*. They're what's left of the *Zacatecas* cartel. After we shut down the Zacatecas operation, there was a power play. Their former turf was split between the remaining members of their security force, who go by the name *Los Alacránes*—The Scorpions—and the Baja cartel."

Monahan passed another photo. "The Russian is a former FSB officer who has ties to the Russian Mafia."

"How did we find out about this?"

"The CIA has been picking up chatter and tipped us off. Working with the NSA, we were able to trace several cell phone calls and eventually identified the two Mexicans. We learned that they had set up a meeting with the Russian. He's someone that we've been watching for some time. We obtained a search warrant and, after recording a conversation where the Mexicans offered money in exchange for the murder, our men arrested them."

"This was in New Jersey?" the president asked.

"Yes, sir. Newark."

"Matthew Richter?"

"He led the team, sir."

The president and Monahan exchanged a glance.

"And the motive?"

"We don't know definitively, sir," Monahan responded. "The two Mexicans aren't talking."

Watson studied the photos for a moment. He laid them on the table then looked up.

"Could this be revenge for Calzada?" he asked.

The president nodded, a scowl on his face. "I was wondering the same thing."

Roberto Calzada, along with the head of the Zacatecas cartel and his key lieutenants, had been arrested two and a half years earlier under a joint operation between Mexican and U.S. forces. Calzada, a former commando with Mexico's Air Force, had deserted five years earlier along with forty of his fellow commandos to form a private army for the Zacatecas cartel. After his arrest, his younger brother, Ramón, a former federal police officer, had quickly stepped in and, with a ruthlessness that would have made the older Calzada proud, taken over the organization. Now, instead of merely protecting, the enforcers had become the cartel.

The older brother, Roberto, along with the eighty-nine other high-ranking cartel members captured under the operation, code-named Project Boston, had eventually been extradited to the U.S. Most, including Roberto, were still awaiting trial.

"It's possible," Monahan responded. "That was my first thought, too." He looked at each of them. "But two cartel hit men arranging for the killing of the head of the DEA?" He hesitated.

"You don't buy it?" the president asked.

Monahan shook his head. "Why didn't they handle the killing themselves? Why outsource it? These guys are assassins. This is what they do."

"Could they be looking to focus blame elsewhere," Watson wondered out loud. "To create some confusion?"

"A diversion?" the president asked.

Watson nodded. "It's possible." He laid the photo on the table again. "If you think about it, since we shut down Project Boston, the DEA has significantly stepped up their focus on cartel operations in the U.S., infiltrating and shutting down cells, disrupting their distribution networks. At the same time, the ATF has put a crimp in weapons smuggling. This has to have hurt them. Maybe not as much as Boston, but with more and more enforcers taking on leadership roles in the cartels, we're dealing with a different enemy now."

"But why use a middleman?" the president asked.

Watson shook his head. "I don't know." He picked up the photo of the two Mexicans. "For years, the cartels have targeted people who have refused to cooperate with them: local and federal officials, chiefs of police, you name it. If they can't be bought, they're killed. The Mayor of Ciudad Juarez has been on their hit list for some time and now lives on our side of the border, in El Paso. But keep in mind, all of their focus has been in Mexico." He tapped the photo. "This might be a subtle way of telling us that if we continue to disrupt their business, they're going to bring their terror campaign here."

The president sat back, thinking. After a moment, he leaned forward and looked from one man to the other. His face was grim.

"We need to understand if this was an isolated incident. Was Calzada seeking revenge for his brother or does this represent a greater threat to us?" He looked at Watson. "We have a National Security Council meeting next week?"

Watson nodded. "Yes, sir."

"This needs to be on the top of the agenda."

Watson nodded again and the president turned to Monahan. "And Joe? I assume he's aware of this."

"He is, sir. He's increased his security. The Secret Service has also put protective details on his wife and kids."

"Good." The president nodded as he stood. "Keep us informed on this one, Pat." He shook hands with both men. "And Pat? Tell Matthew I said, 'Good job.'"

———

Matthew Richter glanced at his watch, checking his speed. A six-twenty pace. *Not bad at four miles,* he thought. He turned the corner, glancing briefly at the hill before him; a steep slope almost two-tenths of a mile long. It had been a couple of months since he'd last run this route, and he wondered for a moment whether he would be able to hold the pace. When he reached the top of the hill ninety seconds later, his breathing was strained, but he recovered quickly. He checked his watch again. *Only lost a few seconds.*

It was two more miles back to his home, a condo nestled in the woods of central New Jersey. After a year in an apartment, he had finally purchased the condo. While he could justify the price—he had paid half of what it had sold for three years earlier—the condo wasn't a commitment by any means. Still unsure of where his life was heading, he had nonetheless exchanged a six-month apartment lease for something a little more—not permanent, he thought, but what? Was there something in the middle?

As he picked up his pace, he thought back to the raid. The fact was, other than the mistake Agent Reardon had made in assuming that the wounded Russian was no longer a threat, the raid had gone smoothly. No one had died. No innocent people had been hurt. Other than Reardon's bruised ego, no one on his team had been hurt either.

He hit the five-mile mark and glanced at his watch, happy to see that his pace was still strong. Even though the uncertainty nagged at him, he enjoyed his job as the SWAT team commander for the Joint Terrorism Task Force. The JTTF was an FBI-led partnership

with the New York City Police Department as well as the departments from surrounding states. The taskforce included representa-
tives from various federal agencies—Homeland Security, ATF, DEA,
Immigration and Customs, as well as his former colleagues from
the Secret Service. They investigated leads related to potential terrorist activity and, since September 11th, the role of the task force
had grown. Intelligence gathering capabilities were significantly
enhanced through the use of paid informants as well as surveillance
and infiltration of the radical groups and terrorist cells operating
in the U.S. At the same time, the task force worked to identify the
funding sources of these operations and to cut off the stream of cash
from sympathizers.

While his investigative partners walked the fine line between
civil liberties and keeping America safe, Richter's SWAT team
focused on enforcement. The team was often called on to execute
search warrants in high-risk situations and, occasionally, to engage
and arrest heavily armed and violent criminals before they could
carry out their plans.

Unlike his old job, where his days could range from the boredom of standing watch to the adrenaline surge and occasional flashes
of panic whenever the president ventured out of the White House,
working for the SWAT team was different. When they weren't on
a call-out, they were either training or briefing. He found he could
lose himself in his work.

After five years in the Secret Service, including eighteen months
on Presidential Protective Detail, he had been on the cusp of leaving
law enforcement altogether. FBI Director Patrick Monahan, newly
named to the job, had made an aggressive pitch to join the Bureau.
More as a courtesy, he had listened as Monahan discussed a variety of
opportunities, all based in Washington.

"You're a good cop, Matthew, and I could really use you here."

At the time, Richter had nodded but said nothing.

"The Bureau has slipped in recent years and, more and more, we
have begun to look and operate like we did during the Hoover era."
Monahan shook his head. "I don't need to tell you that that's some-

thing we can't afford to do. The president has asked me to reorganize the FBI, to reform it."

Richter had waited, certain what was coming next.

"I am creating a new role: Special Assistant to the Director. I want you to help me." Monahan paused. "Then, within the next year, I'm sure a number of positions will open up. While I can't make any guarantees, I'll give you a lot of latitude to choose what you want. So"—Monahan sat back—"what *do* you want? What would you like to do?"

Richter shook his head. "Right now, what I want is to get away from Washington for a while."

Monahan had been persistent, and several months later Richter had finally agreed to join the Bureau but with an agreement that his role—whatever it turned out to be—would not be in Washington. After completing the training course in Quantico, he had requested to train with the elite Hostage Rescue Team. He excelled thanks to the two years spent with the Army Rangers before college. Four months later, when the job as the SWAT team leader for the New York City JTTF opened up, Richter had expressed an interest. He was surprised when, two days later, Monahan told him that the job was his.

Richter hit the button on his watch as he reached the entrance to his condo and slowed his pace to a walk. He wiped his forehead with the back of his hand. The summer sun was hot and he could feel the sweat running down his chest, below his shirt. He glanced at his watch. Not bad, he thought—a six-twenty-one pace overall. He was considering running the New York City Marathon in November and would have to decide soon. Although he had no doubt he could complete it, the training was a large commitment—three months or more—and he was concerned about his job. He was on call twenty-four hours a day and there was no telling when his phone would ring next.

CHAPTER TWO

Pablo Guerrero was known as *El Ocho*. It was a nametag he wore with honor and one he had carried with him ever since he was a boy and had first begun working for the Rodriguez brothers. At the tender age of ten, on his birthday no less, he had been given a task that would prove to be pivotal in his life.

He remembered the day vividly. Alfonso, the younger Rodriguez, had put his arm on Guerrero's shoulder and smiled.

"Today, Pablo, you will become a man."

Alfonso had led him to the back room where *la policía* were waiting. There, Alfonso handed him the gun and nodded. He took the gun and stared at it for a moment and then at the line of men. He stepped up to the first man, knowing what was expected of him. The man was bound and gagged, kneeling on the dirt floor. His eyes were scared, pleading. Guerrero stared into the man's eyes as he brought the gun up, pressing the barrel into his forehead. The man, a federal cop not much older than his brother, began to cry, his sobs choked off by the gag in his mouth. Guerrero pulled the trigger and the man flinched at the metallic click.

Confused, Guerrero pulled the trigger again; still, the gun didn't fire. He turned and stared up at Alfonso, wondering what he had done wrong. Alfonso, smiling, held his hand out and, after hesitating a moment, Guerrero handed him the gun. He watched as Alfonso ejected the empty clip and put a new one in.

"You have courage." Alfonso pulled the slide back, chambering a round. "Maybe, when you're older, you can try again."

"No." Guerrero shook his head, holding his hand out. "I'm ready now."

Alfonso stared at him for a second then smiled and handed him the gun again. Guerrero stepped back to the first man, put the gun to his forehead again, paused to stare into the man's pleading eyes once more, then pulled the trigger. He flinched at the sound, incredibly loud in the small room, and watched as the man crumpled to the floor. He stared at the body for a second, at the lifeless eyes, at the blood that was starting to pool in the dirt below the man's head. Then he stepped up to the next man. Thirty seconds later, eight federal cops lay dead on the dirt floor.

He had earned respect at a young age and had quickly learned that his penchant for violence could get him anything he wanted. At the age of twenty-three he had killed Alfonso Rodriguez—shot him twice in the head as he was dining with friends—and had taken over the Rodriguez drug trafficking operation in the northeastern state of Tamaulipas. Guerrero then quickly and violently eliminated his east coast rivals and consolidated his control over the highly profitable Gulf Coast drug routes. He named the new operation *Las Sangre Negras*. The Black Bloods.

Violence was a useful tool, but one that had to be used carefully. Unfortunately, most of his rivals didn't think that way. He had heard rumors about Ramón's plans before Ramón sent his two *sicarios*—his two hit men—to New York. Information—intelligence—was crucial, and Guerrero's tentacles reached far and wide. He had called Ramón and warned him that it was a foolish idea. But Ramón had always been hardheaded and much too emotional.

"We must teach *los gringos* a lesson!" he had shouted over the phone.

Even though they were competitors, Guerrero had convinced Ramón several years ago that, instead of fighting each other, an agreement to stay out of each other's turf and to occasionally help each other when needed was a smart business decision. *Un alianza de sangre,* they called it. A blood alliance. An apt name, he thought. There certainly was a lot of blood spilled to promote and protect their mutual businesses. But, as he had cautioned Ramón, if they weren't careful, it would be their own blood that was spilled. Besides, there was more than enough business to keep everyone happy, and when they found the occasional barrier in their way, they simply removed it.

Guerrero had no qualms about removing barriers in his way. That was how he looked at it. A government official who refused to be bought? An obstacle easily removed. The Army general who was behind the raid in Monterrey that had resulted in the death of thirty-nine of his men, the arrest of half a dozen others, and the seizure of his warehouse? Another obstacle. These were dealt with in the usual fashion. And civilians? What was the American term? Collateral damage?

But the Americans were different. They were an obstacle—a barrier—that was true. But there were better ways to handle them. What worked in Mexico would not work in *los Estados Unidos*. With the Americans, it was better to be more subtle, to not draw their attention. And in a country that prided itself on safety and being prepared—they had far greater resources and were more sophisticated—a different approach was required. And so he had prepared himself, carefully building a distribution network over the years, finding multiple ways of getting the drugs the Americans craved into their cities. From there, how the drugs got into their hands—and ultimately into their noses, their lungs, and their veins—he left to the local gangs who peddled them in the ghettos, in the dance clubs, and outside the schools. For that matter, he had turned over the local distribution—the wholesale business—to the gangs as well. And when the police or the DEA shut those down, it was easy to find others who were more than willing to take on that role.

Ramón hadn't learned that lesson, or if he had, he ignored it. Guerrero stared out the window at the bright blue sky. Another beautiful day, he thought. But would it last, now that Ramón had succeeded in drawing the attention of los gringos?

CHAPTER THREE

The president swirled his glass, took a sip, and sighed. It was Friday night. Why shouldn't he relax with a glass of wine? Why shouldn't he forget about work for a while? His eyes narrowed. Despite the wine, something was nagging at him. Although the FBI had foiled the planned attack, he couldn't shake the feeling that the game had suddenly changed.

"Dad! You haven't heard a word I said!"

The president turned to his daughter. Michelle was frowning. A junior, her world revolved around soccer, boys, and the trials and tribulations of high school. She believed that despite the fact that he was the president, he was hopelessly lost and out of touch. Or at least, he thought, that's how it appeared. He sighed. So much had changed over the last two and a half years.

"Seriously, Dad! Sometimes, it's like you're in a different world."

He smiled. "I'm sorry, honey. I might be here, but my brain hasn't quite left the office yet."

She shook her head, but he could see the smile.

"What were you saying?"

"I'm going out to a movie."

The president smiled. "What are you going to see?"

"I don't know yet. We'll decide when we get there."

The president took another sip of wine. "Okay. Who's going? The usual gang?"

Michelle shook her head. "No. You don't know him."

The president flinched. He hadn't seen that coming. He looked from his daughter to his wife, Maria, then back again. "Him? What's this? A date?"

"Yes, Dad," Michelle sighed, rolling her eyes. "It's a date. With a boy."

Despite the sarcasm, or maybe because if it, the president smiled. "Do I get to meet him?"

Michelle shook her head. "No way."

She stood abruptly, gave him a kiss on the cheek, waved to her mother, and before he could say another word, she was gone. He shook his head. *School started a few days ago and she already has a date?* The president frowned at his wife.

"Who's this boy? Someone from school? Have you met him?"

Maria laughed. "You sound just like my father when I was her age." She patted his arm. "Relax, Dave. It's just a date. Besides, do you know how intimidating you can be? The poor boy is probably nervous enough knowing there will be half a dozen Secret Service agents in the theater with them."

The president shook his head. "If some boy is going to ask my daughter out, I should at least get a chance to meet him."

Maria smiled, and the president realized that he had missed something.

"She asked him out, didn't she?" he said after a moment.

Maria was still smiling. "Yes, she did. And she didn't want to scare him off by telling him that he had to come here first."

The president held up his hands in surrender. "Okay. Okay." He smiled weakly. "It looks like the two of you had this all worked out beforehand anyway."

"She's almost seventeen," Maria said, holding up her glass. "She's growing up, Dave."

Frowning, the president clinked his glass against hers. "Yeah. Too damn fast."

Maria shook her head again. "You know the girls won't always have you or the Secret Service to protect them."

And that was the problem, Kendall thought. Over the last two and a half years he had learned just how dangerous a place the world could be.

———

As Matthew Richter climbed out of his car, he realized he was nervous. It wasn't the butterflies in his stomach that he always felt before a call-out; the adrenaline-fueled minutes of anxiety before they got the green light, before he and his team burst through the door, guns thrust in front of them, not exactly sure what was waiting on the other side. No, there was no mission tonight, but still, he felt a moment of doubt, a slight uneasiness that told him it had been a while.

He was a few minutes early, he noticed, as he climbed the steps. Inside, he nodded at the grey-haired man in a tux, standing behind a desk.

"Hi. Reservations for two. The last name is Richter."

"Ah, Mr. Richter," the maître d' said with a smile. "Right this way, sir. Your guest is already here."

Surprised, he checked his watch again. He *was* early. He followed the maître d' through the dimly lit dining room past a dozen tables, most occupied. He heard the faint sounds of a piano and, as a waiter passed by with a tray in his hand, he caught the smells of rich French sauces and fresh-baked bread. A sommelier was opening a bottle of wine for a smiling couple, their faces illuminated by the soft light of a candle.

Damn! He thought as he eyed the couple. *Was this what she was expecting?*

He followed the maître d' into another room—smaller, only half a dozen tables—and there was Patty, sitting in front of the fireplace. He smiled, trying to hide his discomfort.

"Hi," he said as he took a seat.

Patty smiled back. "Hi." She waited until the maître d' left then, with a twinkle in her eye, shook her head. "I didn't realize this place was so...fancy."

"The food smells wonderful," he replied, unsure what else to say.

She laughed. "You know, for a brief moment, I thought about meeting you outside and suggesting we go find a pizza parlor or something."

He grinned, relaxing a bit. "I must admit, I was beginning to question your...choice of restaurants."

"You were going to say 'motives,' weren't you?" Her eyes sparkled in the candlelight.

He held up his hands in mock surrender. "I was trying to be diplomatic." She was charming, he thought, as he felt himself beginning to relax. "So, how did you find this place?"

"One of my colleagues mentioned it." She laughed again. "He told me he and his wife come here occasionally and that the food was excellent." She shook her head. "He didn't say a thing about the ambiance!" She shook her head again and sighed. "Men!"

"Did you ask?" He found, somewhat unexpectedly, that he was enjoying himself.

"Okay." She chuckled and shook her head. "I'm guilty." She gestured to the room. "I can see that was a mistake."

He grinned. "So I guess my mistake was letting you pick the restaurant?"

She grinned back. "Are you saying you want to sneak out of here and grab a pizza?"

"Heck no! Not after you made me walk past the kitchen."

The waiter came and they each ordered a glass of wine. They chatted for several minutes and Richter realized that he was glad he'd come. He'd been on only a few dates since Stephanie's death two and a half years ago, each time realizing that he wasn't yet ready. This was the first time, though, where he thought about taking a relationship beyond the occasional cup of coffee or racquetball game. He must have been sending out signals because most women, after one or two dates, stopped calling. That he had never called them either wasn't lost on him.

Patty Curtis was different, though. He never would have guessed that the woman he'd met two months ago in the condominium parking lot was a college professor, teaching political science at Princeton. One Saturday morning when he was strapping his bike to the rack on his car, he noticed her. She was wheeling her own bike out of the building.

"Where are you off to today?" she had called over.

An hour later, he was following her through the trails of a nearby state park. They met twice after that to explore other trails. And even though they had stopped for lunch each time—nothing more than a slice of pizza or a burger at a local diner—this was their first real date.

Richter tasted the wine—a Bordeaux—and found it was better than he had expected. Patty took a sip and he watched as she studied her glass, nodding appreciatively. She set her glass down and leaned forward.

"Okay. So next time it's your job to pick the restaurant."

He grinned. "Oh, so you think there's going to be a next time?"

She smiled confidently. "Oh, I know there will be."

CHAPTER FOUR

Holy shit! DEA agent Juan Ortega thought as he stared down the length of the tunnel. Gun held in front of him, he stood silently for a moment, looking and listening for signs of activity. After a few seconds, he let his hand drop to his side then shook his head in amazement. The tunnel, which seemed to go on forever, was eventually swallowed up by the darkness.

He ran his hand over the six-by-six-inch pressure-treated column, part of the framework that supported the tunnel. And prevented a collapse, he thought. Hopefully. A string of lights, turned off at the moment, stretched along one wall as far as he could see. How long had it taken them to do this? he wondered. Especially without raising any suspicions. He studied the framework and then the walls between the support columns, his night vision goggles revealing scalloped indentations in the packed earth. He frowned until he realized they had been made by a shovel blade. Did they do all of this by hand? he wondered. What the hell did they do with all of the dirt?

He studied the ground below him and the sheets of plywood laid end to end that stretched into the darkness. Through his goggles, he could make out the faint black markings of rubber tires. They were using some kind of cart, he realized. He had heard about tunnels before, but those—at least the majority discovered so far—had been farther west, in Arizona and California. This was the first he had ever seen. The radio interrupted his thoughts.

"Boss. You okay?"

He pulled the wand to his mouth.

"Clear," he whispered into the microphone.

Moments later, he heard movement behind him.

"God damn!" he heard as three more agents joined him. He glanced back, grinning. He saw the looks of amazement on his fellow agents' faces—looks, he knew, that matched his own.

"You got the video camera, Rob?" he whispered.

Behind him, Agent Rob Portman nodded. He held up the camera and flicked it on. Ortega flinched as the red "on" light flashed in his goggles. *Damn!* he thought. They had forgotten about that. Finding what he needed in the pouch on his web belt, he ripped a small piece of tape off the roll and covered the light. He leaned back and studied his handiwork. Satisfied, he looked up at Portman and grinned, then held up the roll of tape.

"Duct tape," he whispered. "Never leave home without it."

"We're really going to do this?" Portman asked nervously.

"Intelligence says that the factory is empty," Ortega responded. Then he smiled mischievously. "No guts, no glory." Before Portman could respond, he turned back to the tunnel. "Camera's on," he said into the microphone.

His radio hissed. "Okay, Juan. We have the feed. Looks good." There was a pause. "Uh, boss? You sure about this?"

Him too? Ortega thought. "Yeah. Let's do this thing."

The radio was silent for a moment. "Okay. Take it nice and slow now."

"Roger," Ortega responded then whispered over his shoulder.

"Stay right behind me, Rob," he instructed.

He took a breath, held his gun in front of him, and began creeping forward. Despite his height—he was five-eight—he had to hunch over periodically to keep from banging his head into the overhead supports.

———

Matthew Richter placed his boots in front of the locker then unzipped his tactical suit. As he slid his arm out of the sleeve, he felt a twinge in his shoulder and cursed under his breath. He hadn't noticed the pain before but, when he thought about it, he realized that he had fallen pretty hard. He grabbed a towel and headed toward the shower.

Camp Smith was located on the Hudson River in Cortland Manor, New York, forty miles north of Manhattan. The FBI, the DEA, and a number of other federal agencies maintained a permanent presence at the National Guard base, and it was a location that Richter's team used for training from time to time.

Moments later, standing in front of the mirror, he thought about Patty. They were supposed to play tennis tonight. He winced as he rubbed his shoulder. As much as he wanted to see her again, they might have to find something else to do. He turned slightly and noticed the reflection. There was an ugly purple bruise extending down the back of his shoulder to just below the shoulder blade. This was why they trained as hard as they did, he thought. Inevitably something went wrong and they had to be able to react instantly to the ever-changing scenario. They had been in the live-fire room—what his team had dubbed the Play Room—which was a large warehouse-like structure that had mockups and flexible building facades that allowed them to run a variety of training scenarios so that when they were called out on a real raid and were facing armed and dangerous terrorists face to face, the odds were stacked in their favor. *Repetition followed by more repetition*, Richter thought, remembering something the HRT trainers liked to say. One day it was an aircraft, the next, a school, the following, a mockup of the UN building.

At the end of the week, he knew, they would be training at the NYPD's fifty-four acre facility at Rodman's Neck in the Bronx. Then, in two weeks, they would travel to the FBI facility at Quantico, Virginia. *Repetition followed by more repetition, in every conceivable scenario*, Richter thought as he rotated his arm. He winced and shook his head. He was going to need some Tylenol.

The training instructor would have to confirm his suspicions, but he knew what had happened. He had been following the point man, an energetic and capable former Marine, as they scrambled through the dark sewer pipes. Right before Agent Reardon, the point man, hit the ladder, he tripped. Richter, who had been following, perhaps a little too closely, had gone over Reardon's heels. If he had to guess, the trainers had placed some heavy obstacle below the water line and the unlucky point man, and in turn Richter, had fallen victim.

He finished packing his gear and glanced over at his men. There were the usual jokes and banter, debates over the Yankees' prospects for the post season, discussions of home-improvement projects, frustrations over a child's illness. They were good guys, Richter thought, with the typical interests, worries, and problems of all middle-class family men.

As he headed for the conference room, he knew it would be an uncomfortable session. There was no room for anything but brutal honesty in the training debriefs, and the reality was that both he and Reardon had made mistakes today. That was okay when the bad guys were paper targets. But when the bad guys were real? Mistakes got people killed.

———

Ortega and his team crept forward silently with no sense of how far they'd gone except for the occasional radio transmission. The DEA plane flying an oval pattern twenty-five thousand feet above their heads was able to pick up their transmitter, even through five meters of packed earth.

"Two-tenths," Ortega heard in his headphones. He clicked his microphone—a signal that he understood—but said nothing. *Two tenths of a mile*, he thought. At a minimum, he knew, the tunnel was three-quarters-of-a-mile long. This they had estimated from the aerial photos and images from Google Earth. But that was assuming, he thought, that the tunnel was a straight line—a direct path from the metal fabricator in Matamoros to the house in Brownsville.

Thirty minutes later, they paused and sat, taking a short break to give their backs a rest. They each selected a column to lean against and sat silently as they continued to study the smugglers' handiwork. Ortega closed his eyes to give them a rest from the eerie green image in his goggles.

Finding the tunnel had taken some time. Thanks to reconnaissance—satellites or airplanes, he wasn't sure—they had been able to track the drug shipments to the factory in Matamoros. But the intelligence analysts were convinced that the drugs were not leaving the factory by truck. Each shipment from the factory had been stopped at the border and thoroughly inspected. Yet the drugs were still making their way north. A tunnel was suspected, and when the analysts noted the unusual traffic patterns at the house in Brownsville, they knew they had found the other end.

The house was put under surveillance and when there was a lull in activity, they had quietly raided the house in the middle of the night. A quick inspection of the vacant house had turned up nothing and they went through a second time more thoroughly. It was then they had noticed the faint scuff marks on the tiled floor— marks that remained despite the strong smell of cleaner and the still damp mops in the laundry room. The trail of scuff marks led from the garage to a closet in the bedroom. Stranger yet, even though the house had been thoroughly cleaned, six empty paint cans, long since dried, had been left on top of a heavy canvas drop cloth on the floor of the closet. Underneath, they'd found the trap door.

Ortega opened his eyes, checked his watch, and nodded to his team. They stood awkwardly and Ortega clicked his microphone twice in quick succession and they began moving forward again. After a while, they came to an opening in the wall. He stepped in and inspected it, noting that it was another airshaft. It seemed there was one every tenth-of-a-mile. *That would make number six*, he thought as he stepped out. A moment later, as they began to move forward again, his radio confirmed his theory.

"Six tenths," he heard in his earbud.

The team continued forward. A minute later, Ortega stopped suddenly and held his fist up. There were scraping noises ahead. The team stood still, silently scanning the tunnel for the source of the noise. *Rats?* Ortega wondered. *God! He hated rats.*

There were two muffled pops and Portman slumped against him, the video camera dropping from his hands.

"We're taking fire!" Ortega hissed into his microphone as he dropped to his knee and frantically searched the tunnel ahead for the shooter. Without looking, he called over his shoulder. "Get him out of here!"

The two agents behind him began to drag Portman back down the tunnel as more muffled pops came from farther ahead. Ortega pointed his gun forward and fired three times, not sure what he was aiming at but hoping to distract the shooter and buy his team some time. A shot slammed into the framework next to his head, and he dropped to his belly.

"We're in the air vent," he heard in his headphones. "Portman's hit! We need to get him out of here!"

Ortega fired three more times, aiming at various spots in the tunnel.

"I'll cover you!" He shouted into his microphone as he fired again.

This time he saw the muzzle flash. He heard the scream behind him as he adjusted his aim. He fired three more times then cursed when he realized his gun was empty. As he reached for a new clip, he saw the tongue of flame and heard the roar of an automatic weapon and realized his mistake.

His last thought was of his wife and newborn son.

CHAPTER FIVE

As he stepped out of the Oval Office, President Kendall spotted Chief of Staff Burt Phillips coming down the hall. His face somber, Phillips nodded toward the door. The president turned and stepped back into his office. Phillips closed the door behind them.

"Four DEA agents were killed an hour ago in a shootout with drug smugglers," Phillips began.

Damn! Kendall cursed under his breath. "Where? What happened?"

"Brownsville, Texas, sir. From what I've been told, they discovered a tunnel under the border and were investigating it when they were ambushed. Apparently the agent in charge made the decision to go in with a small team. He didn't wait for backup." Phillips shook his head. "They were ill-equipped and outgunned."

"A tunnel?"

Phillips nodded. "Yes, sir; from a warehouse or factory on the Mexican side to a house in Brownsville. From what I've been told, it's over three-quarters of a mile long."

"Did we catch any of the smugglers?"

Phillips shook his head. "No. We've notified Mexican authorities. They've promised to investigate, but..." He shrugged.

"Damn!" the president cursed again. "I'll need their names and their service records." He paused, thinking. "And get me some information on their families." He paused again as he thought of the phone calls he would have to make. "I think someone needs to take a look at DEA procedures," he added.

Phillips nodded, making a note.

The president shook his head. The violence along the border—at first isolated and sporadic—had been growing. It was time, he realized, to review their approach to the growing drug problem.

———

A hush came over the room and several members of the National Security Council wore strained looks.

"What does that mean?" the president asked. "The government could collapse?"

Watson nodded. "Analysis by both the CIA and the Pentagon suggests that, left unchecked, the cartels will eventually have the capacity—the money, the firepower, and effective control over major cities and infrastructure—to overtake the Mexican government." He paused, his face grim. "Both think that this could happen within the next five years."

"You're talking about a coup d'état?"

"Yes, sir," Watson responded then paused as a pained look came over his face. He reached for a glass of water. "Excuse me," he said seconds later when he put the glass down. "They've been infiltrating the military for years. We don't know how many of their officers are on the cartel payroll. The CIA is currently doing an analysis of the top brass, but the initial guess is five percent." Watson grimaced and took another sip of water. "That's a conservative guess," he added.

"They already have their tentacles into the police," Burt Phillips stated.

Watson nodded. "They do, both the federal police and some of the state and local forces as well. President Magaña has fired whole departments—the Ciudad Juarez force, the city of Monterrey, whole divisions of the federal police—and replaced them with the military."

"Which may not be any better," the president concluded. He was silent as he considered the implications. "Could this lead to a civil war?"

"It's possible, sir," Watson responded. "But I don't think the cartels would let that happen. It all depends on how much of the military leadership is in their pocket." He grimaced again. "I would think they would wait until they had enough to force a bloodless coup."

The president glanced around the room. "Any thoughts?"

"I think Brett's right, sir," Burt Phillips said. "If the country is plunged into a civil war, it's only a matter of time before the international community reacts and peacekeepers are sent in. They don't want that. Further, a civil war would also disrupt their drug operations." He paused. "They'll wait until they have control of the military."

The president nodded and studied the faces around him. Most were grim, Watson's especially so. Kendall paused as he studied his National Security Advisor. There was something else. He looked pale, the president thought and made a note to speak to him later. He turned back to the room.

"I don't need to tell you that if this were to happen, it would present a grave risk to our national security."

Heads nodded and there were murmurs of assent.

The president stood, then leaned forward and rapped his knuckles on the table. The sound was loud in the silent room.

"I need to know what our options are."

———

Several minutes later, the president waved Burt Phillips into the Oval Office. Phillips, the former CEO of Tandem Capital, a consulting company he had cofounded after serving six years as Deputy Secretary of Defense, was a short man, standing just five-foot-seven. Despite his height, he had the wiry body of an athlete and an intensity and directness that commanded respect. Most who met him assumed, incorrectly, that he had served in the military.

"So in addition to North Korea and Iran," Kendall said as he sat, "we now have to worry about an unstable government right next door?"

Phillips nodded, scowling. "This seems to have escalated pretty quickly." He joined his boss on the couch.

The president was silent for a moment. "What's going on with Brett? He seemed a little off his game today."

Phillips frowned. "I just spoke to him. He's not feeling well. He's going home."

The president arched his eyebrows. The White House had a fully equipped medical facility.

"He wants to see his own doctor," Phillips responded. He had been Chief of Staff for almost two years and, in that time, had come to understand the president well enough that he often knew what he was thinking.

The president nodded then sat back. Hopefully everything was okay, he thought. And hopefully Watson wouldn't be out for long. There was too much going on in the world right now, and he needed the man's guidance.

Phillips leaned forward. "We've been working on a counter drug policy," he said, interrupting Kendall's thoughts.

The president looked up.

"Including a military option," Phillips continued.

The president nodded slowly as Phillips went on to explain that Brett Watson had been working with the DEA and the CIA on a more aggressive approach to compliment the new treatment and education programs proposed by the Drug Czar. President Kendall frowned. In his mind, he could still see the three flag-draped coffins being unloaded from the plane two years before in Dover, Delaware. It was just days later, as the three Navy SEALs were buried, that he had quietly suspended the Project Boston operation. While the operation had shown early success, it had been too narrowly focused on dismantling the cartels without any thought given to what would happen in the aftermath. When the cartels began to fight back, with new players rushing to fill the void, it became clear that without addressing the demand in the U.S. and without addressing the systemic failures of the Mexican government, the operation was destined to fail.

He sighed. One thought continued to nag at him. The game had changed. Now, with the looming collapse of the Mexican government, he could no longer sit back and watch as the situation continued to deteriorate. He looked up at Phillips and nodded.

"Okay. Show me what you have," he said. "The sooner, the better."

CHAPTER SIX

Matthew Richter turned at the sound of the voice behind him and saw Special Agent Mark Crawford coming down the hall. Crawford, the Commander of the JTTF, was a career FBI agent. He wore a troubled look, which wasn't surprising, given that the man rarely smiled, not in the office anyway. Despite that, he was a diplomat and deftly navigated the often tense relationship between the arrogant and overbearing Bureau and the ultra-territorial NYPD.

"You hear about the DEA agents?" Crawford asked.

Richter shook his head. "No."

"Four agents were killed today," Crawford explained, giving Richter the details of the raid.

Richter grimaced. Although he didn't recognize any of the names, he had a number of friends in the DEA. They were all good people. While the FBI, with its vast resources, technical expertise, and regimented training, was often seen as arrogant—a reputation not undeserved given the air of superiority the Bureau cultivated within its ranks—the DEA had a reputation for operating more like street cops. They were far less bureaucratic and much more nimble than the FBI, where operations and raids were, if not centrally planned, centrally scrutinized. Whereas DEA agents were given a lot of latitude, FBI agents often had to wait for a final go-no-go decision from headquarters.

In the last two years the cultural differences had become painfully evident and, on the occasion when FBI bureaucracy frustrated him, Richter wondered what it would be like to work for the DEA. Still, he knew, as he thought about the four dead agents, a cautious bureaucracy wasn't always bad.

As if reading his mind, Crawford put his hand on Richter's shoulder. "The number one job of any leader is to make sure his people make it home safe when the day is done."

Crawford held Richter's gaze until Richter nodded. It was something he thought about every day.

———

Two minutes later, Richter strode into the briefing room. Located in the FBI field office in lower Manhattan, the space was set up like a classroom with rows of tables facing the front. The SWAT team, Richter noted, was already there. He said hello to several of his men, Crawford's words still in his head. A moment later, Crawford himself stepped into the room and made his way to the front. Richter took a seat, and the room quieted as Crawford picked up a remote control.

"I want to brief you on Operation Minuteman." He clicked the remote and a picture of a stern-faced man with a military crew cut appeared on the screen. "This is Gerry Nichols. He's the leader of New Jersey Free Nation, a militia organization operating in northwestern New Jersey, near the town of Sussex. The group has been relatively quiet for the past ten years, mostly attending gun shows, making the occasional ham radio broadcast, and running around the woods in camouflage playing weekend warrior."

There were a few chuckles from Richter's team.

"Nichols took over as the head of this group two years ago and is referred to as 'the Major.' We've seen an increase in activity since then in terms of recruitment, training, the purchase of arms, and more recently, social media. In the past, gun shows were the primary venue for recruiting new members. However, Nichols has leveraged social media—Twitter, Facebook, and blogs—quite successfully. Most of their postings are the typical anti-government, conspiracy theory stuff we've seen before. But," Crawford paused for a second, "the difference is that Nichols has succeeded in not only increasing membership but in soliciting donations from other like-minded people; including people who, apparently, would rather provide financial support than join an armed resistance."

Crawford hit the button and a new slide appeared. The mug shot showed a long-haired man with angry eyes. "This is Dwight Nichols, Gerry's younger brother. He has been—excuse me, make that had been—in and out of jail a number of times for weapons-related charges, assaulting a police officer, and possession of stolen goods. Three years ago, he was killed by a New Jersey State Trooper after threatening the officer with a gun."

Damn, Richter thought as he rubbed his shoulder absentmindedly. That Nichols was a heavily-armed and paranoid right-wing militia leader was bad enough. The fact that he might be holding a grudge made it worse.

Crawford changed slides again, this time to a grinning, ginger-haired man wearing a heavy wool sweater. "This is Terry Fogel. In the late eighties and early nineties, he was active with the Provisional IRA in Belfast. He was suspected of numerous crimes, including the execution-style killing of two British soldiers and the bombing of a police station in Derry." Crawford paused, his face grim. "But, he was never charged in either crime. In 1998, after the signing of the Good Friday Agreement, he fled Ireland for the Middle East where he disappeared for a while. Then, as far as we can tell, he came to the U.S. five years ago, maybe more."

Richter shook his head, fearing where this was going. The next slide showed the two men together, both dressed in camouflage and toting assault weapons.

"Fogel has attended various Free Nation meetings over the last three years, serving, we believe, as a training instructor. In the past month, though, he and Nichols have met four times." Crawford paused. "We've had an informant inside the group for the past five months. He tells us that they're in the early stages of planning an attack."

Richter frowned. He began to think through what was now

looking like an eventual call-out. A direct assault on the camp might not be the best option, he thought, at least not while there were sixty or seventy people running around the woods with assault rifles and semi-automatic weapons. Better to apprehend Nichols alone, somewhere away from the camp. Same with Fogel. If they could plan it right, they might be able to arrange a simultaneous raid of the camp, preferably on a day when there was little or no activity, to seize the weapons. But, he thought, they would also have to identify the command structure and potentially arrest a few of the key lieutenants at the same time to lop off the head. That would be the ideal scenario, he knew. But would they have that option?

There were some murmurs in the room. Richter leaned forward.

"Have we identified the potential targets?" he asked.

Crawford nodded and a hush fell over the room.

"According to our informant, One Police Plaza," he paused, his eyes narrowing, "and this building."

CHAPTER SEVEN

As the helicopter lifted off the ground, Pablo Guerrero smiled at his daughter.

"Are you excited, *mi amor?*"

"*Sí, Papá.* I can't wait to swim in the ocean."

Carolina's eyes were wide with excitement. Eight years old and she already had her mother's beauty. Her regal features, her fine, dark hair, her green eyes, and her olive skin betrayed the traces of European blood in her veins. Guerrero reached out and took her hand.

"You will swim with me, Papá?"

"Yes." He winked. "Of course."

Carolina held his gaze for a moment, long enough to let him know she would hold him to his promise. Then she turned and watched as the ground fell away below them. He glanced over at his wife as she inserted a disk into the DVD player. She was in the process of putting her earphones on when she caught his eye.

"Two hours?"

"Sí. Two hours." He smiled. "We'll be there in time for lunch."

She returned his smile then sat back and turned to the flat panel monitor on the wall of the cabin. He could see that she was happy. His wife enjoyed the finer things in life: the arts, shopping, dining. However, his restrictions over the last several years had been a point of contention. But he knew that the good often came with the bad in life, especially in his chosen profession. Along with the wealth and the notoriety came the restrictions. Safety was never far from his mind and that made it more difficult to travel these days.

While they had everything they needed inside their hacienda— servants, a pool, horses, tennis—she had complained of feeling isolated, confined. They had not been to Europe or South America in years. He had done what he could to make her happy but there were periods where she became moody, melancholy.

He rubbed his fingers along the rich leather of the armrest. This was his second trip in the helicopter, and he was still amazed at how smooth and quiet the ride was. The passenger compartment of the Sikorsky, configured for five, was spacious. Even with Alberto, his chief lieutenant, there was ample room. This was his latest toy; one, so far, that he had managed to hide from the authorities. Or at least those that mattered, he thought.

He looked back at his wife, noticing the faint smile on her face. The smile, he knew, was not because of the *telenovela*—some mindless nonsense she insisted on watching—but due to the anticipation of five days at the beach. And while this would make his wife happy, the truth was, he hadn't bought the helicopter for her.

He squeezed his daughter's hand. She turned and leaned into him, nestling below his arm. When she looked up at him, her eyes were filled with excitement. The smile on her face said it all.

———

"Are we still going swimming, Papá?"

"We can swim after our ride," Guerrero said as he helped his daughter climb onto the horse.

"Papá!" Carolina said with feigned exasperation. She rolled her eyes but smiled nonetheless.

"A ride first, to check on the ranch." Guerrero smiled back. "It's been a while since we were here last."

He waited while the stable hand adjusted the straps on his daughter's saddle. Then, when the worker nodded and stepped out of the way, he turned to Carolina again.

"Listo?" *Ready?*

Carolina wore a mischievous smile. "Sí, Papá."

A minute later, the two riders led their horses on a trot over the rough terrain, the soft breeze from the ocean at their backs. They followed the path that wound through the cactus and sagebrush, past the gullies and washouts. They rode side by side. After a few minutes, they found themselves at the base of a hill. Still trotting, Guerrero looked over at his daughter. She handled her horse, a small Arabian, well. The Arabian was larger than the horse she had back at the hacienda. But was Carolina big enough? he wondered. He glanced ahead as the trail narrowed to a single track and then wound its way up the steep hillside through a series of switchbacks. It was time to see what she could do.

He smiled. "You lead," he said.

Carolina smiled back, gently snapped her reins and pulled ahead. As Guerrero followed, he marveled at how deftly she handled the horse with only an occasional flick of the reins. For the most part, she let the horse follow the path on its own. The small Arabian, he could see, knew that she was in charge, accepted it, and rider and horse had become one. His chest swelled with pride. Yes, she was almost big enough.

———

It was dark as Guerrero strolled along the bluff overlooking the ocean. Walking by himself, he passed the few cows that were still out, lying on the ground, their legs tucked below them. He followed the rough split-rail fence over the uneven ground to the gate. Beyond was the path that led down to the ocean. Resting his hands on the gate, he stared out over the sea. There were no stars or moon tonight—the clouds were rolling in—just the path, the beach, and then a vast black expanse. As he stared out into the blackness, he considered the news.

Earlier, when he and Carolina had returned from their ride, he had found Alberto waiting for him. Now, while Carolina was fast asleep and her mother was ensconced in front of a movie, he was able to consider the implications. The loss of the tunnel was a setback. More important than the loss, though, was the lesson. It may have been nothing more than bad luck. Los gringos—the DEA—had become much more active along the border, with increased surveillance and undercover operations. The local police in Texas had become more wary too. But, as much as he could, he avoided what Ramón faced in Arizona and California by not letting the bloodshed spill across the border. Unfortunately, some of his people, it seemed, had been caught by surprise and had reacted. He would deal with them, but the implications of their actions were clear. The stakes had been raised again, and now he had to wait to see how the Americans would respond.

It had become a game of cat and mouse, a lesson he had learned the hard way. He had built a system of distribution routes to the U.S., over land—and under it too—as well as across the water. This gave him backups should any one be compromised. The problem was, this was the third tunnel he had lost in the last two years.

The Americans were becoming a nuisance, he thought as he stared out at the ocean. He would have to figure out how best to respond.

CHAPTER EIGHT

Brett Watson felt a churning in his stomach and quickly turned and hurried to the restroom. He'd just made it into the stall when he threw up. *Jesus!* he thought. What the hell was wrong with him? A moment later, he stepped out of the stall, noting, thankfully, that the restroom was empty. He washed his face in the sink and rinsed out his mouth as best he could. He looked up at the mirror. His face was pale and his eyes were glassy. Maybe he had the flu, he thought. But that didn't make sense. How could the doctor have missed that? He put the back of his hand to his forehead. He didn't have a fever— or at least he didn't think so.

He stepped back from the sink and felt the burning pain in his stomach. He looked at his watch and swore. He was late. He popped two more antacid tablets into his mouth then grabbed his binder and rushed out of the restroom. *Must be an ulcer*, he concluded. Lord knows, this place did that to a person.

———

The men gathered around the plotting table and stared down at the large four-foot by six-foot aerial photo, an image obtained from Google Earth. Agent Beth Callaway tapped the photo, drawing everyone's attention.

"This was an old hunting camp. It's spread out over four hundred and sixty acres. The camp is bordered by state land on the western side and farmland and undeveloped private property to the north and south." She traced her finger along a two-lane road on the eastern border. "This is Manutonk Reservoir Road." Her finger stopped at a break in the trees, and she pointed to a dirt road that snaked into the forest. "This is the only access road."

Richter leaned in. He saw what appeared to be two columns on either side of the access road with a bar stretching across. Agent Callaway noted his interest.

"That's a gate—a steel, cantilevered slide gate like you might see at the service entrances and private terminals of an airport or"— Callaway looked up—"businesses located in the bad part of town." She traced her finger along the perimeter. "It's difficult to see here, but the entire property is surrounded by a chain link fence topped with razor wire."

She pulled her hand away. "As you can see, the camp is heavily forested, which should work to your advantage." She traced her finger along the access road to a fork then continued down the path that curved south. The road led to an irregular-shaped clearing, curved around it, headed west for a quarter of a mile, then curved north. She tapped the clearing.

"This is the parade ground. It's used for training and also serves as a firing range." Her finger continued along the road to a large structure hidden below the trees.

"This is the main lodge which serves as mess hall as well as a meeting and training facility." Her finger went back to the dirt road and followed it north. She stopped and tapped her finger again.

Richter spotted the twenty-plus small structures hidden amongst the trees.

"These are the bunkhouses," she said. "According to our informant, each can accommodate two to three men." She looked up at the serious faces around her. "Apparently, they prefer sleeping in these versus the barracks." Her finger traced a line over to a larger structure at the end of the dirt road. "The informant indicated that the barracks are only used when the bunkhouses are full, which apparently is not too often. Many members from the surrounding communities choose to sleep at home."

Richter studied the photo. Spread out over a quarter mile, each bunkhouse, he figured, was no more than twelve feet by twelve feet.

"They look rustic," he noted out loud.

"They are," Callaway responded. "Not much room for more than two or three cots or a couple of bunk beds." She tapped another structure close to the barracks. "This is the latrine and shower facility."

Callaway was silent a moment, letting the men study the map. Richter's eyes digested the layout as he considered their options. They would probably come in from the western side where the state forest would conceal their approach. Breaching the fence would be easy. The critical question was where to hit them. The bunkhouses were the obvious choice; while the would-be soldiers were sleeping. He would need more information on the structures: the type of doors, whether there were windows, the materials used in construction. But still, it would be risky, he thought as he counted, finding twenty-six. They were spread out over a large distance. That would require a large assault team, three or more men for each building. A large team would require a lot of coordination and, the larger the team, the greater the chances that someone would spot them. *Not undoable*, he thought, *but not ideal*.

He bent closer, staring at the photo.

"What's this?" he asked.

Callaway turned and frowned. "Dog pen. According to our informant, they have ten German Shepherds, which serve both as security and as a military canine unit. When they leave the compound, when no one's there, the dogs are let out to roam."

"And when the men are there?"

"They're usually kenneled at night."

"Usually?"

Callaway shrugged and Richter glanced back to the photo. The pen was in the middle of the bunkhouses. Unless they could somehow neutralize the dogs, without drawing any attention, attacking the bunkhouses was not an option.

He glanced at the lodge. That would allow a much smaller assault team, but presented different risks. No conditions were ever

ideal, he knew, but his goal was to ensure that the raid was successful, with minimal loss of life. In a perfect world, the men would
surrender peacefully. But the world was far from perfect. Based upon
the propaganda he had read, the surveillance photos of their training, and the profiles of the more vocal and influential members, it
was highly likely that these men would resist. Richter glanced up
at his men, studying each of their faces one by one. Knowing there
would be a fight, he felt the weight of his responsibility to ensure
that each of them made it home safe when the firefight was over.

———

"Do we believe the threat is real?" the president asked.

"Director Monahan and his folks think so," Watson responded.
He explained what the FBI knew about the New Jersey Free Nation.
"They have been amassing arms—assault weapons—and they have
been training with a known Irish terrorist." He paused, his face
a grimace. "Their informant has shared enough details about the
planned attacks that the FBI has no reason to doubt that they're
serious."

The president stood and began pacing. After a moment, he
stopped and leaned forward, his hands on the back of the couch.

"Not on my watch, Brett." His eyes were hard; every word was
measured.

Watson nodded but said nothing.

The president came around the couch. "When are we planning
to hit them?"

"Monahan's team is working through the details now." Watson
winced. "Probably within a week."

The president studied his National Security Advisor for a moment, noting the bead of perspiration on his forehead. "Brett, are
you okay?"

Watson nodded. "I'm fine."

The president sat down next to him. "Are you sure?"

Watson nodded again then suddenly jumped up. "Excuse me,
sir," he blurted as he rushed out of the room.

CHAPTER NINE

It was almost 9:00 p.m. when Matthew Richter pulled into the space in front of his condo. It had been a long week as his team reviewed intelligence on the New Jersey Free Nation and worked through possible approaches to the raid. They had run over a dozen simulations in the forests and fields of Camp Smith. He was beat.

As he climbed out of his car, he hesitated as he tried to remember if there was any food left in the fridge. He wasn't sure if he had finished the rest of the rotisserie chicken. He stood by the car for a few seconds then closed the door. He had no desire to go to the store. There were several cans of soup in the cabinet. So, chicken or soup and a beer, he thought as he walked up the concrete pathway to his door. Then he remembered the four slices of pizza in the plastic bag in the freezer. *Better yet*, he thought. The Yankees were playing that evening, he remembered, and although the game would have started already, he had recorded it. He yawned as he reached for his door. *Who was he kidding?* he thought. He would be asleep on the couch before the seventh inning stretch.

As he pulled the screen door open, he saw the note taped to his door.

Are you up for a ride tomorrow?
Call me.
Patty

He flexed his shoulder—no pain today—and smiled. Yes, he was definitely up for a ride.

———

"You're an adrenaline junkie, you know that?"

"So I've been told," Richter called over his shoulder. He leaned his bike against a tree and slipped off his backpack. He pulled out a water bottle and joined Patty on the rock. Despite the temperature—a chilly fifty-nine degrees—the sun felt warm. They both sat and listened to the rustle of the wind in the trees. Although it wasn't even October yet, the leaves of several trees already showed hints of yellow. *So much for an Indian summer*, he thought.

"I don't know how you do it," she finally said.

"What's that?" he asked with a smile.

"You spend the week kicking in doors and fighting bad guys, and on the weekends, you're doing something active—riding, racquetball. I see you running all of the time. Do you ever sit still?"

He grinned. "I'm sitting still now."

"You know what I mean," she responded.

He wiped the mud off his shin before he looked up. "Yeah, I know what you mean. Partly it's the challenge, you know? Can I do it? Can I finish? Can I win?"

She waited a moment. "And the other part?"

He stretched as he thought about the answer. There were many reasons. For a while, a few years back, it was his way of coping with the tailspin his life had been in, his way of dealing with loss. And now? The truth was, he wasn't sure. He had a great job. He enjoyed the people he worked with. While risky, he thrived on the challenge. There was something that resonated with him—something just about it, a sense of good versus bad, of right versus wrong. Still, he couldn't shake the feeling that his life was on hold, that he was in a rut, unsure which direction he was heading.

"I don't know," he finally responded. "Fighting middle age, I guess."

She laughed. "Yeah. Right. What are you? Thirty?"

"Thirty-two," he answered sheepishly.

They heard voices through the trees and both turned to watch as a group of bikers rode into the trailhead. As the riders dismounted, their banter and laughter carried across the parking area.

"What about you?" he asked. "I imagine you're not like most other college professors."

"No. I guess I'm not." She chuckled. "I'm not really sure how I ended up in front of a classroom. I taught some classes when I was in grad school and found that I enjoyed it. I had done two internships in Washington, and after I graduated, I worked as an aide for Senator Tanner. Then one day, I was invited to Princeton to speak at a seminar. One thing led to another and I found myself in front of a classroom again. It was only supposed to be for one semester." She chuckled again. "Next thing I know, two years have gone by and now I'm not sure I want to leave."

They watched, silent for a moment, as the group across the lot prepared to leave.

She turned back to him and smiled. "I know they say those who can't do, teach. But I'm not hiding behind the ivy-covered walls, stuck in academic discussions and theory all day. We do some interesting research projects. At least I think they're interesting," she added with a grin. "I also do some consulting work. I've done a couple of projects—one in Trenton and one in Washington—both for the challenge and to keep my options open."

He hid his surprise. It was amazing how similar their lives seemed to be, he thought. Could they both be going through some sort of midlife crisis? That didn't make sense. She seemed happy; always smiling, cheerful. But what about him? Was he happy?

He watched as the other riders climbed into their cars. Seconds later, after two or three horn toots were exchanged, the cars drove away. Well, he thought, he wasn't *unhappy*, if that meant anything. More like unsure. He was still trying to figure out what was next for him; where his life was going. But did there always have to be a plan; a goal? Or was it okay to coast for a while? He shook his head. *Too much introspection for one day*, he thought. He turned back to Patty.

"So there's more to the college professor than meets the eye?" he asked.

"Just like there's more to the federal agent than his gun and his badge," she answered immediately.

They shared a laugh and he realized once again how much he enjoyed her company. The discussion left him wanting to know more about her.

"Are you free this evening?" he asked abruptly.

She smiled. "I might be. What do you have in mind?"

"I thought dinner would be nice."

She laughed. "On one condition."

He arched his eyebrows.

"You pick the restaurant this time."

———

Richter listened to the distant sounds of the clock coming from another room. Key-wound, driven by gears and springs, it was an antique in a digital world. Unfamiliar, but not unpleasant, he found the soft ticking of the pendulum reassuring. He stared at the sliver of light on the ceiling, the gap in the curtains allowing a faint shaft in from the streetlight below. A car drove by and then it was silent.

Patty stirred, rolled over, and nestled against him. Her head settled on his shoulder, she draped her arm across his chest. He could smell her hair, the soft scents of her perfume. Her body felt warm next to his. He listened to her breathing, slow and rhythmic—in tune with the clock—as she settled back to sleep.

He thought back to what had led him here, to her bed. Dinner then a stroll along the path behind the condo. The stars bright in the chilly night sky. Another glass of wine. Then a desire to be close; a sharing, slow and gentle.

But it was more than an evening, he knew. For him it had been a journey. Ever since Stephanie, he had felt empty. He hadn't wanted anyone else. And then he met Patty.

"You're awake?"

He turned. Even in the darkness, he could see her smile.

"For a while," he said.

"Everything okay?" she asked, suddenly concerned.

"More than okay," he responded. He was silent for a moment. "I was just thinking…it's been a long time."

She shifted, rolling over so she could see him. "Care to tell me about it?"

He was quiet for a few seconds, unsure where to begin. "You probably didn't know, but before I moved here, I was a Secret Service agent." He paused, searching for her reaction. "I used to guard the president."

She feigned surprise then grinned. "Of course I knew," she said. "Your picture was in every paper. You were on the news."

"So that's why you like me?" he teased.

"Actually," she said, suddenly serious. "What you do, the gun you carry, the world you live in…that stuff scares me." She tapped his chest with two fingers. "It's what's in here that I'm attracted to."

"But that other stuff—my job, my gun—it's part of who I am."

"I know that now," she said. She kissed him, then traced her fingers across his chest. "So why so long?"

He told her about Stephanie. Never far from his mind, he felt the emotions just below the surface as the memories came flooding back. *Save the president or save his lover?* Two years ago, as a Secret Service agent on the president's security detail, he had faced the most difficult choice of his life, knowing that by saving the former, the latter would die. Even today, he still wasn't quite sure why he and the president had managed to survive while everyone else, including Stephanie, had been killed. In the aftermath, he had fled Washington and the agency that had failed him.

"I've been kind of coasting along for the last two years, not quite sure where I was going or what I wanted."

"Until you met me?" she asked with a grin.

"Until I met you," he said with a smile. He kissed her. "Until I met you."

He sighed as she put her head back on his chest. Some things just felt right. They lay like that for a while and after some time he noticed the sound of the clock again. He heard her breathing, slow and rhythmic. After a while, he noticed that his own breaths seemed to match hers. They were breathing together.

Some time passed and he thought she might have fallen back asleep, but then she rubbed her hand across his chest slowly.

"It's been a long time for me too," she whispered.

CHAPTER TEN

"What do you think?" the president asked as they stepped into the Oval Office.

Burt Phillips was silent for a moment as he considered the question.

"I think the difference this time," Phillips responded, "is we would be taking a more holistic approach."

The president sat back on the couch. They had just left a briefing on the proposed change in the war on drugs. Phillips was right, he thought. Anti-drug policy in the past had been inconsistent and piecemeal. Too much emphasis had been placed on attacking the supply, going after the drug dealers here, in the U.S., and trying to dismantle the drug cartels in Mexico and Colombia. Scarce resources had been allocated to reducing demand and those that had been made available had been spent creating a criminal justice system that took a harsh, zero-tolerance approach. But more police and stiffer penalties had only succeeded in filling the jails, disproportionately so with minorities and African Americans.

This was the first time, in his memory anyway, that equal emphasis had been placed on treatment and prevention. What did the studies say? Treatment and prevention were what? Something like twenty times more effective at reducing drug usage than the traditional supply-side focus? And apparently that wasn't new news. But treating drug addiction as a disease had never been the politically expedient answer. That took time and a community-oriented approach, and progress—measured one recovered addict at a time—was slow. It had always been far easier to demonstrate that the government was making progress through a show of force, a *get tough* approach which meant lots of cops, lots of soldiers, and lots of guns.

Not that those weren't necessary too, the president thought with a sigh.

"Do you think we can get the money from Congress?" he asked.

"It will take some selling," Phillips said then smiled, "but I think you might be able to sweet talk it out of them, sir."

Kendall smiled briefly, then his face clouded. "It's not just about the drugs. If the intelligence estimates are right, we could have an even bigger problem on our hands."

Phillips nodded somberly. "I think that's how you sell it, sir. We can't do one without the other."

The president nodded slowly. Phillips was right again. If the drug cartels were on the verge of overthrowing the Mexican government, the U.S. would have no choice but to intervene. National security and the stability of the Americas were at stake, as were the lives of one hundred and twenty-five million people living south of the Rio Grande. But to go after the narco-traffickers—to attempt to dismantle the cartels, as Mexico had been trying to do for years—without addressing demand in the U.S. was foolhardy. And turning a blind eye to the systemic corruption in Mexico's military and police forces, failing to overhaul its weak criminal justice system, and without addressing the foundation of its economy—which despite recent growth, left a large portion of the population still struggling day to day, stuck in poverty—was just as foolhardy. The insatiable and growing demand for drugs in the U.S. was too profitable to ignore and, if the current drug cartels were eliminated completely, it wouldn't be long before other criminal elements stepped in and filled the vacuum.

They exchanged a glance. "Set up some time with Barbara Tanner," the president said. Tanner was the chairman of the Senate Appropriations Committee. Kendall would have to consider the best approach—Tanner could be a challenge at times—but, one way or another, he would have to find a way to get the funds needed. The stakes were too high.

Phillips nodded and made a note.

"How's Brett?" the president asked. Watson had been out sick for the past week.

Phillips frowned. "He's having a series of tests done." He paused then shook his head. "But it doesn't look good."

Kendall let out a breath. "I'll call him this evening."

———

Brett Watson couldn't shake the uneasy feeling as he waited in the examination room. It wasn't the pain in his stomach—a pain he could no longer ignore. It wasn't the queasy feeling that he'd had for the last ten days, the nausea that made him throw up everything he ate.

He looked up at the mirror and didn't recognize the face staring back at him. With sunken cheeks and pale skin, the gaunt look reminded him of the last image of his grandfather, right before he died. He rubbed the stubble on his chin. He hadn't had the energy to shave that morning. As he pulled his hand away, he watched in the mirror as the material of his shirt sleeve swung loosely. Another image popped into his mind: he was eleven years old and his mother was insisting that he wear his big brother's hand-me-downs. He shook his head. His shirts and his pants suddenly seemed to overwhelm his diminishing frame.

He turned at the noise as the door opened. The doctor stepped into the room. He closed the door, turned slowly, then Brett caught his eyes. There was a moment of silence—a split second that said more than the doctor ever could with words. Then the doctor slowly shook his head, and Brett suddenly felt like he was falling.

———

President Kendall stood at the window looking out over the South Lawn of the White House. Although the sun had set an hour earlier, the grounds were illuminated below the soft glow of lights. The marigolds were still vibrant—their yellows, purples, and reds foreshadowing what would soon happen to the trees around them. It was starting already, he noted—a few trees had already begun to turn. With the exception of the marigolds, most of the summer plantings had already been trimmed back.

Two uniformed Secret Service officers stepped into view, a routine patrol, he knew. Despite the serenity of the scene before him, the two officers reminded him that the elaborate security apparatus that protected the White House was ever vigilant. Over the years, the U.S. had become a target for violent extremism and for terrorists from around the world. To many, the White House *was* the U.S. But tonight, the president thought with a sigh as the two officers disappeared from his view, he wasn't worried for his own security. He was worried about the three hundred million citizens who depended on him to keep them safe.

He turned away from the window and stepped back to his desk and the Top Secret folder sitting in the middle. The military operation was being called Night Stalker. He had shared his concerns—a handful only—and felt confident that they would be addressed. Of course, he still needed to meet with President Magaña. Although his phone calls with the Mexican President left him in no doubt that they were aligned, he wanted to meet face to face. There were still one or two aspects that he needed to clarify and, more importantly, he needed Magaña's assurances that the structural reforms Mexico was proposing were real.

His meeting with the chairman of the Senate Appropriations Committee had gone better than expected, and he was optimistic that Barbara Tanner would be able to quietly secure the votes—and the funding—he needed.

Still he was troubled. Operation Night Stalker along with the domestic program—code-named Twenty-Twenty—would represent a dramatic change in the war on drugs. Two years ago, they had tried something similar—to Night Stalker at least—but they had only succeeded in making matters worse. Since then, the situation in Mexico had deteriorated, and he knew that he was largely to blame. He had opened Pandora's box, and now he had to close it.

Not any closer to the clarity he was seeking, he dropped the folder back on his desk and stepped out of the Oval Office onto the West Colonnade. He nodded to the agents outside. He paused for a second as he stared out again over the lights on the South Lawn before he turned and headed toward the Rose Garden. It was cold—he probably should have grabbed an overcoat—but the air felt good. He needed a few minutes to think, and over the last year, he had found that a stroll in the Rose Garden, in any season, often helped to clear his head.

He sighed, chastising himself as he thought about Brett. He should have noticed earlier. He should have said something sooner. Would it have made any difference? The doctors had offered little hope, telling Brett Watson that the tumor was too large, that the cancer had already metastasized. He had called Brett right away and had visited him in the hospital. But he knew there was little that he could say to Brett or to his wife to ease their pain, to ease their fear.

Selecting Brett's replacement wouldn't be easy and, the more he thought about it, his options were limited. Jessica Williams, who had been filling in for Brett, was capable—that was his initial impression at least—but he hadn't worked with her long enough for her to become a trusted advisor. That took time.

He briefly considered someone in his cabinet, but quickly rejected the idea. Half of his cabinet was new; some because hindsight had showed him that the loyalties of people he had trusted lay elsewhere, others because the lives of friends and confidantes had been cut short in the remote mountains of Idaho two and a half years ago.

Building a team was tough, he knew. Finding the right people was critical, and it had taken some time to rebuild his team. The background checks had been far more extensive, something he had insisted on. And although the congressional review of his appointments had been easy—heck, Congress would have given him anything he asked for then—it was still a while before he was able to fill every position. He had the right team now, but several were still learning their jobs and he knew it would take some time before they were fully up to speed.

Trust was built over time. The trouble was, he needed that trust now. He needed some outside counsel, someone independent to bounce his thoughts off of, someone to challenge his thinking, someone who could give him an unbiased opinion. There was one person, he thought—by far the best option he had. *But would it be fair to ask?*

He watched as several leaves fell slowly to the ground. Winter was coming and Washington winters could be cold. Nothing like Colorado, where he had lived for over fifty years; in Washington, the coldness went beyond the weather. People took a calculated approach to relationships here and something was always at stake. There was always something to be gained—support for a bill over here, opposition to a policy over there—and he had come to view most interactions as a game. Many times, it was a zero-sum game where you either won or lost and, sometimes, it wasn't always clear where you stood when the game was over. The lure of power drew some very shrewd operators to the nation's capital, and their agendas were not always what they seemed to be. That had been a painful lesson.

A cold breeze hit him and he shivered. He turned and began walking back toward the Oval Office.

———

"Why don't you ask him?" Maria suggested, "Let him make his own decision?"

"Because I'm afraid he would say yes," President Kendall responded.

They were sitting in the living room, on the second floor of the White House Residence. A fire crackled in the fireplace and, although the TV was on, the volume was muted. Neither paid attention to it anyway.

"You're afraid that he'll feel obligated," Maria said as she sipped her tea.

The president nodded. They had been married for thirty years, long enough that Maria could read his moods as well as his thoughts. She often helped him sort out the pros and cons of tough decisions.

"He'll say yes if I ask him, even if he doesn't want to." And that was the problem, Kendall thought. After their harrowing ordeal two years ago, he had no right to ask. If anything, he was indebted to Matthew—hell, the man had saved his life—and there was no way he could ever repay him. If there was, asking him to come back to the White House certainly wasn't it. Matthew had made his feelings fairly clear two years ago. After the investigation, after the congressional hearings, after the head of the Secret Service and the FBI had both resigned, Matthew had told him that there was nothing left for him in Washington. It had been more than the corruption in the Secret Service, Kendall knew, more than the corruption in the vice president's office. It had a lot to do with Stephanie.

"You miss him," Maria said. It wasn't a question.

"I do," the president admitted. He had come to see Agent Richter as more than his protector—Matthew meant so much more to him. He knew that a psychologist would tell him this was normal, that it was something that soldiers who had survived combat together experienced. After surviving the horrors of war together while others around them came home in body bags, after being forced to make terrible choices as they faced life and death side by side, after being forced to dig deep and find the courage to survive when it seemed there was nothing left, combat veterans shared a bond that few others understood. *Hadn't he and Matthew experienced the same thing?*

Although he had respected Matthew's wishes two years ago, he had carried an emptiness inside ever since.

"Can I make a suggestion, Dave?" Maria said.

Despite his mood, Kendall offered a weak smile, "Do I have any choice?"

Maria smiled back and playfully smacked him on the arm. "Invite him to dinner," she said. "I'd like to see him again too." She put her hand on his. "I don't think I can ever thank him enough for what he did."

"Neither can I," the president responded. "Neither can I."

CHAPTER ELEVEN

Richter glanced around the room, gauging his men. Standing around a scale model of the militia compound, each wore the serious expressions of a warrior preparing himself for battle.

"Does everybody know their job?" he asked then waited until he saw heads nod. "I know I've said this before, but I'm going to say it again. These guys may not be as disciplined as a regular military unit, but they are heavily armed. We need to do this right. We need to maintain the element of surprise. We need to hit them hard and fast. We each need to cover our positions. And we need to be prepared for the unexpected. Things can change very quickly in a firefight." He paused and looked at each man once more. "Anyone have any questions?"

There was a chorus of head shakes.

"Okay, we go in as one and we come out as one."

This was met with several grunts. The meeting broke up and the men walked off to check their gear. Richter followed them into the locker room.

Thirty minutes later, when his gear was ready and he was showered and changed, he saw Agent Kevin Reardon slipping on a suit coat. Most of the other guys were wearing jeans. He walked over.

"Where are you off to, Kevin?"

Reardon sighed. "A wake. Kid I used to coach in little league baseball was killed; shot to death."

Richter frowned. "What happened?"

"Apparently, he got mixed up in drugs." Reardon shook his head like he still couldn't believe it. "I thought the kid was too smart for that."

"I'm sorry, Kevin. Where was this?"

"Trenton." Reardon shook his head again. "I know his folks. They're good people. I can't figure out how this could have happened." He grabbed his bag, slipping the strap over his shoulder. He gestured with his head back to the briefing room and the scale model. "I know these guys are bad, but when are we going to start focusing on some of these drug dealers? Christ! Kids are dying out there!"

Richter put his hand on Reardon's shoulder. "That's DEA territory. We have enough on our plate as it is."

Reardon nodded. "I know. I know. I'm just venting, boss."

Richter studied him a moment. "You okay for tomorrow?"

Reardon's face hardened. "I'm ready, boss."

Richter nodded. *I hope so*, he thought.

———

Guerrero smiled when he saw the message; a confirmation from the bank that the wire transfer had been received. That meant that the third shipment had arrived. Currently, he knew, it was being broken down, separated into smaller loads. It would soon find its way north.

It had taken a long time and a lot of planning, but his efforts were now paying off. Although at first he had been wary, smuggling was a way of life for his new partners. Guns, people, drugs—it didn't matter what the contraband was—the African warlords were proving to be reliable, savvy businessmen. His first two shipments had already found their way up to Italy and to Spain, to markets willing to pay twice as much as los gringos. His third shipment had just arrived safely in Sierra Leone. If it continued to go well, he might eventually ship a full ocean container. It was proving to be an easy and low-cost way to move the product, and the European market provided him with diversification. What was it los gringos said? *Don't put all of your eggs in one basket?*

The bribes he had paid to the police and to the customs inspectors in Veracruz to look the other way had been a sound investment. They also opened up another potential route to the U.S. Borrowing a page from Colombia's playbook, he was exploring the possibility of acquiring a mini-submersible—a submarine. He would acquire it through a shell corporation, of course, claiming the vessel would be used for marine research. But how difficult would it be, he wondered with a smile, to take on a load in the middle of the Gulf of Mexico and then transport it to a rendezvous point off the coast of Louisiana?

This was the lesson Ramón had never learned. Brute force wasn't always the best answer. Sometimes it was better to watch your enemy, to study his moves, to figure out what he was thinking. It required patience but it often revealed weaknesses that could be exploited and opportunities that could be seized.

———

"Marine One is ready, sir."

President Kendall looked up at Burt Philips and nodded. As he handed his bag to an aide, he joined Phillips and together they walked out the door. As they followed the walkway around the West Colonnade, Phillips continued.

"Everything is set with President Magaña,"

The president nodded. He and the Mexican President would meet, out of sight and away from the press. His daughter told him he was old school, but he believed that face to face meetings were critical, especially when the stakes were as high as they were. He and Magaña both agreed that few if any options remained, but he wanted to meet the man in person one final time before he said yes. Phillips's voice interrupted his thoughts.

"Have you given any thought to Brett's replacement?"

"I have," the president responded. "While I think Jessica Williams is certainly qualified, I have someone else in mind."

As Brett Watson's chief of staff, Jessica Williams *was* highly skilled and highly competent. But Kendall was leaning toward bringing someone new to the White House. Well, not new, he thought, but it had been a while. The question was, would he say yes?

CHAPTER TWELVE

In the cold darkness of early morning, Richter snaked forward on his belly, slowly covering the last few yards to the large oak. He lay still for a second and listened to the sounds in the forest. A silent approach was always a challenge, even more so when the ground was covered with freshly fallen leaves. As he searched for telltale signs that their approach had been compromised, the foliage continued to drift down lazily, landing softly around him. Other than the occasional rustle of the wind through the trees or through the leaves on the ground, he heard nothing. He felt a moment of pride—his team was good. He slowly tilted his head to the side, just enough to see the building. Although sunrise wasn't for almost two hours, he was careful to keep his face hidden in the brush. The building—or rather the lodge—stood about sixty yards away. He studied the lodge for a minute, noting the location of the doors, the windows, the electric meter—everything was as he had expected.

Thanks to Google Earth and photos taken from a Bureau plane that had performed a bit of aerial reconnaissance—ostensibly, practicing touch and go's at a nearby airport—they knew exactly what the building looked like. For the interior, they relied on building plans and a handful of pictures their informant had smuggled out. Armed with this data, they had been able to produce a mock-up for training. Although constructed of facades, they had recreated the great room inside, including the circular banquet tables arranged in front of the chalkboards on one end and the couches and easy chairs arranged in front of the fireplace on the other. On one side was a commercial kitchen, next to that a small storage room, and then a restroom.

Information obtained from the county's zoning department told them about the building's construction—standard wood frame with a faux log-cabin exterior—the location of electric and water services, and the type and location of the heating and cooling system.

Richter pulled his head back behind the tree then, after a second, glanced to either side. He spotted nothing unusual. Not that he had expected to. His team was good. He pulled his microphone wand closer to his mouth.

"Blue Lead in position. All clear."

One after another, he received eleven replies. His team was ready. He checked his watch, sliding the sleeve up slightly to expose the luminous dial. It was exceptionally bright in his night vision goggles before they adjusted to the change. Four forty-five. It was time. He pulled his wand close again.

"Blue One. Blue Two. Go."

Although he couldn't see it, he knew that, on the other side of the building, two of his men would begin making their way silently across the twenty-five yards of open ground toward the back door that led to the pantry and the kitchen.

Two minutes later he heard, "Blue One inside." Another minute later, he heard, "Blue Two in position."

He settled back to wait.

Thirty minutes later, he spotted two figures coming down the path on the far side of the clearing.

He cupped his hand over his mouth. "Two inbound," he said softly.

As the two figures approached the building, he could see that both were dressed in camouflage and were carrying weapons; one man held his casually at his side, the other had his slung over his shoulder. Richter's jaw clenched as he studied the rifles, noting that they were fully automatic M-16s. Although he had been expecting this—their informant had indicated that the group had been buying stolen military weapons on a regular basis—it still sent a chill down his spine. He noted that both were also wearing thigh holsters, but from his spot, he was unable to tell what type of handgun each carried.

The men were speaking, but with the breeze rustling through the trees, he couldn't make out what they were saying. The man with the rifle on his shoulder unlocked the main door. It shut behind them with a bang. A moment later, the lights in the main room flickered on, and Richter watched through the window as both men placed their rifles in the gun rack against the far wall. Seconds later, the lights in the kitchen came on. Richter glanced at his watch again. Five-thirty. Right on time. Shortly, he knew, one of the men would start the pot of coffee, while the other would begin to set the tables. They would then begin cooking the eggs and sausages, heating up the frozen home fries, and making toast. According to the informant, breakfast was always the same on a training day.

After a minute or two, Richter knew that the informant had been right as the smells from the kitchen wafted through the trees. The odors also told him that the back door was propped open.

Twenty-five minutes later, in the faint light of dawn, he heard his earbud click: "Two more inbound." A moment later, he saw the two men through the trees, following a different path to the clearing. They were talking softly, but he could hear the occasional laugh. As they entered the lodge, the men propped open the door. Through the window, Richter watched as they too placed their rifles in the gun rack.

Over the next ten minutes, he heard several more calls and watched as the others, in groups of two or three, arrived. All were dressed in camouflage and all were carrying M-16s. And on most he saw shoulder, hip, or thigh holsters as well. They were ready for war.

Daylight grew, and he took off the night vision goggles. It took his eyes a few seconds to adjust. He watched as the men congregated in the great room. The noises of a half dozen conversations carried out the door. By six-thirty, the twenty-two men who had camped out in one of the bunkhouses overnight—all except one—were inside the lodge. If their informant was right, the rest would not show up until much closer to eight. He peered past the men at the gun rack and counted again. Twenty-two M-16s were lined up neatly in a row. He hoped they would stay there. But if they didn't, his team was ready. Each of his men carried a Heckler and Koch MP5 submachine gun with a thirty-round clip and, on a thigh holster, a Springfield .45 caliber pistol with eight rounds in the magazine and one in the chamber. Their weapons, their training, and their method of assault—employing speed, surprise, and violence of action—shifted the odds in their favor. Still, he knew, it was dangerous to assume it would be easy.

He heard another click.

"Visual on Buffalo." Then, "Buffalo inbound."

Thirty seconds later, he saw Gerry Nichols, carrying a rifle in both hands, making his way silently down the path. He was by himself. As he crossed the clearing, Richter saw that he too had a thigh holster and a handgun.

When Nichols entered the building, the conversations abruptly stopped. He placed his rifle in the gun rack. The men stood and joined him in the center of the room. Nichols nodded toward one man who stepped forward and bowed his head. Half the men joined him, while the rest, including Nichols, simply stared straight ahead.

When the prayer was done, the men lined up in front of the serving tables and began filling their plates. Many went for the coffee first and then fell into the back of the food line. Richter pulled himself up into a crouch.

"Yellow." He spoke softly into his microphone, using the pre-arranged code. He watched as the men sat in groups of four or five and began eating. He waited until the last man picked up a tray and placed his food and coffee on it.

"Green," he hissed into his mic.

This was followed instantly by three thumps and the crash of glass as flash-bang grenades were shot through the windows of the lodge. Richter saw startled faces then turned his own a half second before the grenades exploded.

"Go! Go! Go!" he yelled as he jumped to his feet and ran toward the building.

———

"Police! Police! Police!" Richter shouted as he darted toward the blown-out window. In less than a second, his eyes took in the scene. A dozen or more members of the militia were lying on the floor, breakfast trays, plates, and food scattered in every direction. To his left, he noted four men running toward the gun rack. He ignored them. To his right—his assigned zone—four men were crouching, two of them reaching for their side arms. As gunfire erupted around him, he adjusted his aim slightly, centering his sights on the first man. He squeezed off two shots and then swung his arms slightly to the left and squeezed off two more.

He caught more movement in his peripheral vision but ignored it as he swung his gun back to the other two men in his assigned zone. His sights shifted from one man to another, watching their hands, searching for guns, wary of sudden movements. One by one, the men lay face down on the floor. Richter swept his gun over the zone again as shots continued to ring out.

It was so unexpected that it took a moment before his mind registered what had happened. Something slammed into him and he stumbled backwards. He struggled to stand and watched in disbelief as his gun slipped from his hands. He tried to lift his arm but found that he couldn't. *Son-of-a-bitch!* he thought as he glanced at his shoulder and saw the wetness spreading down his sleeve. So dark it was almost black, he noted as he slumped to the ground.

CHAPTER THIRTEEN

President Kendall watched out the window as the coastline approached. He could see a lush, green patchwork of farmland and cattle pastures then a large dune that seemed to extend for miles. This was followed by a rugged shoreline with the occasional narrow stretch of sand. Beyond, he could see the odd house or ranch, but most of the beach, he noticed, was deserted. As they got closer, he noticed two men pushing a large motorboat out into the surf. They struggled for a moment in the waves before the boat began to bob and they were able to climb on board. A few seconds later, the boat was skimming across the water. Farther north, on the horizon, he could make out a cluster of buildings.

Mexican President Filipe Magaña tapped his shoulder and pointed out the other window. They were approaching a group of islands. Beyond, he saw the cargo ships and the cranes of a port in the distance and a sprawling city that stretched beyond and to the south.

"That is Veracruz," Magaña said with a smile.

The helicopter banked and headed north along the coastline. After thirty minutes, they turned inland and began to descend. Kendall noticed the large hacienda nestled in amongst the hills. As they approached, he could see the patio and pool surrounded by several tropical-pink buildings, all adorned with tile roofs. The palm trees were swaying in the breeze. A rough wooden, split-rail fence separated the hacienda from the ranch. There were a dozen horses grazing in the field and then nothing but farmland on either side for miles.

Noticing the look on Kendall's face, Magaña smiled. "I thought this would be more private and," he added, "more secure. This property has been in my wife's family for generations, but lucky for me, she has been successful in keeping that fact quiet."

As they waited for the rotors to stop, Kendall spotted members of his Secret Service detail and the Mexican Security team. This was perfect, he thought. They hadn't publicized the meeting so they were free of reporters and crowds. That had taken a bit of work. He had flown to Corpus Christi, Texas, the day before and, after paying a visit to the naval base, had hitched a ride on a U.S. Navy Seahawk to the USS Kennedy early in the morning. The Kennedy Carrier Strike Group was currently running training exercises two hundred miles off the coast. After a tour of the carrier and a meal with the sailors, a photo opportunity the press had been invited to attend, he had hopped onto the Seahawk once more. The press, having already read the president's itinerary, knew that he had a private meeting with former President George W. Bush and that they would see him the following day for the flight back to Washington.

While his plans did include a meeting with Bush, the press was not aware that the meeting had already occurred, by phone from the Kennedy.

———

President Kendall and Mexican President Filipe Magaña strolled along the bluff overlooking the Gulf. Thirty yards behind trailed a team of agents from both countries. The wind ensured that their conversation would not be overheard.

"I only wish that I could show you Mexico City," Magaña said. "Hopefully, on your next visit that will be possible."

Kendall smiled. "I would enjoy that." They walked in silence for a moment before he spoke again. "I have approval from Congress. We're prepared to move forward with the new plan."

"As we discussed?"

Kendall nodded. "As we discussed. We'll continue to provide you financial support. I have succeeded in getting more money from Congress. We will significantly expand our treatment and rehabilitation programs."

"And the drones?"

"We will provide the intelligence, but you will approve all targets and you will make the final decision on whether your forces will mount an assault or whether we will use the drones."

They continued on in silence for a bit.

"It will get worse in the short term," Magaña finally said.

"It will," Kendall agreed.

Magaña stopped and turned. "The stakes are high, David, but I see no other way. For you, it's about the drugs. For me, it's about the future of my country." He paused, his jaw set, his eyes hard. "I *will* take my country back from these terrorists, one way or another."

———

Through the fog, Richter heard noises. A click. A swoosh. His name. Muffled, close yet somehow far away. Struggling, he opened his eyes and felt a sudden sharp pain as the white light stabbed him. He shut his eyes again and took a few deep breaths before he opened them once more. The room was blurry and seemed to be swimming around him. For a moment, he remembered scenes from his childhood: the shimmers on the pond after he had tossed a rock, the fun house mirror at the amusement park. He felt dizzy but fought it, concentrating until the room came into focus. He suddenly remembered where he was. He heard the noise again and shifted his eyes, searching for it.

Patty stood in the doorway. He could see the tears welling up in her eyes. Her hand flew to her mouth, and she rushed to the bed.

"Oh my God! The instant I heard it on the news, I knew it was you," she said as she wiped her eyes. "Are you okay? How do you feel?"

"Like I've been hit by a train," he said, his voice hoarse.

"Where?" she asked as she sat on the edge of the bed.

He slid the blanket down. His right arm was in a cast. "I was hit in the shoulder. The bullet broke the bone, the humerus. They had to piece it back together." *How did he know that?*

His mind was cloudy, thanks to the Demerol, but he forced himself to concentrate. The surgery had lasted five hours. *That's what the doctor had told him, right?* Then he must have been in the recovery room for a while. He glanced up at the clock on the wall. It seemed to shimmer and move. He gave up trying to read it and closed his eyes, trying but failing to stop the spinning.

"It's nine o'clock," he heard her say through the fog.

He opened his eyes, nodded briefly, then closed them again. *Nine o'clock? In the evening?* When he opened his eyes once more, he saw that Patty was crying again. He tried to smile.

"How long have you been here?" he asked.

"Since eleven," she said with a sniff. She wiped her eyes again.

He struggled with the numbers. *Ten hours? Was that right?*

She gently laid her hand on his. "It might be time to find another job."

Didn't his mother say the same thing? he thought. *Wait, was she here too? Had he spoken to her?*

It was too much effort to think. He closed his eyes again and surrendered to the darkness.

CHAPTER FOURTEEN

Pablo Guerrero let his guest wait. He knew it was a risk to bring the man here, but he was used to taking risks. Besides, the man worked for him. Why should he not come when his boss summoned? He would let the man sit by himself for a while, alone with his thoughts, waiting, wondering.

After reading several reports—he had brought a level of sophistication and order to the operation over the years—he stood, then glanced in the mirror before leaving his office. He was pleased with his new Italian tailor. He made a mental note to summon the man again and at the same time, perhaps, have him bring some of the latest fashions from Paris for his wife.

The colonel was sitting on the terrace. There was a small garden below the balcony, surrounded by a twelve-foot high wall. Under the broad expanse of the roof eave, the terrace was protected from the sun.

"Buenos días, Colonel. Thank you for coming."

"Buenos días, Señor Guerrero. It is my pleasure."

Guerrero suppressed a smirk. Being picked up before dawn, having a hood thrown over his head, followed by a five-hour car ride with armed men at his side wasn't a pleasure, he was sure. But the colonel didn't have much choice. Not if he wanted to continue to earn his pay, now fourteen thousand dollars a month. And not, Guerrero mused, if he wanted to continue to live.

Guerrero poured himself a cup of coffee from the silver service on the sideboard and sat across from his guest. He noticed that the colonel didn't have a cup. That could wait.

"What news do you bring me, Colonel?"

His guest shifted in his seat. "It appears that the Americans are considering a new offensive."

Guerrero nodded and took a sip. The man, he could see, was nervous. Good.

"There has been discussion about using their unmanned spy planes, their Predator drones."

"Only their planes? They will not be putting their troops on our soil?"

"No, señor. From what I learned, it will not be like last time." The colonel shifted again. "But the drones are just as dangerous."

Guerrero sipped his coffee and studied the man for a moment. He put the cup down and brushed a piece of lint off of his sleeve before looking back up at his guest.

"And what is it that you propose to do about this...new development...Colonel?"

His guest shifted again. "The plan's not final yet, but I suspect that we will approve it. I don't know much right now, but I would think that all flights would have to be coordinated with our air force. If so, I should have access to the flight schedules. I should also have access to the mission briefs. I do not know for sure, but I am assuming that I will see them with sufficient time to give you advance notice."

"When do you expect a decision?"

The colonel shrugged. "You know how slow we can be sometimes."

Guerrero suppressed another smile. While this was a potentially troubling piece of news, the bureaucracy of his own government, especially when working with los gringos, might work to his benefit.

"Let's assume the plan *is* approved," Guerrero said.

"Then we can use the email accounts and the codes we've always used," the colonel responded. "Or, in an emergency, the cell phones."

Guerrero nodded. The colonel worked as chief of staff to General

Salazar, the man in charge of Mexico's antidrug efforts. He was one of a number of intelligence sources Guerrero used. They were expensive; his intelligence gathering network alone cost him one hundred and thirty thousand dollars a month. But a business couldn't operate without good intelligence, he had reasoned.

The value of the colonel's information had always been excellent. The colonel had proven to be a shrewd operative as well, suggesting a single email account where he left coded messages in a spam folder that were picked up by one of Guerrero's many lieutenants. Still, trust only went so far in this business.

The colonel continued, providing other pieces of information that he thought might be of interest to the head of Las Sangre Negras. None, though, was as important as the drones. When the colonel was done, Guerrero picked up the bell next to the coffee service.

"You will stay for lunch, Colonel?"

The colonel nodded and Guerrero could see the pained look that the man couldn't quite hide. A heavy lunch, followed by the hood, then a trip down the winding mountain roads and several hours in a car was not something to look forward to.

Guerrero rang the bell.

A moment later, a young woman, wearing the white apron and the plain blue dress of a maid appeared.

"Cecilia, we're ready for lunch."

"Sí, señor."

When she left, Guerrero sat back, looked out over the garden and sighed.

"Such a beautiful day, don't you think, Colonel?"

CHAPTER FIFTEEN

Matthew Richter caught a glimpse of himself as he shuffled past the mirror. He stopped and stared for a second. His face was pale, and his hair was matted down on one side. The other side stuck up at an odd angle. He sighed. None of his half-dozen visitors—most members of the JTTF—had said anything. Nor had Patty. He glanced at the clock on the wall. 3:30 p.m. She wouldn't be back until the evening, after her classes ended. He'd have to wait until then, he thought, unless the nurse had a comb.

He heard the door, but before he could turn—moving quickly made him woozy—the nurse was by his side.

"I told you to buzz me if you wanted to get up again," she scolded as she led him back to bed. She helped him lie down. It took several minutes to tuck him back in and to check his vital signs. She frowned.

"Blood pressure's a little low. Do you feel dizzy?"

"A little," he admitted.

She shook her head. "I don't want you getting up by yourself again." She glared at him for a moment to make sure he understood this time.

He had only gone to the bathroom, he thought, but he was too tired to protest. He nodded slowly, careful not to move his head too fast. She fluffed a pillow, and he grimaced as she placed it, a little roughly it seemed, behind his head.

"You've had quite the stream of visitors today." She shook her head. "You need to rest."

He caught her look and nodded again.

"You're in pain," she said as she studied him.

He grimaced and shook his head. "No more Demerol."

Before she could respond, the door opened and she glanced over her shoulder at the two men in suits standing in the doorway. Their eyes darted around the room. She turned and put her hands on her hips.

"Visiting time is not until..." She stopped mid-sentence, her mouth open, as the two men moved aside and President David Kendall stepped into the room.

———

"From what the doctors told me, it sounds like you're out of commission for a while," the president said some forty minutes later.

Richter nodded. With his arm in a sling for six weeks—quite possibly more, the doctor had warned him—he wouldn't be kicking any doors in for some time. And although the doctor hadn't said anything yet, he knew once the cast was removed, he faced a month or more of rehabilitation before he rebuilt the muscles lost to atrophy, and regained, hopefully, full use of his right arm. Then there were firearms requalification requirements and making up for months of lost training. He was effectively off the SWAT team for four months. He sighed. Maybe more.

The president patted his good arm. "Look, I didn't come up here to make a sales pitch. But if Pat Monahan can't find something for you to do, I could always use your counsel."

Richter nodded. "Thank you, sir."

The door opened and Richter nodded to the Secret Service agent in the doorway. He could see more agents in the hall. After scanning the room, the agent stepped aside and the nurse came in. She hesitated.

"I'm sorry," she said sheepishly, "but I need to change his IV."

Richter noted that the bossy tone was gone. He was too tired to grin.

The president smiled at the nurse. "Absolutely." He stood and turned to Richter. "I don't want to get in the way here, so I'll be going."

Richter nodded. "Thank you for coming, sir." He gestured toward the window and the large flower arrangement sitting on the sill. "Please thank Mrs. Kendall for me."

"I will," the president responded with a smile. He patted Richter's arm again. "Think about what I said. Okay?"

CHAPTER SIXTEEN

As she sprayed the hose across the boat's deck, Agent Maureen Dunn couldn't help but smile. Some days were better than others and, to Agent Dunn, any day on a boat was a good day. And it was one hell of a boat, she thought. The forty-foot Meridian yacht was by far the nicest boat she had ever been on. Seized a year earlier during a drug bust and renamed, the boat was on loan from the DEA. She was one of a handful of ATF agents in her office who were familiar with boats, having practically grown up on her dad's twenty-foot Bayliner. So when she was asked if she wanted to be part of the bust, she had jumped at the chance.

The pair of wires dangling from her ears wasn't an uncommon sight. Her radio, disguised as an iPod, was clipped to the belt of a small fanny pack she wore around her waist. As she washed the seats, she bopped her head and swayed to the beat of the non-existent music. The microphone, nothing more than a small nub, was part of her earphone wire. The fanny pack, or what looked like one, was actually a fast-action gun bag designed with a Velcro-ed front flap that allowed her rapid access to her pistol should it be needed. Even though she was prepared, she didn't think she would need her gun today.

Her earphones chirped once. "Visual on Moonbeam."

Without missing a beat, she casually glanced up as the two trucks pulled into the marina's lot.

"Got 'em," she said.

She turned slightly so she had a better angle on the lot.

The six men climbed out and, after a few stretches and yawns—pretense, she could see, while they surveyed the marina—they opened the rear hatches. They glanced in her direction and she smiled as she continued rinsing off the deck. The men smiled back as they pulled two large coolers from the back of one of the SUVs. She turned, giving them a better view of her tight shirt and shorts. They paused for a second and grinned until one of the men—Grumpy, she decided—said something. They went back to their task, pulling four large duffle bags from the back of the other truck. Moments later, four men began lugging the coolers down to the dock, while two men, laden down with the duffle bags, followed.

Not a smart move, Agent Dunn thought. Their boat, she knew—an even nicer fifty-two-foot Cabo Express—was in the slip next to hers. She smiled again as they neared her boat.

"Where you boys off to today?" she called down.

They paused and all but Grumpy smiled back.

"Fishing!" two replied simultaneously. "What about you?"

She flashed a big smile. "Oh, I don't know. Once I'm done with this, I'll probably pop open a beer and maybe work on my tan."

The men exchanged grins until Grumpy said something. But by then it was too late. Suddenly there were shouts, and the dock was swarming with agents—coming out of the marina office, out of the cabin of Agent Dunn's boat as well as the Cabo Express next door. With their hands full of gear, the men never had a chance. The look on their faces, Agent Dunn would later say, was priceless.

As the six men slowly dropped their gear and lay face down on the dock, Agent Dunn dropped the hose on the boat. She lifted the bench seat and pulled out a nylon vest—black with a large yellow ATF on the back. As she watched her fellow agents, and the men lying on the dock, she slipped the vest over her head. No, she wouldn't need her gun today.

She climbed down to the dock and, while her partners searched and handcuffed the prisoners, she opened one of the coolers. Inside, wrapped in wax paper, she found the guns. Disassembled, oiled, they looked brand new. The other cooler and the duffle bags, she was certain, would be similarly filled. She closed the cooler. She waited a moment for her fellow agents to finish securing the prisoners. Then, one by one, they were led off the dock to the waiting black SUVs with the flashing lights that had, minutes before, suddenly materialized.

"Good job, Maureen," the agent in charge said as he stepped over.

She flashed a smile. "Oh, just another day at the office," she responded. Then, as she climbed aboard the Cabo, she called over her shoulder. "Looks like we just got ourselves a new boat!"

———

One more lap, Guerrero told himself as he reached the wall, turned, pushed off with his feet and began swimming back. When his hand touched the other side of the pool, he stopped and stood, taking a few seconds to catch his breath. He climbed out, grabbed his towel and, as he began drying off, he spotted Alberto. By the look on his face, Guerrero knew something was wrong.

"The boat never arrived," Alberto said.

Guerrero dropped his towel on the chair. "What happened?"

Alberto shook his head. "I don't know. The trawler waited for six hours, but the boat never showed. I tried contacting Jose, but…" He shook his head.

Guerrero cursed. "Anything on the news?"

Alberto shook his head again. "No. Not yet, anyway."

Guerrero cursed again as he considered the possibilities. The trawler had returned safely which meant that, most likely, the Coast Guard had intercepted the boat, somewhere off the coast of Louisiana. And if that were the case, Jose and his men would have been arrested and the shipment of guns would have been confiscated. It appeared that the trawler hadn't been compromised, not yet anyway. But it was only a matter of time. Jose and his men knew the name of the ship, knew the coordinates for the meeting location, and knew the captain.

He looked up at Alberto. "Get rid of the trawler."

Alberto nodded.

Guerrero considered the loss. The supply of guns would take some time to replace. But it could have been worse. Once the guns had been unloaded on the trawler, it would have been easy to send the yacht back to los Estados Unidos loaded with drugs. But he had, wisely it seemed now, made the decision to not mix the gun shipments with the drugs going north.

It could have been bad luck, he knew: a random search by the Coast Guard. But his gut told him that wasn't it. Something had gone wrong and he needed to find out what.

——

Richter shook his head. "No thanks. I'll walk."

The orderly, standing in front of him with a wheelchair, frowned. "I'm sorry. But it's hospital policy."

Richter shot the orderly a look as he picked up his bag. Five days in the hospital—being told what to do, someone constantly fawning over him—was enough. He was anxious to go home.

Five minutes later, he stepped out into the sunshine, the worried orderly close on his heel. Although the air was cool, it felt good and he stopped for a moment and tilted his head up, feeling the warmth of the autumn sun on his face.

"It's good to see you up and about." Mark Crawford smiled as he opened the rear door of the black SUV waiting at the curb.

Richter grinned back. "It's good to be out," he responded.

The driver, another FBI agent, took Richter's bag. Crawford helped him climb in and Richter winced at the stab of pain as he settled into the seat. A minute later, Crawford climbed in the other side and they pulled out of the hospital lot.

"I'm not sure how much of this you've heard already," Crawford said, "but I'll fill you in on the raid."

Richter nodded. He had read the paper. Nine Free Nation members had been killed in the shootout, including Gerry Nichols. Six others, plus one FBI agent—that would be him—had been wounded. Fourteen militia members had been arrested in the lodge. Thirty-three other members had been arrested within hours as they arrived at the training camp. Terry Fogel, it seemed, had vanished.

There had been an initial firestorm of negative press, with comparisons to Ruby Ridge and Waco, the media blasting the government for using excessive force. That had lasted two days, until the U.S. Attorney's press conference.

"We found a large cache of arms," Crawford said. "M-16s, AK-47s, hand guns, grenades"— he ticked each off on his fingers—"as well as a large quantity of ammonium nitrate, primer cord, and other bomb-making materials." He paused. "We also recovered several computers that had surveillance photos, diagrams and schematics, as well as detailed plans for the attacks."

Richter nodded. He was aware of most of this. The U.S. Attorney had released just enough information to douse the public outcry. No one wanted to see another Oklahoma City.

Crawford continued: "We also found something unexpected. It seems they were involved in shipping stolen guns to Mexico."

"Supplying the cartels?" Richter was surprised.

Crawford nodded. "Even more surprising, they were much more sophisticated than we thought. Six months ago, they set up a private trucking operation, handling mostly small shipments for a handful of customers." He frowned. "They were mixing the arms in with legitimate customer shipments. The ATF believes they have identified the routes. The guns were delivered to cartel operations in Texas and Louisiana. From there they were shipped by U.S.-registered pleasure craft to a rendezvous point in the Gulf where they were off-loaded onto a Mexican-registered fishing trawler."

Richter shook his head. The cartel link was disturbing.

"If we hadn't stopped them when we did," Crawford added, "the arms shipments could have become a significant source of funding, and who knows what they might have done then."

Richter cringed at the thought.

"Of course," Crawford continued, "we've frozen all bank accounts, at least those that we've been able to identify so far. But," he sighed, "we're still trying to sort out all that they were involved in."

Richter glanced out the window as the SUV slowed. Although the light was green, the cars in front of them had stopped. He saw a cop in the intersection directing traffic. A second later, he heard the chirp of a siren and watched as the cop waved the ambulance through. Probably an accident up ahead, he thought. He turned back to Crawford.

"What about the shooting inquiry?"

Crawford was silent for a bit. "Ballistics confirmed that the bullet that shattered your arm came from Gerry Nichols' gun."

"How many shots did he get off?" Richter asked. For the last twenty-four hours—once he could think clearly—he had been playing the scene over and over in his head, trying to figure out what had happened.

"Two. We dug one slug out of the wall, inches from your window."

Richter looked at Crawford, waiting for him to continue.

"Reardon was slow getting to his sector."

Richter looked out the window as they began moving again. He had suspected it was something like that. He knew no operation ever went as planned and sometimes things went wrong. And while it could have happened to anyone on the team, Reardon's stumble had almost cost Richter his life. He sighed. At a minimum, it had probably ended his career.

CHAPTER SEVENTEEN

"Mr. Watson?"

Brett Watson turned at the voice and held up his hand. The nurse, wearing the ubiquitous blue scrub pants and multi-colored pastel top, smiled.

"Are you ready for me today?" she asked as she stopped for a second in front of his chair.

He smiled back—a smile that didn't quite make it to his eyes—and nodded.

"How are you feeling?" she asked as she handed him the clipboard and grabbed the handles on his wheelchair.

"Never better," he smiled. *Who wanted to hear the truth?*

She patted his shoulder. "Sorry, we're a little backed up today," she said as she wheeled him through the door into the Nuclear Medicine wing.

She continued talking, more to fill the time than anything, as they made their way down the hall. He nodded and smiled occasionally but wasn't really listening. His brain was flooded with thoughts, as it had been over the past two weeks. There was so much to do, and the treatments would hopefully buy him the time he needed. Still they took a lot of time; traveling back and forth and all of the waiting in between. This was his third radiation treatment and, so far, it hadn't been as bad as he had expected. He had even dozed on and off the last time as the technician made the adjustments. Surprisingly the chemotherapy hadn't been as bad as he'd thought either. That was good. He didn't have time to waste lying in bed or bent over a toilet. His hair was starting to fall out, but he was beyond worrying about that.

The nurse's voice interrupted his thoughts.

"I'll be back for you when you're through," she said with a smile and a pat on his shoulder.

He glanced up, realizing they were in the treatment room. He smiled back, weakly, then nodded at the technician. Thankfully, the technician said little as he helped him climb up on top of the table. He lay back and stared up at the machine. Until a few weeks ago, he had no idea what radiation therapy involved. It was like an X-ray, he decided. The machine contained a radioactive material—some toxic substance that doctors and scientists had figured out how to harness to give people like him a chance. Except in his case, the chance was not one of remission or survival, just a few more short weeks of life. Three months, maybe six was all the doctor could offer. Still, Brett had leaped at the chance.

From a legal and a financial perspective, he thought, there really wasn't much to do. Their wills were prepared. Still they would meet with their accountant and their lawyer, making sure that the plans they had put in place four years ago, plans they never thought they would ever need, were ready. No, the issue wasn't legal or financial. It was even more urgent. What does a husband do to prepare his wife, what does a father do to prepare his kids for the one day when he would no longer be there? How would he make up for the lost time—time he had wasted pursuing a career instead of spending it home with his family—when he had so little time left? What do you say to a seven-year-old girl who was still upset over a missed birthday? Or a thirteen-year-old boy who was struggling with the trials of being a teenager?

He sighed. Nancy was strong. And she was organized. She had left him in the waiting room so she could run errands—pick up his medicine, drop off a forgotten lunch at school—not wanting to waste the time they would have together later when he was home.

It was amazing how quickly life could change. What was important two weeks ago—the growing nuclear threat in North Korea and Iran, the drug cartels and the looming collapse of the Mexican government, and several dozen other risks that he had carried with him every waking moment—seemed trivial now. It almost seemed like a dream, a past life that he wanted to put behind him so he could focus on more important things in the little time he had left.

When Matthew Richter had stopped by the day before for insight into what was happening in Mexico, he had given Richter a few minutes then politely steered him towards his staff. They were capable and competent people and he trusted them. Maybe in a month or two, if he was still around, he might feel he had more time to spare for his country. But for the moment, he needed to be there for his family. And, he knew, he didn't have too many more moments left.

———

It felt strange to be back, Matthew Richter thought as he pulled up to the gate. More of an apprehension than déjà vu, the feeling wasn't unexpected.

Three officers, members of the Secret Service Uniformed Division, turned to study his car. Although Richter didn't recognize him, one of the officers nodded in recognition. Somewhat clumsily, Richter put the car in park then held up his FBI credentials for the officer. He had been out of the hospital for two weeks and was still struggling with the awkwardness of using his left hand for everything.

"Welcome back, Agent Richter." The officer hesitated then offered a weak smile. "I hope you don't mind, sir, but we have to check the car."

Richter smiled back. "I would have been surprised if you didn't." He popped the trunk and unlocked the doors. He watched as one officer with a dog circled the car while the other slid a large portable mirror below his rental. Moments later, the gate opened.

"You know where to park, sir?" the officer asked as he handed Richter a pass.

"I think I can still find my way around," he responded with a grin. He pulled forward, following the curved drive. Seconds later, he parked. Climbing out of the car, the feeling struck him again. With a sigh, he headed for the door.

In the vestibule, he nodded to other officers that he recognized. One of the men handed him a plastic bin. "You'll need to check your weapon, sir."

Richter lifted his right arm; it was in a blue sling. "I'm not carrying," he responded. He dropped his keys, phone, and credentials into the bin, then patted his pockets. He felt the lump in his coat. Feeling awkward and naked without a gun, he still carried a tactical baton. He was putting the baton in the bin when a voice he recognized stopped him.

"He doesn't need to do that. I'll sign him in."

Richter turned to see Keith O'Rourke, the supervisor of the White House Secret Service Command Center.

"Keith! I thought you were planning to retire."

O'Rourke smirked and shook his head. "It seems I've been planning that for the last five years."

Richter struggled for a moment as he gathered his belongings. O'Rourke handed back his visitor's badge. As he followed his old mentor around the metal detector, O'Rourke leaned close and whispered. "I was wondering when we'd see you here again."

Richter grinned. "It's good to see you too, Keith."

After they entered the lobby on the ground floor, O'Rourke stopped. "So, clipped in the wing, huh?"

Richter gave his former mentor a summary of the raid.

"How's the recovery coming?"

Richter frowned. "Slow. It's going to take some time before I know the full impact."

O'Rourke nodded then, thankfully, changed subjects, filling him in on what had been happening in the White House and the Service since he had left.

"It must feel a little strange to be back, huh?" O'Rourke asked minutes later when they were standing outside the Oval Office.

"More than you can imagine," Richter responded with a chuckle.

He shook hands with a few people he knew—somewhat awkward with his left hand—before the door opened.

———

"Hi, Matthew!" Maria Kendall exclaimed as she threw her arms around him. Instantly she let him go. "I'm sorry," she said, her eyes flooded with worry, "I hope I didn't hurt you."

Richter smiled, "It's good to see you too, Mrs. Kendall." He raised his arm slightly, nodding at his sling. "And no—no harm done."

"It is so good to see you! And please," she said, "it's Maria."

Richter smiled and nodded as she took his arm and led him to the couch in the middle of the Oval Office.

"Dave will be back in few minutes," she explained as they sat. "So how have you been?" She asked. "You're working for the FBI now?"

"Yes, ma'am," he answered.

She frowned, but he saw the smile in her eyes.

"I'm sorry, ma'am...Maria." He grinned. "Force of habit."

"I was so sorry to hear that you had been shot," she said, her voice dropping an octave. "How's the recovery coming? What do the doctors say?"

Richter dutifully answered the First Lady's questions then asked a few of his own.

"How are the girls?"

"Oh, they're both doing well, thanks." A proud smile spread across her face. "Angela's a sophomore at Boston University and Michelle is still playing soccer at Brookfield Academy." She laughed. "If you ask Dave, they're both growing up too fast and it's driving him nuts."

Richter laughed. They chatted for a few more minutes before the door opened and President Kendall stepped into the room. Richter immediately stood. Maria stood too, then touched him on the arm.

"Relax," she whispered. "You're no longer on duty."

Richter grinned again and shrugged.

"I'll leave you two," Maria said with a conspiratorial wink. She turned to leave then paused and touched Richter's arm again. "You'll stay for dinner?"

"I wouldn't miss it," Richter answered with a smile.

———

"If we were to take a more aggressive stance against them, how do you think they would react?"

Richter shifted in his seat and tried to shake the feeling that he didn't belong. He had spent a year and a half standing watch on the other side of the door. Now here he was, on the inside, sitting on the couch, discussing national security issues with the president.

"With all due respect, sir, I would think your national security team could give you a much more informed answer."

The president smiled. "Humor me. I need another point of view."

He had seen this coming and had taken the opportunity to meet with Mark Crawford and several other FBI counterterrorism experts as well as counterparts in the DEA. He had also stopped by Brett Watson's house but Watson had steered him toward Jessica Williams, the Deputy National Security Advisor. Then, more as a courtesy, he had spent an hour with Pat Monahan in the morning. When Monahan had nodded knowingly and told Richter he was aware that the president had requested the meeting, he realized that he shouldn't have been surprised.

He leaned forward. "I think we better be prepared for a battle, sir."

Kendall nodded. "Why do you say that?"

"This is a different group than ten years ago, even five years ago. They're much bolder, much more vicious, and there's much more at stake for them."

"So it's like Colombia back in the nineties?"

Richter shook his head. "I think the Mexican cartels are worse, sir. Several are run by former members of their special forces, by people who have been schooled in warfare, who see this from a military point of view. For them, guerrilla warfare is a way of life."

The president nodded and Richter continued.

"If we go after them, I'm not sure what would stop them from bringing the war to us. Those two guys we arrested in Newark four months ago?" Richter paused. "Sir, the war may have already started."

Kendall frowned. "You may be right."

"I also think there's a risk that the remaining organizations will eventually be taken over by their security forces," Richter added. "They play a much larger role now than they did just five years ago."

"Go on," Kendall prodded.

Richter held up his one good hand. "Look, sir, this is really not my area of expertise, but there's a risk that these folks could attempt to take over the country; that they could stage a coup d'état."

He sat silently while the president seemed to consider this.

"How would you handle this?" Kendall finally asked.

"I think the national security folks and the CIA first need to determine how real that threat is." He paused. "But if it is real, then I don't think we can wait."

The president was silent for a moment, and Richter felt a knot forming in his stomach.

The president held Richter's eyes for a moment before he spoke. "I'm not sure you're going to like this," the president began.

Richter nodded, knowing exactly what the president was about to say.

CHAPTER EIGHTEEN

The president read the directive again then paused, his pen poised over the paper. He looked up at his guests. "We're prepared for the fallout?"

Jessica Williams, the Deputy National Security Advisor, and Burt Phillips, sitting across from the president, nodded.

"The heads of Homeland Security, the FBI, NSA, and Customs and Border Protection have been notified." Williams elaborated. "This is obviously classified, so they've been briefed only on what they need to know: that we have reason to believe that the cartels are preparing for an attack against Mexican or U.S. infrastructure or political figures, possibly all of the above."

Kendall nodded. He made a note to call Pat Monahan later and provide the missing details.

"They'll begin putting extra focus on the obvious areas, the borders, critical infrastructure, top officials," Williams continued. "Homeland Security is also reviewing the watch list. NSA will be listening for chatter."

The president nodded then glanced down at the National Security Directive, the document authorizing Operation Night Stalker, lying on the table before him. He wished Richter were here. He glanced at his watch, remembering that Richter had promised to give him an answer today. That would have to wait, he thought as he looked back up at Williams and Phillips. He already knew Richter's position on the operation; like Williams and Phillips,

Richter believed that the cartels were likely to strike back. But he also believed that they didn't have a choice.

The president and Phillips exchanged a glance then Phillips nodded.

As he signed his name, he knew that this simple act would trigger a series of events and, because of it, innocent people would likely die. He only prayed that when all was said and done, it was the right decision.

———

As Patty looked up at him, her eyes moist, Richter felt a flood of emotions, none of them good.

"Is this a permanent move?" she asked.

He sighed. "I don't know yet."

Patty was silent; she averted her eyes, staring down into her coffee.

"Look, I have to face the fact," he said, holding up his injured arm, "that my job on the SWAT team is gone."

"Isn't there something else you could do here? A different job?"

He shook his head. "Patty, I'm sorry, but there are only so many times I can tell him no." He took a deep breath. He had been dreading this conversation not only because he knew Patty would be hurt, but because it hurt him as well. He could see that she was holding back her emotions, fighting the urge to cry. For some reason, that only made him feel worse. He struggled, trying to find the words that would make everything okay, that would make her smile again. He couldn't find any.

He put his hand over hers. "Washington's less than four hours away. I'm trying to arrange it so I can spend the weekends here."

"What about Thanksgiving?"

Only a week away and he knew that he owed her an answer. It wasn't that he didn't want to go—he had been expecting Kendall's call and he knew all too well that for those in the White House, weekends and holidays meant nothing. Hell, there was barely a distinction between daytime and nighttime, with many staffers routinely burning the midnight oil then, jittery from too much caffeine, watching the sunrise through bloodshot eyes as they headed to a restroom with a clean set of clothes kept in their offices for such occasions. He would have to find a way to spend Thanksgiving with Patty.

"I'll be there," he said, smiling, hoping to ease the tension. "I'm looking forward to meeting your sister."

Patty stared at him silently for a moment, then wiped her eyes. "I'm sorry," she said. "I've never been the neurotic, needy type, but this is...I don't know...so unexpected. I thought..." She hesitated and turned her head.

He felt the knot in his stomach tighten. He understood, or at least he thought he did. Ever since he had been discharged from the hospital, except for work, they had spent more time together than apart, sharing meals, long discussions—about anything, it didn't matter—trips to the store, a Saturday excursion to Philadelphia, and most nights together at either her place or his. It had happened so quickly that, before he realized it, he had been swept up in the excitement of a new romance. He finally found someone that he wanted to be with, to share things with, someone he wanted to make happy. His life suddenly had direction again. And now he was jeopardizing it. Wasn't Patty more important? he asked himself again. Before he could answer, Patty interrupted his thoughts.

"Damn it, Matthew! I'm in love with you!"

CHAPTER NINETEEN

It had taken four weeks to set things in motion. The logistical aspects of equipment and men had been easy, a by-product of the trend toward unconventional warfare and special operations that had begun decades ago. The legal aspects had been easy as well. U.S. forces participating in the operation had been temporarily transferred to the CIA. A common practice for such operations, it avoided the thorny issue of armed U.S. forces operating on foreign soil during peacetime. Or, in this case, in foreign airspace.

The intelligence aspects had taken a little longer. The DEA, working with Mexican intelligence, had pieced together a fairly thorough analysis of suspected drug trafficking routes, presumed way stations, and possible crossing points; all intelligence they had been gathering for years. Coordination with Mexican military forces who would be on the ground had taken the most time. But, even then, a history of joint military exercises had established a working knowledge, a foundation that could easily be built upon. Codes and communication protocols were established. Rules of engagement were agreed upon, and the chain of command was clarified. Since the U.S. was merely providing the hardware, the Mexicans were calling the shots.

———

In the mountains of central Mexico, the temperature was dropping as *Teniente* Manuel Ramirez peered through his night vision binoculars at the two buildings inside the walled compound. He watched as the ten-man team of guards prepared for the long, cold night ahead. Another shipment had arrived thirty minutes before, having made the long trip from Colombia, through Central America, before finding its way up to this storage facility hidden in the mountains. By the size of the force, the shipment had been large.

After the truck had left, the guards closed and locked the buildings and then the gate in the perimeter wall. The cocaine would sit for no longer than a day, the teniente knew, before it continued on its way up to los Estados Unidos. He wasn't sure how the cartel was moving the drugs into the U.S. Regardless, he thought, this particular load of cocaine would never make it.

Teniente Ramirez, a lieutenant in the Mexican Navy and the leader of the eight-man special forces team, watched as the last two guards climbed into their SUV, parked just inside the main gate. There was another SUV sitting outside the gate, two more men huddled inside. He panned his binoculars along the wall of the compound, noting the other pairs of guards huddled inside three other vehicles. They would take turns, one napping while the other kept a half-hearted watch. They were getting lazy, he thought, and for that, they would pay a price.

He had no qualms about it. His brother, a journalist, had been killed in retaliation for a series of articles he had written on the devastating effects the narco-traffickers were having on Mexican society. Not satisfied with just his brother, masked gunmen had attacked his funeral, killing his mother, his father, and his sister. The teniente still had a scar on his arm from the bullet that was meant to kill him. How he had survived was still a mystery. But he did, and that was too bad for the men he watched settle in for the night.

———

The MQ-9 Reaper turned gracefully and began another pass over the target area, a section of the Sierra Gorda Mountains, two hundred and fifty miles northwest of Mexico City. The *sensor* marveled again at the stark contrast on his screen. Directly below, the land was rugged, with steep mountains and deep ravines. To the west was a flat plain that stretched for miles; an area that saw little precipitation and was home to scrub brush, cactus, and dust. The eastern side was a semi-tropical environment fed by moisture coming off the Gulf of Mexico.

The MQ-9 was equipped with synthetic aperture radar. Capable of taking near photographic-quality images through clouds, rain, dust, smoke, and fog—both in daylight or total darkness—the SAR significantly enhanced the Reaper's capabilities. And even though the sun had set hours ago—it was several minutes after midnight, the sensor noted—the black and white images on the screen were detailed and crystal clear. It almost looked like a rain forest, he thought, as he spotted a river that fed into a lake and, farther on, a waterfall. The lush vegetation created a jungle canopy that reminded him of Costa Rica. Given the rugged terrain and few access roads, the area was sparsely populated. *A perfect place to hide a drug operation*, he thought. Although they had only been flying for two and a half hours, he rolled his head, stretching his sore neck muscles. This was their seventh flight over the target in the last week, and the tension had been building.

The MQ-9 was the latest generation Reaper aircraft, an unmanned, remotely piloted cousin of the Predator drone. The sensor, as he was called, was sitting three hundred and fifty miles away in a comfortable leather chair in the ground control station at Naval Air Station Corpus Christi in Texas. Six video screens and a keyboard were arranged in front of him. A Navy lieutenant, the sensor controlled the multispectral tracking system, or MTS ball hanging below the nose of the Reaper, as well as the onboard weapons systems. The pilot and aircraft commander, another Navy lieutenant, sat to the right of the sensor. His hand was on the control stick. Like the sensor, the pilot sat at his own station, complete with keyboard, control stick, and six flat panel screens.

"Coming up on target," the sensor announced into his microphone. The mission controller, or MC, was some sixteen hundred miles away in Arlington, Virginia, and was watching the same scene as the pilot and the sensor.

"Roger, Sea Dog. You are clear to engage."

"Copy. Sea Dog clear to engage."

Time to light 'em up, the sensor thought. He flipped a switch, activating the laser guidance system. He deftly moved the control stick, centering the crosshairs on the building, then pressed the switch.

"Laser activated," the sensor stated.

A second later, he heard the pilot's reply: "Copy. Target is sparkle."

The sensor flipped a switch. "Weapons are hot."

"Pilot copies. Weapons are hot."

"Pilot, you are free to engage at your discretion."

"Copy."

The sensor kept his eyes glued to the screen. He could now see the five SUVs sitting in the compound. *Things are about to get a little hot down there, amigos*, he thought.

"Wizard One. Wizard Two." He heard the pilot say after a second.

One after another, two five-hundred-pound GBU-12 Paveway II laser-guided bombs released from the pylons below the wings. After a brief fall, the seeker heads acquired the laser sights, and the bombs began steering themselves—more of a controlled fall than anything else—toward the two cinderblock buildings four miles below.

———

The teniente heard the call then radioed his men. "Cubranse!" *Take cover!*

It was eerily quiet on the mountainside, the only sound the occasional rustle of the wind through the leaves. He quickly panned his binoculars to the left, then right, checking each of his men. Satisfied, he pulled the binoculars away and shielded his eyes. Ten seconds later, there was a tremendous boom, and the ground shook. *So this must be what an earthquake feels like*, he thought for a brief second before leaping to his feet.

"Vamos!" he called over his radio and then began charging down the hill.

CHAPTER TWENTY

There was a knock at the door, and Pablo Guerrero climbed out of bed, grabbing his robe on the way.

He turned to the young girl in his bed, a nineteen-year-old from the village named Lucia.

"Espereme," he ordered. *Wait here.*

"Dónde va?" *Where are you going?* She smiled up at him seductively. He turned again, and her smile suddenly vanished. She pulled the sheet up below her chin as Guerrero slipped into his robe.

There could only be one reason for the interruption. Not his wife certainly. She knew better. He opened the door to find Alberto Espinoza.

"Lo siento, señor." *I'm sorry.* "I have some news."

Guerrero stepped into the hall, closing the door behind him. As he listened, he felt his anger building. *How could this happen? Why wasn't he warned?*

He glanced over his shoulder at the door behind him, knowing that the night he had planned was ruined. He turned to Alberto.

"Take her home," he ordered.

Alberto nodded.

"And find the colonel," he growled. "I need to speak to him."

Alberto nodded again, spun on his heel, and left.

Guerrero stood in the hallway fuming. The message would be passed from Alberto through an intermediary to a third man who would place a coded message in an account that the colonel would access. Guerrero slapped his palm on the small table in the hallway. It would be a while—a few hours at least—before he would be able to speak to the colonel directly, likely later the next day. An unfortunate delay caused by the elaborate security that Guerrero demanded, but one which would give him ample time to decide the colonel's fate.

———

Two days later, Guerrero looked up from his desk as Alberto entered his office.

"He's here, jefe."

Guerrero nodded. Alberto left, closing the door behind him. It had taken a day to arrange the meeting, the colonel unable to leave work on such short notice without arousing suspicion. Despite the delay, Guerrero thought, he still hadn't received the call he had been expecting. After a moment, he stood. He'd see what the colonel had to say first.

A minute later, he joined the colonel on the terrace. The colonel stood; a pained look on his face.

"Lo siento, Señor Guerrero."

"How could this have happened?"

The colonel sighed. "At the last second, there was a change in plans."

"Why didn't you warn me?"

"I didn't see the final plan until that evening," the colonel protested. "I sent the email as soon as I could. And I called." The colonel held up his hands. "You didn't answer."

Guerrero frowned. He hadn't received a phone call. But the colonel would know that he could check this out. And he would certainly know that lying would be a very foolish move. Could he have missed the call? he wondered. He would check the log. The prepaid phones that both he and the colonel had were only for emergencies and had never been used. Until now, apparently. That is, he reminded himself, if the colonel was telling the truth.

The email, following their normal process—picked up by a

cutout, one of Guerrero's many minions, dumped on a USB drive, then passed to a courier for delivery—had not arrived until after the bombing.

He studied the colonel for a few seconds. If the colonel was telling the truth, there was a bigger concern. Why had he not been aware of the change? Could the government suspect the colonel of being an informant? Could they have purposefully not shared the information with him to prevent the raid from leaking? Only a handful of people would have been aware of the raid: General Salazar, the one in charge of Mexico's war on drugs, the attorney general, and the president. Of course, the mission had to be planned and approved by the general and his staff before it was presented to the president. So why hadn't the colonel been aware of it?

Guerrero sat back, his hands forming a steeple below his chin. The colonel looked pale. *As he should*, Guerrero thought.

"They used their navy this time, not their air force," he said, his tone accusatory.

"That was one change, señor. Your storage site was not on the initial target list either. When they learned that a shipment was arriving that evening, they added it. Then, apparently because of the location, they decided on an oversea approach. Their navy has drones in Texas."

Guerrero sat back. The colonel, fidgeting under his stare, continued.

"It seems that they can react to new information very quickly."

Guerrero considered this. He would have his answers soon, when the call came. If the colonel was compromised, then the answer was simple. He would die. If the colonel was lying, the answer was the same. If the colonel was no longer in a position to provide valuable information—*timely information*, Guerrero corrected himself—then he had a decision to make. The logical thing would be to kill him, to eliminate the link. But to replace the colonel would take time.

Could he afford to kill him now? Guerrero wondered. He stared at the nervous man sitting before him. Could he afford not to?

CHAPTER TWENTY-ONE

"Eight men were killed in the bombing," Jessica Williams said. "Two were captured by the Mexican authorities."

Richter frowned. "The men who were killed were part of their security force?"

She nodded. "Yes. According to the gun camera footage, they were in cars next to the buildings at the time of the strike. Somehow, two survived."

The men killed were more than ordinary guards, he knew. Like several of their rivals, Las Sangre Negras employed former members of the Mexican Special Forces. To supplement, they also hired federal police officers—all men who had been corrupted. They were brutal and had no qualms about killing, as the over ten thousand deaths attributed to them alone indicated. Many of those who had been killed by Las Sangre Negras in their turf war with rival organizations and in their ongoing battle with the government had been innocent bystanders.

"How big of a dent will this put in their operation?"

"That remains to be seen," she responded. "Our estimate is that we destroyed close to ten thousand kilos of cocaine. That would have a street value of approximately one point three billion dollars." She paused. "That's billion, with a B."

Richter shook his head. *Billion?*

"The cartel's take would be about a sixth of that, or about two hundred million, still a sizable amount."

Sizable, yes, he thought, but he also realized it was still a long way from breaking them.

"We think this was a major distribution point for shipments to the U.S.," she added.

He nodded and made a note. "Any reaction so far?"

She passed him a series of photos. "These were released by the Mexican government this morning."

He studied the pictures. The first showed a large crater and the still-smoldering ruins of what had once been the warehouse. There were over two dozen police officers, faces hidden behind masks, standing guard. The second photo showed two men, faces bruised, hands cuffed behind them, both wearing bulletproof vests. They were being held by more masked police officers for the cameras. The third showed eight body bags lined up side by side.

"Any response from the cartels yet?"

She shook her head. "Not that we've heard." She went on to explain that she had already asked the CIA and NSA to monitor the chatter, to see if anything turned up.

She was good, Richter thought. As the Deputy National Security Advisor, she was Brett's chief of staff—he caught himself—she was his chief of staff now, at least for the time being. Three years his junior, Williams was African American and bore a striking resemblance to former Secretary of State Condeleza Rice. With penetrating eyes and a meticulous approach to analysis that rarely left her without an answer, she conveyed a sense of confidence.

"They *will* retaliate," Williams added. "It's a matter of when and where."

Richter nodded. She was right. Two hundred million dollars was a huge hit. So was the destruction of a warehouse. That would force them to reroute at least some of their shipments. How big of an impact that would have wasn't clear. He picked up the picture of the body bags. From the cartel's viewpoint, he knew, the eight men were inconsequential. They placed little value on human life, and there seemed to be a steady stream of soldiers and cops ready and willing to join their ranks.

He sat back as he thought about what he would say to the president. The mission had been successful. No innocent civilians had been injured in the process. And a hell of a lot of cocaine would never make it to the streets. Enough, possibly, to temporarily impact street prices, he thought. All that was expected, and the president could easily read that in a briefing document. As Acting National Security Advisor, what the president wanted from him was his analysis, his opinion. And Richter's gut told him that there was a tidal wave coming. They just couldn't see it yet.

———

Richter stared down the barrel, lining up the sights. He kept his focus on the front sight as the target blurred. He moved his left index finger until just the tip—the pad of his finger—touched the trigger. While keeping his focus on the front sight, he let out a breath and maintained constant pressure on the trigger, pulling back slowly. Once again, the noise surprised him and his arm jerked up. He lowered the weapon to the low-ready position and then brought it back up to his natural point of aim. He found the sights, aligned them on the target, then slowly squeezed the trigger again. The shot rang out, and his arm jerked up again. He dropped his gun to the low-ready position and went through the process again.

He had been on the range—the FBI's indoor range at Quantico—for over an hour. The first thirty minutes had been frustrating, his left hand an unwilling partner, particularly so since he could not use his right hand for support. By the end of the hour, some two hundred rounds later, he'd begun to hit the target with some consistency. His shots were dispersed, looking more random than planned, but still they seemed to find the target more often than not.

He had told the president that he would take the job as *Acting* National Security Advisor for the interim, while the president continued the search for a permanent replacement. He knew the president wanted him back in Washington and, now that he was back, he realized the demons he had fled from two years ago were no longer there. The Secret Service had a new director, and many of the old guard—agents who had been there for years—were gone, forced into retirement. And while he had no desire to go back to the Secret Service, he couldn't see himself giving up law enforcement altogether. But whether or not he could return to the FBI, as a street agent and not just as some desk jockey, remained to be seen.

After some basic suggestions, the range instructor had left him alone. Richter changed the clip, somewhat awkwardly nestling the gun against his body with his right arm. After reloading, he checked the safety once more then laid the gun on the bench before him. He flexed his left hand, working out the cramps, as he stared down range at the target, at the holes punched through the paper silhouette. Unlike his own shooting, the drones had hit their first target with precision and no collateral damage. He remembered what he'd read in the briefing on Project Boston, the last time the U.S. had aggressively gone after the cartels on Mexican soil. Then they had deployed Navy SEALs, who along with a Mexican Special Forces team, had succeeded in arresting much of the cartel leadership, destroying vast quantities of drugs, and disrupting their operations. Then, the narco-traffickers had been slow to react. But they eventually did and, after three SEALs were killed, the program had been suspended. This time, he thought as he picked up the gun, the cartels wouldn't be slow. Of that he was certain.

He shifted into a shooting stance again and fired once more. When he finished the clip, he pressed the safety, ejected the clip, and checked to make sure the gun was empty. He laid the gun on the bench in front of him.

"Not bad for a one-armed guy."

Richter turned and spotted the Director of the FBI standing next to the range instructor, behind the safety line ten yards away. Director Monahan said something to the instructor, received a nod in reply, then walked over.

Richter smiled. "Hi, Pat. I hope you didn't come all the way out here just to make sure I didn't hurt myself."

Monahan laughed. "I had to speak to the new class of agents. Someone told me you were out here." He paused as he studied the target twenty-five feet away. "Actually, for one-handed shooting, with your non-dominant hand, that's pretty impressive."

Richter smirked as he nodded toward the range instructor, now visible behind the glass in the observation booth. "I don't think he was too impressed," he said.

Monahan chuckled. "How's the arm?"

"The cast should come off in a few weeks," he responded. "Assuming the bone has healed properly."

Monahan nodded. "When are you headed back to New Jersey?"

"This afternoon." He smiled. "Patty had a paper published and received an award. Her peers are holding a reception in her honor."

"Hey, that's great." Monahan smiled. "Do you have time for lunch before you leave?"

He checked his watch. "I should. What's up?"

"The president briefed me on what's going on in Mexico. In the last twenty-four hours, our JTTFs have been picking up some chatter from informants in Los Angeles, Chicago, New York, Dallas... basically all over. I know NSA and CIA are picking up increased chatter as well. Nothing definitive but concerning nonetheless."

Richter nodded. He was aware of this. In his new job as Acting National Security Advisor he had unlimited access to information from the intelligence community and from law enforcement agencies. Quite possibly, he realized, he knew more than Monahan did. He studied the FBI Director for a moment. Monahan had been involved in Project Boston, Richter remembered. He knew what the cartels were capable of then and he knew what they were capable of now. The FBI Director had tracked him down because the chatter, as vague as it was, had him worried.

CHAPTER TWENTY-TWO

As he climbed the stairs, Matthew Richter heard the music and the dissonant sound of multiple conversations. At the top, he spotted a set of double oak doors, propped open. Even from the foyer, several clusters of people—drinks in hand, mingling—were visible. *This must be the place*, he thought. The room, lined with dark mahogany paneling, an ornate fireplace with a heavy wood mantel, and, on two walls, floor-to-ceiling bookshelves, was both a lounge and a reading room. There were half a dozen antique coffee tables, each surrounded by three or four high-back armchairs. Between the chairs were matching end tables with brass reading lamps. A string quartet was playing in one corner next to a grand piano that held several plants and an arrangement of fresh flowers. This library, Patty had told him, was reserved for faculty.

He saw her across the room. She was smiling, holding a glass of wine, and chatting with what he assumed were colleagues and friends. He scanned the room, his eyes briefly stopping on each person, before he caught himself. *Old habits die hard*, he thought, as he began walking over.

"You must be Matthew Richter."

He turned to an older, gray-haired man dressed in a conservative business suit. A pair of reading glasses hung from a chain around the man's neck.

"I'm Fred Newburg," the man said, sticking out his left hand.

The dean of the department, Richter remembered as he shook the man's hand.

"It's a pleasure to meet you, sir."

Newburg grinned. "Please don't 'sir' me. It's Fred." He laughed. "If anything, I should be calling you sir."

Richter found himself smiling back.

Newburg nodded toward Patty. "She's quite a lady. We're lucky to have her."

That makes two of us, Richter thought before he caught himself. He glanced over at Patty. Hopefully she was still feeling the same way.

Newburg continued to chat as he steered Richter toward the bar.

"Now, I don't want you to get the wrong impression," Newburg said in mock seriousness. "I don't want you to think that this is all we academics do: wine and cheese parties every night." He laughed again. "Your boss might decide to cut funding for education."

"Your secret is safe with me," Richter answered with a grin. The man was charming, he thought. He had an easygoing approach and was clearly skilled at the small talk circuit. Not unlike a politician. Well, he was the head of the Political Science department, Richter thought.

As the bartender prepared their drinks, Newburg asked, "So how's the arm doing?"

"Not bad," he responded. "The challenge has been learning to use my left hand for everything."

Newburg smiled and nodded. They chatted for a moment.

"You know, I'd like to ask you about Iran or North Korea, but Patty told me that I couldn't."

Richter smiled back but said nothing. There wasn't much he was allowed to say about either other than that they continued to monitor the situation closely; a polite way of saying, no comment.

With a glass of wine in his hand—a glass he probably wouldn't drink—he let Newberg introduce him to Patty's colleagues.

"You've been avoiding me all night." Patty was smiling, but he could see that it was forced.

Richter held up a hand in mock protest. "Hey, your boss cornered me. I kept trying to sneak away."

She frowned and rolled her eyes. His attempt at humor, he noticed, had fallen flat.

"I'm sorry," he said as he took her hand, hoping to ease the tension. "But I'm here now."

She smiled briefly. She seemed about to say something but, instead, averted her eyes, seemingly drawn to the laughter coming from the conversation behind her. She dropped his hand.

"What did you think of him?" she asked when she turned back.

"Your boss?" he asked. He was relieved that she had changed the subject. "Actually, he's very charming."

She smiled briefly again. "Speaking of bosses, I want to show you something."

She led him over to the grand piano, several Poinsettias sitting on top. At the end was a large arrangement of flowers.

"*Your* boss sent those."

He picked up the card, the Presidential Seal on the outside.

Patty-
Congratulations!
David & Maria Kendall

That wasn't surprising, he thought. It was something he had seen the president do numerous times during the eighteen months he had served on his security detail.

"He also called me," she said.

He turned. That was a surprise.

She took his hand, and he could see her eyes were moist. "*Your* boss can be very charming too. And persuasive. After I talked to him, I think I know why you couldn't say no. He needs you." She paused a moment as she stared up into his eyes. "But that doesn't mean I have to like it."

He shook his head. "I'm not happy about it either."

Then she smiled, a real smile this time, and he felt the tension ease.

She let out a sigh. "So, I guess, as long as this is only temporary," she said, her eyes steady on his until he nodded, "Then I can make the sacrifice for my country."

He grinned. "That's very patriotic of you."

She grinned back, hesitated for a second, then leaned in and whispered, "Well, you better take me home and reward me for my patriotism before I change my mind."

CHAPTER TWENTY-THREE

"You're asking for too much." Guerrero stated, careful to keep his voice even.

"But I'm the one taking the risk. Am I not?" Ramón responded. "Besides, you don't have an alternative, do you?"

Guerrero was seething. This wasn't what they had agreed to when they'd shaken hands almost three years before. He considered his position. It would take two or three weeks to reestablish his supply route to the U.S. He had other warehouses: two on the southern border with Guatemala, two in the state of Veracruz to the east of Mexico City, and one to the north in the state of San Luis Potosi. But the warehouse in Tamaulipas had been his main terminal for shipping product north. It was a risk, he had realized earlier, and one he was in the process of addressing. But he had not been quick enough.

Through a shell company, he had signed a contract on a submersible. But it would take several months to finalize the deal, and then there were the modifications that would have to be made to suit his needs. It could be four or five months before the submersible was ready. Conversely, for his overland routes, it would take him several months, at a minimum, to find another warehouse that far north, and quite likely much longer if he had to build.

He had made a mistake, and now he was stuck.

"One half?" he asked.

"One half," Ramón responded.

Ramón's men would pick up the product in Guatemala. Ramón

was even willing to cover the transportation costs and the bribes required to move the product to the U.S. In return, Ramón wanted half of the shipment for himself. The lost profits weren't the issue, Guerrero knew. Rather, it was the impact on his distribution network. When wholesalers and dealers in the U.S.—people who had come to rely on him for a steady flow of quality product—realized that he wasn't capable of supplying all of their needs, they would quickly look for alternatives. And there would be Ramón, with an abundant supply.

"One half," he finally stated.

After he hung up, he sat back thinking. He knew Ramón would continue to squeeze him, likely demanding a greater cut of the next shipment. This would further strengthen Ramón's position in the U.S. as Guerrero's own network shrunk. If he couldn't replace the lost warehouse quickly, or find another alternative soon, he would have to concede territory: first somewhere like Atlanta, then maybe Boston or Chicago, and the dominoes would start to fall. If he were able to re-establish his own supply routes quickly, he could win those dealers back.

But with his foot in the door, would Ramón ever give him that chance?

———

"Are you sure you're ready for tomorrow?" Richter asked.

"How bad could it be?" Patty asked as she snuggled up next to him on the couch. Both held cups of cocoa as the soft sounds of an orchestra playing holiday music drifted across the room. Half a dozen presents lay open below the tree, the lights twinkling off an errant bow and several small pieces of wrapping scattered below. Several other larger boxes, still wrapped, were stacked in the back.

"Have you ever heard of *enhanced interrogation techniques?*"

"I don't buy that, not even for a second." Patty said as she leaned into him. "I'm sure your mother's a wonderful person."

Righter grinned. "Oh, you two will get along just fine. I'm the one who should be worried."

Patty laughed then snuggled up again and let out a contented sigh. The following day, they would travel to Ohio for a second holiday dinner with his mother, his sisters and their families, and several cousins. They would fly, but not without several Secret Service agents on the plane with them. Once they landed, agents from the Columbus, Ohio, field office would meet them at the terminal, two armored SUVs full of gun-toting agents ready to haul Richter and Patty wherever they wanted to go.

Although he had resisted at first, with the classified information he was exposed to daily, he was considered a vulnerable target, and security protocol dictated that he have protection. It was an ironic twist that he found discomforting and more than once he had to remind himself that he was no longer the *protector,* he was now the *protectee.*

It was a role that did not come easily to him.

———

Guerrero studied his daughter. She was speaking softly to the cat, scratching its belly, seemingly more interested in the white Persian than the game on the table between them. The cat was purring, content in her lap. He cleared his throat and Carolina looked up at him, the lights from the Christmas tree reflected in her eyes. She smiled. Then she glanced down at the chessboard and, after a moment's study, moved both her rook and her king at the same time. She looked up at him and smiled again.

Guerrero tried to hide his own smile but couldn't. Carolina had just castled on the kingside. He was still surprised at how quickly she had picked up the game, learning critical opening moves, seeking to control the center of the board, developing her pieces, formulating a strategy, all while treating the game as a diversion from her main interest, whatever that happened to be at the time.

Carolina was speaking softly to the cat. They had played for the first time only two months ago, he remembered with pride. He had shared only the barest of details: the names of the pieces, their positions, their movement, and the objective of the game; to capture the king. The first two games, Carolina had moved her pieces seemingly randomly, and had quickly lost. By the third game, she began asking questions. He explained certain moves, a few basic strategies, but kept his answers brief.

Now she rarely studied the board for more than a few seconds. He suspected that she had a photographic memory. She would look away, at the TV, at her iPod or whatever else seemed to be more important at the moment. A minute or two later, she would glance back at the board and make her move. She was methodical, having taken after him.

She had her mother's beauty, yes. But from him she had inherited an athletic ability that her mother had never known. And she had inherited his ability to analyze, to reason, to plan, and to plot.

Chess was something he had first learned at the age of five from a Canadian missionary who had spent six years living and working in his barrio in Monterrey. From the missionary, he had also learned English. When the man had left, just before Guerrero had turned ten, he had given Guerrero a chessboard, telling him that he had an exceptional talent. And it was a talent, he thought with pride, that Carolina had as well. She was more intelligent than most of the people he dealt with on any given day, he thought, remembering his recent conversation with Ramón. He knew that she could do anything she wanted, that the barriers that held most people back couldn't hold her.

That thought made him proud but troubled him nonetheless. His wealth gave them everything they wanted: a huge ranch—actually, ranches—and dwellings in multiple cities, beach houses and servants and a lifestyle that was the envy of most. But as his success grew, he could feel his freedoms slowly slipping away. His wife had been the first to notice, complaining that she could no longer visit Mexico City for a long weekend, could no longer travel to the U.S. or Europe, was no longer able to dine at the restaurants she loved. It was a small trade-off, he had reasoned at the time. After all, they had everything they wanted right there.

But now, he thought as he studied his daughter, it wasn't

enough. Not for her. His own success had resulted in one barrier still standing, one that he had yet to figure out how to move out of her way. That he would figure it out was never in doubt; it was only a matter of time.

He realized Carolina was looking at him, and he smiled. She had a mischievous twinkle in her eye.

"What is it, mi amor?" he asked.

She laughed. "It's your move, Papá."

CHAPTER TWENTY-FOUR

It was three in the morning when the ambulance came to a stop at the traffic light. The driver yawned and stretched. He glanced in his mirror and noted the black truck behind him, his companion for the last six hours. He could just make out the two men in the cab, nothing more than dark shadows through the windshield. Behind them, he saw two more men leaning over the cab of the truck. Their faces hidden behind masks, they scanned the intersection nervously, their weapons ready. He knew there were two other men behind them, watching the rear. It had been a long ride, the driver thought. But for those men standing in the back, he knew, the ride had seemed much longer, for it wasn't too long ago when he had been back there himself.

The light changed and he pulled forward, while the black truck, with the emblem of the *Policía Federal* on the side, followed closely. At the next intersection he turned, then, at the end of the block, pulled through the gate into the fenced-in lot.

The police truck slowed behind him, then after a quick nod from the guards at the gate, continued on. As the ambulance pulled into the warehouse, the security guards closed and locked the gate and then the large overhead door was pulled down. This too was locked.

The driver hopped out, stretched his tired back, and nodded to the six guards waiting for him.

"Buenos días." *Good morning.*

"Buenos días. Todo bien?" He was asked. *Everything okay?*

He nodded. "Todo bien."

While the driver went to use the restroom and to find a much-needed cup of coffee, the guards opened the rear doors of the ambulance and began unloading the boxes.

Several minutes later, in the small kitchen, the driver poured his coffee and thought about the day ahead. He wanted to sleep, but by the time he got home, it would be close to five. His wife and his mother would already be up and would have his breakfast ready. Then, while they cleaned and cooked, he would play with his son, almost two years old now, until it was time for his son's nap. Then he too would take a *siesta*.

He had thought about moving closer to the city—with his new job he could afford to now—but Ciudad Juarez had become a battleground. He couldn't risk his family being caught in the violence. He poured a second cup of coffee for the ride home and headed back to the warehouse.

The shipment, he saw, had already been unloaded.

"So you are an ambulance driver now, Jorge?"

He smiled at the guard, a former *capitán* in the police and the man who had recruited him.

"Sí. I am an ambulance driver." Last week it had been a plumber's van and, before that, a farm truck, the shipment hidden below a mound of beans. Each week, something different.

"Listen. Don't go on Avenida Tecnología. There is a raid in progress."

He nodded and thanked his former boss for the warning. Ignoring the pain in his back, he climbed back into the ambulance and considered his alternatives. It would take a little longer, maybe thirty minutes at this hour, to reach the storage facility near the airport. There, he would drop off the ambulance and retrieve his car. So he would be home a little later, he knew, but it was better than finding himself caught in a shootout.

He was fumbling with the key when a blinding flash rocked the building and his world went dark.

———

It was a few minutes before 4:30 a.m. when Matthew Richter kissed a still sleeping Patty goodbye. He stepped outside to find a light dusting of snow and two Secret Service agents waiting for him on his front stoop. The first snow of the new year, he thought, a fine way to end the holidays.

"Good morning," he said. He held his hand out and caught a flake. "Going to do this all day?"

"No sir," Special Agent Wendy Tillman answered. She smiled. "At least not in Washington."

He followed Tillman to the waiting SUV, the second agent trailing behind. Tillman held the door. As Richter stepped up, his foot slipped on the slick pavement and he awkwardly grabbed the passenger assist handle to keep from falling. He felt Agent Tillman's steady hand on his back.

"Are you okay, sir?"

He nodded and thanked her as she helped him into the seat. The cast was supposed to have been removed—on the morning of New Year's Eve no less—but after seeing the results of the CAT scan, the doctor had taken the cautious approach and told him the cast had to stay on for another six weeks. He cursed silently as Tillman closed the door. He hated not being in control.

Richter's security detail consisted of three agents: a driver, an agent riding shotgun—an appropriate description of the well-armed agent who climbed into the front passenger seat—and Wendy Tillman, who climbed into the rear seat next to him. Tillman was the agent-in-charge.

Although he had been uncomfortable at first, there were some benefits to a security detail, he reluctantly admitted. With the number of classified reports and briefs he received each day it gave him more time to read. And there was always a lot of material to get through in a day. Today was no exception, he thought, as Tillman handed him the morning briefings. He turned on the map light and scanned the documents, performing his own form of triage and selecting the most critical ones to read first. With the three-and-a-half-hour ride to Washington, traffic permitting, he should be able to get through the bulk of the pile. He glanced at his watch. They should arrive in Washington by eight, just in time for a short meeting with his staff before his daily briefing with the president.

The SUV had just pulled onto the highway when his phone rang. He glanced at the phone, seeing Jessica Williams's name in the display. The SUV was equipped with a secure telecommunications unit—STU in government parlance—which allowed him to discuss sensitive matters without fear of compromising national security.

"Last night's operation was successful," she said then told him about the raid in Ciudad Juarez. They had been tracking the shipment since it had left Guatemala five days before. This shipment belonged to the Alacránes cartel, which controlled much of the central part of the country from north of Mexico City up to the State of Chihuahua. Rather than let the Mexican authorities intercept it, they had allowed the shipment to reach the warehouse in Ciudad Juarez. That was the real target, a location they had been searching for, for over three weeks.

"Preliminary estimates are nine dead and four thousand kilos of cocaine destroyed." She paused. "There were no survivors."

"We need to include this in the brief." Each morning, Richter provided a summary of breaking international events and situations—typically those that had security implications for the U.S. and for its major allies—in the president's daily brief.

"I already did," she responded. She was silent for a moment then added, "I have some bad news."

He waited.

"The two men from the Sangre Negras raid? The two survivors? They were killed yesterday while in government custody. Right now Mexico's position is that, while they were being transferred to a military prison, there was a scuffle; they tried to overpower their guards and were killed in the process."

Richter frowned. U.S. agents had been hoping to question the two men, and the U.S. Attorney's office was currently working on an extradition request. Williams promised to follow up with her contacts in the CIA, the military, and the U.S. Embassy in Mexico City to see if she could get any more insight into what had happened.

Ten minutes later he hung up. He stared out the window as dawn broke over the hills to the east. He didn't buy the story. The two men would have been handcuffed with shackles on their arms and legs. They would have been under heavy guard. It was highly unlikely that they had been able to free themselves to attempt an escape. More than likely, his gut told him, the Sangre Negras cartel had just covered their tracks by bribing the police guard.

He wasn't surprised—frustrated, yes—but not surprised. He sat back and closed his eyes and considered how difficult the war was going to be when their number one ally couldn't be completely trusted.

CHAPTER TWENTY-FIVE

There had to be a spy, Ramón thought. That was the only explanation. How else could the government have learned about his warehouse? How else could they have learned about the shipment? He picked up the pictures again, flipping through them, growing angrier with each one. There had to be a mole.

He glanced up at Eduardo. They had been together for nine years, having worked together for *los Federales*—the Federal Police—before joining the cartel. And when he took over seven years ago? Eduardo had been by his side. It couldn't be him, Ramón thought. They were like family. And what could the government offer? To be an underpaid federal servant, always struggling to put food on the table. That was the life they had both left. Why would Eduardo want to go back to that?

He glanced at the pictures again. It had to be the DEA. One of their agents had infiltrated his organization. He would find the mole. Of that he was certain. Then he would learn as much as he could from him before he sent the Americans a message. He had seen the videos posted by the Taliban. The tearful American pleading for his life. The three armed men standing behind him, weapons held ready. The tears running down the American's face as he read from the paper, listing all of America's sins. The long curved knife. The sickening scream. Then the Taliban fighter holding the severed head for the whole world to see. He smiled for the first time that day. What he planned for the mole would make the Taliban cringe.

His thoughts were interrupted by the phone. He glanced at the number, hesitated a moment, then picked up.

"The Americans are becoming a problem," he said before Guerrero could speak. "But I will handle it."

"The key to success in business," Guerrero stated as if he hadn't heard a word that Ramón had said, "is to find the opportunities before your competitors do."

Ramón frowned. He looked up at Eduardo. Eduardo's face was blank.

"Oftentimes the best opportunities come during adversity," Guerrero continued.

Ramón frowned again then felt the hairs on the back of his neck stand up. He looked back at Eduardo. Eduardo's face was still blank but then he suddenly pulled his hand up from below the table. In the half second before the flash, in the half second he had left to live, Ramón realized his mistake.

———

In the gray light of early morning, the twin white vans turned the corner, the grill lights and taillights flashing. People on the street glanced up nervously as they passed by. An old woman made the sign of the cross then clutched her sweater tightly around her throat as she hurried inside. The vans, with *Unidad Especializada de la Escena del Crimen*—Crime Scene Unit—stenciled on the side, had become a daily sight in Ciudad Juarez. Ominous and foreboding, everyone knew it meant another body had been discovered.

Two miles up the road, the vans turned another corner then signaled again as they approached the entrance to the highway. Several cops held the yellow crime scene tape up, letting them through. As the lead van pulled onto the highway, the investigator sitting in the front passenger seat craned his neck to see the overpass. Eight bodies hung motionless from the pedestrian bridge. The investigator shook his head; it had already been a long night and now eight more.

The van pulled up behind the police truck, and the investigator climbed out. As he walked to the middle of the three lane road, closed now to traffic, he glanced up at the clouds then adjusted the setting on his camera. He took several wide angle shots first to capture the full scene before zooming in. He worked fast. The eight men, their faces bloated in death, their shirts all stained with blood, weren't going anywhere. Still, he hurried. Several were missing shoes, he noted. All had their hands bound behind their backs. And all, he could see from here, had been shot in the head. He zoomed in on the first man, staring through the viewfinder at the face, at the broken nose, at the black hair matted with blood. Even with the bruising and bloating, it was a face he knew well. Victim number one was *el capitán*, the head of the Los Alacránes operations in Ciudad Juarez. He snapped two pictures then one of the sign around the man's neck. *Ciudad Juarez belongs to Las Sangre Negras,* the sign proclaimed in Spanish—a stark warning to all that the ever-shifting landscape of narco-trafficking had changed yet again.

Ten minutes later, when the investigator finished taking pictures, he walked back to the van to grab his crime scene kit. As he pulled on a pair of gloves he sighed. The night had started out like most. The first call had come not ten minutes after his shift had begun: a twenty-two, meaning a body had been discovered. That one had been shot inside a small *mercado*. Then an hour later, two more had been gunned down in a car. The driver was dead but the passenger, despite having been shot four times had survived, for a little while at least. The men who shot him found him later, a mile away, where they stopped the ambulance, pulled the wounded man out, and shot him eight more times in the head.

That was followed by three more, killed on a soccer field in front of their families, then another two while drinking beer in a bar. Eight victims in the first three hours. He should have known then that it would be a difficult night, he thought with a sigh as he climbed the steps to the overpass.

Then came the call at midnight. Eight severed heads tossed into a crowded restaurant—one favored by Los Alacránes henchmen—and the banner hung up outside: *Ciudad Juarez belongs to Las Sangre Negras.*

Eight, eight, and eight, the investigator thought as he waited for the capitán to be hoisted up to the bridge. He would perform a quick inspection of the body here before it was loaded into the van and driven back to the lab. Twenty-four in total. The first eight were likely a coincidence, he knew, but he couldn't help but wonder. Eight. *Ocho*.

More would come, he knew as he squatted down by the body. A lot more. El Ocho now owned Ciudad Juarez.

CHAPTER TWENTY-SIX

As the colonel read the email again, he felt his stomach lurch. *Be ready at six*, the note said. Just four simple words, but he couldn't shake the dread that it meant so much more. *Be ready at six*. He had to work tomorrow. El Ocho was aware of that, he knew. How would he explain his absence? He sat back, stared at the ceiling, and wondered. Why would El Ocho want to meet now? Whatever the reason, it wasn't good.

He stood and began pacing. After a minute he stopped and walked quietly to his son's room. He stood in the doorway and listened to his son's breathing. Fourteen years old and already a soccer star, his son led his high school team in goals. He smiled then quietly closed the door. He tiptoed down the hall to his daughter's room. He gently opened the door and saw that she had left her light on. He turned it off then carefully pulled the covers up to her shoulders. She rolled over and, a moment later, she was breathing peacefully again. He closed the door and stood for a while in the darkened hall. It was all for them, he thought.

After a moment, he hurried back to his computer. Fifteen minutes later, after he had transferred the funds, he began to make a list. That took some time. When he was done, he read it twice to make sure he had considered everything. He added two more items, then read it again before he finally glanced at his watch. He stood abruptly. He had a lot to do and the clock was ticking.

———

One hundred miles south of San Diego, in a food processing facility on the southwestern edge of Ensenada, the guard inspected the load once again. The two rows of pallets, each stacked with dozens of cases of strawberries, filled the truck. The pallets were double-stacked, just a foot of space between the thick corrugate boxes on top and the ceiling of the refrigerated trailer. He glanced between the two rows and nodded to himself. The strawberries, while expensive and quite profitable, were not the critical items on board.

He closed the door, locked it, then affixed the seal. He checked the manifest once again, signed it, then walked around to the front of the truck. He rapped his knuckles on the window.

"Listo," he said to the driver. *Ready.*

He handed the driver the manifest, the FDA certificates, and customs paperwork required to transport the berries across the border. As the driver closed the window and put the truck in gear, the guard pulled the chain, opening the door to the warehouse. He stepped out of the way as the driver eased the truck forward. The guard waited to close the door. But in mere fractions of a second, before he could pull the chain, his brain registered the burst of light and, in his last moment alive, images of his wife and children flashed through his mind.

———

"Any more problems?" Guerrero asked.

"No," Alberto answered. "The city is ours."

Guerrero merely nodded. That Ciudad Juarez would fall quickly had been expected.

"And the colonel?"

"He disappeared," Alberto stated, then added, "His family is missing, too."

"Do you think he's been arrested?"

"It's possible. But wouldn't we have heard about it?"

Perhaps, Guerrero thought. *Perhaps.* If the colonel had been arrested, there was little he could do to cause Guerrero harm. He had been careful. The colonel had always been blindfolded and had never known the location of their meeting sites. And the colonel would have learned little, if anything, about his operation. Any information exchanged had always flowed in the other direction: from the colonel to him.

He would get rid of the phone. That was easy. The cutout—the man who passed their email messages back and forth—that was the only link. He was no longer useful and now posed a risk. But that problem was easily solved too, he thought. He would get rid of him just like he would get rid of the phone. And if the colonel was in custody, he would easily find out through his other contacts. Then it would be a simple matter of a payment to the right person, and the colonel would be dealt with. And the message to the others would be clear.

He frowned. But if the colonel had run? That he couldn't let happen.

He locked eyes with Alberto. "Find him."

———

Tomas Mendoza didn't notice the blood on his hand, didn't feel the pain. He slammed his fist against the desk again.

The man sitting in front of him, across the desk, flinched. He nervously rubbed the scar on his cheek but said nothing. He had learned the hard way to keep his mouth closed when *el jefe* was angry.

Mendoza was oblivious to his aide's discomfort. Someone would have to pay, he thought. His own government had permitted the Americans to fly their drones and to drop their bombs on Mexican soil, on *his* soil. And now, one of his warehouses was destroyed. Hadn't he paid enough in bribes to ensure his protection? Yes, someone would have to pay.

He stood, his dark eyes piercing his aide for a moment. Then he stepped to the window and looked out over the city of Ensenada as he decided where to direct his violence.

———

On the roof of a building, half a mile away, Teniente Ramirez let out a breath. *Finally*, he thought. He had been perched on the rooftop for the last six hours.

He spoke into his radio "Target spotted."

"Roger. Sniper One has target."

He watched through his binoculars as the man stood in the window. He wondered for a second whether the glass would deflect the round but quickly put the worry out of his mind. The sniper team on the adjacent building would account for this, as they did for the wind, for the humidity, the distance; the various factors that could affect the rise and fall of the bullet.

"Sniper One has the shot," he heard in his earbud. "Waiting for authorization."

Ramirez knew they had a small window of opportunity, before the target stepped away.

"Green light, Sniper One. Take the shot."

A second later, Ramirez heard the boom and watched through his binoculars as the round punched through the window and slammed into the target's chest. A split second later, another shot rang out and he watched the target crumple to the ground.

CHAPTER TWENTY-SEVEN

Richter jotted down one final note then read through the page again. There was a lot to talk about today. After years of claiming that their nuclear development program was intended for peaceful purposes, Iran had just conducted a test of a small nuclear warhead. Although they had no intelligence yet to indicate whether the test had been successful and although Iran had yet to develop the missile technology required to deliver the warhead to its enemy—Israel being the most likely target—this was a disturbing piece of news.

More disturbing, North Korea, which had already demonstrated its ability to produce a nuclear device, had conducted missile tests of its own. Ostensibly the launch of a communications satellite, their test had been unsuccessful as the rocket failed to achieve the desired orbit.

Then there was factional fighting in Somalia, civil unrest in Egypt and Syria, Venezuela's Nicolás Maduro was once again threatening to send troops into neighboring Colombia, while China and Japan were sparring over who owned some barren rocks in the East China Sea. He sighed. Since he had briefed the president on the Ciudad Juarez raid three days ago, the situation continued to deteriorate. Murders had skyrocketed in the city with over sixty killings in seventy-two hours as rival drug factions battled for control. The violence had spread to other cities, particularly along the border.

His phone rang, interrupting his thoughts.

"He's ready for you," the president's secretary said.

"Thanks, Arlene. I'm on my way."

He stuffed his notes and the folder into his sling—at least it was useful for something, he thought—then grabbed a binder and headed down the hall.

———

"Next is Mexico, sir."

The president nodded as Richter filled him in on the latest drone strikes and the resulting violence that had ensued.

"We've been able to confirm that Ramón Calzada has been killed," Richter continued. "We also have unconfirmed reports that Tomas Mendoza is dead."

The president frowned. "The Mexican government?"

Richter shook his head. "They insist they had nothing to do with Calzada's death." Mexican President Filipe Magaña had declared the cartels and their leaders enemies of the state. But so far, that had only served as a newsworthy sound bite.

"Calzada appears to have been killed as part of a turf battle," Richter continued. "The Sangre Negras cartel is trying to take over Alacránes—that's Calzada's—territory."

The president nodded. "Seizing the opportunity?"

Richter shook his head. "Yes and no, sir. I think it's a sign that Night Stalker is starting to have an impact. The strike several weeks ago shut down a key Sangre Negras supply route. We think they are trying to replace that by overthrowing the Alacránes cartel."

"What do we know about the Sangre Negras?"

Richter handed the president a photo. "This is Pablo Guerrero. He's the head. He's violent and ruthless but he's also shrewd and calculating. He's had no formal education, at least not since elementary school, but he appears to be highly intelligent. Since taking over, he's quietly grown the Sangre Negras organization, taking over smaller rivals, building his distribution network. He's managed to avoid drawing attention to himself through a network of informants in the police and the military and by brokering peace deals with his larger rivals, including Ramón Calzada and the Alacránes cartel."

The president frowned. "Calzada was behind the attempt on Joe Delia's life, not Guerrero, right?"

"That's correct, sir. But we think Guerrero is a more formidable enemy. He's just as brutal but his moves appear to be well thought out."

The president sat back. "What's your recommendation?"

Richter had been considering this for some time. "If Guerrero does take over the Alacránes organization, he poses a far greater threat. He would double his resources almost overnight: the size of his private army, the arms at his disposal, the infrastructure he controls. Even though we've succeeded in shutting down some of their routes, the combined business would give him a huge war chest," he paused, "one that would give him a greater ability to wage a war against Mexico's government." He hesitated.

"Go on," the president prodded.

"We can't give him that opportunity."

———

The two cops leaned against their car, arms folded across their chests, and watched as the team of agents loaded the boxes into two vans. Despite the fact that February was still a few days away, both cops wore their short sleeved uniform shirts. The mild winter had left the southern states relatively unscathed—so far at least—and in Atlanta the daffodils and crocuses were already starting to bloom. Today, however, neither officer was in the mood to appreciate the early spring.

"Fucking Feds," one said.

His partner grunted.

Assigned to crowd control—their part in assisting the federal agents with the raid—there was little for them to do but watch. Patrol cars were stationed at both ends of the block, closing it off and, behind them, two other officers kept the half-dozen gawkers behind the yellow crime-scene tape that had been stretched between the telephone poles and street signs. Many more curious onlookers chose, thankfully, to watch from windows. That was fine with the two cops.

"They got the whole damn alphabet out for this one," the first cop said.

His partner grunted again.

Across the street, in the parking lot of the courier service, agents in different-colored wind breakers and shirts streamed in and out of the building. Mostly DEA, there were one or two FBI and ATF agents as well.

"The idiots are tripping all over each other," he said as they watched several agents move out of the way of two others carrying computers.

That elicited another grunt.

"Sergeant said they were running drugs out of there. You believe that shit?"

The courier service was a perfect setup, the second cop thought, but he let it go. He shrugged. "I've been on the job for fourteen years. Nothing surprises me anymore."

Their captain stepped out of the building. Both cops grinned. He was still arguing with one of the feds—over being cut out of the operation, they knew. The first cop glanced down the block. Their SWAT team had already packed up and left. They too had been pissed. They had been asked to stand by but ultimately hadn't been needed. No shots had been fired and the feds had quickly subdued the employees. Now, they were in the process of seizing evidence.

He shook his head. They didn't know much; the feds hadn't provided any information. But earlier they had seen five people being led away in handcuffs and a number of boxes and bags being carried out. Likely, they suspected, the feds were in the process of confiscating the cash, the accounting and financial records, and any drugs found on the premises.

They both turned at the noise and glanced down the block as a patrol car was moved to let the tow trucks through. They stood there for the next half hour and watched as the half-dozen courier vans were towed away.

Ah, what the hell, the first cop thought as he glanced back at the crowd which had grown. They were being paid to watch and they had front-row seats.

———

Richter glanced at the clock. It was almost 8:00 pm and Patty would be home soon. He would call her then. In the meantime, he thought as he glanced down at the report he had just finished reading, something was nagging him. He placed the report on his desk then sat back, thinking. As expected, the violence in Mexico had intensified. A week earlier, a convoy of soldiers had been ambushed just north of Mexico City and twenty-nine had been killed. Then, a police station in Matamoros had been firebombed and when the cops tried to escape, they had been cut down by gunfire. Sixteen had been killed. Three days later, the chief of police in Reynosa, after his child had been kidnapped, had ordered his men to abandon their posts before he himself resigned. Then, yesterday, a grenade had been tossed into a crowded nightclub in Tijuana, killing seven and wounding many more while, outside, a banner bearing a warning fluttered in the breeze. In contrast, though, the violence in Ciudad Juarez had begun to slow. Ciudad Juarez had been taken over by the Sangre Negras cartel. Pablo Guerrero now controlled the city.

Operation Night Stalker was clearly having an impact, Richter thought, as was Mexico's own campaign. Mexican snipers, he had confirmed, had killed Tomas Mendoza. And the latest intelligence indicated that Guerrero was in the process of moving into the Baja Cartel's—Mendoza's—region. Although Mexico had not shared their specific targets with the U.S., Guerrero had to be on the list, he thought. Looking at the remaining major players, Guerrero was the largest one left.

Meanwhile, the incidents and the bodies continued to pile up. In many cities, shootouts had become daily events. Bodies hung from overpasses. Headless corpses lay on the side of the highway. Police investigators would no sooner arrive at one scene when they were called to another. Parents were afraid to send their children to school. Business owners were nervous. The governors and mayors in the states and cities along the border, where the violence was particularly bad, had publicly condemned President Magaña, demanding an end to the carnage. The situation was deteriorating and the Mexican government was struggling to stem the bloodshed. In the U.S., the State Department had issued warnings about travel to Mexico and had suggested that Americans living in Mexico consider leaving for their own safety.

Still, as bad as it had become, Richter thought as he flipped through several pages of the report again, it wasn't as bad as some analysts had predicted. The violence had yet to spill over the border. He sighed as he sat back again. He couldn't help but wonder. Was this the calm before the storm?

CHAPTER TWENTY-EIGHT

Guerrero looked up at Alberto, his eyes dark.

"Can we get to them?"

Alberto shook his head. "I don't know, Jefe. They're being held by the DEA."

Guerrero considered this. Except for the potential that they could identify members of the Sangre Negras organization who were supplying them, the fact that some local wholesaler had been arrested was inconsequential. Like the gangs that sold the drugs on the street, the wholesalers were not part of his organization. With a little time, he could replace both. But if his distribution operation in Atlanta—the people who supplied the wholesaler—was compromised, that could be an issue.

It was no secret the drugs were coming from Mexico and, with Mendoza and Calzada gone, it was a reasonable guess that Las Sangre Negras was the source. What los gringos didn't know, he hoped, were the names, addresses and locations of the people who worked for him in Atlanta. What they didn't know was the logistics of his operation: how he was moving the drugs across the border, where he was storing them and how he moved them to local markets, like Atlanta. But if the wholesalers—operating under the guise of a courier service—were being held by the DEA, it would be difficult to silence them before they told everything they knew. The question was, what did they know?

The Alacránes cartel had a separate operation in Atlanta. He had decided, for the time being, to keep it separate from his own operation. Now he realized how wise that decision had been.

"Shut down our operation," he instructed Alberto. "We need to break the link."

Alberto nodded. "And our men?" he asked, referring to the three people who managed the distribution business.

No one else, Guerrero knew, understood how the supply chain worked. The three had been careful about that. He stared at Alberto for a moment before he responded. "Dispose of them."

After Alberto left, Guerrero sat back, thinking. The three men who ran the Atlanta operation had always been loyal, had always done whatever they had been asked to do. And along the way, they had become wealthy. But they knew the risks.

He stood. A minute later, he found himself in front of the chessboard. Carolina, he noticed, had made her move—last night, he assumed, before she had gone to bed. He studied the board, staring at her pieces, at the knight and the rook that she had deftly positioned, boxing him in. She would force him to sacrifice his queen. He smiled but the smile quickly faded.

The situation was becoming dangerous. After decades of turning a blind eye to the cartels, publically pretending they didn't exist while secretly sharing in the spoils of their trade, the Mexican government now considered him an enemy of the state. They had leveraged the resources of los gringos and were now waging a full-scale war against him and the other smuggling organizations. Their goal, he knew as he stared at the chess board and his now exposed king, was his destruction.

Sure, los gringos were becoming a problem. They had recently changed their tactics, working closely now with the Mexican government to bring their war here. But that was because the Mexican government was weak. They hadn't stood up to los gringos. Instead, President Magaña had sold out to the Americans; had become their puppet.

It wasn't all bad, he realized. In the short term, he would benefit. He had taken over a large portion of the Alacránes operation and now, with Mendoza dead—killed supposedly in a shootout with Mexican soldiers—he would move into Baja territory. But, he knew, that would also make him a bigger target.

He sat back, his hands forming a steeple below his chin. Yes, he thought as he stared at the chessboard, he would have to carefully consider his next move.

CHAPTER TWENTY-NINE

General Diego Salazar dined alone. Normally, when his wife was away, he dined out with one of his aides. Even though the maid at home would have food prepared, he hated an empty house. The children were adults now, living on their own; one in Toronto, and one in Madrid. His wife was in Egypt, her third trip overseas without him in the last year. She was touring the pyramids and the museums; taking the trip they had planned to take together, but with her sister instead of him. It was his own fault, he knew. But, he couldn't leave, not now, not with the threat his country faced.

He glanced up at the waiter, standing expectantly ten feet away. The general nodded and the waiter hurried over to clear away the dinner plate.

Normally, when his wife was away, the colonel would dine with him. Normally. But the colonel was missing and the general was worried. The colonel's family was missing too and it was beginning to look like they had fled, hastily, in the middle of the night. Now, he realized, he had been a fool; that the colonel had been playing both sides. At first, it had been difficult to accept; to believe that the colonel had deceived him. The man had been a good soldier, a capable aide, and someone that he had considered a friend. But the colonel would forever remain a colonel, not having the political skills and polish required to receive a star. Maybe that was why, the general thought.

He sipped his coffee and sat back thinking. He was worried.

Not about the colonel's fate. Traitors deserved their justice and if the cartels were after him, then justice would be served. No, he was worried that his operations against the cartels were compromised. Mexico was at a tipping point and the next few months would decide the country's fate. They had made considerable progress against the cartels: Calzada was dead, Mendoza was dead and, working with the Americans, they had shut down several key distribution routes and destroyed more drugs than he had ever imagined—somewhere now in excess of ten billion dollars according to the report he had read.

Yes, they had made progress, but Pablo Guerrero and Las Sangre Negras were still operating, growing stronger with each passing day. Although there were still a handful of smaller organizations— the Carrillo family in Acapulco, the Campeche cartel in the Yucatan, *Los Arquitectos* in Michoacán—Guerrero was the worry. He had profited from the attacks as he quickly stepped in and took over rival operations. If they could succeed in capturing or killing Guerrero and dismantling the Sangre Negras operation, the rest would fall. Guerrero was the next target.

President Magaña, while pleased with the progress, was pressuring him for a large-scale push; an assault that would be a decisive blow against Guerrero. The risk, though, was how much of their current plans were compromised? How much did Guerrero know? And if the colonel had been corrupted, who else on his staff had been?

He took another sip of coffee and glanced up at the man hurrying across the room. The man stopped five feet from the table and saluted.

"General." The military aide said, holding up the briefcase. Salazar nodded toward the empty chair next to him. The aide placed the briefcase on the chair, saluted again, and withdrew. The general sighed as he signaled the waiter. He needed to review the latest intelligence reports but he couldn't do that here. He would wait until he got home.

———

Outside, the military aide climbed into the car and let out the breath he had been holding for the last five minutes. The man sitting be-hind the wheel glanced over.

"It is done?"

The aide nodded as the driver put the car in gear. As the driver pulled out into traffic, the aide pulled his cell phone from his pocket. He waited until they were at the end of the block before he dialed the number. He didn't bother to hold the phone to his ear. He didn't bother to listen for the ring. He stared ahead and waited. A second later, the car shook from the loud explosion behind them.

———

Richter sat on the examination table and stared at his arm. There was an ugly scar curving around what was left of his bicep from the bullet wound and the surgery that had followed. He shook his head as he cautiously flexed his muscles, or what was left of them. His arm was now thin and weak, the muscles having atrophied after too many weeks in a cast. The hairs were matted and the skin felt clammy. He cautiously moved his arm slowly up and down and to the side, hoping that his days in a cast were over. Unable to make the trip to New Jersey, he had gone to Walter Reed Medical Center instead.

He looked up as the door opened and the orthopedist stepped in.

"The good news," the doctor began, "is that everything looks like it healed properly." She dropped the file on the table beside Richter and took hold of his arm, one hand on his elbow, the other holding his hand. She gently moved Richter's arm up and down and to the side, watching his face for signs of pain. She lifted his hand above his head—far more than he had done moments earlier—and, despite the pain, he gritted his teeth and said nothing.

The doctor, an army captain, frowned.

"Look, Mr. Richter. I've consulted with the surgeons in New Jersey and I've seen the films. The bullet did a lot of damage, above and beyond the obvious damage to the bone. There was extensive soft tissue damage as well as some nerve damage." She searched his face for comprehension.

Richter nodded but said nothing.

"You've lost a lot of muscle mass, and that will take time to rebuild, six months or more. And we won't know whether or not you've lost any range of motion until you complete physical therapy."

"What are you saying, doc?"

"I'm saying that you were lucky. The surgeons who operated on you did a marvelous job. But I don't want you thinking that you can strap on a Kevlar vest tomorrow and go back to bagging bad guys." She put her hand on his shoulder. "This is going to take time. There's no reason to believe that you won't regain full range of motion"—she held his eyes for a second to make sure he understood—"*if* you follow the therapist's orders. But whether you can return to active duty?" She paused again. "I just don't want you to set your sights too high. Not just yet."

———

It was late at night when Mexican President Filipe Magaña left his second-floor office in *Los Pinos*. Located in the center of Mexico City, in the Chapultepec Forest on land that was once ruled by Emperor Maximilian from his castle nearby, Los Pinos was often referred to as the Mexican White House. The name came from the many pine trees that still adorned the sprawling property.

Magaña wasn't thinking about that as he stepped outside. It was a cool evening, though he hardly noticed. He passed the fountain and followed the cobbled lane through the lush gardens. His security detail trailed close behind. As he passed a statue, he thought of the string of events that brought him here, walking the grounds of Los Pinos, the burden of the presidency weighing heavily on his shoulders. He had never wanted to be president. Three years ago, just four months shy of the national election, Luis Lara, his party's candidate, had been killed while campaigning. After three days of internal turmoil, the party selected Magaña, a relatively young foreign-educated engineer currently serving as a campaign policy advisor, as their candidate. Although he had initially refused, party elders had eventually persuaded him, convincing him that no one else had the skill, the vision to succeed. They must have been right, he mused later. He had beaten his opponent by a full two-point margin and had been dubbed *the accidental president* by the press.

Having served in the navy, something unusual for a technocrat, he knew well the burden that commanders carried—a burden that came from having to order troops into harm's way, knowing, as he did so, that some would never return alive. General Salazar was dead. Investigators suspected that the bomb had been in a briefcase, delivered to the general's side by an aide who was now missing. While it was obvious that the cartels were behind the attack, he knew that he too was to blame; as he was for the twenty-eight other people— waiters and patrons—who had been killed along with the general.

It was a war started by his predecessor, a war that he had inherited when he took office three years ago. But it was also a war that he had escalated after evidence was uncovered linking the cartels to Lara's assassination. He had approached the cartels as he had the many challenges facing Mexico: as problems that could be solved only after understanding the root causes. Then, with sufficient resources and the right legal structure, solutions could be applied. The underlying causes for the cartel problem were related to a failed educational system and lack of economic opportunity coupled with widespread corruption in the criminal justice system. That and an almost insatiable appetite for drugs from the neighbor to the north.

While he knew that reforms were sorely needed, he also knew that Mexico was on borrowed time and that the country would not be able to survive for however long it would take before the reforms took effect. He saw the war now for what it was: a war for survival. The social fabric of Mexico was being torn apart and the country was on the verge of collapsing.

The general was—had been, Magaña corrected himself—a capable man in a difficult job. He knew that Salazar was an idealist and had never been tempted by the lure of cartel spoils. Instead, he had committed himself to restoring security within the fragile state.

With Salazar leading the charge, they had made great strides, but now the enemy was fighting back. And the general had been killed in the latest battle. Magaña sighed. Like any good commander, he knew, he had to order someone else to take the hill. The war was far from over. He had to appoint someone to take the general's place.

By the time he returned to his office, he was steeled in his resolve.

CHAPTER THIRTY

The knock finally came at ten in the morning. Terry Fogel had been waiting, ready. He opened the door and found the guard; a new face this time. Behind him, a second guard stood further back, his gun ready. Fogel grinned. They had come prepared. The first guard signaled with his hand and Fogel grinned once more before he turned. He could sense the guard's nervousness as the hands slid up and down his legs, then onto his waist. Still grinning, Fogel turned and held his arms out. The guard slid his hands up under his arms then back to his waist again.

Finally, the guard stepped back and Fogel dropped his arms.

"Enjoyed yourself now, did you, lad?"

The guard's dark eyes narrowed, but he said nothing. He stepped back and motioned with his head and Fogel followed. He could sense the second guard behind him.

He was led out to the courtyard, to a table in the middle. The guard pulled out a chair.

"Wait here," he ordered.

Fogel sat. The guard glared at him again, the warning unmistakable. Fogel glanced around the garden, noticing the six men standing along the perimeter. There were two more, he knew, standing behind him by the archway. All were heavily armed, he could see. He remained seated, remembering the guard's look. He could follow orders when it suited his purpose.

He waited patiently and after a few minutes was rewarded by

the sound of footsteps behind him.

"Señor Fogel." Pablo Guerrero suddenly appeared; his tone was sharp.

Fogel nodded in greeting. "Señor Guerrero. It's nice to see you again."

Guerrero scowled. "I wish I could say the same, Señor Fogel."

Fogel said nothing as Guerrero sat in the chair across from him.

Guerrero considered him for a second then held up his cell phone and passport and slid them across the table.

Fogel bowed his head in acknowledgement.

Guerrero smiled briefly. "If I remember correctly, you drink tea."

Fogel nodded again. "That would be nice."

Guerrero snapped his fingers and, moments later, two men appeared with place settings and a tea and coffee service. Not waiters from the hotel, Fogel noticed. Serious, cautious, he knew Guerrero was not a man to be trifled with. Or crossed.

He had met with two of Guerrero's associates in Mexico City two days earlier. Both he and his luggage had been searched and his passport and cell phone had been confiscated. Then, unexpectedly, there had been a flurry of phone calls, hushed conversations and a long wait before he was finally shoved into the back of the car. Two hours later, sometime after midnight, they had arrived at a hotel or a house, somewhere outside the city he guessed. With the blindfold on, he wasn't exactly sure. Although he didn't speak Spanish, he sensed the tension; he caught the cautious tone, and knew that something had happened. Then, on the TV in his room, he learned of the bombing. No one had to tell him who was behind it.

Late the next morning, he was blindfolded and thrown into the car again. Four hours later, they arrived at a second hotel. The room he was given was small but comfortable. Sometime after he arrived, a meal had been delivered. He had fallen asleep easily—a soldier's habit—and slept soundly. He woke early and had already showered and dressed when breakfast was delivered at seven. Although he hadn't left his room, he hadn't seen or heard any other guests since his arrival. Guerrero, he had concluded, had taken over the entire hotel.

Guerrero took a sip of coffee then sat back. "The loss of the guns was disappointing."

Fogel nodded, hiding his smirk. Although they had discussed the FBI raid on the militia group in New Jersey months ago—in a short and somewhat cryptic phone call—this was the first time they'd had a chance to meet face to face. Fogel had realized a while back that Guerrero ruled by fear and, therefore, felt the need to occasionally remind Fogel what befell those who displeased him. "An unfortunate occurrence," he paused, "But this is a dangerous business, Señor Guerrero; not one without risks."

Guerrero glared at him. "Your choice of business partners? Was that too an unfortunate occurrence?"

Fogel was quiet a moment before responding. "You knew their intent." That wasn't exactly true, he knew, but the militia's hatred of the U.S. government was no secret. That they would take their hatred beyond talk—that they would develop detailed plans, scout sites and pick their targets—hadn't been a surprise. Gerry Nichols, he had sensed from the beginning, was different. A zealot to be sure, Nichol's eyes had told him all that he needed to know. The man was ready to die for his cause.

Nichols had provided him with the funds and asked him to acquire certain critical components on their behalf. It had taken some time for research and he had eventually figured out a way. Then the FBI had killed Nichols. Frankly, it was only through luck that he hadn't been there when the FBI raided the compound.

An outsider, he had initially been approached to help with training. Then he had helped set up the smuggling operation, more out of boredom than anything else. It was a challenge and the cash was good. Then, when Nichols had told him his ultimate goal, he was intrigued. As in Ireland, ideology played no role in what he did. Any beliefs he had once held had been lost long ago. To him, it was all a game; a very dangerous one to be sure, but a game nonetheless.

Guerrero's eyes narrowed. "Have you made alternative arrangements?"

Fogel nodded. "I have," he paused, "But I'm not sure it's more guns you need."

Guerrero glared at him.

"I'm a student of history." Fogel smiled then shrugged. "How could I not be growing up where I did?" His smile vanished. "And the Americans are an interesting lot."

"Meaning what?" Guerrero demanded.

"The environment has changed," Fogel said. "The Americans have become much more aggressive. And they seem to be working with your own government, more so now than in the past."

Guerrero studied him for a moment. "And your point?"

Fogel sat forward, resting his arms on the table. "Let me answer your question this way, Señor Guerrero. The American policy toward Mexico has been inconsistent, has it not? Their approach has been fragmented and many times contradictory. But, in the 1990's, what became clear was that combating the growth of the drug trade was their top priority. Not NAFTA. Not immigration." He paused. "But drugs. That had not been a good time for the cartels, had it?"

Guerrero frowned but said nothing.

"But on September Eleventh, all of that changed. They turned their focus to Iraq and to Afghanistan." Fogel took a sip, studying Guerrero over the rim of his cup. He knew he had the man's attention now. He took another sip.

Guerrero's eyes narrowed. "But, what was it? Three...four years ago? They sent their Navy SEALs here. Their focus has been shifting back."

"It has," Fogel said as he put his cup down. "But what happened when several of their SEALs were killed? They have no stomach for the sacrifices required; not after Iraq and Afghanistan." He paused. "And when the SEALs were killed, they changed their policy yet again. They began to target the distribution networks you have throughout their cities. Perhaps they thought those represented a bigger threat to them because they are much closer to home. Or perhaps," he paused, "it was a way to appease the voters, to provide some footage for the news stations, to show they were doing something."

Guerrero sat back, his hands steepled below his chin. "And their drones?"

"Another shift in strategy. And a low-risk way to go after you again. You might be able to shoot down a few of their planes, but no American blood will be spilled." He smiled then reached for his cup again. About to take a sip, he stopped, the cup inches from his mouth. "Wouldn't it be nice, Señor Guerrero, if Al Qaeda struck again?"

———

Matthew Richter, sitting in the fourth row, was only half-listening. His eyes were on Nancy Watson and her two children, huddled together in the front row. The boy, he noticed, was sitting stiffly, staring straight ahead. Wearing a dark suit—one that, Richter guessed, had been purchased recently in anticipation of a day that no one wanted to come—he seemed oblivious to his mother's arm, to the words whispered in his ear. On the other side, the little girl, her blond ponytail just visible above Nancy's shoulder, was lost in her mother's embrace. He had met them once, at the hospital. It had been an awkward moment, he remembered.

The president said something and he heard a few chuckles. Nancy's shoulders shook and for a second he thought she was laughing. Then someone, her mother he guessed, handed her a tissue. She sobbed quietly. When she looked up, she wiped her eyes and glanced over at her husband. The coffin, draped in an American flag, sat directly in front of the altar.

He had met Brett Watson four years ago, the last time he had worked in the White House. At the time, Watson had been the Deputy National Security Advisor; someone he saw frequently when he was standing watch in the West Wing. He always seemed to be rushing somewhere; his head down, his face full of worry, a stack of reports in his arms. He had devoted his life to his country, the president said, first as an officer in the Coast Guard, then, after getting his master's degree, as an analyst for the CIA. He had left the CIA to join the National Security Staff some fifteen years ago.

His last meeting with Watson had been brief: a ten minute visit in the hospital where it became clear that Watson no longer had any time to devote to his country. Forty-nine years old, Richter thought, shaking his head. And now, his wife Nancy was left to raise two children by herself.

As the president continued, Richter's mind drifted. He wanted to call Patty; she was still upset that he had cancelled their plans for the prior weekend—a Valentine's weekend away, no less—and he knew he had to find a way to make it up to her. But she would ask when he was coming home and he wasn't sure what he could tell her. Mexico was reeling after the assassination of General Salazar. At the same time, a CIA report indicated that the Sangre Negras and remaining cartels were stockpiling food, water, gasoline and supplies—an ominous sign. Richter and the president had discussed the possibility of increasing the DEFCON level from Five to Four. The change would signal a heightened state of alert, an increase in intelligence gathering and greater national security measures. Military commanders would increase troop readiness to a level above that normally maintained in peacetime. It was not a move to be taken lightly. But one, Richter thought, that they might have to make.

CHAPTER THIRTY-ONE

Carolina Guerrero glanced out the window at the blue sky and smiled. She had been waiting a long time for this day and, over the last week, the days had seemed to stretch longer and longer, each taking forever to end. She checked the calendar on her bureau a second time, just to make sure she wasn't dreaming. February 21st. She *wasn't* dreaming—today she was nine!

She hurried as she changed her clothes, excited for the day ahead. She couldn't wait to see the surprise Papá had for her. She glanced at her riding pants and her boots, which Cecilia had laid out on her bed. She hadn't planned on wearing those today—she had planned on wearing a dress—but Cecilia had told her that she would look pretty in them, very grown up.

"Your papá will be so proud when he sees you!" Cecilia had said.

She quickly pulled on the pants then the boots and stood. She glanced at herself in the mirror and smiled again. She *did* look good. Papá *would* be proud.

She found Papá outside by the pool. He was speaking on the phone but turned at the sound of her footsteps. He smiled and held up one finger. She waited for him to finish; not an easy thing when she knew that he had a surprise. Thankfully, she didn't have to wait long.

"Mi amor!" he said holding his arms wide.

She ran into his hug.

"Happy birthday!" he said as he wrapped his arms around his daughter. After a moment, he stepped back holding her at arms' length. "Let me look at you!" he said, beaming. "You look beautiful!"

She leaned in and hugged him again.

"Are you ready?" he asked.

"Sí, Papá!" she said.

"Well then," he said as he led her to the stone path that curved past the house, "come on!"

Half way down the path he stopped, by the stone bench below the trellis, and rubbed his chin, feigning confusion.

"Where were we going again?"

"Papá!" Carolina protested playfully.

After a second, a smile spread across his face. "Wait here, mi amor," he said in a whisper. "I'll be right back."

"Papá!" she protested again, but she sat anyway, knowing it was part of the game.

She watched as her father turned and continued down the path.

———

"Target spotted," Teniente Ramirez called softly over his radio. He watched through the binoculars from almost half-a-mile away as the man emerged from around the building. A second later his radio hissed.

"Sniper One has target," he heard in his earbud. "Setting up shot."

"Hold for authorization," he ordered.

"Sniper One holding," he heard in reply.

Ramirez knew it would take some time for the sniper and his spotter to dial in on the target. The spotter would calculate the wind speed and the bullet's drop over the twelve-hundred-meter distance between his perch in the mountains and the target below. The sniper would make minute adjustments to his scope and his aim to compensate.

Ramirez watched as the target disappeared into the stables.

———

Carolina fidgeted, wondering what her Papá was doing. She knew it had to do with the surprise. But he had been so playful lately, leaving little clues, most of which, she knew, were false. It was a game they often played. After a few seconds, she stood and began walking down the path that her Papá had followed. When she rounded the corner, she spotted the stables and realized that was where her Papá had gone. That was why Cecilia had prepared her riding clothes. And she knew, in that moment, what the surprise was.

———

Inside the stables, Pablo Guerrero took the reins of the sleek black mare from the stable hand.

He whispered softly, "Tranquila, chica." *Easy, girl.*

The horse snorted in reply and nudged him with her nose. She could smell it, he knew. He pulled the apple from his pocket and held it out to her. He hadn't named her yet; he would let Carolina do that. He smiled as he anticipated the look on her face. When the horse finished the apple, he patted her softly.

"Listo?" he asked her. *Ready?*

The horse snorted again, and he turned and began leading her toward the stable door.

———

Ramirez stared at the stable door through his binoculars. It wasn't an ideal shot given the distance, the angle, and the short gap between the trees that lined the path and the stable door, but framed by the doorway, the sniper had told him, it would be a clean shot. The sniper, some four hundred meters behind him, higher up in the mountain, had a better vantage point, he knew. He would have already dialed in on the doorway, estimating where the target's center mass would be inside the frame. Once he reappeared, it would take only a moment to make a few slight adjustments.

———

Carolina stopped for a second when she saw her father emerge from the stable. When she saw what was behind him, what he was lead-ing out of the stable by the reins, she shrieked and began to run.

———

Two seconds after Guerrero reappeared, Ramirez heard his radio.

"Sniper One has a clean shot,"

He studied the scene for a second before he answered.

"Green light, Sniper One," he responded. "Take the shot."

A second later, Ramirez saw a flash of color through the trees lining the road to the stable and cursed.

"Sniper One hold!" he hissed into his microphone.

The words had barely left his mouth when, to his horror, he heard the crack of a rifle and, a fraction of a second later, saw the young girl crumple to the ground.

CHAPTER THIRTY-TWO

"Jesus! How could this have happened?" The president demanded.

"We don't know, sir." Richter paused. "They deployed a sniper team. These guys are very good, well-trained, extremely disciplined." He nodded at his cast. "But in any operation, there's always a risk."

The president let out a sigh then nodded. "How old was the girl?"

"Nine," Richter responded.

The president rubbed his face. "I need to call Magaña."

Richter waited. The president seemed lost in thought.

"Sir?" He waited for the president to look up. "It wasn't our operation."

"I know. I know." The president waved his hand dismissively. "But Jesus! A nine-year-old girl?"

Richter waited. The president sat forward, elbows resting on his knees. Richter knew that he felt that he was partly responsible. After a second, the president looked up. There was a pained look on his face.

"He's going to want revenge," he finally said.

Richter nodded but said nothing.

"Okay," the president said as he sat up straight. "I want our folks working with the Mexicans, sharing any intelligence we have, anything we pick up…" His voice trailed off. "Do you think Guerrero will target us?"

"I don't know, sir." He paused. "There's been some press recently—mostly editorials in Mexican newspapers and online blogs—questioning Magaña's ties to us. One even called his administration a puppet government, beholden to the U.S." Richter frowned. "It's possible that Guerrero shares this sentiment. He must know that it was our drone that took out his facility several weeks ago. He must also know that many of their units, especially their elite units—their special forces—train with our guys," he added as he sat back. "It's possible that he could see us as partly responsible for his daughter's death."

The president considered this. "We need to be prepared. Homeland Security. The FBI. We need our folks working together on this; no turf wars."

Richter nodded and made a note then looked up. He caught the president's eye. "I think we need to discuss at what point and under what circumstances do we send our own forces in, to help them."

The president shook his head. "I'm not prepared to do that. Not yet. I've agreed with President Magaña that we would only do that as a last resort, and only if he requests it."

Richter said nothing for a moment, then put his pen and pad down. "I'm not saying we're at that point yet, but we need to define what we mean by 'last resort.' And our troops need to be prepared before we reach that point."

The president sighed and sat back. After a few seconds, he nodded.

Richter studied him for a moment. "We also need to speak to the National Security Council," he said softly.

After a second, the president nodded slowly. Unsure before, it was clear now that it was time to change the DEFCON level.

———

"It wasn't your fault, Dave," Maria said as she studied her husband. He was standing in front of the fireplace. He picked up a picture of Angela and Michelle and ran his fingers lightly across the glass.

"Then why do I feel like it was?" he said as he put the picture back on the mantle. "She was only nine years old." He sighed. "Just nine."

Maria stepped over and wrapped her arms around him. He shook his head and let out a heavy sigh. "There are some things about this job that I absolutely hate," he confessed. "It's tough to hear something like that and know that I played some role, however small, that led to her death." He shook his head. "Hell, she was just a kid."

She rubbed his back.

"How's Matthew doing?" she asked, grabbing his hand.

Kendall realized what his wife was doing, but he joined her anyway as she led him to the couch.

"He's doing a fantastic job," Kendall answered as they sat. Although Matthew hadn't been trained as a national security analyst, he had learned quickly, one of the risks every president faced was how information and analysis tended to morph and change as it made its way through the hierarchy and ultimately to the Oval Office. Along the way, the spin doctors changed the slant, deleted this, added that, and by the time it was presented to him, any semblance of reality was questionable. Because of his investigator's background, Matthew routinely challenged the analysis and opinions of the intelligence agencies and the military. He was able to sort through the BS, and Kendall knew that Matthew would always bring him an objective answer. He had ruffled a few feathers along the way, but that was what Kendall wanted. Brett Watson had done the same.

Matthew was one of the few people that Kendall trusted implicitly. And he couldn't have been happier when Matthew had told him about Patty.

"What?" Maria asked.

He raised his eyebrows.

"I saw the hint of a grin."

"Oh." He shook his head. "I didn't realize I was that transparent." He smiled conspiratorially. "Matthew has a new lady friend." He told Maria what he knew. Although he and Matthew were close, Matthew normally didn't offer up such personal information. A lot,

Kendall knew, had to do with the setting. Advisors to the president had learned to leave their own personal worries and concerns as well as their joys and successes at the door when they stepped into the Oval Office.

"You know," Maria said with a smile. "I suspected something when I met him a few months back. He seemed happy." She looked up and Kendall nodded. "I'm glad for him," she continued. "He needs someone."

"That sounds like a mother speaking."

Maria laughed. "We ought to invite them both to dinner."

"I wouldn't mind meeting her myself." He sighed. "But with everything going on right now, it may take a while to arrange."

They sat in silence for a moment before the president put his arm around his wife. She leaned in.

"Thank you," he said softly.

She turned and looked up. "For what?" she asked, feigning ignorance.

"For helping me put all this in perspective," he said. He kissed her. "But mostly, just for being you."

———

As Terry Fogel made his way through the crowds, he could sense that something had happened. There was always a tension in the airport: missed connections, delays, people hurrying to catch planes. But he could sense something else, even if he couldn't speak the language.

He stepped into the restaurant and smiled, then shook his head at the hostess as he made his way to the bar. As he sat, the bartender asked him, in broken English, what he wanted.

"Jameson's," Fogel said with a grin, nodding toward the bottles on the back of the bar.

He smiled again when the bartender placed the shot in front of him.

They chatted for a few minutes, then Fogel nodded toward the TV in the corner and asked what had happened. The bartender, a

dark-skinned Mexican, with more Aztec than Spanish blood running through his veins Fogel guessed, shook his head. He glanced
cautiously at other patrons then leaned forward.

"They killed his daughter," he said softly.

Fogel feigned surprise as the bartender filled in the blanks.
Nothing shocked him anymore.

The bartender held his gaze for a moment then turned and
walked to the end of the bar to serve another customer. Moments
later, when he returned, he picked up a glass and polished it with a
towel. He glanced around once more then leaned forward again. "El
Ocho will get his revenge," he said with a knowing eye and a nod.
"Just wait."

Fogel asked several questions and the bartender, in a quiet voice
and with more than a touch of reverence, answered. Fogel wasn't
surprised. He had seen the same thing from some of the boys back
home. The exploits of some of his colleagues had become legend.
His own had too, for a while anyway. And here in Mexico, in the
barrios, amongst the working class, amongst the poor, El Ocho was
a hero.

It was a strange thing, Fogel thought. El Ocho was viewed as a
hero. But then again, maybe it wasn't so strange. Although many
innocent civilians had been caught in the crossfire over the years,
El Ocho had provided where the government had failed. He offered
jobs where there previously had been none. He built schools and
medical clinics and provided housing to people who had no means
to support themselves. And, because of him, people who would otherwise go hungry had food on their tables. And he did this by sat-
isfying the depraved needs of the Americans; a people Fogel knew,
who had too much time and too much money on their hands.

And so the game would continue, as it always did, as it always
had for thousands of years: the Arabs and the Jews fighting over
the same piece of dusty desert; the heavy-handed Chinese government suppressing a people who wanted nothing more than to have
a small measure of control over their own lives; ethnic cleansing in
the Balkans; apartheid in Africa; slavery and a brutal repression of

the Native Americans in the U.S.; the list went on and on. And in his own country, almost eight hundred years of oppression under the British.

It always came down to four things: economics, race, religion, and ideology. In his own life, he had found the key to economic success by serving as a hired gun, a mercenary available to the highest bidder. He would never become rich, but he lived comfortably and always had enough in his pocket for a good Irish whiskey. The differences in race, he never understood. And as for religion and ideology, he no longer had time for such nonsense.

When the bartender left to serve another customer, Fogel glanced up at the TV, certain that Guerrero would call again.

CHAPTER THIRTY-THREE

Patty sighed. It wasn't supposed to be like this. She had planned a quiet dinner for the two of them. Then, in the morning, Matthew had promised to take her to New York City, to make up for the Valentine's weekend they had missed. They had planned to visit the Museum of Natural History, have a late lunch in Little Italy, then check into a hotel. In the evening, they had tickets to a play—a Broadway production she had been looking forward to.

Now, she thought as she stared down at her half-packed suitcase, he wouldn't be coming home at all. Although Matthew hadn't said much—security procedures typically prevented him from sharing all but what was already on the news—he had told her that an operation in Mexico had gone badly. What exactly that was, she wasn't sure. There had been nothing on the news, not yet at least, but whatever it was, it was causing concern within the White House.

She knew that Matthew had been looking forward to the weekend too; they had talked excitedly last night. She also knew that world events were out of his control. Still, she sighed as she began putting her clothes away, she couldn't help feeling disappointed.

———

Guerrero sat stone-faced as his wife wept openly beside him. He didn't notice her sobs. He didn't hear the cries of the others behind him. He didn't hear the words of the priest. He didn't see the large arrangements of flowers, almost overwhelming the small, white casket. He didn't see the ring of men, all armed with automatic weapons, all nervously scanning the crowd.

His father had once told him that all a man had in this world was his family and his God. His father, an old man then, close to death himself, had been wrong. He had no family. His Carolina was gone, stolen from him. And he had no God. What kind of God would permit this?

The sun shimmered off the casket, the reflection painful to his eyes. Still, he didn't blink. He continued to stare at the white box that contained his only child. He would no longer see her smile. He would no longer see her eyes sparkle. He would no longer hear her laugh. The image of her lying on the ground, her head destroyed, was forever burnt into his brain. He sat and stared, no concept of time passing.

Sometime later, he wasn't sure how long, he startled as the casket began to blur. Confused, he continued to stare as his vision clouded. He shook his head, a small movement, reluctantly taking his eyes away from the casket, away from his Carolina. His head hung on his chest and he stared down at his hands, blurry but folded neatly in his lap, as they had been for the last four hours. Something splashed, and he saw that his hands were wet.

He looked up again, noticing for the first time that he was alone. The sky was beginning to darken and a moment later he felt the first drops of rain. He wiped his eyes then put his hands on his knees and stood slowly. He took two steps and then his hands were on the casket. He stood there for some time, his own tears mixing with the raindrops that splattered off the polished wood.

The rain stopped just as suddenly as it had started. He wiped his eyes again and straightened. It was a while before he spoke.

"Sí, Carolina," he finally said. "It is my move."

———

Matthew Richter studied the aerial photos. The ranch, over one thousand acres, was nestled in the mountains north of Ciudad Victoria in the state of Tamaulipas. He studied the rugged terrain, the mountains along the eastern border, the patches of desert scrub brush and dirt to the west, the cluster of buildings and, beyond, the stables, riding trails, and cattle pastures.

His soldier's eye went first to the security, noting the layers: the outer perimeter fencing, the high walls farther in, the roving teams of guards, and the second wall surrounding the buildings. The guards, even from the aerial shot he could see, were all heavily armed, many on ATVs. He picked up another photo. A young man, eyes hard, wearing the bush hat and the combat fatigues of a Special Force unit of the Mexican Air Force stared back at him. He was part of a total security force estimated at two hundred and twenty, all suspected to be deserters of the same unit. *A small, highly trained, and heavily armed enemy*, he thought with a frown.

He glanced at the aerial photo again. Along the outer wall were machine gun nests—bunkers concealed in the heavy brush and supposedly manned twenty-four hours a day. There was a chance, CIA analysts had said, that some of the bunkers were also equipped with surface-to-air missiles. Yet, despite the security, another Special Forces unit, this one from the Mexican Navy, a unit that routinely trained with U.S. Navy Seals, had been able to insert a sniper team. No doubt since then the elaborate security at the compound had been increased. He studied the cluster of buildings and then individual photos of each. He read the descriptions on the back, reviewing what he had heard earlier.

The final series of photos were of Pablo Guerrero; his chief of staff, Alberto Espinoza; and those of various members of the Sangre Negras hierarchy. Richter stared at Guerrero's face for a moment then sat back thinking.

He could not fault the Mexican government for their decision to deploy the sniper teams. President Magaña had declared the cartels an enemy of the state, and that made the leaders legitimate military targets. That Guerrero's daughter had been killed was a tragedy, an unfortunate accident that could have been avoided had the sniper team chosen a better angle. However, as he knew, conditions in the field were often different from how they appeared during planning sessions, and a soldier in the field often had to improvise.

Although Mexico had suspended any further sniper missions while they completed the investigation, President Magaña was undeterred. The Mexican military was considering several options, including an assault of the compound, but had specifically requested the use of U.S. drones to minimize the casualties.

Richter had to give President Kendall an answer. He was against using the drones where non-combatants were present unless they were only being used for surveillance. But the Mexican government had requested armed drones. Unless they could isolate Guerrero— something the Mexican sniper team had tried, unsuccessfully, to do—his instinct was to say no. There were too many servants, gardeners, chauffeurs, and others whose only crime was working for the Guerrero family. That made a drone strike risky. An aerial assault of the compound was risky too, he knew, both because of the suspected SAM capability and the risk that innocent bystanders would get caught in the ensuing firefight.

He sat back and, without thinking about it, began a series of exercises, moving his arm as the physical therapist had instructed. He raised his arm above his head, feeling the sudden sharp pain. He ignored it, holding it there while he counted to ten. He dropped his arm again and let out a breath. It had been two weeks since the cast had come off, and he was frustrated with the rate of progress.

He continued to move his arm slowly as he stared down at the photos before him. He was still not sure what he would say when he met with the president in two hours.

CHAPTER THIRTY-FOUR

The van crawled at a snail's pace through the streets of Mexico City as the first signs of daylight began to filter through the buildings and the smog. Not quite six in the morning, the streets were already clogged, but the driver didn't mind. Today, the city's congestion would work to his advantage.

Forty minutes later, the driver—a sound technician—finally turned on *Paseo de la Reforma* and followed it northeast. Modeled after the Champs-Élysées in Paris, the wide boulevard cut diagonally across the city, at one time providing Emperor Maximilian a direct route from his castle to the National Palace. Maybe then, the driver thought, a trip across the city had been easy. It took another twenty-five minutes before he reached the *glorieta*. At the roundabout, he turned again then followed a zigzag route toward the *Zócalo*, the main square in the heart of the city, the place where his Aztec ancestors had gathered seven hundred years ago.

It was just after seven when he finally spotted the plaza through the gaps in traffic. He followed the line of cars and trucks as they turned right at the square, passed by the Federal District buildings and, then, turned left at the next intersection as the road curved around the plaza, past the National Palace. He maneuvered his van into the left lane and, at the end of the square, he turned left again, passing the cathedral. At the end of this side of the square, he turned left once more and pulled into the empty spot in front of the tent.

Within seconds, two police officers were at his window. He

showed his permit and identification and, after several questions, they seemed satisfied. The barricade was moved, and he pulled his van into the plaza. Even though the concert was not for another twelve hours, the square was crowded as workers set up the stage and installed temporary lighting and sound systems while the food vendors began setting up their booths around the perimeter. Normally crowded on most days, over one hundred thousand people were expected to descend on the Zócalo by late afternoon.

The driver parked by the back of the stage and stepped out into the chilly morning air. He took his time unloading the cables and equipment. *No sense rushing*, he thought. He had more than enough time. As he stacked the cables on the ground, the supervisor hurried over.

"You're late."

The driver shrugged.

The supervisor glanced at the cables and then in the back of the van.

"These are the replacements they gave you?" he asked, indicating the two large speakers in the back.

The driver nodded, knowing that he had been asked to bring the newer, smaller set.

The supervisor shook his head. "Did you test them?"

He nodded again. "Yes. And I brought another soundboard just in case."

"Okay. Get these set up and test them again. Leave the van there. If something goes wrong again, we'll need our tools."

The driver shook his head. "The police told me I could only park here temporarily, just to unload."

"Don't worry about them," the supervisor said; his frustration was evident. "I'll take care of it."

The driver nodded again. He hadn't planned on that. He would have to improvise.

———

Richter flexed his arm, feeling the slight twinge in his shoulder.

Ignoring it, he picked up the gun. It felt heavy in his hand. He brought up his left hand to support his right. Flicking off the safety, he took a shooter's stance then lined up the sights. It took him a moment to steady his aim. He let out a breath and gently squeezed the trigger. The gun jumped in his hands. He dropped his arms to the low-ready position and stared out at the target. There was a hole in the upper right hand corner, an inch from the silhouette torso, and even farther, he frowned, from the center of the chest where he'd been aiming.

Shit! He swore under his breath. The cast had been removed almost a month earlier and although he had diligently followed the physical therapy schedule, he wasn't progressing fast enough. At least not according to his own expectations. Consequently, several days earlier he had decided that he needed to accelerate his therapy and, ignoring both his doctor's and his therapist's advice, he began lifting weights—once early in the morning and again late in the evening—trying to rebuild the muscles that he'd lost. It wasn't much, just five and ten pound dumbbells. But it was a start. He could not accept the doctor's warning that his days as a federal agent—at least the type of agent he wanted to be—might be over.

He stared at the target. Based upon his first shot, he had a long way to go. He took a breath, brought his arms up again, and fired.

After two clips, he was able to hit the target consistently. But his shots were spread out across the torso. Only one had hit the cross in the center mass. Not good, he thought, as he rubbed his aching arm. Frustrated, he switched hands, this time holding the gun with his left hand and using his right for support. Two clips later, he felt better. After almost three months of shooting with his left hand, his useless right arm trapped in a cast, he had improved significantly. He wouldn't win any shooting competitions, but he could hit what he was aiming at. Now, using his right hand for support, it was like night and day. There was a cluster of holes around the center mass.

Not bad, he thought. But the target was only twenty-five feet away. He attached a fresh target to the frame and pressed the switch.

The target slid away, and he watched it pass the twenty-five foot mark. He stopped at thirty-five feet. Tomorrow he would try again with his right arm. But, for now, he wanted to see just how good he was with his left.

———

By 3:00 p.m., there were sixty thousand people in the plaza. Although the Zócalo was one of the largest city squares in the world, people were already jostling for space, trying to find a spot closer to the stage. Despite the crowd, people were in a festive mood, many singing and dancing, others laughing, playing, all excited for the concert still hours away. A line of seventy-five policemen were stationed in front of the National Palace while another two hundred were ringed around the square across the street. More wandered amongst the crowd, a visible presence designed to keep order. As the evening approached and the crowd grew, so would the number of police.

Wiping his brow, the driver dropped his tool belt on the floor of the van, then shut the door. He locked the van and, when he turned, noticed his supervisor frowning, glancing at his watch.

"It's not time for your break yet."

The driver nodded in the direction of the line of Porta-Johns at the edge of the square. "I'll be back in a few minutes."

"Did you check the last connection?"

The driver nodded again. "I tested everything twice. Everything is working properly."

He motioned the supervisor over to the soundboard. He punched a few buttons, slowly increased the volume, and music began playing though the speakers. The crowd began to cheer. He adjusted the balance and fade controls, effectively cycling through the channels, sending music to the two main speakers he had replaced, first the right and then the left. Then he channeled the music through the side speakers one at a time, before rebalancing the system.

The supervisor nodded, made a note on his clipboard then, without a word, headed to check on the lighting system. The driver shook his head and walked over to the Porta-Johns.

Five minutes later, he stepped out, casually glanced around and, noting that his supervisor was nowhere to be seen, ducked under the barricade and crossed the street. Two blocks away, he hailed a cab.

CHAPTER THIRTY-FIVE

Christina Thompson stood in front of the cathedral across the street from the Zócalo. She checked her watch again, knowing as she did that it couldn't have been more than a minute since the last time she had looked. Miguel wasn't late, not yet at least. *And not according to Mexican time*, she thought with a grin. He would probably show up with that happy-go-lucky smile of his any minute now and chide her for being a typical impatient *gringo*.

Confident, outgoing, and adventurous, being here at the concert summed up her time in Mexico. She could have stayed in the States as her parents had wanted. *More like pleaded*, she thought. But she wanted to experience life, to experience another culture: the language, the food, the music, the customs, the people. And the opportunity to study abroad, to spend a semester in Mexico City, had given her that opportunity in a way that the local Mexican restaurant in Princeton never could.

She wasn't normally impatient, but as the crowd across the street continued to swell, she worried about finding a spot. She glanced at the crowd around her. Most had already staked out spots on the sidewalk and on the steps of the cathedral. This was probably a good spot to see the concert, she realized. It was less crowded than the square and, when the concert was over, leaving would be much easier. *Not bad*, she thought as she noticed people spreading out blankets on the sidewalk and unfolding chairs. Not bad, but not good enough for her. She wanted to experience the concert—to really be a part of it—and that meant getting up close to the stage. To feel the heavy thumping of the bass. To see the sweat on the singers as they gyrated below the lights. To get caught up in the moment with the crowd, swaying to the music.

"Mi amor!"

Christina turned with a smile and saw Miguel winding his way through the crowd.

He stopped a foot away and spread his arms out. "See! I'm right on time!"

She threw her arms around him. "Hardly," she said before she gave him a kiss. She stepped back, slid her hand down his arm, and grabbed his hand. "But I forgive you. Now, come on. If we hurry, we still might be able to find a spot!"

Hand in hand, they crossed the street and made their way through the crowd. It took almost fifteen minutes, with her leading Miguel by the hand, before they slipped through one final group of people and found themselves in front of the rope barricade, ten feet from the stage.

"This is perfect," she yelled.

Miguel leaned forward and kissed her once more. "No. You're perfect." He smiled. She smiled back then, hand in hand, they began swaying to the music.

They never heard the explosion. They never saw the shrapnel— the jagged pieces of the speaker frame, the ripped metal of the stage—rocketing toward them at supersonic speeds. They never felt the red hot metal slicing through their bodies. Thankfully, when the first shockwave hit them, their world went dark.

———

The president smiled as he stepped into the room—a small gathering of a select group of administrators, deans, professors, and students from Howard University. He was feeling good. The speech had gone well, and the audience had seemed receptive to his thoughts on education.

He was chatting with the Dean of the Law School and his wife when he felt a hand on his arm. He turned, shared a glance with

Burt Phillips and knew immediately that something was wrong.

"Please excuse me," he apologized with a smile as Phillips led him several steps away.

Philips leaned close. "Sir. There's been a bombing in Mexico City. We don't have much information yet, but it's bad."

"How bad?" he asked, tight-lipped.

Phillips shook his head slightly, almost imperceptibly. His face was grim. "Could be thousands, sir."

Shit, Kendall thought. *It's started.*

———

On the large plasma screen in the Situation Room, Matthew Richter watched the image flicker before a live video of the carnage in Mexico City appeared on the screen. The image came from one of the National Reconnaissance Office's Lacrosse satellites.

He studied the screen. The first thing that struck him was the emergency vehicles. Like the spokes on a wheel, flashing lights from the hundreds of fire trucks, police cars, ambulances, and military vehicles lined up in rows on the streets leading into the Zócalo. The spokes extended off the screen. Around the square, there was a ring of vehicles, those that had arrived first, he realized. They were parked randomly at odd angles.

The scene reminded him of an anthill as thousands of rescue workers swarmed over the square. He could see the walking wounded being led away by rescuers and dozens more being carried away on stretchers. They disappeared at the edge of the screen. He glanced at a second monitor and saw the triage center, set up in the park a few blocks away. He turned back to the first screen. There were hundreds of soldiers carrying automatic weapons, but the majority seemed to be involved in the rescue effort.

Surprisingly, the buildings surrounding the Zócalo did not appear to be damaged. But in the middle of the square, he saw the twisted metal of the stage and a half-dozen scorched vehicles, lying upside down or on their sides. Firefighters were dousing them with hoses; the steam and smoke rising into the sky.

Richter noticed Jessica Williams by his side.

"I just had a meeting with the embassy and with the CIA," Williams said.

Richter nodded, and she gave him a summary. The estimated number of casualties was staggering. The CIA was working on several theories for who was responsible for the bombing.

"It's possible that one of the leftist groups is behind this," Williams continued. "Remember eight or nine years ago there were a series of attacks on gas pipelines and oil infrastructure?"

Richter nodded. Unhappy with the last election and with claims of tampered ballots and voter fraud, a rebel group had carried out a series of attacks over the span of six months. No one had been killed and the movement had just as quickly dissolved. He frowned then noticed Williams was frowning too.

"You don't buy that," he stated.

Williams shook her head. "No, I don't." She paused, her eyes steady on his. "My gut tells me this was Pablo Guerrero."

The conversations around them suddenly died out, and Richter looked up as President Kendall entered the room. Behind him was Burt Phillips. The president stared at the screen for a second then turned to Richter.

"Do we have any estimates?"

Richter nodded, his face somber. "Very preliminary at this point." He paused. "Mexican authorities estimate between one and two thousand people killed and another six to seven thousand wounded."

The president's face went pale. He nodded slowly.

"I have independent estimates from the embassy and from the CIA. They both support this." Richter paused. "Preliminary analysis indicates some kind of plastic explosive, likely hidden somewhere near the stage."

The president gestured toward the screen and the still-smoking car frames. "Not a car bomb?"

Richter shook his head then explained the analysis by the ATF. "They were caught in the blast. The fuel was likely ignited by live power cables or as a result of the explosion. ATF believes that a car bomb would have resulted in structural damage to surrounding buildings, and a much larger crater." Richter nodded toward the screen. "The crowd absorbed the bulk of the blast. This was designed to maim and kill, not destroy buildings."

The president stared at the screen for a moment.

"Mexico has instituted a no-fly zone over the city," Richter continued. "Inbound flights are being turned around and rerouted. The FAA is working with them, and we may need to handle the overflow along the border."

The president nodded.

"Communication networks are swamped and can't handle the volume," Richter added. "They're putting patches in place, but it's likely some will fail. They've mobilized three army divisions, both for rescue and for security. They've indicated that they're going to shut down the city." He nodded to the screen. "And they're going to need medical help."

"Has anyone claimed responsibility yet?"

Richter shook his head.

"But you have a hunch?" the president asked.

Tight-lipped, Richter nodded. "Guerrero," he said.

The president glanced at the screen for a second then turned. "My first reaction too."

CHAPTER THIRTY-SIX

"We need rescue personnel. We need medical personnel. We need doctors, nurses, whatever you can spare. We need medical supplies. And we need blood." President Magaña's voice sounded hollow.

"I have two military transports with medical response as well as search and rescue teams," President Kendall responded. "They're in the air over Texas. I also have a FEMA team airborne. They're waiting for my final instructions. I'll send them immediately."

"Thank you, David."

"I'm also told that the Red Cross has been working on getting blood to you. We'll do whatever we can to help them do that as soon as possible. We're also mobilizing medical personnel from the private sector."

"Okay, we'll take whatever you can send." There was a pause. "I believe you have medical ships? Floating hospitals?"

"Yes, we do," Kendall responded after a moment. "But they're both in port. I've ordered the USS Mercy to launch as soon as possible." He glanced at Richter.

Richter held up four fingers.

"But the earliest they can sail is four days." He paused. "I'm sorry, Filipe, but that's the best I can do."

There was silence, then a long sigh. "I understand. I'll take whatever help you can provide."

"I'm sorry it came to this, Felipe."

There was a pause on the line. "We knew something like this

could happen, David, but what choice did we have?" There was another pause. "We can't stop now."

It was a difficult decision, but the president knew that Magaña was right.

"No, we can't," he said. He knew that if they did stop now, it would only get worse. He waited a second then asked, "What else, Filipe? What else do you need?"

There was a long pause. "Your prayers, David. I need your prayers."

———

Pablo Guerrero stared at the TV as the announcer repeated again what little the authorities knew at the moment. President Magaña had declared a state of emergency, and Mexico City was virtually shut down as travel was restricted to rescue and recovery efforts. This was required, the announcer said, as authorities struggled to handle the casualties. When hospitals in the center of the city, near the Zócalo, were overrun, those injured were being transported to other facilities all across the sprawling city.

The death count, the announcer said, now stood at thirteen hundred killed and eighty-two hundred injured. Many of those who perished or were wounded had been on the periphery of the square and had been hurt not by the bomb, but by the stampede that had followed as the panicked crowd fled the area.

Authorities were aggressively pursuing leads, the announcer said, as the screen showed masked soldiers and police storming a compound in the southern state of Chiapas. However, no one had yet claimed responsibility. It was old news footage, Guerrero realized, from a raid last year. Cheap theatrics by the media, or more likely, he thought, government propaganda intending to show that they were aggressively pursuing those responsible. He turned off the TV and stood. There was no need for him to claim responsibility. The government knew who was behind this.

Two minutes later, after he changed his clothes—donning a peasant's work shirt, pants, and boots, the wide brim of the hat pulled low over his face—he stepped outside into the bright sunshine and followed the path past the pool and around the house. He had let his guard down. It was clear now that the government had been aware of his ranch and had been watching him for some time. And now Carolina was dead.

When he passed the stables, he didn't look up at the black mare on the other side of the ring. His wife had left him, more bitter and angry at him than at the government and the soldiers who had stolen their daughter. Still, he had taken care of her, made sure that she was safe. At the same time, he had quietly leaked word that they had both fled the ranch and, fearing for their own security, were now in hiding. But he would never leave.

He opened the metal gate and stepped gingerly across the recently disturbed soil. He took a deep breath and laid his hand on the marble cross, still hot below the fading sun. A single tear ran down his cheek. *Thirteen hundred deaths*, he thought as he wiped it away. That didn't even come close.

CHAPTER THIRTY-SEVEN

Patty tried the phone again, frustrated but not surprised when it went to voice mail. She didn't leave a message. Matthew was probably huddled with the president at the moment, consumed, she guessed, by the crisis in Mexico City.

She had spoken to him last night, or rather, she reminded herself, early in the morning. Still at work, he had sounded tired. She had told him about the students, about the seven Princeton kids who were in Mexico City for a semester. She only knew one of them, an outspoken and outgoing young lady named Christina that had been in her International Relations class two years ago. With communication networks swamped, the university still didn't know whether Christina and the other students were safe. Matthew had promised to pass the students' names on to embassy officials.

She told herself to be patient, to wait for him to call, knowing that it wouldn't likely be until late at night again. She turned to the TV in her office. The images on the screen and the announcer's description were horrible. But she knew that what Matthew was looking at was probably worse. With the satellites, the intelligence agencies, and who knew what else he had access to, he would know far more than the news announcer. And he had sounded pretty grim last night. She hoped he would call again that evening. Even though he was only a few hours away and she knew he was okay, it would be reassuring just to hear his voice. She let out a breath. *He's extremely busy and he will call when he has a chance*, she told herself again.

The images on TV triggered something in her brain and she spun her chair to the computer on the credenza behind her desk. She pressed a few keys. After a few minutes, she found what she wanted. She glanced back at the TV and then at her watch. Only forty-five minutes until her next class. If she hurried, she thought, she might make it. She turned back to her computer and started typing, forgetting the lecture she had planned for today. Instead, she thought as she began to cut and paste, she would talk about the use of violence as a political tool.

———

Guerrero studied the face on the screen. The American president was standing behind the podium, facing a room full of reporters.

"Scott," he said, pointing to the man from ABC.

"Mr. President, do we have troops in Mexico?" the reporter asked.

Guerrero leaned forward, staring at the TV.

The president shook his head. "We do not have any combat troops in Mexico."

There were numerous shouts.

"But we have troops," the reporter persisted.

"We have national guardsman in Mexico City—primarily medical personnel and search and recovery teams—as part of a humanitarian effort to provide relief and medical assistance in the wake of the bombing. We also have specialized teams such as the Army Signal Corps, which is working with the Mexican government to reestablish communication networks. In addition, FEMA has sent people to assist in recovery efforts, and the FBI and the ATF have sent teams, at Mexico's request, to assist in the investigation."

There were more shouts, attempts to get the president's attention. He pointed to another reporter. "Gretchen."

"Sir, over the last two or three months, there has been a significant increase in Mexican police and military activity directed at the cartels. A number of cartel leaders have been killed, allegedly by covert sniper teams. Has the U.S. played a role in this?"

Guerrero's eyes narrowed.

"The bombing in Mexico City," the president said, "is a frightening reminder of the stranglehold that the cartels have on Mexican society. And, frankly, we must share the blame. Our growing demand for drugs, our inconsistent policies, our unwillingness to commit the funds needed to deal with this problem, our inability to police our borders, our focus on prohibition here while, in essence, treating the cartel problem as Mexico's worry, our lack of focus on education, treatment, and recovery programs," the president paused and waved his hand, "all of these things have contributed to the problem." He shook his head. "We can no longer turn a blind eye to what's happening south of our border."

The American president, Guerrero noted with a scowl, had evaded the question.

There were more shouts, and the president pointed to another reporter.

"There have been unconfirmed reports" the woman said, "that the U.S. has been indirectly involved in these recent conflicts. Some say directly involved. Would you care to comment, sir?"

The president's eyes narrowed. "Make no mistake about this. The cartels are terrorist organizations. This is something that deeply concerns us. Not only does it present a threat to Mexico, it presents a threat to us and to the world community. Consequently, we continue to work closely with President Magaña and with the Mexican government on this issue. But unlike our approach several years ago, we do not have covert teams operating in Mexico."

There were several shouts.

"However," the president paused until the room quieted, "we do provide various forms of military assistance including sharing intelligence, providing aerial and satellite reconnaissance capabilities, establishing training programs for police and military personnel on the front lines of this battle, and sharing certain technologies, including certain weapons and surveillance systems to support those efforts."

The American president had sidestepped the question again,

avoiding any specific mention of the drones. *It would be easy,* Guerrero thought, *to provide dates and specific information about the bombings and the people killed to the press. But would that embarrass the Americans?* he wondered. *Would it force them to reconsider the use of the drones? Probably not.*

But there was another question that nagged at him. He watched as the conference ended and the American president left the podium and stepped out of the room. A question that had been at the back of his mind for weeks. What was the price for the hundreds of millions of dollars of financial aid that los gringos provided to his country each year? The American drones, flown by American pilots, were taking orders from Washington, no doubt. Was Magaña taking orders from Washington too?

He stood abruptly. Two minutes later, he found Alberto.

"Find the Irishman," he ordered.

CHAPTER THIRTY-EIGHT

Richter shook his head. "The last time he was spotted was at the funeral. We've been picking up chatter that indicates that both he and his wife may have fled, that they may be in hiding. Nonetheless, we're maintaining round-the-clock surveillance on his ranch in Tamaulipas." He passed a group of photos to the president. "However, there's been no sign of him. Just normal activity: guards, domestic servants, gardeners..." His voice trailed off.

The president flipped through the photos for a moment. "What about phone calls, that sort of thing?" he asked.

Richter shook his head again. "None. No phone calls, no emails, no texts, at least nothing that we've been able to connect to him." He paused. "We suspect that he has houses elsewhere in the country, places where he can hide but still maintain control of the drug operation."

The president sat back, thinking. "So, what are our options?" he asked after a moment.

"We keep looking," Richter responded. "He's bound to turn up at some point."

"And when he does," the president said with a sigh, "I need to make a decision."

Richter shook his head. "I think you need to make the decision now, sir. If we spot him, by the time we get your authorization, we could lose him again."

The president held Richter's gaze for a moment then nodded

slowly. He turned to Jennifer Williams and Burt Phillips.

"What do you think?"

"I agree with Matthew," Williams answered immediately. "Give the order now."

Burt Phillips nodded. "I agree too."

The president was silent for a moment. "I'll need to speak to Magaña first," he said more to himself than anyone else.

After a moment he looked up. "In the meantime, prepare the directive," he ordered.

———

The sensor watched on the video screen as the two gardeners climbed on their bikes and began to pedal away from the hacienda. Bored, he zoomed in on the riders but was unable to make out their faces below the wide brims of their hats. The bikes were old, the lieutenant saw; both had coaster brakes and only one gear, reminding him of the bicycles his grandfather fondly talked about. The wide tires, he could see, were well suited for the ruts and bumps in the dirt road.

The two peasants pedaled slowly, taking their time. Ten minutes later, they passed through the first guard booth and then, after another fifteen, they passed through the outer wall. The lieutenant glanced briefly at his watch. It was 1:30 p.m. local time and the two, as was the custom, were likely going home for the midday meal.

Looks like siesta time, he thought then yawned. A nap right now sounded good. He watched as the two men pedaled slowly down the dirt road toward the small village two miles away. *Lucky bastards*, he thought again as he moved his joystick, directing the camera back to the hacienda.

Intelligence now believed that Guerrero had fled. There had been no sightings since his daughter's funeral. Still, the drones were maintaining round the clock surveillance on the chance that the drug boss would return.

The sensor sighed as he began another scan of the compound, again searching for signs of something—anything—that would indicate where Guerrero had gone.

———

"*Buena suerte*, my friend," Felipe Magaña said.

"Thank you, Felipe. Good luck to you too."

The president hung up the phone and nodded. Richter passed him a folder that bore Top Secret stamps. The president opened the folder and began to read. Two minutes later, he pulled a pen from his pocket. As he signed the Presidential Directive, he knew that he had just signed Pablo Guerrero's death warrant.

———

As the peasants rode up to the cantina, a young boy stepped out of the shade. The men climbed off their bikes and, after a quiet word with the boy, one of the men stepped into the cantina. The other, his face hidden behind the brim of his hat, waited outside in the shade with the boy. A moment later, the man who had gone inside came back out and nodded.

The man who had been waiting outside stepped into the building and stopped for a minute, just inside the doorway, waiting for his eyes to adjust to the dim light. As the boy and the other man wheeled both bikes around the side of the building, he threaded his way through the tables—all empty despite the hour—and through the doorway to the patio out back. The patio too was empty, except for a lone man sitting at the table next to the ring. The peasant took the chair across from the man and nodded. Then he frowned when he saw the empty bottle.

"I have a job for you," Pablo Guerrero said in English, his words meant only for the man sitting across from him. The boy, he knew, spoke only Spanish as did his mother in the kitchen. Even though the boy, his mother, and Alberto were the only other people in the cantina, and even though he trusted all three completely, Guerrero was cautious.

Terry Fogel nodded but said nothing as the boy suddenly appeared with two plates of food and a basket of tortillas. The mother followed, and Guerrero frowned again as she set another bottle of beer in front of Fogel. She placed a glass of water in front of Guerrero. He nodded once, and the boy and his mother quietly retreated to the kitchen. Then he nodded at Fogel and, as the Irish terrorist began to eat, he explained what he wanted.

CHAPTER THIRTY-NINE

"You're full of surprises," Patty said as she leaned into Richter. They walked hand in hand, following the path behind the condo through the woods. Almost midnight, impulsively they had climbed out of bed and set out for a stroll. The night air was relatively warm, and the earthy smells of spring wafted through the air. The sky was bright with the half moon, and they could see the new ferns on the forest floor waving in the mild breeze.

Richter's text had surprised her and he had showed up, just as he had promised, at eight o'clock. She had dinner waiting and, after they'd had a pleasant meal and split a bottle of wine, they'd made love. She had fallen asleep immediately afterwards, content to be in his arms. But she had woken an hour later, sensing something was wrong, only to find him staring at the ceiling.

"How's the arm?" she asked as they walked around a bend.

He flexed it, holding it above his head. "Not bad," he said. "Just slower than I thought it would be."

They continued walking in silence. Patty occasionally stole a glance, trying to read his mood.

"Things are bad?" she asked, knowing she was treading on delicate ground.

He was silent a moment. The call of an owl floated across the air.

"Well, for one," he said, drawing out the suspense, "I missed you."

She leaned in, "I missed you too," she responded as she wrapped her arms around him.

"Anything else bothering you?" she asked tentatively.

He was quiet again for a moment.

"I think the attack in Mexico is just the beginning," he finally said as they crossed a small wooden bridge. A stream gurgled below them. Patty nodded but said nothing, her instinct telling her that he needed to talk.

"We have no credible evidence, but my gut tells me there's something there."

Patty knew he was talking about his sixth sense, something he had told her many cops possessed, an ability to feel the danger that was around the corner. They walked quietly for a minute before he spoke again.

"I think the next attack is going to be here. Somewhere in the U.S." He was quiet for another minute before he let out a sigh. "Look, the last thing I want to do is worry you. The reality is we face threats every day—Islamic terrorists, right wing militias, Iran, North Korea—the public just doesn't know it." He paused. "And it's my job to sort through all of those and figure out which ones are real, which ones aren't, and what we need to do." They continued walking as a dog barked somewhere off in the distance. "When I was in the Secret Service and even in the FBI, I thought I'd seen it all." He shook his head. "But now..." his voice trailed off. "And I'm only an advisor. I can only imagine the burden of having to make the decision."

Patty knew he was referring to President Kendall. They continued walking in silence.

Sensing he was done, she pulled on his arm, turning him, and they began walking back towards the condos.

"Know what I think?" she asked playfully after a moment.

"What?"

"I think I should visit you in Washington next weekend."

He hesitated. "What if something happens and I get tied up in work? I'd hate for you to come all the way down and me not be there."

"I'm sure I can find something to do. Besides, we'll still have the nights," Patty answered as she squeezed him. "Right?"

He grinned. "I sure hope so."

———

Bobby Fleming glanced at the clock while he waited for the light to change. Was there enough time, he wondered. He could be a few minutes late, maybe fifteen, and no one would say anything. And if anyone asked, he could blame it on traffic. Besides, today was a slow day. He only had one more run scheduled in the afternoon. His mind made up, he pulled out his cell phone and pressed a number, preset to speed dial Tina. She wasn't his girlfriend, not exactly. But whatever she was, he certainly enjoyed the benefits.

"Hey, babe. It's me. You free?"

He heard a yawn, then, "I thought you had to work today."

Her voice was thick with sleep, and quite likely, he suspected, a hangover as well. She'd been out late again last night.

"I'm working now. I just made a run, but I might have some time to stop by and pay you a visit before I head back to the shop." He grinned at himself. "You know, just to say hi."

She laughed. "Honey, you always want to do a lot more than just say hi." There was a pause. "How much time do you have?"

"Forty-five minutes. Maybe an hour."

He heard a laugh. "Just enough time for a quickie, huh?"

He grinned. "Hey. What can I say? I miss you."

There was a pause and he heard some rustling, then: "I'll tell you what. I'm hungry and I need to take a shower. Stop by the deli on the way and grab me a sandwich. You know the one I like, with the cheese?"

He laughed. "Sure. I'll be there in fifteen minutes."

"Thanks, Bobby," she purred. "That should give me enough time to get ready. But that doesn't leave us much time. You better hurry."

As he hung up, he heard a honk behind him and realized the light had changed. He eased the van forward as he calculated the quickest way to Tina's apartment. He glanced in his side view mirror then pulled into the left lane and turned at the next light.

Sixteen minutes later, he parallel parked in front of Tina's building. As he hopped out, sandwich in hand, he hit the button on the key fob and heard the chirp as the doors locked. He glanced quickly at the van, at the new logo for Billings Medical Devices on the side. *The future of medicine...now,* the tagline proclaimed, followed by an artist's depiction of an atom. He wasn't sure how much the company had paid some marketing firm for that design, but whatever the price, it had been too much.

He shook his head. Anyway, he had more important things on his mind at the moment, he thought with a grin, as he pictured Tina waiting for him upstairs. As he mounted the steps to her building, he didn't notice the white truck pull into the space behind him.

———

"Passport, please."

Terry Fogel smiled as he handed his documents to the immigration officer and then watched casually as the woman flipped through the pages, past the numerous entry and exit stamps from around the world. All were expert forgeries, of course, and he was certain they wouldn't raise any suspicions even to her trained eye.

The officer studied the photo, and Fogel smiled again when she glanced up to scrutinize his face. She wore the perpetual scowl of someone who sees hundreds of faces each day, never quite trusting a single one. He wasn't worried. With dark brown hair now, instead of his natural ginger, and wearing a pair of colored contacts, he looked sufficiently different than whatever picture they might have on file.

"Did you visit any other countries besides Brazil?"

"No," he responded with another smile. "Just Brazil on this trip."

She grunted as she slid his passport though the bar code reader.

While he waited, Fogel thought about the day ahead. From the airport, he would catch a cab to the hotel. After checking in, he would take another cab to Walmart, where he would buy several phones—prepaid models that didn't require that you provide any information. He would pay in cash. Then he would call his contact again. The man, someone he had worked with many times in the past, was confident that by the time Fogel arrived, he would have everything that he needed.

The officer looked up and Fogel smiled again as she handed his documents back.

"Welcome home."

———

Bobby left Tina's building, humming a tune. He was later than he expected and he knew his supervisor was going to chew him out. Especially since he had ignored the two calls. He could tell by the second message that he was in trouble. *Oh well*, he sighed. *It was worth it.*

As he stepped to the sidewalk, he pulled his keys from his pocket, thumbed the unlock button and climbed in. When he started the van, something in the rearview mirror caught his attention. He glanced in the back at the box. The heavy case that stored the canisters was at a slight angle. He frowned as he climbed between the seats to the back. He stared down at the box. *He hadn't left it like that, had he?* Then he noticed the lock. It was broken. *Oh, shit!*

CHAPTER FORTY

As the train pulled into the station, Patty stood up and reached for her bag.

"Here, let me help you with that."

She turned at the voice and smiled back at the handsome man standing next to her.

"Thank you," she said.

The man grinned as he lifted her bag off the storage rack and placed it in the aisle. After he extended the retractable handle, he looked up and nodded once, not quite a bow.

"And here I thought chivalry was dead," Patty said with a laugh.

"Not where I'm from," he said, holding her gaze.

Where's that? she wanted to ask, but caught herself. She didn't want him to misinterpret her gratitude as flirting. After all, she wasn't. *Was she?*

He grinned and she caught something in his eyes, a look that was intriguing. *Let it go*, she told herself.

"Well, thanks again," she said with a smile as she reached for the handle of her bag.

"Enjoy your stay in Washington," he said with another grin as he turned and, pulling his own bag, stepped out onto the platform.

She followed him off the train. He turned once and smiled at her again then she lost him in the crowd. As she followed the stream of passengers into the main concourse, she realized what it was that she had seen in his eyes: a look that said he found life amusing.

———

Terry Fogel stopped by the coffee shop and ordered a cup of tea. As he was paying, he saw the woman walk by. She was attractive. For a second he thought she had been flirting with him. But then something in her eyes had changed and he realized that the moment was gone. *Oh well*, he thought as his phone rang. He didn't have time for that now. As he watched her disappear in the crowd, he answered.

A minute later, he hung up. He smiled. His contact had what he needed; more than enough really. But it would take some time— perhaps a month—to finalize plans and to assemble the device.

He thanked the bearded young man behind the counter as he was handed a cup of tea. Now would be a good time to send a message, he thought; something both to warn but also to create a diversion. It was a risky move, but what was life without a little risk?

He took a sip of tea. *Not like home but not bad*. But then again, after all of these years, maybe he had just grown used to weak American tea. He took another sip as he watched the crowd streaming by. A woman, in the black full body cloak favored by some Muslims, passed by the coffee shop. Only her face was visible, the rest of her body hidden by the burqa. He watched as she walked past a police officer. The officer turned and followed her with his eyes until she disappeared in the crowd. *Perfect*, Fogel told himself. He took another sip and smiled. Life was just a game.

CHAPTER FORTY-ONE

The man disconnected and dropped the cell phone into his pocket. He climbed out of the car and locked it. This was Brooklyn after all, and he wanted it to be there when he got back. Not that locks meant much to thieves these days. But he was prepared; he patted his side, feeling the reassuring bulge of the gun under his Consolidated Edison uniform. He walked up the block. At the end, he stepped into the store and was immediately assaulted by the strong odors. Specializing in Middle Eastern foods, books, movies, newspapers— the little things that made the transplanted Arabs that had taken over the surrounding neighborhoods feel a little closer to home— the store was busy.

He smiled as he took in the two aisles of shelves, seemingly randomly stocked with various cans, boxes, and jars. His dark skin didn't fool those inside. He wasn't one of them. He could feel the eyes on him as he walked up the first aisle, his hand on his chin. He stopped by the small refrigerator and looked inside. In the reflection in the glass door, he noticed that the two men playing backgammon at the small table in front had turned their attention back to their game. The man behind the counter though, he could see, was still watching him. He took a step to the side and was able to see more of the store. He heard the bell on the door and watched as two women, covered completely except for their faces, entered. They were followed by three children. He listened to the conversations, all in Arabic, and heard the usual topics: politics and food. He could speak fluent Arabic and could imitate several different dialects well enough to fool the locals. This skill had been learned over the years, first as a child, thanks to six years spent in Egypt, then Saudi Arabia, when his father's company, an engineering firm, had sent him to work on hydroelectric projects. His later training had come courtesy of the foreign ministry. Other than listening, though, he had no plans on using his ability today. He turned and walked to the counter, a smile on his face. The clerk behind the counter stared blankly back at him, not quite hostile but certainly not friendly.

"Hi," the man said, still smiling. Without seeming to, he studied the clerk's face. This was the one, he concluded, the owner. "I was looking for the grape leaves?" he said hesitantly.

Without a word, the owner pointed to the shelf across from the refrigerator case.

The man turned and looked, his forehead creased as if unsure, then a second later, he turned back. He shook his head. "No, not the jar." He held his hands up, as if holding a plate. "I'm looking for the stuffed grape leaves. You know, the dish? I forget what it's called."

The owner shook his head.

The man heard the bell again and turned, noticing three more men enter. They too regarded him warily as they walked over to the two men playing backgammon. He turned back to the owner.

"No?" He sighed. "Darn. My wife loves them." He shrugged, offering another smile which wasn't returned. "Do you know anyone who makes them?"

The owner shook his head once more.

"Oh," the man said, deflated. "Thanks anyway."

A minute later, he stood on the sidewalk and glanced up and down the block as if searching for something. *Where to hide it?* he wondered. Two more people passed him and entered the store. He turned and walked to the corner, then turned right and headed down the side street. There was a small lot behind the building. He glanced once behind him and, seeing no one, quickly ducked into the lot. The single car, a Honda minivan, was sitting in front of the rear door. Twenty seconds later he was inside. A quick glance at the registration confirmed that the minivan belonged to the store owner.

A minute later, he was walking back to his car. No one had seen him break in. No one had seen him hide the phone—his prints wiped clean—below the driver's seat. He hid his smile as he climbed back into his car. He had just earned five thousand dollars.

———

With Special Agent Wendy Tillman at his shoulder, Matthew Richter scanned the crowd streaming through the main concourse of Union Station. He had considered asking his security detail to arrange for Patty to be driven to Washington—something they were authorized and would have been glad to do—but she had insisted on riding the train.

His schedule that day had been hectic, with meetings with the CIA, the NSA, and the other intelligence agencies lasting longer than he had expected. As usual, he and his team had regrouped after, to sort through what they had learned. No sooner had he taken his seat than Agent Tillman had interrupted his meeting, letting him know that Patty's train would be on time.

So, with Agent Tillman and three other agents, he made the quick trip over to the station, while Jessica Williams, his top aide, managed the meeting.

When he saw Patty coming through the crowd, he knew he had made the right decision.

CHAPTER FORTY-TWO

Closing the gate, Guerrero put the tools in the small cart. With one last look at the cross, he turned and began pushing the cart back toward the stable. He had spoken to the gardeners. They had understood. Or maybe not; it didn't matter. Regardless, they had provided him with the tools. And so, once a day, sometimes twice, he checked the grass. He cut it when it was long, then pulled the weeds, tended the flowers, and polished the stone, making sure everything was as neat and orderly as he could make it. It had to be, for Carolina.

He left the gardener's cart in the stables and made his way up to the house. He walked slowly, another laborer taking his time below the hot midday sun.

Minutes later, he stepped below the trellis-covered walkway and made his way around the house to the patio by the pool. There, he spotted Alberto waiting for him. Alberto nodded once but said nothing and Guerrero followed him into the house.

In his office, Guerrero placed the hat on the corner of his desk. Taking the USB drive from Alberto, he slid it into the port of his computer. After he read the message, he stood and looked out the window. Although he could only see leaves, he knew that beyond the trees was the stable, and, beyond that, the grave.

Soon, Carolina. Soon.

———

"So, Matthew tells me you worked for Barbara Tanner," the president said.

"I did," Patty answered, "For a couple of years." She smiled. "But I think I was a few years too early. I would have liked to have worked for the senator after she became the chair of the Senate Appropriations Committee."

Richter and Patty were dining with the president and the first lady in the residence section of the White House. A Saturday, he had only worked for a few hours early in the morning, then he had taken Patty on a tour of Washington. Prearranged by the Secret Service, they had bypassed the tourist lines and were given private tours of the Capitol building, the Supreme Court and the Lincoln Memorial. Then they were treated to a rarely seen view of the Washington Monument, bypassing the elevator and taking the stairs—something that had been closed to the public for decades.

"What did you think of Barbara?" Maria Kendall asked.

"I think she's fantastic!" Patty answered. "I admire her for standing up, for making her voice heard, especially in a male-dominated organization like the senate."

"I'll drink to that," Maria said with a twinkle in her eye as she raised her wine glass.

The two ladies engaged in small talk as white gloved members of the butler's staff cleared the dishes. The ladies continued talking when the servants left and Richter and the president exchanged a glance. The first lady was keeping the conversation on lighter subjects, not wanting to spoil the evening with a discussion of the threat just south of the border. The conversation shifted to Princeton and Patty's classes.

"Do you enjoy teaching?" Maria asked.

"I do," Patty said then laughed. "It wasn't what I intended to do but I somehow fell into it." Patty took a sip of wine. "So what is Angela studying?"

"She's in premed. She has a long way to go, but if she could pick her dream job, she would travel the world with Doctors Without Borders, providing emergency medical care to people impacted by conflict, disasters...," the first lady gestured to the president. "Dave doesn't like the idea, but she's determined."

Richter and the president exchanged another glance. He understood all too well the president's concern.

"That's impressive and admirable," Patty said then turned to the president. "But I can understand your worry, especially given what you must see."

The president nodded. "You can only bring them so far and then you have to let them go. I am proud—what dad wouldn't be?—but still it makes me nervous."

"Did Matthew give you the tour?" Maria asked, changing subjects again.

"Of the White House?" Patty asked. "Not yet."

"Well then, let's go." Maria said as she pushed her chair back. "I'll give you an insider's view, show you some things that Matthew doesn't even know about."

The two women stood and the first lady leaned over to Richter. He noticed the twinkle in her eye.

"I like her," Maria whispered.

Richter smiled and it struck him just how alike Patty and the first lady were. They both were comfortable in social settings, able to make small talk with anyone and, when animated, they both had a sparkle in their eye. As the two women left—their excited chatter and laughter ringing off the walls—he and the president exchanged another glance. The president, he could see, had noticed it too.

———

The analyst clicked the icon on his screen and listened to the call again. Despite the fact that both phones were cell phones, it was surprisingly clear. That, he knew, had less to do with the quality of the phone or of the platform of the local cellular service providers and more to do with the sophisticated enhancement of the computers. He had never seen the legendary NSA supercomputers and likely never would. He wasn't sure if they were even located in his building in the vast, sprawling complex in Fort Meade, Maryland. Everything was need-to-know and what he needed to know, and knew very well, was radical jihad.

Translation wasn't a problem. He was fluent in Arabic, having spent the first fifteen years of his life in Lebanon. Members of a small and dwindling Christian community, his father finally decided it was time to leave when their church was burned to the ground. It was one of the rare occasions when he, his parents, and two younger brothers hadn't attended. His older sister, married and living several blocks away at the time, hadn't been so lucky.

No, translation wasn't a problem, he thought. Still he glanced at the English-language transcript that the computer had spit out. He shook his head. It always amazed him how the system was able to detect subtle nuances in tone and accent and handle the differences between the seemingly endless dialects. He could, but he wondered again how long it would be before the agency told him his services were no longer needed.

He shook his head again then focused on the task before him. The call was troubling. Although he listened to many calls and read many postings and emails where angry parties discussed the *Great Satan* and how, one day, God willing, they were going to bring the wrath of Allah to America's shores, this one was different. It was more than the rant or the blowing off of steam of a disaffected and disenfranchised people, a people who had neither the means nor the conviction to act. This one hinted at a plan that was underway.

He listened another time to see if he had missed anything.

"We have acquired the necessary materials."

"Allah be praised. Where are they now?"

"In Ohio."

"What is the next step?"

"We have to remove the critical components. This takes time. We have to be careful."

"Allah will protect you. When?"

"Soon, my brother. Soon."

There was a pause and, in the background, he could hear street noises: a car horn, a shout, the rumble of a truck.

"Allah willing, this machine they use to stop their cancers will now give them cancers instead."

He glanced at the transcript again. No, he hadn't missed anything, he thought, as he began to type. He needed to get this one out immediately.

CHAPTER FORTY-THREE

As Richter climbed into the back of the SUV, he yawned. He was tired. The previous afternoon, he had decided to return to New Jersey with Patty. She had made the trip to Washington, then decided to stay for two days, something which had surprised him. Some sort of holiday at the university she had said. Whatever the reason, he was glad she had come. And so while he had worked, Patty had played tourist, seeing the sites they hadn't been able to visit together. The evenings had been nice, he thought with a smile. After two days, he realized that he didn't want her to leave and, although she had insisted on taking the train to Washington, he had decided to drive her home. Or rather, the Secret Service drove her home while he and Patty sat in the back. After another late dinner, this one in New Jersey, they returned to her apartment close to midnight.

It was a long time before they finally fell asleep.

The next morning, after he climbed into the SUV, Agent Wendy Tillman handed him his morning briefings and a cup of coffee.

"Thanks," he said with a smile as he took the cup. "I was going to ask you to stop along the way." He took a sip and sighed. The briefings could wait.

Tillman smiled back. "I figured you would, so we stopped on the way over." Her eyes shifted back to the road as the driver signaled for a turn. She glanced back again. "Got a second cup up here for you too."

Richter raised his cup in salute. "You go above and beyond the call of duty, Agent Tillman."

Ten minutes later, they had just pulled onto the New Jersey Turnpike when the phone rang. He glanced at the number then frowned. When he hung up moments later, he felt a chill running up his spine. He leaned forward and gave the agents a new address. It was always better to get information directly from the source, he reasoned, and he was so close. As the driver made a U-turn—illegal, but it hardly mattered since they were cops—he sat back and considered the news.

Fifty minutes later, he was sitting in Mark Crawford's office in the federal building in lower Manhattan. Crawford's face was grim as he filled Richter in on the theft.

"Are you familiar with cesium-one-thirty-seven?" he asked.

"The basics," Richter responded as he remembered the training he had received while with the FBI. "Give me the summary."

"It's a man-made element, a radioactive isotope created in nuclear fission. It's used in industrial gauges and certain types of measurement devices and," he paused, "in radiation therapy for treating certain cancers."

Richter frowned as he briefly thought of Brett Watson. He shook his head and gestured to Crawford to continue.

"In these devices," Crawford said, "it's referred to as sealed-source radiation. In brachytherapy devices—the machines used for cancer treatment—it's in a stainless steel tube, about three quarters of an inch long."

Richter's eyes narrowed. And it was dangerous and lethal even in such small quantities, he knew, as he recalled an incident in Brazil where one such device had been stolen. After the scrap metal, the thieves had nonetheless been intrigued by the radiation capsule. They punctured it, no easy task, and in the ensuing chain of events, a handful of people had been killed and several hundred sickened. All from just a few small grains, he remembered.

"This stuff, obviously, is regulated," Crawford continued. "The canisters are stored and transported in a sealed lead container.

Records must be maintained each time the lead container is opened, serial numbers of each canister recorded..." He waved his hand. "Long story short, a medical equipment and supply company in New Jersey had one of their trucks broken into in Newark. And although they had ten of these canisters in a sealed lead container in the back at the time, only one was taken."

Richter was silent for a moment as he considered the implications.

Crawford nodded as if he could read his mind. "I think that we have to assume that the threat we've been worried about for the last decade is real."

———

Five hours later, Richter, Pat Monahan, and the Secretary of Homeland Security sat down in the Oval Office across from the president. They all wore the grim faces of those who bore bad news. Burt Phillips joined them a moment later.

"Sir," Richter began, "we have credible intelligence that an Islamist terrorist organization is planning to detonate a radiological dispersal device—a dirty bomb—somewhere in the U.S." He paused, his eyes locked on his boss's. "This is not just chatter, sir. We believe the group now has the necessary materials."

He turned to Monahan and, as the director provided details on the theft and the FBI investigation, he thought again about what little they knew. The ride back to Washington had been spent on the phone, checking with his team, then with the intelligence agencies, and learning as much as he could about dirty bombs. It was then that he had learned about the intercepted call. But, outside of the thefts and phone call, they had nothing specific to tell them where or when.

"And the tie to Islamist terrorists?" the president asked.

Richter handed him a piece of paper.

"We've intercepted a phone call that appears to reference the thefts." He nodded toward the paper. "That's the transcript."

A moment later the president looked up. His face was pale. "God help us." He paused. "Why Ohio? Are they targeting Cincinnati? Chicago?"

Richter shook his head. "We don't know, sir. Ohio might just be a location where they plan on disassembling the machines and building the bomb. It's far enough away from New Jersey that anything peculiar noticed might not be linked back to the thefts. And if they're in a rural area, on a farm for instance, they might not draw attention to themselves."

Monahan leaned forward, frowning. "A farm would also have access to fertilizer."

The president grimaced. "Ammonium nitrate? Like the Oklahoma City bombing?"

Monahan nodded. "Yes, except, for a dirty bomb, the blast wouldn't have to be as big." He took a breath. "While the blast itself will cause some immediate deaths, the intent of a dirty bomb is to sow fear and panic."

Richter nodded. "Pat's right. This is not the same as a nuclear device. There would be no nuclear chain reaction. But even with the radiation from just one of these canisters, such a bomb, if constructed right, would contaminate a fairly large area, as much as thirty or forty city blocks." He paused. "And that's from a small explosive device; something equivalent to ten or fifteen pounds of TNT."

The president's face hardened. "Tell me about the radioactive material," he ordered.

Richter nodded. "Cesium-one-thirty-seven is a radioactive isotope with a half-life of thirty years. It's in powder form and is stored in a small, stainless-steel rod, about this long." Richter held his thumb and index finger an inch apart.

"The stuff in one of those could contaminate thirty or forty blocks?"

"Yes, sir." Richter said. "Above the current acceptable limits, potentially well above."

The Secretary of Homeland Security leaned forward. Her face was scrunched in a perpetual scowl, like she had just eaten something bitter. Despite the pundits' commentary, the former governor of South Dakota and former lawyer had a firm hand over the vast and sprawling Homeland Security organization.

"Cesium emits both beta and gamma rays," she said. "For people in the immediate vicinity of the blast—those who weren't killed by the explosion—the risk would be radiation poisoning: either external burns if it comes into contact with the skin, or internal damage, if it's inhaled. Then, depending on several factors like wind and the amount of explosive material used, most of the dust would likely settle over a five or ten block area, but some of the fallout would travel farther. Apparently, this stuff would adhere to surfaces like buildings and roads. It would hide in crevices and cracks. It might be carried farther away from the contamination zone by cars and trucks, increasing the risk. It would get into sewers, air ducts, the soil, the food supply, the water supply," she paused, "and although there is some debate in the scientific community, it would likely render a large area of any city—Washington, DC for instance—uninhabitable."

"So we would have a mass evacuation," the president stated, his eyes narrowing.

The Homeland Security Secretary nodded somberly. "It's likely, sir. But in the short term, we might have a mass quarantine."

The president's face clouded.

"Because this stuff would be virtually impossible to clean up," she added, "it would continue to emit gamma rays for a long time, creating a long-term cancer risk in the area." She put her pad down and took a breath. "Because of public fear, many suggest that the best way to deal with the contamination is to abandon the area, potentially demolish it."

The president nodded. "And that would have a devastating effect on the local economy," he added as the implications became clear. "Quite possibly the national economy as well."

The president stood and began pacing back and forth across the room, seemingly lost in thought. Abruptly, the president stopped and turned.

"So let me see if I've got this straight." His voice was sharp. "We know that someone stole a radiation source, and we believe two Islamist terrorists are planning an attack." He stopped, stared hard at the people before him. "We don't know where or when. The only things we do know is that this stuff is apparently in Ohio and that one of the men on the call is, or was, in New York and the other was in Chicago. Is that it?"

The Homeland Security Secretary frowned while Richter and Monahan both nodded slowly. Kendall held their eyes for a moment then turned to Burt Phillips. "I want the National Security Council in the Situation Room," he growled. "Right now."

CHAPTER FORTY-FOUR

As the bus passed through the toll booth, Terry Fogel couldn't help but notice the police. In addition to the cars and trucks—even the unmarked ones were obvious—there were a dozen cops from various jurisdictions standing in the median at the entrance to the Lincoln Tunnel. Besides the two or three Port Authority police officers who were normally stationed by the entrance, there were three New Jersey State Police cars and two from the New York City Police Department. He glanced up at the wall to his right and saw another half dozen cops standing on top. Then, just before they entered the tunnel, he spotted the black SUV and three men in suits. Even the Feds were here, he thought. He sat back as the bus was swallowed up by the darkness.

A few minutes later, as they pulled into the Port Authority Bus Terminal, he made another count. There were four cars and seven officers, all NYPD. And those were the ones that he could see, he mused. The terminal, as usual, was crowded, and the constant stream of buses coming and going blocked much of his view. He climbed off the bus and made his way over to the subway entrance. As he swiped his MetroCard, he saw the clusters of cops eyeing the harried commuters. The commuters didn't seem to notice the extra police presence, but he did. He nodded to two as he jostled his way through the crowd, following the signs. He would catch the train to Penn Station. And, he thought with a grin, when he got there, and later when he visited Grand Central Terminal, he was certain that he would see the same thing.

He hid his grin. His message had been received.

———

The sliver of a moon hung low in the sky as Pablo Guerrero followed the path past the cantina, past the cages for the roosters, and then on to the stables. Outside, the boy had the four horses ready. Guerrero climbed onto the spotted stallion, several years past his prime, but still strong. As Alberto and two other men climbed onto their horses, he looked down at the boy.

"You know what to do?"

The boy nodded. Guerrero studied him for a second then, with a nod, turned his horse. With Alberto in the lead, the four men followed the path through the trees. They kept the horses to a walk, partly because of the uneven terrain and the darkness, but more so as to not draw attention. Four *vaqueros*—cowhands—headed out for another long day in the hills would not look unusual.

The tip had come from one of his contacts in the government. It was a difficult decision to leave Carolina behind. But he had no choice. The troops, an elite unit, were staging for the raid, and the noose around him was tightening. It was time to leave.

An hour later, as the sun was poking above the peaks in the east, they came upon the group of buildings; a handful of rustic, single-story concrete structures common to the barrios, the farms, and the ranches that dotted the landscape. For the men who worked the small ranch nestled high in the hills and for their families, this was home.

They dismounted, and while Alberto and the two men loaded the saddle bags into the back of the waiting pickup trucks, Guerrero glanced behind, down the long dusty trail they had followed. For weeks he had been preparing himself, knowing that this day might come. The safe house, another smaller but secluded ranch he owned on the coast, was ready. By the time the sun was setting, they would be there.

He glanced over the hills across the grey of the early morning and into the distance. He felt sick. In his grief, he had made a mistake. But what choice did he have at the time? He had to bury his daughter. And what choice did he have now? He had to flee.

I'll be back, Carolina. I promise.

After a moment, he turned and climbed into the truck, knowing that until he returned, the boy would make sure Carolina's grave was tended properly.

———

"We were able to locate both phones," Monahan said, referring to the recorded conversation between the two jihadists. He went on to explain that agents had been able to triangulate the GPS chips in each phone. "We found one in Brooklyn, in the car of a Syrian immigrant named Mandhur Husam al Din. He runs a Middle Eastern food store in Bay Ridge. He belongs to the Syrian Cultural and Dawah Center, which is a Mosque headed by Sheik Ramzi Abdul-Muqtadir."

Richter grunted. He remembered the imam from FBI briefings. A radical preacher known for his anti-American views and a suspected recruiter for the Al-Aqsa Martyrs Brigade—a terrorist organization allegedly funded by the government of Syria—he was being closely monitored by the New York City Police Department and the JTTF.

"He insists that the phone is not his," Monahan continued. "But we've taken him into custody."

There was a pause, and Richter heard a shuffle of papers.

"The second phone was located in Chicago in the possession of Murad Al-Asadi. He's someone we've been watching as well. He's from Yemen, and we believe he's involved in recruiting displaced Muslims for jihad training. We also have reason to believe he serves as a middleman by funneling Al Qaeda money to cells in the U.S. He too swears that the phone is not his." There was another pause. "Both men claim to know nothing of the cesium thefts or of any plot."

"So what's our next step?" Richter asked after a moment.

"Their lawyers are screaming and yelling, but I've spoken with

Ben Kiplinger," he said, referring to the attorney general. "With the evidence we have—the phone calls, the record of suspected financial transactions in both cases—we can hold them for a while as we investigate and execute search warrants." He paused. "Ultimately, we would need to charge them, let them go, or potentially transfer them to the military."

Richter made a note. He knew that under the provisions of the National Defense Authorization Act, the men could be detained indefinitely. They would have to be transferred to military custody where they would be treated as enemy combatants, prisoners of war. But would that accomplish anything? The cesium was still missing, and finding that was the priority.

"What about accomplices?" he asked.

"We're interviewing known contacts, influential people in their communities," Monahan replied. "But that's a long shot."

Richter frowned as he made another note. He knew this was likely to be met with open hostility, that many in the community—the business leaders, the sheiks, and the faithful—would refuse to answer any questions until the men were set free.

They spoke for another few minutes. When he hung up, he considered the news. Locating the cell phones had been the easy part, he knew, a simple matter of triangulating the embedded GPS chips. Now they faced the challenge of learning what the potential suspects knew and the legal hurdles of detaining them. Meanwhile, the FBI and Homeland Security were moving as fast as they could.

He hoped it was fast enough.

CHAPTER FORTY-FIVE

As Jerry Watkins climbed down the steps, she smelled the familiar
sour smell, an unpleasant odor from years of grime, grease, urine,
decaying garbage, and dampness that seemed to be forever trapped
in the stairways, platforms and tunnels of the subway. She swiped
her MetroCard and pushed through the gate. She normally wouldn't
have noticed the smell, having grown immune to it over the years.
But, ever since the treatments began, many things seemed to make
her nauseous now. Odors she previously found pleasant, especially
certain foods, now left her gagging. She stepped away from an old
man who reeked of cigarettes and garlic.

Seconds later, she heard the rumble of the train. It was her first
day back at work after two weeks off. It had been a whirlwind that
had begun with a routine medical test and an apologetic look in
her doctor's eye. This was followed by CT Scans to confirm the
doctor's suspicions. She had spent several days learning as much as
she could about breast cancer and treatment options, speaking to
her doctor, to other women, to support groups, and then spending
hours online. Thankfully, according to her doctor anyway, the
cancer had been caught early enough and she had more options.
The surgery, a lumpectomy in her left breast, had been followed by
chemotherapy—which she knew was the cause of her nausea—and
the implantation of radioactive seeds where the tumor once was. The
seeds would remain for another week.

After three days spent on the couch, she was anxious to go back to work. A computer programmer, she worked for an investment bank in lower Manhattan. Not exactly on Wall Street, she thought, but it didn't matter. With the amount of transactions her firm handled daily, they had the ability to move the markets, if not rattle them occasionally. *What was the term now? Too big to fail?* She had joked with a friend that at least it provided job security.

The train pulled into the Wall Street station and her anxiety grew while she waited with other passengers for the doors to open. She needed to get out; out of the subway, away from these people, away from their odors, away from the stink of the station, into fresh air. She climbed the stairs and felt a sense of relief when she made it to the top. There, she spotted the two police officers, not an unusual sight in Manhattan.

As she passed, one of the cops frowned and stepped toward her.

"Ma'am. May we have a word with you?" The female cop asked.

———

"I think I got something. Let's go back."

The pilot nodded and began to bank. As he came out of the turn, he spotted the barn directly ahead. The weathered siding and missing roof shingles indicated that it probably hadn't been used in some time. He glanced at the nearby house. The front porch was missing a step, the screen door was bent at an odd angle, and most of the windows were boarded over. The farm looked abandoned. Yet the fresh, dark soil, neatly sculpted as if a giant comb had been dragged through it, indicated that the fields had been recently tilled. Someone was farming the land. And in the driveway sat a rusty and dented late-model Ford pickup truck.

"Go right over the barn this time," the young patrolman said. Then he turned and glanced at the pilot. "Can you get any lower?"

The pilot, a twenty-eight year veteran of the Ohio State Police nodded as he turned slightly and began to descend. He leveled off at two hundred feet. The young cop sitting next to him hadn't even been born yet when he'd joined the force, he thought once more. That made him feel old, and he tried once again to chase the thought from his mind. A mission was a mission he thought, and he would rather be flying than on the ground. Usually called out for search and rescue, sometimes a missing person, other times a wanted fugitive, this was just another form of reconnaissance, he told himself. The difference was, his eyes wouldn't help him much today, except for keeping the plane in the sky.

As they passed over the barn, the kid watched the meter then smiled.

"Bingo!" he called out.

The pilot began to fly an oval pattern over the barn while the kid confirmed his readings. It was amazing technology, he thought. From two hundred feet in the air, the meter was able to pick up radiation. That both amazed and frightened him. The kid had assured him that they were safe, although he still wondered. What the heck did the kid know anyway? If that meter was able to pick up the radiation from this far away, were the levels high enough to affect him? He glanced over at the kid again. He was excited and didn't seem the least bit troubled by being so close to something so dangerous. The pilot sighed. The kid was too young to remember the emergency drills, the fallout shelters and bomb cellars of the Cold War. Just a young kid himself in the 1970s, the pilot remembered the teacher telling students to put their heads below their desks, as if the eighteen-inch by two-foot piece of wood over their heads would protect them from an atomic blast.

He glanced over at the kid. "Do we have enough to confirm?"

The kid smiled and nodded.

"Call it in," the pilot instructed as he began to climb. He wanted to put as much distance between whatever was in the barn and his plane as he could. He leveled off at one thousand feet. From here, he was still in position to support the response team on the ground. That is, if they arrived within the next hour, he thought as he checked his fuel gauge. After that, they would have to bug out.

He glanced over at the meter in the kid's hands and noticed that, although the radiation levels had dropped, they were still registering something. He glanced at the fuel gauge again and then at his watch, anxious as the seconds passed by at a snail's pace.

———

When Jerry Watkins reached her building, her face was still red. She hesitated outside the door for a second, then turned and walked to the bench by the small fountain. She was embarrassed and she was angry. She had felt guilty when the two cops had questioned her, like she had done something wrong. The female cop had finally asked her if she had recently undergone any medical treatments. *How could they know?* She had wondered at the time. She felt as if her privacy had been violated. She stared back at the cop, unsure what to say as both cops glanced down at their gun belts. It took her a moment to realize what they were doing—she had read something about this in the *New York Times*, hadn't she? It was then that she remembered the card.

"I'm sorry," she stammered and fumbled in her purse. The nurse had told her that she should carry the card with her; that certain detectors could be sensitive, especially in airports. She had absent-mindedly stuck the card in her purse, less concerned about it and her future travel plans at the time than the cancer inside her.

The cops had been polite, professional and had even apologized for the inconvenience. That didn't make it any better, she thought. *God damn it!* There was something wrong with the world when she was forced to explain her medical condition to two cops, to two strangers carrying meters that could sense what was going on inside her own body.

———

Rusty Morgan saw the plume of dust in the distance, rising above the Nevada desert. He grabbed his radio and alerted his crew to the inbound load. After thirty-six years in the business, he had begun thinking that it might be time to sell out and retire; especially now, with scrap metal prices as high as they were. The last two years had been great for his business. Everybody attributed it to the demand from China, but, he thought as he squinted into the sun—trying to make out the truck—whatever it was, he had a decision to make. Sell now, while his business was profitable or ride out the next few years of high prices and pocket as much cash as he could. The trouble was, he thought as he stared at the truck rumbling across the desert, what would he do instead?

He grabbed the meter and walked down to the scales. By the time he got there, two of his men were waiting. The truck pulled through the open gate and drove up to the scale.

"What you got today, Pete?" Rusty called up to the driver.

"Copper pipes, various lengths, some coils of tubing, and some wiring. Also got some iron pipe and some metal workbenches."

Rusty shook his head. "Where did you get this stuff, Pete?"

"Aw, come on, Rusty. You going to grill me every time?"

Rusty shook his head. Maybe it was better if he didn't know. He wiggled the meter at Pete.

"Jeez, Rusty. The meter too?"

Pete hopped out of the cab. Rusty ignored him and climbed up into the truck bed. He turned the meter on and, after a moment, it began to chirp. Rusty's head spun. He shot Pete a dirty look as he quickly climbed out.

"What the fuck's wrong with you, Pete?" he screamed in the driver's face. "You trying to kill me? You trying to kill my boys? You trying to destroy my business?"

Pete backed up, his hands held, palms out, in front of him. "I swear, Rusty," he pleaded. "I didn't know. I got it from some guy in Reno."

"Get this shit out of here!" Rusty snarled.

"Aw jeez, Rusty! What am I supposed to do with it?"

Rusty took a step toward him; Pete flinched then scrambled back into the truck.

Seconds later, the truck drove out through the gates. Rusty, still angry, watched as it headed back across the desert. That was the last time he would do business with that guy, he told himself. He still remembered, all too vividly, the dirty load he had received several years back; the one that had almost shut down his business.

He shook his head and hurried back to his desk, searching for the card. It took him a moment to find it. The visit last week from the stern-faced woman and the two doom-and-gloom men from the Nuclear Regulatory Commission had frustrated him. With her hair pulled back into a bun so tight she couldn't even smile, she had come into his yard unannounced with the men in tow waving their meters. She had demanded to see his records, treating him like an uneducated redneck.

He dialed the number. It was Pete's turn for a taste of bun lady.

CHAPTER FORTY-SIX

"We have teams all over the country searching," Pat Monahan began, "and while we've found a number of things that concern us, we haven't found the missing canister."

Matthew Richter frowned. He was sitting in the Oval Office with the president and the Secretary of Homeland Security while Monahan provided an update. It was like looking for a needle in a haystack, he thought. Still, they had to try.

"The Department of Energy, the EPA, the NRC, and state and local authorities are working with us," Monahan continued. "Our initial focus has been on highways, transportation routes, and waterways. We've followed up on hundreds of leads so far, but most have turned out to be illegally or improperly disposed of industrial equipment or industrial waste." Monahan paused. "All of that has to be dealt with properly. And if some of it were to wind up in the hands of terrorists," his voice trailed off; the implication was obvious. "At a minimum," he continued, "we've identified a dozen issues that the NRC and EPA will need to follow up on."

"What about the Ohio connection?" the president asked.

"We're doing aerial and drive-by surveys, taking readings of farms, factories, warehouses, and rural properties," Monahan responded. "But..." he shook his head.

"This stuff is in a sealed container, right?" the president asked.

Monahan nodded.

"So it may not emit radioactive waves," the president continued.

"How sure are we that we'll be able to detect it?"

"Unless they break open the containers," Monahan answered, "it's going to be a challenge to find this stuff. But, we have a lot of resources out there searching, and some of the equipment they're using is highly sophisticated and can detect sealed-source materials. Still," he paused, "there's a lot of ground to cover."

The president glanced over and caught Richter's eye. Richter could see the frustration and worry on his face. He knew what the president was thinking. One of the options they had discussed was mobilizing the National Guard. That was a tough decision. The president had already quietly raised the DEFCON level, but that fact had become public fairly quickly. Now, if they mobilized the guard, there was no way to prevent the public outcry that would ensue as people reacted to the sudden presence of troops all over the country, troops with Geiger counters and detection equipment searching for an unknown threat. And what could the government say? No matter how carefully they crafted a statement, speculation and conspiracy theories would dominate the news and internet chatter, potentially leading to panic. Still, they might not have a choice.

In the silence that followed, Richter heard a mechanical noise and glanced up at the mantel above the fireplace. The clock was ticking.

———

The sensor zoomed in on the boy's face. Even from twenty thousand feet, he could see the boy clearly. The boy appeared to be pleading. He held up his possessions for the soldier to inspect. The sensor knew that the boy had been waiting for hours in the darkness just beyond the roadblock. Turned away the day before, he had returned before sunrise to try once more. Now, as the sun peeked over the horizon, it seemed, he had succeeded in making it to the gate where, once again, he held his possessions up for another soldier to inspect.

From his comfortable chair in the ground control station at Naval Air Station Corpus Christi, the sensor watched as the soldier inspected the pair of pruning shears, then the trowel, and, finally, the small bundle. This, the boy unrolled to reveal a small, colored glass. The sensor stared at the screen. It took him a moment to realize that the boy was holding a votive candle. He had seen them frequently in Texas, occasionally in Mexican restaurants, but more often on the side of the road in makeshift shrines. On one side, he knew, was a colorful picture of a saint dressed in flowing robes, a halo overhead. On the other: a prayer.

He watched as the soldier handed everything back to the boy. The soldier pulled out his radio. After a minute, he stepped back and let the boy through, directing him to a truck. Another soldier lifted the boy up into the back, where he sat on the bench sandwiched between two heavily-armed men. The sensor chuckled as the truck began bouncing up the long road toward the hacienda. The boy had made it through.

He had been wondering who would tend the grave. It had become a routine. Every day at noon, and sometimes in the early evening, a gardener would shuffle to the stables where he would retrieve his tools then make the long slow walk out to the grave. There, he would spend a half hour making sure everything was neat and orderly. Then, he would say a prayer, the lieutenant remembered, his hand resting on the marble cross.

But two days ago, the gardener, like many of the other workers, had failed to show up. Sensing their raid was blown, the heavily-armed troops had stormed the gates yesterday, in the darkness before dawn. There had been a brief firefight—a couple of dozen guards killed or wounded—but far less resistance than everyone had been expecting. The sensor hadn't been on duty then; this he had learned from the briefing. Now, it appeared that many inside the compound had gone home or fled, having somehow caught wind of the pending raid. How so many had managed to flee, under the watchful eyes of the satellites and drones, was still a mystery. And from the frustrated looks on the faces of his officers, the sensor knew that Guerrero and his henchman were still missing.

The sensor followed the truck as it made its way past the house, past the stables, eventually stopping by the wrought iron fence. Two soldiers jumped out then, after helping the boy down, stood to the side as the boy made his way to the gate.

CHAPTER FORTY-SEVEN

It was six-ten in the morning when the brown-haired man wheeled his small suitcase onto the platform. He found a spot against the wall and stood behind the crowd that was forming on the platform. Although the train was still three minutes out, people were already jostling to be first in line for a good seat.

He glanced down the track, then back at his watch. There was a sharp odor of burnt metal mixed with the pungent smell of grease, coming from the tracks he suspected. Almost June and the morning sun was already warm. The platform continued to fill: men and women dressed in suits, lugging briefcases or computer bags, some carrying newspapers folded below their arms, others sipping from steaming cups of coffee, some doing both. Many wore bored expressions, while the fingers of others danced over their phones' screens, oblivious to the world around them, as they checked their latest messages or what additional nonsense disguised as news had been posted on CNN. They were like sheep, he thought, as he glanced from one to another. If they only knew how radically their lives were going to change that morning.

The woman next to him glanced over and he smiled. The woman frowned and quickly turned back to her book. A moment later, the woman glanced up again then stepped forward, jostling her way toward the edge of the platform. The others around him stepped forward as well and the man glanced up the track. In the distance, he saw the light. Thirty seconds later, the southbound Metro-North train pulled into the station. He joined the crowd and jostled for a space in front.

When the doors opened, he was tenth in line. He felt the blast of warm air as he stepped into the car. The air conditioning must be broken, he suspected, or perhaps Metro North hadn't bothered to turn it on. Finding a seat three rows back, he lifted his travel bag. The wheel caught on the bottom of the overhead rack then began to slip from his hands. For a second, he thought he might drop it. An arm darted up, helping him shove the suitcase into the rack. He turned to a young African American man, in his early twenties, dressed in a business suit. The man smiled.

"Thank you." He grinned at the younger man. "Wouldn't want to go dropping that."

The young man smiled back. "No problem," he said as he headed down the aisle.

As the car began to fill, the brown-haired man shifted the bag slightly. He noticed a young woman next to him, waiting. He smiled as he stepped out of the way. She gave him a quick glance and nodded her thanks as she slid into the window seat. She seemed more interested in the music or whatever she was listening to in her earphones.

Fifteen minutes later, the train pulled into Stamford and he spotted his opportunity. The elderly woman stopped in the aisle and glanced down the length of the car. She was dressed elegantly in clothes that said money wasn't a concern. She frowned, sighed loudly, then began to turn, when he jumped up.

"Please," he said with a smile. "Take my seat."

She smiled stiffly as if frustrated that it had taken him—anyone—so long. "Thank you," she said dismissively as if she were talking to a servant.

He smiled nonetheless as she brushed past him, then made his way to the doorway, joining two other people who had resigned themselves to the fact that there were no seats left.

Thirty-five minutes later, he heard the static of the speakers and the conductor announced that 125th Street was the next stop. As the train began to slow, he turned and noticed the young man who had helped him stow his suitcase. They shared a brief smile.

The doors opened, and he let the man and several others step off, then just before the doors closed again, he followed them onto the platform. He trailed the line of people to the stairs when someone grabbed his arm.

"Hey! Your suitcase!"

He turned, a momentary look of confusion on his face. "Damn!" he said, frowning as the train pulled away.

The young man who had helped him earlier checked his watch. "Another train should be along in a few minutes. If you catch it," he said, as he nodded toward the departing train, "that train should still be in Grand Central and hopefully you can find your bag."

"That's a good idea," he said. "Thank you."

He smiled as the young man turned toward the steps. He waited on the platform and a minute later, another train pulled in. This one was headed northbound. He hopped on. He had no intention of going anywhere near Grand Central Terminal today.

———

In the years after September 11th, the detectors had been quietly installed at the entrance to the tunnels at 96th Street, where the Metro-North train tracks dropped below Park Avenue. They were strategically placed so that they were able to take multiple readings from each passing car. Similar to other systems on the George Washington Bridge, the Holland Tunnel, and every other heavily traveled route into and out of Manhattan, the detectors initially installed were sodium iodide devices, designed to detect only gamma rays. But later enhancements, the addition of thin-window Geiger-Mueller probes, allowed the system to detect the shorter, heavier beta and alpha rays as well.

However, as the 6:14 out of Westport rumbled by, the detectors registered nothing unusual.

———

The conductor walked through the cars, ignoring the discarded newspapers, coffee cups, and soda cans. The crew waiting on the platform—the Coach Cleaners—would get those. He was interested in what else he might find. It was amazing what people left behind. Cell phones, calculators, iPods, watches, laptops—even the occasional wallet or purse. Most of these never made it to the lost and found, unless they were big and bulky—like laptops—and were likely to be picked up by the security cameras on the platform. The bulky items and the wallets and purses, he turned in. Of course, the money would have been removed by then, but that was usually the least of his forgetful passenger's worries. He had learned long ago that they were often relieved to get their driver's licenses, their credit cards, the pictures of their kids, their passports, and other personal information back and didn't normally make a fuss over the missing hundred dollars.

Today was a light day, only two cell phones so far. He smiled to himself. It wasn't every day when he found a diamond tennis bracelet, like he had three years ago. That had been a great day and just in time for his anniversary! So he took the light day in stride, knowing that it meant he was one day closer to another big find.

As he stepped into the next car, he spotted the suitcase up on the shelf. He shook his head. He wouldn't have time to rifle through it, and it was much too big to hide, unlike the phones in his pocket. Those he would sell to the kid down the block. What the kid did with them, he didn't know, but the kid would pay him thirty bucks. He glanced up at the suitcase as he pulled out his radio. Although his supervisor would reprimand him—delays were unacceptable for the commuter railroad—he believed in doing his part. They took unattended packages and luggage very seriously in the airports; to his way of thinking, the railroad should do the same. What could his supervisor do? Fire him? Not likely with the union at his back.

"Base. This is Sixteen on track Twenty-three. I got a suspicious stray bag here."

CHAPTER FORTY-EIGHT

The Metro-North cop walked down the platform, dodging between the commuters who were waiting to board the train for the outbound leg back to Connecticut. Most, like him, worked the third shift, but, unlike them, he still had another thirty-five minutes before his shift ended. He had been on patrol, on the adjacent platform, when the call came over the radio.

He stepped inside the car and spotted the two conductors chatting. He knew both. Behind them, on the overhead rack, he spotted the bag.

"Hey, Ed, Tom." He gestured toward the bag. "That it?" he asked.

The conductors turned.

"Hey, Steve," one said. "Yeah, that's it."

The cop studied the carry-on bag for a few seconds. He glanced down at his gun belt, checking his "radiation pager"—the portable detector most cops in the city carried. Nothing.

"You see who put it there?" he asked. "Any reason it's suspicious?"

Ed, the conductor who had discovered the suitcase, shook his head. "No. I didn't notice it until after we pulled in." He shrugged. "But it was left behind..." The unfinished sentence was clear.

The cop nodded, glanced at his watch, then keyed the microphone on his lapel. "This is Unit Two-Nine. I'm going to need the portable ETD and K-9 on track Twenty-three."

"Copy Two-Nine. Stand by."

The cop exchanged a glance with the two conductors; Ed pulled his own radio out and called the dispatcher, notifying him of the delay. As the cop stepped back onto the platform, he heard enough of the dispatcher's angry response over Ed's radio to know he wasn't happy. *Tough shit*, he thought. He wasn't paid to make the dispatcher happy.

The train would wait as the dog sniffed the bag. Then, to be sure, they would swab the bag then run the swab through the detector, checking for trace elements of explosives. Even though he had been trained, he rarely got a chance to use the machine. Besides, he thought as he glanced at his watch again, if he played it right, he would probably earn some overtime.

He turned and scanned the crowd. Many were glancing at their own watches, frustrated at the delay. A moment later, he heard the crackle of the speaker, then the announcement. This was followed by a collective groan from the crowd. The passengers, most wearing a weary, resigned expression, turned, en masse, and began heading toward the new track.

Two of his fellow officers, one leading the German Shepherd on a leash, the other carrying the ETD unit, threaded their way through the stream of passengers. He nodded to both then tilted his head toward the open door next to him. Then, as he turned to step back into the train, there was a bright flash and he was slammed into the steel pillar behind him. He was dead before he knew what hit him.

———

Jean Dunlap sighed as she turned and began to shuffle slowly with the crowd to the next platform. She glanced at her watch and sighed again when she realized that she would be late for class. She pulled out her phone. A legal secretary, she worked the overnight shift at a law firm where the associates and many partners worked brutal hours, especially when there was a deal underway, as there always seemed to be. She was one of five secretaries who catered to their needs. More of a concierge than a secretary, really—the filing was handled by the paralegals, the lawyers did their own typing, and the phones were answered by a team of receptionists—her job was to arrange for the food, to handle the laundry and to run assorted errands for the overworked lawyers. She made travel arrangements and prepared their expense reports when necessary, and generally made life as easy as she could for the twenty-one associates and five junior partners who often caught only a few hours of sleep in their offices. When she had first taken the job, she had been amazed at the number of businesses that operated around the clock: restaurants and caterers, dry cleaning and laundry services, messengers and overnight delivery services—all available anytime. Her firm was one of seven law firms in the area that operated on a similar schedule, and the service industry in the surrounding neighborhood had grown and prospered along with the lawyers.

She accepted the hours because it allowed her to take law classes during the day. Tomorrow, she planned on speaking to her boss. With the first year of law school behind her, she was hoping to become a paralegal. Then, if she did well in school, in three more years, she would take the bar, and, hopefully, join the other associates who demanded freshly made pasta and fruit smoothies at three in the morning.

She left her professor a message then, as she put her phone away, told herself again that it was worth it. That was her last thought before the bright flash. She never heard the bang. When the first shockwave hit her, she was hurled like a rag doll onto the tracks. In a sense she was lucky: the blast killed her instantly, sparing her a more painful death when her limp body landed on the third rail.

———

Rebecca Matthews grabbed her husband's hand even tighter and grinned.

"Isn't this amazing?" she asked.

Her husband, looking like a deer caught in headlights, shook his head.

"This is crazy!" he responded.

Rebecca glanced at him again and could see that he was grinning too.

They stood still for a moment and watched as harried commuters streamed out of the arched passageways that led to the commuter trains and spilled out onto the main concourse. There the commuters darted left or right, heading off at every angle; many talking on phones or texting, somehow narrowly avoiding collisions as they shot across the floor toward the marble steps of the ornate staircase or around the corner, to where or what, Rebecca didn't know. She turned and watched as others headed down yet more passageways to yet more mysterious places. *They must lead to someplace important*, she thought. Seconds later, she realized she was right when she spotted a sign on the archway through which a stream of people disappeared. That one led to the subway.

A man brushed past her, and she turned and watched him make his way over to the shops and restaurants along one wall. The noise was deafening but no one seemed to notice or mind, she thought, as she spotted people sitting and eating at the tables that seemed to be set up like a sidewalk cafe.

She shook her head in wonder before the ceiling caught her eye. She stared up at the picture of the night sky above her, the arched ceiling held up by enormous stone columns. She was jostled again and smiled nonetheless as the serious-faced man brushed by. He glanced at her momentarily, mouthed a *sorry* before turning his attention back to his phone and scurrying away. She shook her head as he was swallowed up by the crowd.

"We better ask at the information booth," her husband said, "before we get run over."

Rebecca, still grinning, nodded. "I guess we just do like they do. Right?" Her eyes were full of adventure. "Ready?"

Her husband grinned back and, with Rebecca leading, they began to snake their way toward the booth.

Visiting the city for only two days, there was a lot they wanted to see. But first on the list was the Empire State building. Then, shopping on Fifth Avenue, taking in the glitz and glamour, before stopping by St. Patrick's Cathedral. Then they would make their way up to Central Park, maybe take a horse drawn carriage ride, before working their way back to Rockefeller Center. Unsure whether they should take a cab, try their luck on the subway, or simply walk, they decided to ask for advice. Although, Rebecca thought as she stepped around another group of tourists taking pictures, if the subway was anything like this, a cab or even walking might be better.

She had just reached the booth when the ground shook and a loud bang echoed through the building. There was a momentary silence—a fraction of a second when she was unsure what had happened—before she heard the screams and panicked cries echoing around her. Suddenly there were shouts, and people began pushing and shoving against her. The panic she saw in their eyes only fueled her own.

She turned to her husband, caught the panic in his eyes too, when, suddenly, she lost his hand. She screamed once and reached out for him when she was knocked from behind and fell to the ground. She saw a flash of blue light as her head slammed into the stone floor, then everything went black.

She never saw the smoke that began to billow out of the commuter train passageways.

CHAPTER FORTY-NINE

Charlie McGuire deftly stepped over the third rail, ducked below the small arch and stopped in front of the electrical panel. He opened the panel and pulled the meter from his belt. Standing six-foot two and topping the scales at two hundred and twenty pounds, the archway was a tight fit. He didn't mind. A big man, he was surprisingly dexterous in the nooks and crannies and small passageways of the subterranean station.

As he connected the meter, the ground shook as a loud bang echoed through the tunnels. He braced himself in the archway as debris—dust, soot and small pieces of stone—rained down around him. Almost immediately, he heard the klaxon; the electronic whooping of the emergency alarm. An electrician by trade, he was one of hundreds of tradesmen—plumbers, mechanics, elevator repairmen—who kept Grand Central Terminal operating seven days a week. But when the alarm sounded, he became a fireman. He quickly stuffed the meter back into his utility belt and backed out of the small passageway.

Moments later, back up on the platform, he began to weave his way between the startled passengers, then turned and jogged down the passageway toward Track Fourteen. One of twenty volunteers—all certified firefighters and licensed emergency medical technicians—he was a member of the Grand Central Terminal Fire Brigade. The Brigade was the first responder to any emergency within the forty-seven-acre complex. With almost seven hundred and fifty thousand people passing through each day and over one hundred restaurants, eateries, coffee shops, and retail stores, Grand Central Terminal was a city within a city. Not surprisingly, medical emergencies were common, and the brigade responded to the frequent slips and falls of rushing passengers as well as the occasional dizzy spells and heart attacks.

And while the number of fire incidents had dropped dramatically since the brigade's inception a quarter of a century ago—thanks to their vigilance in fire prevention—they still responded to almost two dozen fires each year. Usually the result of trash on the tracks or the occasional transformer failure or grease fire, these were dealt with swiftly and professionally, the fire often extinguished by the time the New York City Fire Department arrived.

The klaxon continued to blare as McGuire turned again. Probably a transformer explosion, he thought. As he turned another corner, he spotted a group of men and women from his unit in front of the garage that housed their gear. They were pulling on the white hazmat suits. Must be a steam pipe explosion, he thought. Installed, in some cases, almost one hundred years ago, it was assumed that the pipes were covered in asbestos.

"What's up, Chief?" he called.

A man ten years his junior, an elevator mechanic who usually had a joke and a smile for everyone, looked up. There was no sparkle in his eyes today.

"Suit up, Charlie." The chief ordered then paused, his eyes narrowing. "An explosion on Track Twenty-three. Francine's over in the area. She's picking up high levels on the PRD."

Charlie dropped his belt in front of his locker and began pulling on his gear. *High levels on the personal radiation detector*, he thought, cursing under his breath. As he hurried to pull on the suit, he thought about his wife and sons. For the first time in his career as a firefighter, he was scared.

———

Sergeant Joe D'Agostino was sitting in the driver's seat of his patrol car at the corner of East 44th Street and Vanderbilt Avenue. He glanced over at the rookie—the young kid he had the misfortune to be babysitting—and yelled out the window.

"With cream and two sugars!" He paused then added, "Don't screw it up this time!"

The rookie, standing in front of the pushcart, turned and grinned. "Got it, Sarge," he yelled back.

D'Agostino shook his head and grinned. The kid was all right. He listened. He asked the right questions. And he had a good sense of humor. But, he was a rookie officer with only four months on the job. He had a lot to learn.

D'Agostino watched as the kid paid the vendor and carried two cups back to the car. He took the coffee from the rookie without a word. He shifted in his seat and took a sip. Eighteen years on the job, he had grown immune to the long stints in the car and the hemorrhoids that came with it. He had grown immune to his doctor's warnings about the food he ate, especially while on patrol. All great tasting—over eighteen years he had learned where to eat and where not to—it had too much fat, too much salt, too much of all the things that made food good. And he had grown immune to the silence. He could sit for hours at a time with a partner, both having figured out that they didn't need to say anything to fill the void, and that, after all of the time they spent together, there really wasn't much left to say anyway.

He glanced over at the rookie and sighed. Unfortunately, he couldn't remain silent today. The kid had to learn, and the only way that was going to happen was if someone like him—a seasoned veteran who knew his way around the streets and around the department—took the kid under his wing and taught him what he knew.

But that could wait until he finished his coffee. He watched the stream of pedestrians heading up Vanderbilt, passing the MetLife Building, and glanced down at the doors to Grand Central where the stream began. It would be like this until shortly before nine, when it would start to trickle but never quite stop. Then, in the afternoon, the stream would reverse, starting shortly before four as the commuters headed back to Grand Central to catch trains to Stamford and White Plains and God knew where else.

He grinned as the young woman in a very short skirt began to cross Vanderbilt, heading directly toward their car. Despite the cool weather, her jacket was open, and he could see the plunging neckline of her blouse. The rookie, he noticed, had spotted her too. The kid was catching on. He was about to say something when there was a muffled boom and he saw the young woman flinch, a confused expression on her face.

"What the hell was that?" the rookie asked.

Ignoring him, D'Agostino scanned the street, searching for the source, his eyes drawn to the doors of Grand Central a block away. Startled, pedestrians had stopped mid-stride, some glancing over their shoulders, others turning and hurrying away. Several ran. Seconds later, people began to pour out of the doors.

One handed, D'Agostino hit the lights and the siren then slammed the gearshift into drive. He handed his coffee to the rookie.

"Call it in," he said as he turned onto Vanderbilt and sped down the block. "Possible Ten-Thirty-Three. Explosion in Grand Central Terminal. Unknown source," he added as he chirped the siren, scattering pedestrians in the process. The rookie, unsure what to do with the coffees, dropped them out the window then reached for the radio. As he made the call, D'Agostino crossed the double yellow line and pulled up to the entrance across from East 43rd Street.

"Let's go," he yelled to the rookie then shot him a warning look. "Stick with me."

The kid nodded.

D'Agostino climbed out of the car and took two steps when the radiation pager on his belt started to vibrate. *Oh, shit!* He stared down at it for a moment to make sure the pager wasn't malfunctioning, then reached for his radio.

He looked up just in time to see the rookie disappear into the terminal.

———

Seven blocks north of Grand Central, Anthony McGrath, sitting in his office on the second floor of the firehouse, glanced at the calendar then bowed his head. It had been thirty-four years ago to the day, but not a day went by when he didn't think about Vinny Demarco. And each year on the anniversary, regardless of where he had been stationed over the years, he visited the cemetery on Long Island where Demarco had been buried and he said a prayer. Today, he would do so again at the end of his shift.

Thirty-four years had done nothing to soften the image. He could still see the stairway, he could still smell the smoke—hell, he could still *taste* it. He could still hear the roar of the fire and the screams for help as if it had been yesterday. Chief McGrath had been a probie then, just nine months out of the academy, just nine months since he had graduated from *The Rock*. They had responded to a routine call—a Ten-Seventy-Five—for a structural fire in Queens. He had been following Demarco up the steps of the burning building, behind the nozzle, humping the hose, when Demarco stopped and turned to explain something. Suddenly the ceiling caved in. Had Demarco not stopped, had he not taken a moment to explain something to the probie, it would have been him, not Vinny Demarco, who had been buried below the burning rubble. And it would have been him who thousands of firefighters had donned their dress uniforms for, to pay their final respects. One second and some luck had been all that had mattered and, as a result, the fire had taken Vinny Demarco instead of him.

His radio crackled, interrupting his thoughts. As he reached for it, the alarm sounded in the stationhouse. He took the call. A moment later, he grabbed his hat and coat and hurried down the steps to the watch center. Over the loudspeakers, he heard the watch officer's voice telling the station what he already knew.

"Box Zero-Seven-Eight-Nine, Park and Forty-Second," the loudspeaker crackled. "We've got a report of an explosion at Grand Central Terminal. Everybody goes."

He took the ticket from the watch officer. *A transformer explosion?* he wondered seconds later, when he stepped onto the apparatus floor. *Or a steam pipe?* He had seen his share of both over the years. He glanced at the men as they hurried to pull on their bunker gear. They wore the serious faces of a brotherhood that so few understood, one that put their lives on the line daily in a never-ending battle against death. He had attended too many funerals, had buried too many brothers over his thirty-five years on the job to take anything for granted. Even routine fires could turn ugly real fast. The difference between life and death, he knew all too well, often came down to seconds and sometimes, despite the skill, training, and unparalleled bravery of the firefighters responding, to sheer luck.

Now though, he thought with a sigh as he watched the men, it wasn't just burning buildings they had to worry about. Now, hazardous materials, accidentally spilled or otherwise, as well as terrorists and the threat of all of the chaos and destruction they could bring kept him awake at night. He exchanged a glance with the captain as he headed for the door. The captain nodded. The message was always the same: *Let's bring our boys home safe from this one.*

Thirty seconds after the alarm was received, Engine Eight pulled out onto East 51st Street. Two firefighters stood in the middle of the street, blocking traffic. Ladder Two, referred to as Two Truck by the men in the firehouse, came next. The chief, already in his Suburban, glanced at his aide as he reached for the radio.

"Battalion Eight to Manhattan. Box Zero-Seven-Eight-Nine."

As the chief waited for the reply, he watched as the last two firefighters hopped onto the back of Two Truck. His aide pulled out behind them.

"Battalion Eight," the radio said in reply. "Engine Sixty-Five is first due. You've also got Engine Twenty-One, Four Truck, Rescue One, Engine Eight and Two Truck responding."

"Contact the Transit Authority and Metro-North," the chief ordered. He needed information, the more the better. A transformer or a steam pipe explosion could be tricky. A high-voltage third rail, narrow platforms and tunnels, and the high likelihood of asbestos added to the challenge. He would need to speak to Con Ed as well.

The aide chirped his siren as the light turned red. Ignoring it, he leaned on the horn as he followed Two Truck, turning south onto Lexington Avenue. Like the trucks he followed, the aide alternated between the horn and the siren, a vain attempt to move the traffic out of their way. A minute and a half later, they crossed 45th Street when there was a cackle on the radio.

"Engine Sixty-Five to Battalion Eight."

"Battalion Eight," McGrath responded.

"Battalion Eight, we're getting hits on the rad meter."

"Ten-Five?" The chief asked as he glanced at his aide. The aide frowned.

"We're getting hits on the rad meter. Both at the main entrance at Park and at Vanderbilt." There was a hiss. "Very high readings, boss."

"Shit!" the chief swore under his breath. "Hold your position, Sixty-Five." He pictured the scene in his mind. The Park Avenue overpass created a canopy over the main entrance on Forty-Second Street, but the south side of the station was also accessible at the corner of Vanderbilt Avenue on the west side, both at Forty-Second Street and at Forty-Third. It was also accessible from below ground.

"Engine Sixty-Five. Establish a perimeter. Take readings at the subway entrances." Those, the chief knew, were across the street. He made another call, instructing Engine Eight and Two Truck to stop at 43rd Street. The Graybar Building had a passageway that led to the main concourse. Seconds later, as his aide pulled to the curb, men were already hopping out of the fire trucks in front.

As the chief climbed out of the Suburban, the firefighters were jogging toward the entrance. Suddenly, they stopped short and the captain began waving them away from the doors. The chief could hear the shouts.

"Get back! Get back!"

Shit! The chief thought as the captain herded his men to the other side of the trucks. He didn't need to be told; the meters had gone off and the captain was using the trucks as a shield. He saw the people streaming out the doors, panic and confusion on their faces.

"Chief, this entrance is hot," McGrath heard the captain say on the Handy-Talkie, confirming his suspicions. He glanced across the street at the captain, at the firefighters, at *his* men, praying the levels were low, praying the exposure was brief. Then he turned and signaled to his aide. As he did, he heard the voices behind him. *But, Cap! There're people inside!*

"Manhattan wants the signal on the box," the aide said.

"Ten-Eighty," the chief barked without hesitation. His face was hard. "Code Four."

There was a scream, and he glanced back at the door. It was the first time in thirty-five years that he had ever made such a call. He watched firefighters lifting a mother and her two kids off the sidewalk. They had apparently been knocked down by the surge behind them. Before they could be trampled, firefighters had rushed to their aid. Ten-Eighty was a hazardous material incident. Code Four indicated large-scale contamination of both first responders and civilians. The signal would result in the automatic deployment of the Mass Decontamination Task Force as well as specialized HazMat and Rescue battalions and a huge contingent of support personnel. The chief prayed that they would get there quickly.

He turned back to his aide. "And, God damn it, I need TA and Metro-North. Now," he snapped. Leaving his aide to make the call, he turned back to the door. Firefighters were carrying the mom and her children away from the building's entrance. He saw the terror in the little girl's eyes. He held the Handy-Talkie to his mouth.

"All units responding Box Zero-Seven-Eight-Nine," the chief radioed. "All second and third due units to check the entrances north of Forty-Second Street, along Vanderbilt, Park, and Lexington, including the northwest and northeast passages. Call in your readings prior to entering the scene." He paused then added. "Command post is at Forty-Third and Lexington, in front of Graybar Building. Staging area one block south."

The chief turned and watched as panicked commuters, tourists, and office workers continued to pour out the doors. How many people were in the terminal at this hour? he wondered. And in the connecting passageways and office buildings? Ten, fifteen thousand? More? The firefighters were directing the fleeing crowd across the street, finding anything solid to hide behind. There were likely injured and dying people inside, he knew, and potentially a fire still burning. But the squads and the HazMat teams were the only units equipped with radiation suits and Level A protective gear. Until the special teams arrived, there was little he could do.

CHAPTER FIFTY

President Kendall climbed down the steps to the cheers of the small crowd. He returned the salutes of the Air Force officers and enlisted airmen at the bottom of the steps then walked over and shook hands with the mayor, the governor, and then the assembled U.S. and state senators waiting for him on the tarmac.

In Atlanta to celebrate the opening of a new series of treatment centers, part of a public-private-partnership to expand drug education, treatment, and rehabilitation, the president planned to meet with state and local officials and the leaders of almost a dozen churches and community organizations that had brought the vision to life. Then he would tour two facilities where he would meet with those who were in dire need of treatment and recovery services, and with those on the front lines who were devoting their time and energy to provide hope for a better tomorrow. He would deliver his comments from the second facility, praising the people involved and the progress they had made, before flying back to Washington in the afternoon.

He waved to the reporters and posed briefly for pictures with the governor and then the mayor. Then the trio began walking toward the motorcade. Out of the corner of his eye, the president saw Burt Phillips hurrying over. He caught the look in his Chief of Staff's eye, something most would miss, and then felt rather than saw the subtle change in his bodyguards.

The hair on the back of his neck stood up. He smiled and excused himself, then stepped back to join Phillips as a dozen Secret Service agents formed a ring.

Turning the president away from the cameras, Phillips leaned in and whispered. "There's been an attack in New York City, sir. A bomb was detonated in Grand Central Terminal just a few minutes ago."

"Do we know the extent of the damage? The number of casualties?"

Phillips shook his head.

The president nodded slowly. "Okay. See if you can get the mayor or the governor on the line. If you can't, try to reach Pat Monahan. He has a lot of people in Manhattan. We need to find out what's going on."

Phillips nodded.

"Let's regroup on the plane," the president said after a moment. "If it's big, it'll be on the news shortly."

Phillips nodded again then gestured toward the local officials huddled in their own group. "Invite them to join us. They'll probably hear the news in a minute or two, if they haven't already. If we can't reach officials in New York, they might be able to give you a perspective into what their counterparts in New York are facing."

As Phillips headed back to Air Force One, the president turned toward his hosts. He heard his name, the sudden shouts from the press, and could see in the governor and the mayor's faces that they had just heard the news.

———

Matthew Richter pressed the button on the speaker phone. While he waited for Burt Phillips to come on the line, he glanced briefly at the members of the cabinet with him in the Situation Room. Several, including the vice president were absent. After a few seconds, they connected, one-by-one, to the call. The vice president, Richter didn't have to be told, was in the PEOC—the Presidential Emergency Operations Center, below the East Wing of the White House. More secure than the Situation Room, which itself was located in the basement of the West Wing, the PEOC was designed to withstand all but a direct nuclear attack. However, it was normally only used as a temporary bunker before evacuating to a more secure location outside of Washington. The vice president, he suspected, wouldn't be there for long.

There was another click on the line and, after a quick roll call, Phillips began.

"The president has ordered continuity of government to be put into effect immediately." There was a murmur in the room as Phillips continued. "The vice president and the following members of the administration will be moved to the designated standby locations: the Secretary of State, the Secretary of Defense, and the Secretary of Homeland Security. For everyone else, the president requests that you remain in Washington and that your designated deputies be moved to the secure locations."

Each department, agency, and function, Richter knew, had their own continuity plans that stipulated chain of command. He scribbled the name *Jessica* on his pad. Jessica Williams, along with key members of the National Security team, would be sent to one of the secure bunkers. Knowing Williams, he thought, this wouldn't come as a surprise. He remembered the exercises from when he last worked in the White House. In the event of an emergency, key leaders within the government and military were moved to secure, underground bunkers to ensure that government was able to function in the event that there was a direct attack on the White House or on the president. There was no credible evidence of an imminent attack, he knew, but it was a precaution that was warranted under the circumstances. From the underground bunkers, the leaders would remain in touch and in control of their agencies and departments. Those deputies and the seconds-in-command sent to the bunkers would be ready to take over should their bosses on the outside fall victim. All told, there were some one hundred governmental officials who would be moved to one of various locations around the country within the next few hours. None though, Richter thought, was more important than the vice president.

"Where is the president now?" he heard the vice president ask.

There was a click on the line, and they suddenly heard the president's voice.

"I'm on my way to New York to meet with the mayor and the governor. I will be back in Washington by early afternoon at which time I plan to address the nation."

There was another murmur in the room.

"This will be followed by a joint National Security Council and cabinet meeting." There was a pause on the line before the president continued. "I understand Burt has already relayed my COG order." There was another pause. "You all know the plans. You've practiced this and you know what to do."

Richter could hear the steel in the president's voice. It was clear that he was in charge.

"Our country needs us," the president continued, "now more than ever. We will not let them down."

CHAPTER FIFTY-ONE

As he re-zipped his carry-on, Terry Fogel noted the National Guard troops beyond the screening tables. They were carrying automatic weapons. He had seen more outside earlier, after he had hopped off the rental car bus. He slung his bag over his shoulder. The security check had taken longer than normal as nervous TSA screeners checked every piece of luggage, and every passenger was subject to a pat down while wary cops and soldiers watched. He hid his smile as he headed for the bar. The drive to Philadelphia, just over two hours, had been easy, and with fifty minutes before he had to board, he decided that he had time for a drink. Just one. To celebrate.

All of the seats at the bar were taken and there was a small cluster of people standing to the side. Everyone was watching the TV. The screen showed fire trucks, police cars and vans, and the EMS Units lined up along 42nd Street. The announcer, a disembodied voice, described the scene and, after a moment, Fogel realized that they hadn't learned anything new. It was the same thing he had heard on the radio. The station played again a brief statement from the mayor. In a voice that sounded tinny but very much in charge, the mayor announced that it now appeared that a bomb had been detonated. The city's emergency response plan had been implemented immediately, and first responders were on the scene. All train service had been suspended and the mayor had ordered people to stay away from the area. There was no estimate yet on the number of casualties.

On the screen, Fogel saw dozens of firemen in hazmat suits streaming in and out of the building. The announcer speculated that it was a precaution for the potential lethal dust in the air. Or, she said, to guard against the noxious fumes from the plastic, rubber, and oil that were apparently still fueling the fire inside the building. Fogel knew that wasn't the reason.

He turned, caught the bartender's eye, and ordered a beer. While he waited, he listened to the conversations around him.

"Can you believe it, man? Fucking Muslims!"

"We should nuke the whole God-damned country!"

"Which one? Iran? Libya? Syria?"

"Hell! Bomb them all! It's time we show those fuckers that we won't put up with this shit!"

Fogel hid his grin. They were so predictable.

"How long ago did this happen?"

He turned at the sound of the voice. The man was dressed in a business suit, a computer bag slung over his shoulder. He wore a worried scowl.

"I think shortly after eight," Fogel responded. He gestured to-ward the TV. "At least that's what they said."

The man shook his head as he punched a button on his phone. "My brother takes the train in every day," he said softly as he brought the phone to his ear. "But I haven't been able to reach him."

That's life, Fogel wanted to say. And with life came death. It was something he had seen so often in his twenty-eight years in Belfast that he had grown numb to it. Friends, relatives, and neighbors killed by the police, by the British Army, all because they wanted to be free. And the U.S., with all of its talk of democracy, of free-dom, had always sided with the British. Fogel didn't mention this. Instead, he shook his head and shared the man's pained look.

He glanced at his watch then swallowed the rest of his beer. As he left the bar and made his way to his gate, he knew that what had happened in New York that morning was just the beginning. He would be in Mexico City by evening and tomorrow he would find out what his client wanted to do next. That there would be something next was a given.

———

"Because this occurred in the tunnels, we think the fallout has been somewhat contained," the fire chief said. There was a hint of the stereotypical Irish brogue that had once been common across the ranks of cops and firemen alike. The Chief of Department was the highest ranking uniformed officer and had been a fireman for forty-three years.

The president, wearing a silver radiation suit, nodded. He was standing with the mayor, the governor, and a handful of emergency management officials, all similarly dressed, around a table, on top of which was an elaborate three-dimensional scale model of the city. In a secure bunker that housed the police command and control center in lower Manhattan, they were over three miles from Grand Central and the radioactivity. Still, the Secret Service had been nervous and had warned against the trip; the president had ignored the warnings and had come anyway. How couldn't he, he thought.

"What about the subways?" he asked. "Aren't they connected?"

The chief nodded, his face grim. "That's one of our concerns, sir. There are connections to the Lexington Avenue line, to the Number Seven which goes out to Queens and to the Times Square Shuttle and on to the Javits Center." He paused and frowned. "But we're more concerned about the air vents. As soon as we knew that this was radiological, we shut those off. However," he paused again, "there were a number of trains coming and going at the time of the blast: the subways, Metro-North. As those trains move through the tunnels, they move a lot of air, kind of like a bicycle pump. It took a little while, but we shut off the third rail on Metro-North and on the affected subway lines."

The president nodded somberly.

"That's one of the challenges as well," the chief continued. "When we shut off the power—that stopped the trains wherever they were. Most were in the middle of tunnels at the time and we're still working on evacuating the people on board."

He pointed to several spots on the model with his finger. "We've set up decontamination centers at multiple points around the city," he added, explaining that those who were in or near Grand Central or were on the subway and commuter trains had been herded into temporary shelters. There they were ordered to remove their clothes and to shower before they were given a fresh set of clothes. Then they were quarantined until emergency workers were able to record their personal information and verify their exposure levels. Emergency medical personnel, in white hazmat suits, were on hand to deal with medical emergencies. There was no antidote for cesium-137, the chief added; only something called Prussian blue which might help victims who had ingested the radioactive material from absorbing it in their bodies. The city had been prepared, and the decontamination centers had ample supplies of the pharmaceutical form of the blue dye on hand.

The chief gestured toward the map and drew a circle in the air. "We've declared the area around Grand Central, some twenty square blocks, a hot zone," he said, explaining the elaborate emergency response procedures that the city had put in place after September 11th. He traced his finger around several other areas, including where major air vents were located and where the Metro-North tracks exited the tunnels below Park Avenue at 96th Street. Although the initial readings had been low, those areas, he told the president, were being treated as hot zones as well.

The president nodded as local officials went on to describe an amazingly quick and organized response to the bombing. Specialized teams of firemen, policemen, and EMTs from all five boroughs had responded immediately. Travel into and out of the affected zone had been restricted, effectively quarantining those inside. The emergency communications plan had been activated, and cell and landline circuits in the hot zone had been restricted to emergency calls. Hospitals city-wide had implemented their own disaster response plans and were dealing with the spike of heart attacks, broken bones, concussions, burns, and assorted injuries in the wake of the bombing as well as monitoring all new patients for radiation. Police helicopters and unmarked SUVs equipped with sophisticated detectors—what the Police Commissioner referred to as the *radiological suite*—were canvassing the city, checking for hot spots. Emergency response teams were deployed immediately to those areas where readings indicated higher than normal levels of radiation. Both the mayor and the governor had declared states of emergency, and the governor had mobilized the National Guard who, with the police, were in the process of securing critical infrastructure: the bridges and tunnels around the city, the aqueducts supplying the eight million residents with water, as well as Kennedy and La Guardia airports. Subways, bus stations, the Empire State Building, the Freedom Tower, Wall Street, police headquarters, and key sites throughout the city were all operating under a heightened state of alert.

The president turned to the mayor. "What can I do to help?" he asked.

"We need FEMA, sir," the mayor responded immediately.

The governor nodded in concurrence.

"They've already deployed," the president responded. "I'm told that they're in the air and circling, waiting for your order. They can be on the ground within the hour."

———

Five minutes later, after a brief huddle with the mayor and governor, the president climbed into the waiting helicopter. Fifteen minutes after that, for the third time that morning, he climbed the steps to Air Force One where he made a brief statement to the reporters on the plane then retreated to his office.

As the president sat back in his chair while the plane taxied, his mind raced with what he needed to do. He had been amazed at how quickly and efficiently New York City had responded. Ever since September 11th, they had been preparing for when, not if, the next strike would come. And city officials and the police and fire departments had been well prepared. FEMA teams had landed and were in the process of offloading their equipment. The FBI had dispatched their HazMat team as well as a specialized Evidence Response Team to assist in the forensic investigation. The Nuclear Regulatory Commission's NEST, or Nuclear Emergency Support Team, was on the scene, and FBI Tactical Aviation units had been deployed, not for medical evacuation but to assist New York officials in their search. The idea that another dirty bomb would go off at any minute weighed heavily on everyone.

He leaned forward and glanced at his notes. He had sketched the outlines of a speech. Once back in the White House, he planned to address the people of New York City, the nation, and the world. Then he had numerous phone calls to return to world leaders who had offered their condolences and pledged their support. But first and foremost, he told himself as he sat back again, he had to prevent the terrorists from striking again. He pushed the speech aside and grabbed the phone. The Air Force communications specialist sitting behind the cockpit on the deck above him answered immediately.

"Get me Matthew Richter and Pat Monahan," the president ordered.

While he waited for the call, he realized that he didn't need to script his speech. He knew what he wanted to say.

CHAPTER FIFTY-TWO

President Kendall stared somberly at the camera for a moment before he spoke.

"Earlier today, America was attacked by terrorists in yet another incident that reminds us of the fragile hold we have on peace. This morning, in New York City, our fellow citizens were attacked on their way to work, on their way to school, and as they were going about their daily lives, enjoying the freedoms that we as a nation have come to cherish. As most of you know by now, a radiological device was detonated in Grand Central Terminal in the middle of the morning commute.

"To those directly affected by these terrible and tragic events, and to those who lost loved ones, who lost friends, neighbors, and coworkers, America offers its deepest condolences and its prayers for healing and for peace." He paused, his eyes firm on the camera. "At the same time, America offers you this commitment: we will stand by your side until those who were responsible for these criminal acts are brought to justice."

The president stared hard at the camera.

"Make no mistake. These were criminal acts, acts of murder and terror committed by cowards who once again seek to test America's resolve. To many around the world, America represents freedom, America represents democracy, America represents equality and, more than anything, America represents opportunity. Our prosperity has been earned through our own sweat, our own ingenuity, and through our own hard work and sacrifice. While most around the world admire these traits, those very things which make us a leader among nations, there are those who seek to destroy them. There are those who seek to use the blood of innocent people to spread their message of hatred, their message of intolerance. There are those who seek to destroy our way of life."

The president shook his head. "They will never succeed. They will never take away that which makes us a great nation, for our resolve is firm, our faith is unshakable, and our commitment to freedom knows no bounds."

He paused a moment, but his eyes never left the camera.

"I want to assure you that we are doing everything we can to assist those affected by today's tragic events. This morning, I met with officials in New York City, and I was comforted by the level of organization and professionalism of those in charge and by the magnitude of the response that they were able to bring to bear in a very short period of time. To the brave men and women of the fire and police departments in New York City, to the dedicated medical personnel working as emergency medical technicians and as doctors and nurses in the many hospitals around the city, to the relief agencies, and to the ordinary citizens who responded today to help their fellow man, we salute your heroic efforts. Your bravery gives us hope. Yet we know that our task has only just begun. After meeting with the mayor and the governor, I activated the federal emergency response plan, and units of the federal government are currently assisting in the rescue and recovery efforts.

"Unlike September Eleventh, and unlike the recent terrorist attack in Mexico City, this was a radiological attack designed to sow fear, designed to shake our faith, designed to make us run and hide." He paused and his eyes narrowed. "We will never run. We will never hide. We will never cower in fear. We will never give up our faith in America."

He paused again as he took a breath. "As I speak, specialized units of the federal government, working with state and local officials, are working to assess the impacts of this event and the extent of the damage. They are working diligently to contain the radiological materials that were released. This will not be easy, and I ask for your patience. But the teams I met with this morning are up to the task, and the plans I reviewed give me comfort that we will succeed."

He lay his hands flat on the desk and continued. "I have ordered all agencies of the federal government to do everything in their power to ensure that an event like this never happens again."

He paused once more, his eyes still on the camera.

"New York City will come back. We will recover, and both New York City and America will be stronger than ever before because you can never extinguish the lights of freedom and you can never break the character of our great nation.

"I want to thank the many leaders from around the world who have offered their condolences and who have pledged their support. Your friendship and your compassion is a comfort in our time of need. And to those behind these cowardly acts, I say this: Your day will come. I have authorized the full resources of federal intelligence and law enforcement agencies to do everything in their power to bring those responsible to justice. And we will not stop until we have done so." His eyes narrowed again. "*You* may run and *you* may hide, but *you will* be caught. And *you will* pay the price."

The president looked down for a moment before continuing.

"For many this morning, their peaceful world has been shattered. And as a nation, we mourn your loss and we offer our prayers and our continued support. And with you, all of America is united in our resolve for justice and peace. We will restore. We will recover. And our freedom will ring loud and clear for all to hear.

"Thank you and God bless America."

CHAPTER FIFTY-THREE

While she stared at the screen, Agent Mona Baylor grabbed her cup and took a sip before she realized that it was empty. It was six in the morning and she was coming up on twenty-four hours without sleep. She glanced over at the coffee pot, just twenty feet away. *Not yet*, she told herself. One more station. She clicked on the icon and copied the three files onto her computer. Then she sat back and rubbed her neck while she waited. This was her seventh station and she was tired; all the more so since each station had multiple cameras. She had checked almost thirty already and while she found a number of matches that were concerning—a handful of people currently wanted for parole violations and one former Wall Street investment banker wanted on charges of security fraud—she hadn't found what she was looking for.

The copy complete, she leaned forward again and clicked the mouse several times, checking to see that all three files had copied properly. Each contained the security footage from one of the three cameras in the Westport, Connecticut, Metro-North station. Westport was next on the list, she told herself, and it had to be either here or Stamford. Then she caught herself as she remembered. Or Harlem. She selected the file for the camera on the westbound platform. That was the best place to start, she knew. The person she was looking for, whoever that might be, had to have boarded the train at some point.

She opened the file with the viewer and scrolled through in fast forward, watching the time stamp until she got to 6:14 am. She stopped and the picture froze. She saw the train in the station, the clusters of people waiting to climb on board. Then she scrolled in reverse, watching as people seemingly walked backwards, literally and in time: stepping off the train instead of on, into the station instead of out. She kept scrolling until the platform was empty. She checked the time stamp: 6:09 am. That was when the first person stepped onto the platform. She clicked the mouse again and began to watch the video in slow motion from that point forward.

She was searching for someone with a bag. Male or female, young or old; she wasn't sure. But someone had climbed on board with a bag—*a carry-on suitcase, with wheels,* the now dead conductor had radioed.

She stopped on a woman. She scrolled forward then backwards a few times, searching for the best image. Then she studied the bag. It was on wheels and it looked like a computer bag, the modern-day version of a briefcase. She enlarged the image, placing the box around the woman's face. She clicked the mouse and the image brightened and sharpened automatically. She saved it. She would check it against the database when she was done.

An hour and a half later, when she had finished with the Westport station, she had nine images that were of interest. She looked at them all again, one at a time, but kept coming back to the man. He had waited on the platform for three minutes before the train arrived. What struck her was his smile. Whereas most people wore resigned looks—the toll of years of commuting—he had smiled and nodded at several people before boarding. She would run him first.

Three hours later, Agent Baylor knew that she had him. The grinning man had boarded the train in Westport at 6:14 am, pulling a suitcase on wheels behind him. It was the type of soft-sided nylon case seen frequently being pulled by harried passengers in airports around the world. Then she saw the man again, on the 125th Street platform, at five minutes after seven. He had just exited the train and, minutes later, after speaking to someone on the platform, he had caught another train north. His carry-on was nowhere in sight.

What clinched it for her was when she ran the face through the database. The facial recognition software had compared his face to the millions of images of convicted felons, suspected terrorists, law enforcement officers, government officials and federal employees, foreigners visiting the country on visas, and ordinary citizens whose image had been captured for one reason or another. In the man's case, the computer had matched the face on the train platform to that of Terry Fogel, Irish terrorist and explosives expert.

She reached for the phone to call her supervisor, making a note as she did so to run the face of the young, well-dressed black man that Fogel had spoken to on the 125th Street platform. The FBI would have to track him down and find out exactly what his connection was to Fogel and to the bombing of Grand Central Terminal.

———

The NRC agent frowned. "Three canisters are unaccounted for." She stared at the manager, waiting for an explanation.

"That's impossible!" the owner insisted.

The agent spun the papers then pushed them across the desk. "Here's the latest inventory. We opened all of the containers and checked each serial number against the log then against invoices and return orders." She tapped the sheet. Three canisters were highlighted. "These three are missing."

The owner shook his head. "There must be some mistake!" He stared at the documents, then flipped through the thirty pages of sales records, trying to find it. By the time he got to the end, he felt sick. "These are the paper records," he said, looking up. "Have you checked the computer?"

"Of course," the agent responded, sliding another report across the desk. "We've gone back eleven years," she said. She folded her arms across her chest and waited.

The owner grabbed the report, stared at it for a second, then dropped it on the desk. *Eleven years*, he thought. A medical doctor, he had seen the opportunity years ago. His first investment was in an imaging center, providing X-Rays, MRIs, and CAT scans. While that had proved to be lucrative, he had quickly realized that many of his colleagues were thinking the same thing. Then he discovered he could make just as much money—more actually, a lot more—helping them to set up their own imaging centers. His company provided the equipment, the software, the training, and the service. Imaging had branched into nuclear medicine and soon hospitals were knocking on his door. And they had been doing so for eleven years, ever since he sold his first brachytherapy system.

He glanced up at the agent, a look of panic in his eyes.

CHAPTER FIFTY-FOUR

"The Islamist angle appears to have been a diversion," Monahan began. "We've uncovered evidence indicating that this was ordered by Pablo Guerrero."

Richter waited for the FBI Director to explain. Monahan handed him a series of photos. Richter picked up the first: a black and white security camera shot of a man waiting on a train platform. The second, the same man on a train platform again. But the platform looked different, Richter realized. He flipped to the next. It showed the man, dressed differently this time, in a crowd. He had a small bag slung over his shoulder. In all three pictures, Richter noticed, he wore a lopsided grin. Richter started to flip to the next then paused to study the man's eyes more closely. Scowling, he looked up.

"Terry Fogel?"

Monahan nodded. "Correct. The first is a picture of him on the train platform in Westport, Connecticut." He pointed at the picture. "Notice the carry-on."

Richter glanced back at the first photo and spotted the bag that Fogel was pulling behind him. He had missed that earlier.

"The second," Monahan continued, "is on the 125th Street platform."

Richter flipped to this and noticed that the bag was missing. *Son of a bitch!* He glanced at the third photo.

"That's in Philadelphia, in the airport." Monahan held up another group of pictures. "Long story short, after he hopped off the train in Harlem, he somehow made his way to Philly. We suspect that he had a car waiting somewhere in the city. From Philly, he flew to Houston; we have pictures of him there. Then he caught a flight to Mexico City"—Monahan flipped through the photos and pulled one out—"where he was met by one of Guerrero's contacts."

Richter shook his head as he glanced at the photo. Unfortunately, all of this came from reviewing security camera footage after the fact. Apparently no one had noticed Fogel or anything suspicious at the time. Which, he realized after a moment, raised a question.

"False passport?" he asked.

Monahan nodded and slid another photo across the desk.

Richter picked it up. The passport photo—a U.S. Passport, he noted—was in color. Fogel, he could see, had changed both the color of his hair and of his eyes. Other than that, he looked the same. *Christ!* he thought. The man was arrogant.

"There's something else," Monahan said.

Catching Monahan's tone, Richter looked up.

"More cesium canisters are missing."

Oh, shit! Richter thought. "How is that possible?" he asked, then his eyes narrowed. "How many?"

"Three," Monahan said. "Apparently, record keeping at the medical supply company was spotty."

Richter frowned as Monahan continued.

"These things are shipped and stored in lead containers. When the driver reported that the van had been broken into, the company only inventoried what was on the van. They opened the container and validated that only one canister was missing."

"But they never inventoried the warehouse," Richter guessed.

Monahan nodded. "Correct. As I said, these things are stored in lead containers. Initially the company checked the containers in the warehouse, made sure that all were accounted for, checked to see that the seals were intact and thought everything was fine. It wasn't until an NRC team went in, opened all the containers and compared the contents inside with the company's records and *with their own records*, that they noticed anything missing."

Richter's eyes narrowed. "Is there any way we can measure how much cesium was released in the blast?"

Monahan shook his head. "I don't know. I've asked the same thing. Most of the blast was confined to the tunnels. We're taking samples from the blast site outwards: in the main concourse, in the surrounding vicinity, the tunnels, the air vents..." His voice trailed off. "Based upon that, we'll do some mathematical modeling." He shook his head. "But I'm not sure how much confidence we can place in the results."

Richter nodded slowly as he considered the implications. Fogel might have used only one canister of cesium in his dirty bomb. Or he might have used all four. And without knowing for certain, he had to assume the worst.

He and Monahan shared a glance. The possibility of a second dirty bomb attack already weighed heavily on everyone's minds. And now the risk of another attack had suddenly increased.

CHAPTER FIFTY-FIVE

Ginny Martinelli pushed the hair out of her eyes and wiped her brow from the stifling air as she stared out the window. From the forty-eighth floor of the Chrysler Building, she had a bird's eye view of Manhattan. In the fading light, she saw the reflection of the still blinking lights of the emergency vehicles down on the street below. She sighed. This was her first time visiting the building and she hated it. Tired, hungry, in need of a shower and a change of clothes, she had been trapped here for almost two days. What was worse, though, was not knowing. *How much radiation had she been exposed to? Would she get sick? Would she die?*

A photographer, she had been hired by a real estate agent to take pictures of the vacant sixty-fourth floor. Not the type of job she was expecting when she decided that she might be able to carve out a living as a photographer, she had taken the job nonetheless. Still building her client base and her reputation, she rarely turned down work. Now, she regretted that decision.

She had asked for an early morning shoot—to capture the morning sunlight coming through the windows, she had told the agent. But the real reason was that she had another appointment at 9:30 all the way uptown. And so, they had met at 7:30 and, while she toured the space, considering angles and light, the young agent was on her heels, whispering suggestions into her ear. He wasn't even the listing agent, she suspected, just one of the junior agents assigned to prep the property. She had politely and diplomatically given the

overly helpful young man a five-dollar bill and sent him downstairs
for two cups of coffee. Then, with him out of her hair, she pulled out
her camera. She had only taken a dozen pictures when she heard the
muffled bang. It sounded like an auto accident—not an uncommon
sound in the city—and she had ignored it. Then came the sirens.
These were commonplace too and she had ignored those as well. It
wasn't until she had finished taking pictures and uploading them
to her laptop that she began to wonder what had happened to the
agent. She had tried calling his cell and when she heard the tones
and then the message that all circuits were busy, she began to pace.
She didn't want to leave without showing him the proofs. After
repeatedly glancing at her watch, she walked over to the window
and stared out at the beautiful morning. The skies were a brilliant
shade of blue. She heard the sirens—they had been going nonstop
she suddenly realized—and she pressed her face up against the glass,
straining to see what was happening. Frustrated that she couldn't
see anything due to the angle, she began pacing again.

Ten minutes later, angry and not wanting to be late for her next
appointment, she packed up her computer. It was probably better
that she was unable to reach the agent, she thought. If she told him
what she was thinking, as she had a very strong urge to do, she probably would have lost the client.

"Goddamn it!" she said five minutes later as she pressed the
elevator call button again. With a sigh she tried her phone. When
she heard the same message, she hit the disconnect button angrily
and turned toward the stairs. With her backpack slung over her
shoulder, she began making her way down, all the while cursing the
agent and the sixty-four floors. Seven floors later, she met a handful of people. She asked what was wrong with the elevator and one
woman shrugged her shoulders and said something about a fire at
Grand Central.

"How does that affect us?" Ginny asked.

The woman merely shrugged.

It was then that Ginny began to wonder whether something
was wrong.

She joined the group as they made their way down. By the time they got to the fifty-second floor, they heard voices below. The sound grew until they finally joined a larger group four stories below. Stopping on the crowded landing just above the forty-eighth floor, they spotted two men in white hazmat suits—firefighters or cops, she wasn't sure. Using a bullhorn—their voices muffled by the hoods—they instructed people to return to their offices. They explained that there was an emergency situation at Grand Central and that once that was under control they would allow people to leave. They shook their heads at most questions and after a lot of protesting and grumbling the crowd began to disperse. Many began to make their way back up the stairway.

As Ginny flattened herself against the wall, she tried her phone again. Hearing the busy circuit message once more she hung up and pushed her way through the people coming up the steps. She was met by the two white suited men at the top of the stairwell on the floor below.

"You need to go back to your office, miss," one had said. "You'll be safer there."

She lodged her own protest and, when that fell on deaf ears, she was directed through the doors onto the forty-eighth floor and into the offices of an investment firm. There she had remained for a long day and even longer night, sleeping fitfully on several chairs lined up side by side. The seven people in the office treated her well, and their well-stocked refrigerator meant that she wouldn't go hungry. The water cooler and the half-dozen spare carboys meant she wouldn't go thirsty either, at least not yet.

The large-screen TV in the conference room was tuned to CNN and from it they had learned about the attack. Hours later, they learned about the radiation. Most of the staff had congregated around the set throughout the day, some continuing to sit there through the night. Several were there right now, but Ginny had seen enough. It was bad enough to be trapped in the building, but to watch the same images over and over again, to hear the endless speculation was too much.

The firemen in suits had stopped by four times to check on them, to take headcounts and to see if anyone needed medical attention. Then there were the constant announcements over the building's public address system, at least one per hour, Ginny had noticed, even during the long night. They were reassured that they would be evacuated soon, but she was beginning to resign herself to the fact that it might be another day or two. She had tried to send emails, to her friends, to her family, to let them know she was okay, but the servers seemed to be overwhelmed.

The staff had long abandoned their business attire, ties and suit jackets gone, shirts and blouses untucked. The air conditioning had been turned off early yesterday and the temperature had climbed during the day. People drank tea and coffee by the gallon, the caffeine not helping already frazzled nerves. Most grumbled, and one or two were angry, but Kathy, the senior partner, had done her best to reassure everyone, to calm the tension. She had even set up an exercise schedule and, once every two hours, led everyone through calisthenics and deep breathing exercises, both to take their mind off the terrible news on TV and to ease the tension over their plight. Ginny had to admit, Kathy was doing an admirable job under the circumstances.

She sighed and stepped away from the window, thinking that maybe she would go to the ladies room to splash water on her face then try to send an email. Again.

"Telephone service has been restored. Computers are up too."

Ginny turned. Kathy stood in the doorway. Even the strain was staring to get to her, Ginny noticed. There were lines around her eyes, but still Kathy offered a smile. She was worried like everyone else, Ginny realized. She probably had a family, kids. *God,* Ginny chided herself. *She was so preoccupied with her own worries that she hadn't even thought to ask about Kathy's.* Through it all, Kathy had been more than accommodating to the stranger who had barged into her office a day and a half ago.

"Thanks, Kathy," Ginny smiled as she reached for her phone.

She glanced at it and cursed silently. The battery was dead.

"Feel free to use that one," Kathy said, gesturing toward the office phone on the table.

Ginny picked up the receiver and waved her thanks as Kathy left. Then she hesitated. Overwhelmed by being out of touch for almost thirty-six hours, she was suddenly unsure who to call. She stared at the phone for a minute and her hand shook as she punched in the number. She heard two rings before the phone was answered.

"Hello?" The voice was shaky, tentative.

"Mom?" Ginny said and then she began to cry.

CHAPTER FIFTY-SIX

Terry Fogel resisted the urge to laugh. With the high-pitched call of the gulls, the sound of the surf, and the smell of seaweed and salt in the breeze, if he closed his eyes he might have been standing on a quay back in Belfast. Yet, here he was, in the shade of a small covered cowshed with the angry head of one of Mexico's most ruthless cartels, both dressed as if they were the *vaqueros* hired to mind the horses and cattle. He enjoyed the charade; no one would mistake them for the men who had plotted and carried out the bombing in New York. But as he had found in Belfast, the tit for tat cycle of revenge—a three-way match between the IRA, the Prods, and the British alike—left a seething anger in men for whom the latest retribution by bomb or bullet brought no more sense of relief than the one before it. Guerrero was no different.

Fogel wondered if he had overestimated the man. Guerrero didn't get it. Certainly, while the loss of life was nowhere near what Guerrero himself had been able to inflict in Mexico City, a half a loaf, as his grandmother used to say, is better than no bread at all.

Guerrero, his eyes filled with menace, said nothing as he waited for an answer.

"I told you the number of deaths would be small," Fogel said. "The purpose of this wasn't to kill people, but to bring New York City to its knees."

Guerrero continued to glare.

Fogel held up his phone, a newscast playing on the screen.

"Radiation is a scary thing. People are nervous. Right now, there are hundreds of thousands, possibly millions of people wondering not if but when they will become sick. Maybe not right away, but ten years from now, twenty years from now"—he drew a steep line in the air with his finger—"cancer rates will shoot up." He sniffed dismissively and shook his head. "They have no idea how to handle this."

Guerrero said nothing.

He was no different than the boys back home, Fogel thought.

"Think of the impact this will have on their economy," he continued, nodding to his cell phone again. "New York City is shut down and, right now, they don't know when they will be able to return to normal. Or if they ever will. People will stay as far away from the city as they can, uncertain whether the government is telling them the truth when they say it's safe.

"Think about it," he added with a wave of his hand. "Restaurants, theaters, stores—they'll all be forced to close. Businesses for blocks around Grand Central will move out—either because they are forced out by authorities or because they're scared. Real estate prices in the surrounding blocks will plummet, and a relatively small but once very expensive piece of real estate in the heart of Manhattan might be deemed uninhabitable." He held his phone up again. "Some of the newscasters are already suggesting that officials might not have any other choice but to tear buildings down." He stared down at his phone for a moment before he continued. "Imagine that," he said, almost to himself. "Some of the most expensive real estate in the world bulldozed to the ground and fenced off for years to come." He looked up at Guerrero and smirked. "And what about the people who live there? They'll leave the first chance they get. There'll be a mass exodus as they move to Virginia or Pennsylvania or Ohio; somewhere far away from New York." He twirled his finger. "And the death spiral will begin."

He paused to study the Mexican. The angry glare was gone. Guerrero was thinking. "And it won't just be in New York," Fogel continued, knowing he had him now. "Chicago, Boston, Houston,

Atlanta—all of their big cities will see the same thing. People will no longer feel safe living or working inside a giant target." He grinned. "A terrorist sows terror, and that is precisely what I've done."

Guerrero was silent for another moment before Fogel thought he noticed the hint of a smirk.

"How many more canisters do you have?" Guerrero asked.

CHAPTER FIFTY-SEVEN

With a frown, the president hung up the phone and turned to Matthew Richter.

"The mayor has imposed a curfew. There's been some looting."

Richter nodded. He had already been briefed. The looting was not just in Manhattan but in the outer boroughs as well and was primarily focused on survival items: water, food, medical supplies. It hadn't taken long, though, before it had spread to items of opportunity: electronics, furniture, anything people could get their hands on in the midst of chaos.

This had been expected. The city's emergency response center had run scenarios and looting was, unfortunately, one of the anticipated aftereffects of a major calamity.

"There's also been a spike in crime," the president added.

Richter nodded again. Violent crimes—muggings, robberies, and rapes—were all up. It was a tug of war between those looking to cash in on opportunity and the basic survival instinct of the masses. People were hoarding supplies, and stores in turn were jacking up prices. Meanwhile, the violent element had taken to the streets, preying on the masses.

"Yes," Richter agreed, "but the fortunate thing is that most of what's happening was expected. From what I can see, the mayor and the governor have done a good job in anticipating these challenges and responding appropriately."

The number of cops on duty across the city, Richter explained, had increased twofold as shifts had been extended and, under emergency procedures, overtime became mandatory. Not that it had been necessary. Many cops had refused to go home at the end of their shift. The governor had deployed the National Guard and the State Police to assist. And in addition to the hundreds of federal agents working on the investigation, thousands more had been sent to assist New York City Police in restoring order.

"Still," the president continued with a sigh, "the mayor assures me that it's not been as bad as they had expected." He came around his desk and sat down on the couch. He gestured for Richter to do the same.

"Are they moving fast enough in evacuating the hot zones?" the president asked.

"From what FEMA and the NEST teams are telling me, they're moving as fast as they can, sir. Everyone has to be checked by medical personnel, and they've been working their way through, building by building. They expect to have that done in two more days. In the meantime, they're making sure that the people who are trapped have enough food and water. They're also dealing with a spike in medical emergencies, which frankly isn't unusual during a disaster such as this."

"A full moon?" The president asked.

"Sort of, sir," Richter answered. "Disasters tend to bring out both the best and the worst in people." New York City, he explained, had been preparing for this day for years. As part of the Joint Terrorism Taskforce, he had participated in numerous scenarios, mock disasters, and drills. Ever since 9/11, the city had been holding these exercises, preparing hospitals, clinics, medical personnel, as well as city, state, and federal health and emergency personnel for the day that no one ever wanted to see but knew was coming nonetheless.

After another minute of discussion, the president waved his hand, dismissing the matter. New York was in capable hands. He and Richter had other things to discuss.

"What's the latest?"

Richter let out a breath then told the president about three additional canisters of cesium that had been stolen and the scramble to determine if all or only some had been used in Grand Central.

The president's eyes darkened. "We need to find Fogel," he said. "Pretty damn quick."

———

Terry Fogel glanced out the window as the bus slowed. Seeing nothing but scrub brush on the side of the road, he leaned over into the aisle and peered out the driver's windshield. Over the line of cars in front, he saw the flashing lights. *An accident?* he wondered. *No matter*, he thought as he glanced at his watch then sat back. *Nothing to worry about*. He still had plenty of time before the flight.

As the bus pulled forward, he could see the orange cones out his window, then the black trucks with their flashing lights, the men in black tactical gear, only their eyes and mouths visible through their masks. Most were cradling automatic weapons in their arms while a few others held leashes, the German Shepherds sitting patiently at their sides. *Los Federales*. The Federal Police. *Well that answers one question*, he thought. It wasn't an accident; it was a roadblock.

Beyond them, he spotted the two larger trucks, both painted a dull, army green. Standing in a line in front were a dozen soldiers, also carrying automatic weapons. They were serious about this, he mused.

He casually glanced around the bus. Most other passengers, he noticed, looked up briefly and, seemingly unconcerned, turned their attention back to their books or their cell phones or the conversations they were having. He glanced over at the girl across the aisle, the teenager who spoke English. He caught her eye.

She smiled. "It's just a routine stop," she said as she pulled out her ID card. "They do this all the time."

"What are they looking for?" he asked with a smile.

"Drugs," she responded. "But it shouldn't take long. We'll be on our way soon." The girl, fourteen or fifteen he thought, was sitting next to an older woman. Probably her grandmother, he guessed. Recognizing him as a foreigner when they had boarded earlier, she had decided to practice her English until her grandmother scolded her.

The old woman glowered at the girl again, then looked back down at her lap as she worked her fingers over the rosary beads, silently mumbling the same prayers she had been muttering since the bus had left two hours ago. For a brief moment his smile faded as he thought of his own grandmother, long dead now. Coming home late in the evening, or sometimes very early in the morning, he would find her in front of the wood stove, her fingers playing over the beads. Praying for him, he knew.

"You have nothing to worry about," the girl said then smiled. "Unless you have drugs."

He grinned back. "And what would I be wanting drugs for?" he asked, the lilt in his voice, the Belfast accent slipping out in a momentary lapse.

She laughed, and her grandmother gave her another dirty look and said something in Spanish. The girl rolled her eyes and Fogel grinned as he pulled out his passport. It was an Australian passport, the edges and cover slightly worn as they would be for a frequent traveler. However, despite its appearance, the passport was new as was the tourist visa folded inside. The passport that he had used when he fled the U.S. after the bombing was now nothing more than ashes in an incinerator. Even he wasn't foolhardy enough to try and use it again.

The bus stopped and Fogel heard the hiss as the doors opened. A federal cop, this one not wearing a mask, climbed on board and barked out an order in Spanish. The passengers around him began to gather their belongings.

"They want us to get off," the girl said. "They want to search the bus." She nodded at the bin over his head. "You have to take your bags."

Fogel nodded and smiled as he stood and grabbed his carry-on. He followed the girl and her grandmother as they made their way up the aisle and then down the steps into the hot sun. As his eyes adjusted to the glare, he noticed the line of masked policeman. The one who had ordered them off the bus was shouting and pointing at the two tables set up on the side of the road. Fogel joined the other passengers as they obediently formed a line.

A cop with a dog circled the bus, the dog sniffing the tires and the wheel wells. Two more cops with dogs waited by the storage compartment while the driver pulled out the luggage and lined it up on the side of the road next to the bus. Fogel hid his smirk. He glanced farther up the road and saw the line of soldiers and, to the side, the sandbag emplacement and the dark-eyed soldier standing behind the machine gun. He felt like he was back in Belfast. *Jesus*, he thought. They were serious.

The line moved quickly. The police glanced briefly at the passengers' documents, asked one or two questions, hastily searched their hand luggage, then directed them to the side of the road where they waited. They would soon be on their way again, Fogel thought. When he reached the table, the man standing behind said something, and Fogel shook his head.

"I don't speak Spanish," he said, smiling.

The cop who had ordered them off the bus stepped over. "You're American?" the cop asked in English.

Fogel shook his head. "I'm Australian."

"Your passport." The cop held his hand out.

Fogel handed over his documents.

"Put your bag on the table please," the cop instructed.

Fogel did as he was told and watched as the cop behind the table unzipped the bag and began pulling his clothes and toiletries out. That his luggage was being inspected more thoroughly was obvious to both him as well as the other passengers who now seemed to regard him warily. Out of the corner of his eye, he watched the English-speaking cop flip through the pages in his passport, studying each for a moment before turning his attention to the tourist visa. The cop looked up.

"Your purpose for visiting Mexico, Mr. Abbott?"

"Business," Fogel responded.

The cop studied him for a moment before he nodded.

"Wait here," he ordered, staring for a second to make sure Fogel understood before he walked away.

Fogel watched as the cop climbed up into one of the trucks. He could see the glare of a computer through the window and, after a few moments, he saw the cop speaking on the phone. This was more than a random drug inspection, Fogel realized as he casually glanced around. All of the other passengers, having already passed through the inspection, were standing to the side. Fogel could feel as well as see that all eyes were on him. He smiled at the girl and began to weigh his options.

———

Pablo Guerrero walked along the bluff overlooking the ocean. By himself, he passed the cows and the few horses that were out grazing. He followed the rough split-rail fence over the uneven ground to the gate. Beyond was the path that led down to the ocean. Resting his hands on the gate, he stared out over the beach. He could still picture Carolina, laughing as they swam in the surf. She had enjoyed the smell of the salt water, floating on the gentle waves, splashing and playing with her papá. The wave had hit them from behind—he hadn't seen it coming—and Carolina had tumbled out of his arms. He felt a flood of panic as she disappeared below the surface. She had resurfaced moments later, dazed and scared, ten yards from him, and he had lunged before she disappeared again.

That day, for the first time in his life, he had known what fear felt like.

He pictured Carolina again moments after he had pulled her to the beach; she was laughing and running across the sand, her wet hair flying in the breeze.

"Catch me, Papá!" she had called over her shoulder.

As he stared out at the beach, a single tear slid down his cheek.

CHAPTER FIFTY-EIGHT

Dressed for war with masks and body armor, the two Federal Police officers grabbed Fogel's arms. With his hands cuffed behind him, his legs bound by shackles, and wearing a bulletproof vest, he shuffled forward awkwardly. Three dozen federal cops, all masked and holding automatic rifles, formed two lines leading to the small stage. As Fogel was led through the gauntlet, he suppressed a smile. This was the perp walk, an opportunity for the police and the government to parade their prisoner in front of the cameras. He was led up the steps where the procession stopped and he was turned to face the cameras. A man wearing a business suit, the attorney general for the state of Tamaulipas, stepped up to the microphone. He made a few comments, glancing periodically at the notes in his hand. Fogel understood none of it.

He grinned for the camera, knowing it would give the press, the commentators and the news shows something to analyze, to discuss. The media show was brief—cut short, he suspected—and he was led off stage to an armored van. Out of sight of the cameras, he was roughly shoved into the back. The police, it seemed, had expected him to show the defeated look of a prisoner: a crestfallen, confused face for the cameras. The grin had pissed them off.

Two cops pushed him down to the bench then took up positions across from him. Their dark, menacing eyes stared at him from behind their masks. He ignored the cops as he considered his predicament. This was a tough scrape, he knew. But he had been in worse. The Mexicans would likely extradite him to the U.S. or, at a minimum, turn him over to U.S. authorities. He might be taken to Guantanamo or to one of the CIA black sites in Asia or Africa. There, he would be waterboarded, or worse. He had no illusions. The Americans would use whatever means they had to—legal or otherwise—to find out what he knew.

But he had a bargaining chip: he had only used two of the cesium canisters in New York. The remaining two canisters were in a self-storage locker near Buffalo, in upstate New York. It wasn't much, and it was unlikely to remain a secret for long once the CIA got a hold of him. But it was something he might be able to use. And as far as Guerrero was concerned, he had no loyalties. Guerrero was simply a source of funds, someone to finance a game that Fogel had been playing for as long as he could remember.

He shifted in his seat and the cops' dark eyes bore into him. He grinned. One of the cops suddenly lunged forward and struck him in the face with the butt of his rifle. He saw stars as his nose exploded in a shower of blood and his head was slammed into the wall of the truck. Dazed, he slumped to the floor.

He lay still for a while as the white hot pain danced in his head. Unexpectedly, he gagged—an involuntary reaction—and rolled onto his side. He coughed up a mouthful of blood. Rough hands grabbed him and pushed him back into his seat. One of the cops— he couldn't tell which one through the tears in his eyes—held a cloth to his nose, pinching the bridge to stop the bleeding. He sat still for a while and his head began to clear. It was a predictable response, he thought, as he eyed the cops. And it was one that he might be able to use to his advantage. As rough as the Mexicans were likely to be, they represented his best option. As the truck rumbled along, he closed his eyes and began to think.

CHAPTER FIFTY-NINE

As the National Security meeting ended, the president glanced over at Richter and nodded briefly. Richter caught the message and, moments later, he followed the president back to the Oval Office. The president had something on his mind, Richter guessed, something that he didn't want to share with the other NSC members.

"We need to speak to Fogel," the president said once the door was closed.

Richter nodded but said nothing. Talking to Fogel was going to be a challenge. Despite appeals by both the State Department and the U.S. Attorney General, the Mexican government had refused to consider an extradition request. Further, they had refused to allow the FBI to interview him. Apparently, they believed that Fogel had a role in the Mexico City bombing and, so far at least, the U.S. had been denied access. Even the president's own appeal, Kendall had told him a day earlier, seemed to have fallen on deaf ears as President Magaña promised, somewhat vaguely and uncharacteristically, to see what he could do.

"I spoke to Magaña again this morning," the president continued. "I think there might be a small window of opportunity but," he paused, frowning, "the situation is very delicate right now."

Richter nodded again. This was something they had discussed. In the wake of increasingly negative public sentiment, there was a risk that Magaña's own administration might be turning on him. Tired of the violence, critics were strongly encouraging the Mexican government to negotiate a ceasefire with the cartels. Yet those same critics still demanded that someone be held accountable for the deaths in Mexico City. Was Fogel the sacrificial lamb?

"I want you to go down there," the president continued. "Publically, they cannot be seen as caving to U.S. pressure. But privately, I'm hoping you can negotiate an arrangement with President Magaña and with their attorney general."

Frustrated with the pace of diplomacy, and perhaps, Richter suspected, realizing the futility given the tenuous situation, the president wanted to try a back channel. He understood the urgency. There was a risk that Guerrero would get to Fogel before they did. What would happen to the cesium then? Had Fogel made any arrangements just in case he was captured? Something to show the U.S. that he would have the last laugh? Did he have someone working with him or for him as the FBI suspected? Potentially someone connected to Guerrero? Did Guerrero know where the canisters were and no longer had a need for Fogel? The possibilities were frightening, and finding out exactly what Fogel knew was crucial.

"Don't push for extradition," the president continued. "We'll worry about that later. Our priority is getting access to Fogel and finding out what he knows."

The president sat down behind his desk and began to scrawl a note.

While he waited, Richter thought about Magaña. He had met the Mexican President three years before when he had visited Washington. It was a meeting he remembered well. On President Kendall's security detail at the time, Richter had been standing watch outside the president's private dining room while the two leaders enjoyed lunch. He had been the first one through the door when he heard the crash of a chair. He remembered the look on President Magaña's face. Standing, with his hands on his throat, Magaña's eyes had been wide with panic as he choked on a piece of chicken. It was a story that only a handful of people would ever hear. What could have been an embarrassing situation for the White

House had been avoided when Richter performed the Heimlich maneuver. Magaña had been gracious and had gone out of his way to show his appreciation. At the time, Richter remembered, he had dismissed it as routine response, something he had been trained to do. Then, a week later, he had been surprised when he received a hand-written thank you note.

The president stood. He folded his own note and stuffed it into an envelope bearing the presidential seal. "President Magaña understands the urgency. The issue will be working out the details with the attorney general." The president handed him the envelope. "Give this to President Magaña. Tell him that I've reconsidered." The president paused. "Tell him that I'm ready to send the SEALs in to help find Guerrero."

———

As she sipped her tea, Patty thought about how quickly life had changed. She hadn't known anyone personally who had been in Grand Central that morning but, once again, she thought through her list of friends and acquaintances, making sure she hadn't missed anyone.

As a result of the bombing in Grand Central, cops were now visible everywhere. Security was more visible on campus too, she thought. But as dire as it looked, the situation in the U.S. was not nearly as bad as it was in Mexico.

Mexico had become an extremely dangerous place over the last six months and her former student, Christina, had joined the growing list of casualties in the escalating violence. News stories and personal accounts of the atrocities had become a daily occurrence. That the government hadn't yet declared a state of emergency was not a surprise. A curfew and martial law would mean nothing in those cities that cops and soldiers—vastly outnumbered and outgunned and fearful for their own lives—avoided. And those that did venture in, to cities like Matamoros, Monterrey, Ciudad Juarez, were suspected to be on the payroll of one cartel or another.

From an academic standpoint, the potential collapse of the

Mexican state was an interesting event to watch unfold. What would happen if the country did collapse? And how would it happen? Would military and police forces simply *walk off the job*? Or would they aid in the overthrow by imprisoning key leaders?

There was a risk that, at some point, basic governmental institutions would simply cease functioning. And what would happen then? A failure in the maintenance and operation of roads, railways, airports, harbors, and other physical infrastructure would have a significant negative impact on the business environment and on the economy. The petroleum industry was state run, a governmental monopoly. What would the tens of millions of citizens and businesses that bought gasoline and diesel fuel for their cars and trucks each day do if supplies were interrupted? And what about electricity and water and other key utilities? Some of those were controlled by the government too, weren't they? What would happen if those services simply ceased? Would communication networks—phone and Internet service—still function if the government collapsed?

In the ensuing economic turmoil, would the central bank ultimately lose control over the currency, leading to the eventual collapse of the monetary system? Would the judicial system— the operation of courts and the criminal justice system—go next, further weakening the rule of law in an already weak state? Would government coffers be looted, if not by the cartels, by greedy bureaucrats? Would the educational system crumble when unpaid teachers were forced to find other ways to feed their own children and the lights in schools were no longer lit? What would happen when state-provided medical care and food for the poor and other critical social programs collapsed, leaving large segments of the population, already living below the poverty line, to fend for themselves?

Ultimately, unless the cartels stepped in and quickly established order, the country would be plunged into chaos. Civil disorder— widespread looting, rioting, and violence—would follow. How would the cartels manage to prevent that? she wondered. Or is that what they wanted? Would they band together and forge an alliance? Could that work? Did they even have a plan?

How far, she wondered, was Mexico from that doomsday scenario? A year? Six months? The United Nations was debating how best to respond to the growing threat. Would they send peace-keepers in? What would that accomplish? Would Mexico end up like Somalia, as an ungoverned collection of territories controlled by regional warlords?

She stood. It was only for a day or two, she told herself as she poured the rest of her now cold tea in the sink. And no one understood the risk better than Matthew. The Secret Service did all it could to avoid dangerous situations, and even an ex-agent like Matthew, having been trained well, would take the necessary precautions. He was more than capable of protecting himself. Besides, he would have a team of Secret Service agents with him to keep him out of trouble. There was no reason to worry.

So why was she?

———

The pilot held the aircraft low as he raced at close to two hundred miles per hour toward the coast. Less than one hundred feet over the waves, he relied on his skill and the sophisticated navigation system to keep him out of trouble. The MH-65C, a multi-mission Coast Guard helicopter used in search and rescue and for armed interdiction, was equipped with a forward looking infrared display that allowed the pilot to see at night and hopefully keep his aircraft from plummeting into the waves that were a blur in the darkness below.

He saw the dark shadows of the coastline appear on his display. After six minutes of skimming high speed just above the water, the real fun was about to begin. He glanced at his copilot and grinned. The copilot grinned back, not just from the excitement of flying but from a sadistic streak that he shared with the pilot—one seemingly at odds with their standard search and rescue mission. When plucking a drowning victim from the water, the two were all business. But when they became glorified taxi drivers, they liked to have some fun.

If the VIP sitting in the back wasn't turning green yet, the pilot thought as the coastline rushed toward them and he pulled up on the collective, he soon would be. The helicopter shot up, barely clearing the bluff, then decelerated rapidly as the pilot put the aircraft into a hover. Moments later, as he landed softly on the ground, two dozen men who had been waiting surrounded the aircraft. He noticed the weapons held ready. Let's hope, the pilot thought, that they really were friendlies as he had been told to expect.

A minute later, his VIP discharged, he increased the throttle and pulled up on the collective again. The helicopter lifted off and, after a graceful turn, accelerated off into the night. Seconds later, it was lost in the darkness over the water.

CHAPTER SIXTY

For a brief moment Matthew Richter felt like a criminal. Dressed in a Coast Guard flight suit, standing in the middle of the helipad in the darkness, surrounded by twenty-plus men—all carrying weapons, all watching him with wary eyes—he felt exposed and helpless. It was an uncomfortable feeling for a man who was used to being on the other side. Where the hell were his people? he wondered.

He heard his name, a familiar voice, and turned as Agent Wendy Tillman and seven other Secret Service agents stepped into view. With the Secret Service agents were a handful of plain clothes Mexican security agents, part, Richter presumed, of the Mexican President's security detail.

"This way, sir," Tillman said, pointing to the path that led to the lights and the buildings beyond the trees. As they walked, Tillman provided an overview of the security arrangements.

"They have a force of thirty from the Presidential Guard," Tillman said.

Richter gave her a look. That, plus the eight Secret Service agents assigned to protect him, wasn't much.

"It's a little light," Tillman acknowledged, "but, as you know, this meeting is supposed to be a secret. From what I've been told, as far as most people know, including most of President Magaña's security team, he's asleep in Los Pinos."

Richter nodded but said nothing.

"He arrived about an hour ago," Tillman continued then added,

"The attorney general should be here shortly."

Sneaking the president out of Mexico City without anyone knowing must have been a challenge. But, as Richter also knew, secret
presidential trips were not unusual. As one of his former colleagues
had told him, shortly after the fall of Saddam Hussein's government,
President George Bush had flown to Baghdad to meet with the U.S.
troops who had secured the city. Most Americans, including a number of the Secret Service agents assigned to protect him, only learned
of the trip after Bush returned. The hapless agents had no idea that
President Bush had left his ranch in Crawford, Texas. With a little
bit of subterfuge, Bush had been able to sneak away.

Richter's own trip had been a charade. Dressed in a Coast Guard
flight suit, he had been secreted onto a chopper in Corpus Christi
and flown to a Coast Guard cutter patrolling several hundred miles
off the Texas coast. Later, sitting in the captain's quarters as the
cutter sailed south, the captain had explained the plan. Shortly after dark, the cutter would receive a distress call from a capsized
boat twenty-three miles off of the Mexican coast. As expected, they
would dispatch a helicopter—with Richter in the back, sandwiched
between the rescue swimmer and hoist operator—to search for the
stranded crew. After making a show of flying search patterns over
a patch of ocean, the chopper would drop low, below the radar, and
make a beeline for the coast. If all went well, fifteen minutes later,
the chopper would be back on station searching for the non-existent
boat and no one would be the wiser.

Elaborate, yes, but the ruse had been necessary. There had been
a growing anti-American sentiment in Mexico, many claiming
Magaña's close ties to the U.S. President were responsible for the
bombing in Mexico City. The Mexican President could not be seen
publically to be caving in to American demands to turn over the
Irish terrorist. In private, though, Richter hoped that some accom-
modation could be made.

His eyes scanned across the open ground of the ranch, at the
darkness of the forests beyond, and then back toward the sea from
which he had come. He had wanted to grill Tillman, to better un-

derstand the security procedures in place and how the small security force would defend the Mexican President, and by extension himself, from a potential assault. But he didn't. He had other things to worry about; Tillman would have to take care of the rest.

———

"Mr. Richter," President Magaña said with a smile. "It's a pleasure to see you again."

Richter nodded as he took Magaña's outstretched hand. "Mister President. Thank you for agreeing to meet with me." Magaña's smile, Richter noted, was a politician's facade. His eyes told the real story. They reflected the burden and worry of a man fighting to hold his crumbling nation together.

Richter glanced around the room. There was a sitting area, several comfortable chairs and a couch in front of a large square marble table that was bathed in the soft glow of reflected light. The tile floor extended out to the veranda, creating an extension of the living room when the large glass wall panels were retracted, as they were now. He could see light reflecting off the ocean in the distance.

A servant appeared and took his drink order. Richter asked for iced tea, something he knew from his briefing was a favorite of the Mexican President's. As the drinks were served, one of Magaña's bodyguards stepped into the room and said something in Spanish that Richter didn't comprehend. Magaña nodded then turned.

"Come," he said, standing. "The attorney general will be here momentarily."

As he followed Magaña out onto a large veranda, Richter could hear the pounding of the surf in the distance. The veranda was illuminated by the light of the living room and the low voltage lighting along the railing. Magaña led him around the side, where the veranda wrapped around the house. Standing at the railing, Richter realized they were facing the now dark helipad beyond the trees.

"I watched you land," Magaña said. He pointed over the trees and began to describe the ranch. Richter smiled and nodded but said nothing. Mexican customs were different, he knew, and he suspected

that Magaña wanted to wait for the attorney general before discussing Fogel. Once the attorney general arrived, Richter decided, he
would let Magaña initiate the conversation. The man clearly understood what was at stake for both countries and the urgency of
speaking with the Irish terrorist.

His thoughts were interrupted by the staccato sound of rotors
slapping at the air and, seconds later, the lights around the helipad
were turned on, illuminating the contingent of soldiers standing
around the perimeter. The sound reverberated off the building and
the forest and hills beyond and, for a moment, Richter was unsure
which direction it was coming from. Then he saw the faint outlines
of the aircraft coming in low over the hills to the west. Like the
Coast Guard helicopter that had ferried him here, this one too was
flying without its anti-collision lights.

The helicopter hovered momentarily and then, as it began to
descend, a streak of orange light flashed up from the ocean. In a
fraction of a second, Richter's brain registered the tongue of flame
and, operating on instinct, he spun away from the railing. He could
see the orange streak reflecting off Magaña's eyes as he pulled him
down, away from the railing. Suddenly, the night was lit up by a
brilliant flash as the helicopter exploded in a fireball. The shockwave
slammed into them, tossing them like rag dolls into the side of the
building. Glass from the shattered windows rained down on their
heads. There was a split second of silence—a feeling like his head
was stuffed with cotton—then the muffled roar of an inferno behind
them. Richter shook his head and, as he pushed himself up to his
knees, he heard the first screams of the men near the helipad as the
burning debris rained down on them. He grabbed President Magaña
below the arms and hustled him into the house where they were met
by the security team. As Magaña was led away by his agents, Agent
Tillman grabbed Richter's arm. There was blood running down her
cheek, from a cut above her eye.

"We need to evac now, sir!" she shouted as several agents moved
him toward the stairs.

Suddenly, the room exploded in a flash of light.

CHAPTER SIXTY-ONE

Silently, slowly, Richter crawled forward over the cold ground, sliding up behind the tree. There, he lay, still for a moment, listening to the sounds around him. Other than his own breathing and the occasional rustle of the wind through the trees, he heard nothing. He slid quietly to the side and lay still again. Then, slowly, he turned his head, sweeping his eyes across the field before him, looking for the thing that didn't belong; looking for movement. The sound seemed to catch him by surprise. The soft drumming, fast and steady, grew. He listened to the beating, finding solace in the rhythm. It was his heart, he realized. The sound grew and soon he could feel it in his chest, then after a moment, in his fingers and his toes, his whole body thumping. He could hear the blood pumping through his arteries, the sound building, the beats coming faster, until it sounded like a stream, a river, a rushing red torrent, the roar building in his head.

Startled, Matthew Richter woke to an agonizing pain. Wanting to scream but holding it in, he struggled with the kaleidoscope of images in his head. Slow, oozing, shifting, the scenes flashed before him, each vividly sharp for a brief instant before clouding, blurring then vanishing into the darkness only to be replaced by a new flash, a new image. He struggled to figure out what it all meant, but his thoughts seemed to form slowly then slip away. He knew what it was, he told himself. But when he tried to find the word, when he tried to explain it, the answer was just beyond his grasp. *What the hell?*

Patty suddenly flashed before him. *How long will you be gone?* He opened his mouth to answer, but no sound came. *Is it dangerous?* He tried to shake his head, tried to form the words, but his tongue seemed lost in his mouth. *It's just for a day,* he wanted to say, *maybe two.* He could see the fear in her eyes as she started to fade. She grew darker, fainter, until the only thing he could see was her face, her eyes incapable of masking her fear. He tried to reach out, but suddenly there was nothing left. She was gone.

He lay still for a while and concentrated on his breathing, trying to make order of the confusion in his head. Struggling to focus, he took inventory. His ears were ringing and there was a pounding drumbeat of pain in his head. His chest felt like it was in a vise. *What's going on?* He opened his eyes, or tried to, but something sticky was blurring his vision, weighing his eyelids down. He tried to sit up, slowly this time, flinching at the jolt of pain that shot through his body. He lay still for another moment. Then he tried to move his arms and when he couldn't, he struggled to understand why. *Something was wrong. Very wrong.* Then, he sensed something, more of an intuition than anything else. His arms were pinned. *What?* He was sure of it. His arms were pinned below something. *Below him?*

He lifted his head slightly and felt another sharp stab of pain and, as he put his head back down, he felt something sticky on his cheek. After a while, he realized it was blood. The coppery taste was in his mouth, the smell was in his nose. *His own blood!*

He was jostled, and he felt the pain coursing through his body again but he also felt something else. *He was moving.*

———

After a while—he didn't know how long—he woke again. The fog lifted somewhat, and as he lay there an image began to form in his mind. A helicopter. While he struggled with what that meant, President Magaña flashed before him. Then, as if a dam had broken, the thoughts came rushing back in a cascade. The secret meeting. The explosion at Magaña's ranch. *What happened to Magaña?*

Knowing he wouldn't find the answer to the Mexican President's fate until he found the answer to his own, he took inventory again. He tried to move his arms and legs and realized that he was bound and then, a moment later, that he was gagged. He felt a flood of panic, a fear so deep that he couldn't breathe, that he would suffocate. He fought it, concentrating, slowing his breathing until the panic faded. Then he realized why he couldn't see; he had been blindfolded as well. But he could smell and taste blood and knew that he must be injured. *The explosion!* That was why he was in pain. Okay, he told himself, pain he could deal with. He analyzed what he knew and the realization dawned on him. He had been kidnapped.

What happened to Agent Tillman? What happened to the other agents? Where is President Magaña? He felt a stab of pain as he was suddenly jostled to the side. *Has he been kidnapped too?*

———

"It hasn't hit the news yet, sir, and the Mexicans aren't saying much, only that there has been a security incident involving President Magaña and that they are investigating."

President Kendall, sitting in the darkened living room in his pajamas, let out a breath. "What about Matthew?" he said into the phone.

"We haven't been able to reach him," Phillips said. "We're trying to contact his security detail..." His voice trailed off.

Kendall frowned as he stared at the phone. "What about the drones?"

"From what I've been told," Phillips said, "the Mexicans have denied us access, claiming its restricted air space." There was a pause on the line. "Maybe we can get something from the satellites?" his Chief of Staff asked.

"It'll take care of that," the president said then paused a second, thinking. "I want to meet with the cabinet. And the NSC staff." He glanced at his watch. Most were likely home asleep, unaware. It would take some time to get them back to the White House. "In two hours," he added.

"Yes, sir," the Chief of Staff responded. The president heard a car horn as Phillips continued. "Word of the meeting will get out. We'll need to prepare something for the press when they start asking questions."

"Let's get on it," Kendall ordered then paused. "But our first priority is Matthew. I want to brief our ambassador and have him formally request more information. We need to find out what's going on." He paused again, thinking. "In the meantime, who's in charge?"

"From what I understand, there's no automatic succession," Phillips said. "Their Congress would need to elect an interim president."

The president heard more noises: a truck's horn and then the chirp of a siren. Phillips was on his way in.

"Okay," the president said as he stood. "I'll be down in the Situation Room."

———

When Richter woke again he was shivering. The air was bitterly cold, and he pulled his knees up to his chest, trying to preserve what little body heat he had. His arms were still bound behind him and he had a pins-and-needles sensation radiating down both. There was an intense pain in his right shoulder, and he wasn't sure if it was from the explosion, from lying on his side for so long, or a lingering pain from the gunshot wound he had suffered what now seemed like ages ago.

He struggled to roll over and, after several attempts, succeeded. He instantly felt better as the pain in his right shoulder subsided to a dull throb. He took inventory again. The ground was cold, and he felt the packed earth against his cheek. Had he been dumped outdoors? The ringing in his ears was gone and he strained to listen, searching for the sounds of people, of a road or highway, anything. After a moment, he heard the trill of a bird followed by a flutter and then a cooing sound. There was a bird's nest nearby, he realized, and that meant he was outdoors, or close to it.

He noticed a distinct odor: an earthy, dusty smell that reminded him of the root cellar at his grandfather's farm. This was mixed with a faint, lingering sweetness that reminded him of animals, of hay, of manure. It wasn't strong, but it was there nonetheless and he realized that he was in a barn or some sort of enclosure where farm animals had once been penned.

He put that thought aside and continued. He was still blindfolded and gagged, but, as he shifted his position slightly, he caught a small sliver of light along the bottom of the cloth. He rubbed his face against the cold earth, ignoring the pain, and, after a few attempts, succeeded in moving the blindfold slightly. The sliver was bigger now.

He saw a shaft of light coming in through an open window, the dust particles flittering and dancing in the air. The window was nothing more than an opening in the cinderblock wall—no glass, no shutters. He spotted a tree outside and, from the angle of light, he knew that the sun was low on the horizon. Other than the sounds of the birds there was a stillness that told him it was morning.

He lifted and turned his head slightly for a better view when he heard a soft moan behind him. He rolled over again, ignoring the pain that shot through his shoulder. He bent his head back as far as he could and, through the slit, he saw a bloodied, gagged, and blindfolded face. He recognized the nose and chin. They belonged to Felipe Magaña.

He heard noises, muffled voices, and then someone was in the room. Suddenly, there were hands below his arms and he was being lifted, his feet dragging on the dirt floor as he was carried. *Where?* He feigned unconsciousness, his head lolling to one side, as his senses catalogued what they could. Even with the blindfold, the sudden brightness told him that he had been carried outside. He focused on sounds and smells, trying to get a sense of his surroundings—and his options—when he heard a car door opening. He was thrown in the back and covered with a heavy blanket and suddenly everything was dark again.

CHAPTER SIXTY-TWO

When he learned that Magaña and the American National Security Advisor were still alive, Guerrero had cursed and immediately thought that he would have to eliminate a few of his own men for failing him. But they had survived and now Guerrero realized how much better that would be.

His prisoners were now on their way to Monterrey. Guerrero would soon be leaving for Monterrey as well. There were some jobs, some tasks that were better handled personally.

Magaña and the American National Security Advisor were being taken to a business that Guerrero owned on the outskirts of the city; a legitimate business that provided services to ranches like his. *How fitting*, he thought with a grin.

He didn't waste time congratulating himself on his foresight. To him, at least, it had been obvious that one day he would have to leave the drug trade behind and, knowing this, he had quietly purchased dozens of businesses around the country. Most were secluded ranches or farms, but others were small manufacturers, restaurants, metal fabricators, or car dealerships operating and even thriving in the cities. They had been purchased through shell companies, and he had paid all of his taxes and complied with the government's many regulations. They had been useful as a way to launder money and, as he had planned from the very beginning, they would one day provide a legitimate income during his retirement when the day came that he decided it was finally time to leave the drug business; the day when he decided that he could retire comfortably. But that day had come and gone years ago and he was still here.

Over the years, some of the businesses, especially those in the border cities and in the major ports, had been converted to serve as bases for smuggling. And his drug business continued to grow. He had also purchased numerous beachfront properties, both on the Pacific and the Gulf coasts and large houses—private haciendas really—in the larger cities. Some were for speculation, others were meant to be a second or third home, and then a fourth or a fifth. At the time, he knew the day would come when he might have to run, and he realized that he would need a place to run to, a place where he could forget the drug business, reinvent himself as a legitimate businessman and continue to live in the lifestyle he had grown accustomed to.

But that wasn't going to happen, he knew, not now. His wife had left him. She was living now in one of his houses in Mexico City; living the life that he had planned for them both and for Carolina. His wife was in mourning too, but it hadn't taken long for her to flee. Although she had never said anything, he knew that she blamed him for Carolina's death. And so he had helped her, had his men deliver her safely to the house. She had servants and access to cash and he had made sure that she had a handful of men to provide for her protection. Lost in the masses of Mexico City, she would be able to hide in plain sight.

And so, he had been shrewd, he had been wise years ago when he'd begun to acquire businesses and properties. But no congratulations were deserved. For despite all of his planning, there was one thing that he had never contemplated. And now, he owed it to her, he owed it to Carolina, to make them pay.

He rang the small bell he kept on his desk and, seconds later, one of his maids was standing at the door, nervously wiping her hands on her apron.

"Find Alberto," he ordered.

Guerrero stood when the servant left. It was time to visit the pigs.

———

Burt Phillips sat down heavily on the couch. "There's no official word, sir," he said softly. "Unofficially, the Mexicans believe that they may have been taken hostage. Publically, they're stating that President Magaña is taking a well-deserved vacation."

The president let out a breath. "So, we don't even know if they're alive?" he asked, his voice rising.

Phillips shook his head. Jessica Williams, sitting next to Phillips, leaned forward. "The only thing we know for certain is that eight of our people—Matthew's Secret Service detail—were killed," she said. "We've confirmed this through diplomatic channels. State is working to arrange to have the bodies turned over to us as soon as possible, but that may take some time." She went on to explain the challenges with the Mexican criminal investigation and the desire by Mexican authorities to perform autopsies. The FBI, she said, was anxious to send a team of investigators, but, so far at least, the Mexican government had not granted permission.

"Guerrero?" The president looked at each of them.

Williams nodded. "That's what the CIA believes, sir. The little we've been able to get from Mexican Intelligence—all through informal channels—is that they believe so as well."

The president sat back as he considered the news. "No word on succession?"

Phillips shook his head. "From what we understand, they've scheduled an emergency session of Congress, but nothing yet."

The president ran his hand through his hair then looked up. "Could this be the beginnings of a coup d'état?"

Phillips and Williams both shook their heads. "We don't believe so," Williams said. "The government seems to be functioning as normal. Their military has been put on high alert and, so far at least, the generals are following orders. But strangely enough, their Navy has been running a training exercise in the Pacific and, based upon satellite images and signal traffic, the exercises are continuing as scheduled. And this morning, based upon Night Stalker intelligence we provided, they raided a warehouse on the border with Guatemala."

The president considered this for a few seconds. "So we don't think Guerrero is making a play?"

Williams shook her head. "No, sir. Not yet at least." She paused then added, "We've heard nothing from him. No public statements. No internet videos. Nothing."

The president's eyes narrowed. "And the motive?" he asked. He was afraid of the answer.

Williams let out a breath. "Revenge, sir," she said. "We believe that he wants revenge for his daughter. The bombings in Mexico City and in New York apparently haven't been enough. The CIA believes—I believe—that this is no longer about drugs. I'm not saying that he's giving up the business. He's still moving a lot of drugs, and word on the street is that he may be making a play for Los Arquitectos turf in Michoacán." She paused. "But we believe that this is about revenge, plain and simple."

The president shuddered as the image of Matthew's body swinging from a highway overpass flashed through his mind. He was silent for a moment before he abruptly stood.

"The game has changed," he said, more to himself than anyone else.

Phillips stood. "Can I ask what you intend to do, sir?"

The president turned back and stared at his Chief of Staff for a second before he answered. "I'm going to pull all Night Stalker assets. As of right now, they have new orders: to search for Guerrero and for Richter and Magaña. That goes for all military, all intelligence, and all law enforcement teams we have down there. I want all hands on deck leveraging every intelligence network, every source we have." His eyes narrowed. "We have a SEAL team training for Guerrero?" he asked.

Phillips glanced over at Williams.

She nodded. "Yes, sir. They've been deployed to Texas. They've been training, running scenarios in the desert."

The president's eyes narrowed. "I want them ready to go on my command."

———

A steady rain fell as President Kendall stared into the Rose Garden. Standing below the portico, he listened to the hiss of the rain splattering off the leaves, the staccato tapping off the drops on the roof, the patter of the raindrops splashing off the stones. Several Secret Service Agents stood watch at a respectful distance.

The dark, grey skies matched his mood.

Harry Truman had a sign on his desk that said, *The Buck Stops Here.* Kendall had seen the pictures, had heard the story. *The president,* Truman had said, *whoever he is, has to decide. He can't pass the buck to anybody. No one else can do the deciding for him. That's his job.* And, Kendall thought, the president had to live with the consequences of those decisions, as difficult as they might be. Truman certainly knew that, having issued the difficult order to drop atomic bombs on Hiroshima and Nagasaki, instantly killing ninety thousand people and forcing a Japanese surrender to end World War II.

President Kendall had made his own decision, a series of them actually and, as a result, people had died as well. Thirteen hundred people in Mexico City, fifty-nine in Manhattan. Scores injured and countless more exposed to radiation. And as difficult as it was to accept—as difficult as the loss of innocent life was—he knew he had had no choice. He could not ignore the threat of a terrorist organization that was capable of overthrowing an ally right next door. The consequences for the U.S., for the world, were too grave. And as long as there was a risk that they would explode another dirty bomb, he had to do everything he could to stop them.

And so he had sent Matthew Richter. He would not be alive today if not for Matthew. Richter, then a Secret Service agent, had risked everything to save him two years ago. He was much more than a friend, Kendall thought as he choked away a sob. He sighed as the weight of his decision hung heavy on his shoulders. Had he sent Matthew to his death?

CHAPTER SIXTY-THREE

The battered pickup came to a stop. Seconds later, after the dust plume settled, two men climbed out. Dressed in the long pants and long-sleeved, button-down plaid shirts of day laborers, they drew no more than passing attention from the old man sitting in the shade. Two young boys, not more than ten, looked up once before they went back to kicking a soccer ball in the dust on the side of the building. The driver walked over to the building: a small mercado with the ubiquitous *Coca-Cola* sign in the window. The mangy dog, lying at the old man's feet, picked its head up briefly and watched the driver as he stepped inside. Then the dog yawned, put his head back on his paws, and closed his eyes again.

The passenger looked around casually then, turning away from the building, took his hat off for a few seconds. He pulled a rag from his pocket and mopped his brow; he spit into the dirt, then wiped his mouth. As he put the rag away, he spotted the small shrine: nothing more than a white cross, decorated with flowers and blue ribbons. On the ground, at the base, stood three votive candles. He took a step, hesitated, then took several more until he could read the handwritten note attached to the cross. Te extraño, mi hijo. Te amo. *I miss you, my son. I love you.*

A small cry escaped his lips, and he shuddered once before pulling the rag from his pocket again and wiping his eyes. He squinted up at the sun for a moment and shook his head before he put his hat back on. After a moment, he turned away.

He walked to the other side of the building, away from the soccer game, and followed the path to the cistern out back. He stopped by the cistern and nodded to the old woman. Avoiding her eyes, he thrust his hand into his pocket, handed her a few coins, then he disappeared into the outhouse.

A minute later, he stepped out, washed his hands then took his hat off again. He splashed the water on his face, rubbing the week's worth of stubble on his chin. As he put his hat back on, he turned to see the driver coming down the same path he had followed moments before. Without a word, he took the two bottles of *Coke* from the driver; the driver then paid the woman and stepped into the outhouse himself.

Three minutes later, in a small cloud of dust, the pickup truck pulled out onto the road again and headed north.

———

"The team is ready, sir," Williams said.

"How soon can they deploy?" the president asked.

"I'm told four hours. But I think it will depend on how solid our intelligence is. The more intel we give them up front, the better they can prepare."

The president nodded. They didn't know where Guerrero was, but his gut told him that if they could find Guerrero, they would find Magaña and Richter. Once they did, assuming Magaña and Richter were still alive, the SEALs would have to deploy immediately. Would he be putting more lives in jeopardy if he sent them in? Did he have any other choice?

He glanced over at the noise and saw Burt Phillips answer his phone. Phillips mumbled something, then walked over to the TV.

"Ernesto Alameda was named interim president," he said as he turned.

Damn, the president cursed under his breath. Alameda was left-of-center, a member of PRD—the National Democratic Front that was the successor to the corrupt, one party system that had ruled Mexico for almost sixty years before finally falling from grace in the

1990's. He was a vocal critic of Magaña's campaign against the drug cartels and publically opposed U.S. drug policy. It was believed that he was preparing to run for president himself when Magaña's term was done.

The screen showed Alameda standing behind a podium flanked by the Mexican flag. They listened as the announcer described the scene.

"Ernesto Alameda made his first public appearance less than thirty minutes ago when he addressed reporters from the Presidential Palace at Los Pinos. In an emergency session of Congress earlier today, Alameda was selected to serve as interim president following the apparent abduction of President Filipe Magaña. Alameda provided few details about Magaña's abduction, claiming that it was a national security matter. Meanwhile, other sources tell us that Magaña was vacationing at a private location on the Gulf Coast when his compound was overrun by armed terrorists. In the process, President Magaña was taken hostage and, as of yet, his whereabouts and condition are unknown.

"Alameda would not comment on who might be behind the abduction or the possible motives, but our sources tell us that it is widely believed that one or more drug cartels are responsible. In the past, Alameda has publically voiced his disagreement with Magaña's drug policy and with the heavy influence that the United States exerts in Mexican national matters."

As the news announcer continued, the president turned. "He'll likely renege on our agreements," he stated.

Phillips and Williams both nodded somberly, and the president's face clouded. As he watched Alameda on the screen, any lingering doubts he had about sending in the SEALs faded.

———

Sitting in her office at Princeton, Patty tried to focus on her work, to push Matthew from her mind. She had to keep busy, otherwise the worry would consume her. She had been unable to reach him but assumed he was consumed with national security issues. Was he on his way to Mexico? she wondered. Was he already there? She felt a chill. Was he safe? She shook her head. No, she told herself, with the situation in Mexico, his trip had been cancelled. He was probably huddled in the Situation Room trying to assess what was happening right now. Felling a little better, she turned back to her work.

But after several failed attempts to focus on the papers she was grading, she gave up and switched on the TV. The channel, as was her custom, was set to a twenty-four hour news program. She watched for several moments, hoping to learn something new. Mexico had named an interim president. The transition of power was an interesting topic, she thought. Mexico's constitution dictated a transitional process, she knew, but the unfolding of the transition, especially under the circumstances, would make for timely discussions. And especially when she considered all of the things that it signaled. The PRD had seized power. Although through a democratic process, they had seized it nonetheless by coercing enough votes for Alameda. And now it was likely that there would be a significant shift in foreign policy and, likely, she thought, domestic policy as well. She knew Alameda was a critic of the current approach to combating the narco-traffickers. The last time that the PRD was in power—or rather, its predecessor the PRI—the government had turned a blind eye to the narco-traffickers, quietly accepting the cartels as a fact of life in exchange, some said, for a share of the spoils that came with it. One of her colleagues had published a paper last week that suggested the political landscape in both North and South America, and ultimately the world, could change if Mexico succumbed to a violent revolution. The cartels, no longer content with the tacit approval they once had, might try to seize power. And she wondered: with the PRD now in office, was that still a possibility?

Her cell phone rang and she spun away from the TV, hopeful that it was Matthew. But when she saw the number she was confused.

"This is Patty Curtis," she said.

"Ms. Curtis, this is the White House operator. Please hold for the president."

The president? Before Patty could respond, the line clicked. A moment later, it clicked again.

"Patty?" she heard.

"Yes...yes sir...this is Patty."

"Patty, this is David Kendall." There was a pause and Patty could feel her heart hammering in her chest.

"Hello," Patty responded as the dread rising up inside her continued to build.

"Patty, I'm afraid I have some terrible news."

CHAPTER SIXTY-FOUR

Four miles over the Mexican landscape, the Reaper banked gracefully while, a thousand miles away, the sensor's eyes scanned the six screens in front of him. He suddenly leaned forward. *Holy shit!* He zoomed the camera in and studied the man as he stared up at the sky, his face contorted in pain. The sensor cursed silently when the man put his hat back on. But two minutes later, now by the outhouse, he took it off again as he washed his face. *That's him!* the sensor thought. He tracked the man as he walked back to the truck. Then, he kept the camera on the truck as it pulled onto the road, a wake of dust billowing behind.

"Possible visual on Banjo!" the sensor said into his mic, more excitement in his voice then he intended. "Designate as Target One."

"Copy, Sea Dog," he heard the mission controller's reply. "Wait for confirmation."

"Copy," the sensor replied.

The sensor felt a rush of adrenaline. The intelligence pukes would have to verify it, of course. But he felt the excitement that always came before they engaged a target. He glanced over at the pilot. After a moment, the pilot looked up, then nodded once before turning back to the screen. It was show time.

———

When they pulled the blindfold off, it took a moment for Richter's eyes to adjust to the light. He blinked once or twice as the guard checked his hands, then his feet, making sure they were bound securely to the chair. The guard—terrorist, Richter corrected himself—gave him an evil look, a warning. Richter exchanged a glance with President Magaña. The Mexican president's face was a mask of stone. Subdued but not intimidated, he showed no fear as the guard checked his bindings. Throughout it all, Richter noted, Magaña had maintained a dignified silence.

The guards left, and he took the opportunity to study their surroundings. As he took in the cavernous room, he felt sick as adrenaline flooded his body. He fought the feeling—pushing it down, hiding it—knowing that panic would do him no good. He glanced over at Magaña. He saw the flash of fear in the president's eyes then a quick, almost imperceptible nod. Magaña's face hardened. They exchanged another glance and Richter found strength in the president's resolve. He nodded at Magaña then turned, taking some time to study the room, cataloguing what he saw, weighing their options.

Directly over their heads was a rail system, suspended from the ceiling, with large hooks—shackles—hanging down. The rail continued, then turned and passed into another room. He looked down, knowing what he would find. At his feet was a six-inch wide trough that ran the length of the floor, following the pulley system as it curved into the next room. It was called a collecting trough, he remembered.

The trough and the floor around it were stained brown, and there was an unmistakable stench, a coppery smell that brought back images from his childhood. He glanced to the far corner, where the rail system began. There, he saw the door that led to the hog pens. Just inside the door, below where the overhead rail began, was where the *sticker* stood when the plant was operating. Then the scalding tank and the tumbler where the hair was removed. And the area where he and Magaña were sitting would normally be occupied by a team of workers. Dressed in boots, wearing hardhats and large aprons, each had an assigned task. Using enormous knives, the first was responsible for removing the heads, the next person, the entrails, before the pigs, hanging by shackles, passed on to the next station. There, the carcasses were split, sometimes with a chainsaw, before they were washed. Richter's eyes followed the rail again to where it curved out of the room. Although he couldn't see it, he knew the rail curved into the chilling room, a large refrigerator where the carcasses were stored temporarily to cool them before they were further processed in the cutting room. He glanced back down at the collecting trough and the stains on the floor and the muscles in his face tightened. This, he remembered, was called the *kill floor*.

That they had been brought here was not a good sign, he told himself unnecessarily. The building was full of weapons: knives, hooks, saws, things that could do considerable damage to a human body. He pulled at his arms unsuccessfully then tried to move his legs. He had to find some way to get his hands on those weapons before they were used on him.

———

President Kendall stared at the faces around the table.

"We cannot let Mexico fall," he said. "And we will *not* abandon one of our men."

The Secretary of State hesitated. "We have an appointment, sir"—she glanced at her watch—"in six hours."

The U.S. Ambassador, Kendall was aware, would meet with the Mexican Secretary of Foreign Affairs and learn what he could. But by then, he knew, both Richter and Magaña could be dead, killed by Guerrero directly or by corrupt Mexican troops during a rescue attempt. Would Guerrero hold them for some form of ransom? Or, as Jessica Williams had suggested, would he kill them for revenge? Would he torture them first? Were they dead already or, worse, would Guerrero make their deaths a public display, a sign both of his power and of the impotence of the U.S. and Mexican governments? The problem was, without any solid intelligence on where Guerrero or Richter or Magaña might be, he was powerless. The only thing he could do was prepare for the chance that they would find them, and when they did, ensure that U.S. forces were ready to react.

"We run parallel courses," the president said. He nodded at the Secretary of State. "We pursue diplomatic channels, find out what Mexico knows, what intelligence they have," he paused. "Whatever they're willing to share," he added dryly. "We need to know what they're planning. Meanwhile..." his voice trailed off and he looked up as Jessica Williams rushed in.

"Sir! We've located Guerrero!"

CHAPTER SIXTY-FIVE

Jessica Williams slid a photo across the table. As the president picked it up, his eyes narrowed. The peasant, a hat in his hand, his hair matted down, was wiping his brow. The man had several days' worth of growth on his face. Was this really Guerrero? he wondered. As he studied the man's face, something about the eyes caught his attention. Instead of the weary look of an overworked laborer he had been expecting, there was an intensity in the man's eyes that was menacing. *Damn*, the president thought, as he looked up.

"Are we sure it's him?"

Williams nodded. "Yes, sir. The CIA has confirmed it."

So that was why they hadn't seen or heard from him for the last few weeks, the president thought. The man was clever; he had been disguising himself as a peasant.

"Do we know where he is right now?" the president growled.

"Yes, sir. We tracked him to a building on the outskirts of Monterrey." Williams made a face. "It appears to be a slaughterhouse, sir."

The president's face darkened as Williams shook her head. "We don't know if Matthew Richter and/or President Magaña are there, sir," she added, her voice trailing off.

"But?" the president prodded.

"But," she said after a deep breath, "something drew him out of hiding. Why else would he travel there?

The president nodded as Williams continued.

"Currently, the slaughterhouse is not operating. The hog pens are empty." She paused. "Which is odd," she added, "since it appears that the plant normally runs two shifts, five days a week." She explained that CIA and NSA aerial reconnaissance from the last several months showed shipments arriving once or twice a day, animals being offloaded into pens and, on the other side of the building, refrigerated trucks leaving on set schedules. "Then last night, they abruptly shut down," she continued. "When our people called the main number, a recording indicated that the plant would be closed for two days due to an agricultural inspection."

"Regardless," the president said with a wave of his hand, "we're certain he's there?"

Williams nodded and the president turned to the chairman of the Joint Special Operations Command.

"And the SEAL team, Admiral?"

The Navy Admiral, a steely faced man with close-cropped silver hair, stated that the SEALs were already reviewing the intelligence, learning as much as they could about the target location. They would likely insert by air, he added, and were working through alternate scenarios for infiltration—storming the building—and not only capturing Guerrero alive, if possible, but rescuing Richter and Magaña as well.

"They will be ready to go on your command," he assured the president.

———

Like a rag doll, Terry Fogel was dumped in his cell. The door banged shut with a metallic clang. Naked and curled in a fetal position on the cold floor, Fogel's breath came in gulps. His hands were protectively cupped over his genitals. It took a while for his breathing to slow. When he got up the nerve, he opened his eyes and pulled his hands away. His penis and testicles were swollen, and there were burn marks where the electrodes had been attached. He could feel the blood seeping out of his rectum. Still, he told himself, it wasn't as bad as he had been expecting. He had seen worse at the hands of the British.

His nose was still swollen; one eye was puffy, an ugly purple bruise extending down to his cheek. That had been courtesy of the soldier in the truck, after the hastily shortened press conference, he thought with a small smirk. Since then, they had stayed away from his face, preferring instead to target more vulnerable, more sensitive areas. They seemed convinced that he had a part in the attack on Mexico City. The fools. Had he, he had told the two men from CISEN—Mexico's Center of Investigation and National Security— the death toll would certainly have been higher. They hadn't appreciated that answer but, between the shocks, he had seen something in the men's eyes. *A glimmer of doubt?* he wondered.

Still, he knew, they might use him as a scapegoat, a vehicle for the vengeance that many Mexicans were demanding. He had initially been surprised that they hadn't let the Americans near him. *They must know by now*, he thought. But it seemed the Mexicans wanted to exact their own pound of flesh before inviting the Americans in.

He heard a door banging followed by scraping. Then a hushed conversation followed by footsteps before the creak of his own door. Another hushed word and then two arms lifted him up; gently, this time. A blanket was draped over his shoulders. A man he had never seen before stood in the doorway as a soldier helped him to his cot. Another blanket was draped over his naked body.

The man in the doorway said something and the soldier left, closing the door behind him. Fogel heard the click of the lock. The man stepped forward, and Fogel noticed the black bag in his hands. His heart started to pound, and he fought the panic.

"Oh, no!" the man said in perfect English. "I'm not here to hurt you." He shook his head, making a tsk-ing noise. He pulled a chair over by the bed and placed his bag on the floor. He reached for the blanket then stopped.

"May I?" he asked.

Fogel hesitated, then nodded, and the man lifted the blanket.

Fogel watched the man's face change; he heard the sudden intake of breath. The man shook his head again.

"What have those fools done to you?" the man said softly.

"Ah, now," Fogel said. Despite the pain, he grinned. "I've had worse."

CHAPTER SIXTY-SIX

The jolt of electricity hit Richter like a bolt of lightning. His body arched uncontrollably, straining at the restraints until his chair tipped and he slammed into the floor. Every nerve in his body was on fire. He struggled to breath, gasping in labored pants. After a while, he opened his eyes. Pablo Guerrero stood over him. He held the cattle prod up and nodded at it.

"Now you know what the pig feels like, eh, Señor Richter?"

Richter said nothing and, after a moment, Guerrero turned toward Magaña.

"We will speak in English, *Señor Presidente,*" he said. There was no mistaking the contempt in his voice. He turned back to Richter. "I want Señor Richter to know exactly what's going to happen to him." He smiled, a perverse grin that did nothing to mask the hatred in his eyes. He turned back to Magaña and sneered.

"And I want you to watch so you know exactly what's going to happen to you."

Magaña said nothing. Guerrero scowled at him then turned and barked an order in Spanish. Richter felt arms grabbing him and gritted his teeth as he was roughly hauled up. Sitting upright once again, he looked up at Guerrero.

"You see, Señor Richter, the pigs come here in trucks. When we put them into the pens they start to squeal." Guerrero smiled again. "Do you know why?" he asked after a second.

Richter said nothing.

Guerrero leaned in, his face inches away. Richter could feel the man's hot breath.

"Because they know. They can smell it. They can smell death and they are scared. An animal knows when he is about to die, Señor Richter." He paused and sneered. "Do you feel like a pig now?"

Richter said nothing, and Guerrero thrust the prod into his chest again.

His brain exploded in a flash of white light, and his body slammed into the floor again. Then there was a blue flash as his head hit the concrete. His body convulsed, and he felt like he was going to be sick. He had to fight the darkness creeping over the edges of his vision. He concentrated on breathing. *In then out. In then out.* Slower, he told himself. *In then out.* It was something he could focus on instead of the pain coursing through his body. After a while, he opened one eye—a slit below a swollen lid—and looked up at Guerrero again.

"The pigs don't like it either, Señor Richter. But fortunately, for them, it's over quickly." His eyes narrowed. "For you, *unfortunately*, things won't be so quick."

Richter remained silent. He wasn't sure if he had screamed when the prod hit him, but he was determined to not give Guerrero the satisfaction if he could help it. Guerrero nodded once at someone and Richter felt hands under his arms again as he was lifted up. He winced as pain shot down his right arm, and he suddenly felt woozy and nauseous. He wasn't sure if his arm was broken. He closed his eyes, trying to force the dizziness and pain away. His head hanging low on his chest, he focused on his breathing again. Guerrero was saying something, but he ignored him as he took inventory once again. His right shoulder was on fire, and he could taste the blood in his mouth. He must have bitten his tongue, he realized. He slumped forward to spit the blood out, then hesitated when he felt it. He let his head drop like he was drunk. He moved his arms again; nothing more than a twitch. The ropes had loosened somewhat, he realized. He hadn't been able to lean forward before. His head down by his knees, he opened one eye—nothing more than a slit again—and could see that two of the cross supports for the chair's legs were broken. The rope hung loose around his ankles. What about his hands, he wondered. He resisted the urge to try to free his hands, knowing that one or two of Guerrero's men were standing behind him. *Wait for the opportunity*, he told himself, hoping one would come before Guerrero zapped him again. He wasn't sure how many more shocks from the cattle prod he could take.

There was a noise outside and Guerrero barked an order in Spanish. Richter heard footsteps and turned his head slightly and watched out of the corner of his eye as Guerrero's two men went through a doorway. He coughed once and spit a mouthful of blood on the floor. Then he sat up slowly, acting more dazed than he was. He opened his eyes—squinting—and saw Guerrero before him. The man's eyes were like daggers. He glanced over at Magaña. The Mexican President held his gaze for a second then nodded once and gestured with his head toward Richter's chair. Turning back to Guerrero, Richter moved his arms slightly, and although he could still feel the rope biting into one wrist, the binds were looser than he thought. *But loose enough?* he wondered.

Guerrero's eyes bore into him. He could feel the man's hatred; he could feel the rage. He waited, bracing himself for what was coming.

"You took her from me!" Guerrero suddenly hissed. "She was nine years old, and you took her from me!"

Richter said nothing. Guerrero was responsible for thousands of deaths—for taking the lives of innocent men, of innocent women and even children whose only crime had been being in the wrong place at the wrong time. But that fact seemed lost on him, Richter realized. He stared at the cattle prod in Guerrero's hands, judging the distance. The possibilities played out in his head, but no matter how he looked at it, Guerrero was still too far away.

Richter sighed. "You had your revenge," he said, his voice weak. "Mexico City...New York..."

"Do you think any of that comes close?" Guerrero hissed back then lunged forward.

Richter saw a flash of light as the fire exploded in his body again.

———

The black and white image from the synthetic aperture radar was crisp and clear.

"I have target building in sight," the sensor said into his microphone. "Designate as Target Two."

Two seconds later came the mission controller's reply: "Copy, Sea Dog. Building is Target Two."

The sensor centered the crosshairs on the building and locked in the laser designator. A second later, he heard the pilot.

"Pilot copies. Building is Target Two. Target is Sparkle."

Their role, the sensor knew, was to support the special ops team. The firing solution on the building was a precaution; the decision to destroy it would come from the men on the ground. His eyes slid off the building to the parking lot and fenced-in area surrounding it.

"There are four vehicles in the lot," he said as he spotted the three SUVs and the battered pickup parked side by side. "Designate as Target Three." *One five-hundred-pound bomb should do it*, he thought.

"Copy, Sea Dog. Target Three identified."

"Pilot copies. Target Three."

The sensor continued to scan the screens. He spotted the men standing by the gate.

"I have four men, all armed, by the gate."

"Copy, Sea Dog. We see them."

Two more men exited the building. The sensor called it in.

"Sea Dog, how many are in the building?" the mission controller asked.

The sensor switched on the ultrasound system. Referred to by the crews as the X-Box, the prototype system used sound waves at specific frequencies to penetrate solid surfaces, seemingly impenetrable surfaces such as the reinforced concrete of the slaughterhouse below. The sound waves bounced off the lower-density objects inside, then, using complex algorithms, the system's computer converted the reflected energy into the three ghostlike figures that suddenly appeared on his screen. Two appeared to be stationary—

nothing more than oozing white blobs—while the third appeared to be moving. The third blob seemed to shift, dissolve, then reappear as the figure moved across the room.

One was definitely Banjo, the pilot knew. He had followed the truck for two and a half hours until it had pulled into the slaughter-house lot and he had watched Banjo go inside. The other two could be terrorists, but he and everyone on the operation were hopeful that they were the two friendlies they had been searching for. Codenamed Spartan and Aztec, the two men—high value VIPs—had not yet been located. The sensor glanced briefly at the two pictures provided to him by the intelligence analysts. He hoped they weren't too late.

"Looks like we have three inside."

"Copy Sea Dog. Three confirmed inside Target Two."

CHAPTER SIXTY-SEVEN

Lying on the floor, the chair in splinters below him, Richter fought the waves of darkness washing over him. He forced his eyes open and stared up at his tormentor. Guerrero glared down at him, his dark eyes filled with venom.

"You don't look like a man now," he taunted, waving the prod in Richter's face.

Richter flinched.

"Do you think your government will help you, Señor Richter? Your army? Your Navy SEALs?" Guerrero shook his head. "Instead of fighting like men, you send your remote control planes to spy on us, to drop your bombs on us." He shook his head again. "No, Señor Richter. You are on your own. And so that is how you will die. On your own. Then your body will be strung up from a pole, left for the birds to eat."

Guerrero leaned over, shook the cattle prod again, and Richter saw his opportunity. With every bit of energy he had left, he lashed out with his foot, catching Guerrero between the legs. Guerrero's eyes went wide and he grunted as he doubled over. Richter scrambled up, shaking to try and free his arms from the ropes. He was still struggling to free himself when Guerrero—gasping—reached for the cattle prod lying at his feet. Richter stepped forward and thrust his knee into the cartel leader's face. Guerrero let out another grunt as his nose exploded and he fell to the floor.

Richter glanced up at the door, praying that Guerrero's men

were still occupied outside, and then concentrated on the ropes. With Guerrero lying in a fetal position moaning at his feet, Richter succeeded in loosening the rope around his right wrist. He flexed his right arm and gasped at the sharp pain in his shoulder.

"Look out!" Magaña yelled.

Guerrero pushed himself up to his knees. Richter lunged forward. Grabbing the cattle prod with his left hand—a two-foot piece of rope dangling from his wrist—he thrust the contact points into Guerrero's neck, sending nine thousand volts through his body. Guerrero screamed and, like a rag doll, dropped back to the floor. As he lay writhing on the ground, Richter hurried over to President Magaña.

He began working on the ropes that bound Magaña's legs and arms when there was a shout outside. He stopped and stared at the door.

"Hurry!" Magaña hissed.

Richter watched the door for another second before turning his attention back to the rope. After a moment, he loosened one of the president's wrists and began to work on the other when he heard a door slam.

———

The two MH-60S Knighthawk helicopters flew fast and low over the ground. Using nap-of-the-earth navigational systems, both helicopters jerked up as they approached the small hill then plunged down the other side, hugging the ground as they skimmed over the dips and rises of the uneven terrain. Equipped with stealth technology, designed to suppress engine and rotor noise as well as to reduce their radar profiles, the Knighthawks had passed into Mexican airspace undetected.

Each Knighthawk carried a crew of four: two pilots, a crew chief, and a gunner manning the door-mounted M-60 machine gun. The passengers, eight Navy SEALs in each Knighthawk, were dressed for war. Codenamed Jackhammer, they were on a kill or capture mission. The preference was to take Banjo alive, if possible, but the mission planners were realists, and the Knighthawk carried body bags just in case. Secondarily, the Jackhammer team would, if possible, execute a rescue operation. With no direct evidence that Spartan and Aztec were in Banjo's custody, the team was prepared for that possibility.

The SEAL platoon leader, a lieutenant in the lead helicopter, glanced back at his men. Once the building had been identified, they had little time to prepare. A few satellite images, a floor plan, a map, and a rushed briefing by a CIA analyst were all the intelligence and preparation they would get. Not ideal, but they would have to find a way with the information they had. While no mission was routine—in the last two years, his team had rescued a downed pilot in Afghanistan, killed a warlord in Somalia, and rescued a kidnapped ambassador in the Philippines—this was what he and his men did and did well.

Two of his men, he noted, were studying the pictures of their target. The rest were quiet, several with their eyes closed, others staring straight ahead. Some already had on their warrior masks: eyes hard, muscles stretched tight across clenched jaws. Each man, he knew, was going through his own pre-game ritual.

The communications specialist sat next to the lieutenant, a computer perched on his lap. He tapped at the keys then looked up.

"Got Sea Dog online, boss."

———

"Sea Dog." The sensor heard the voice of the mission controller. "Jackhammer inbound. Jackhammer has assumed mission control."

"Sea Dog copies," he said into his mic. "Jackhammer assumes mission control."

A second later he heard a click.

"Sea Dog, this is Jackhammer."

"Copy, Jackhammer," the sensor responded.

"Jackhammer inbound to LZ Whiskey. ETA one-three minutes."

"Sea Dog copies. Jackhammer ETA one-three minutes."

The sensor's eyes flicked across the screens. On the upper right hand screen, he saw the dust plume of a vehicle on the access road to the slaughterhouse.

"Jackhammer, we have company. Standby."

He zoomed the camera in and saw the four armed men in the back of the truck, the federal police emblem clearly visible on the side.

"Jackhammer. Be advised we have federal police approaching on the access road from the west."

He watched as cartel guards fanned out around the gate, their guns held ready. The truck came to a stop twenty yards from the gate. An officer in the front passenger seat hopped out, and the four masked cops in the back jumped down. The sensor centered the laser designator on the truck.

"The police truck is Target Four," the sensor said as he clicked the button on his joystick.

"Jackhammer copies. Target Four. Jackhammer ETA eleven minutes."

"Pilot copies. Target Four."

———

Grabbing the cattle prod, Richter jumped up and rushed to the door as a man burst into the room. Richter shoved the prod into the man's neck. The man let out a grunt as his body arched before his legs buckled. Richter grabbed the man by the shirt—gritting his teeth against the pain that shot up his arm—and yanked the man in, then banged the door shut. He took the man's weapon, an automatic rifle, then hesitated and shocked the man again. The man screamed and, as he jerked and twitched on the floor, Richter ran his hand along the man's legs then around his waist, up his sides toward his chest. He found the handgun in a shoulder holster. Sticking the handgun in his waistband, he thrust the prod under the man's chin and pressed the trigger again and the man went still. He dragged the unconscious man away from the door, his right arm on fire. Then, slinging the rifle over his shoulder and grabbing the cattle prod, he hurried back to the Mexican President.

Kneeling on the floor behind Magaña, his eyes darted from the ropes to the door to Guerrero then to the ropes again as he struggled to free the Mexican President.

"How many are there?" Magaña whispered.

"There were two in here earlier," Richter responded. "And I heard at least two other voices outside when they brought us in." He grunted, then, steeling himself against the pain, finally succeeded in loosening the last knot. "But I think there may be more."

Magaña stood and rubbed at his sore wrists. "So what's our plan?"

Richter thought for a second. "You were in the navy?"

Magaña nodded. Richter handed him the rifle, knowing that with his injured shoulder, the gun was useless. Then his eyes darted around the room, first to the door, then to the opening behind them where the rail system curved into the next room. He glanced back at the door and saw the electrical box, the series of light switches, and then the wash station near the corner. His eyes traveled down the wall to where the overhead rail began and to a second door that led to the hog pens. He glanced back at Guerrero, motionless on the floor, and spotted the radio.

"Okay," he said after a moment. "Here's what I need you to do."

———

The sensor's eyes flicked back and forth from the five cartel guards to the building then to the federal police. The cartel guards were fanned out in a large semicircle inside the gate, their weapons held cautiously. Outside, the police truck was idling; the four masked and armed officers who had been riding in back had also fanned out, two taking defensive positions behind the truck. The driver remained in the cab. One cop, a tall, heavyset man who was not wearing the usual face mask was standing on the other side of the gate. He was speaking to one of the cartel guards—the one, the sensor noted, who appeared to be in charge. The cop was gesturing toward the truck. After a moment, the head guard turned and spoke to the man next to him. The man nodded, then turned and jogged across the lot to one of the SUVs.

The sensor saw the rear hatch open. The man was apparently
looking for something in the back, but the rear hatch blocked the
camera's view. After a moment, the guard closed the hatch, then
jogged back across the lot with, the sensor could now see, a backpack in his hand. The man handed the backpack to the head guard.
The head guard opened it, glanced inside, then nodded to the tall,
heavyset cop on the other side of the gate. The heavyset cop returned
to the police truck and, a moment later, dragged a hooded figure
from the cab. The figure's hands were bound behind his back. The
heavyset cop led the prisoner to the gate and, after a few words were
exchanged, pulled the hood up.

The sensor adjusted the camera but the cop's hand and the
scrunched up hood blocked the prisoner's face. The head guard nodded as the cop slid the hood back down. The gate was opened, and
the sensor realized that an exchange had been negotiated. The guard
handed over the backpack as the cop pushed the prisoner forward.
The cop pulled a bundle of bills from the backpack—U.S. currency,
the sensor noted—fanned it once in his fingers, then dropped it back
inside. He nodded once then turned back toward the police truck.

The sensor's eyes caught movement, and he glanced back at the
screen that showed the sound wave images from inside the building.
The figures there were moving. Something was happening inside.
As if reading his mind, he heard a hiss in his earphones.

"Sea Dog, this is Jackhammer. Police truck is priority. Vehicles
in the lot are secondary. We have the building."

"Sea Dog copies. Target Four is priority," the sensor responded
as his eyes shifted back to the police truck. "Target Three is secondary. Jackhammer has Target Two."

"Pilot copies," he heard a moment later.

He flipped a switch. "Weapons are hot."

"Hold for clearance, Sea Dog."

"Sea Dog copies. Holding."

CHAPTER SIXTY-EIGHT

Crouched in front of the plastic strip curtains hanging at the entrance to the chilling room, Richter peered around the corner. The only light came from the window in the door that Guerrero's men had used. The door, Richter had determined, led to a hallway and then outside. But the small shaft of light was enough. Once his eyes had adjusted to the relative darkness, he had a clear view of the kill floor. Guerrero, like a rag doll, lay motionless in the middle of the floor; the lone guard, also unconscious, was ten feet away next to the wall.

Richter glanced back at the Mexican president then pointed across the room to the scalding tank.

"I'm going to take up a position over there," he whispered.

Magaña nodded his reply, and Richter handed him the radio.

"Call them inside. Make something up. Tell them you need help. Make it sound urgent."

Magaña nodded and Richter stood. Suddenly, the bang of a door interrupted the silence. Instinctively, Richter crouched and trained his gun on the door. Half a second later, the door opened partway. There was an exchange of words in the hallway, something in Spanish that he didn't understand, then the door opened wide and two men stepped into the room. Wary of the darkness, they held their guns ready. Richter, his own gun in his left hand, centered the sights on the first man's chest. He fired twice, the sound incredibly loud as it echoed off the concrete walls. As the man fell, Richter swung his gun to the man behind him. He squeezed the trigger again and the man staggered. As the man began to fall forward, Richter tracked him with his gun and fired once more. As the second man crumpled to the floor, a third man burst into the room. Before Richter could swing his gun back, there were two sharp cracks behind him and the third man's head exploded in a spray of blood.

Richter glanced back at Magaña. The Mexican President, his head angled as he squinted down the rifle's sights, had his weapon trained on the door. After a second, he lowered the rifle and glanced over at Richter. Even in the darkness of the room, Richter recognized the eyes: stone-cold and without remorse, they were the eyes of a soldier.

———

The sensor saw the men running toward the building. Two of Guerrero's men remained by the gate.

"Jackhammer," he said into his radio. "We've got three Tangos entering the building. Looks like they have a prisoner with them."

"Jackhammer copies. We see them. Do you have an ID on the prisoner?"

"Negative, Jackhammer."

"Okay, Sea Dog. Hold on Target Four."

"Copy. Sea Dog holding on Target Four."

The cartel guards and the prisoner entered the building where they suddenly became white blobs on the sensor's screen as the X-Box picked them up. They seemed to shift and ooze as they moved inside, then, a moment later, they all went still.

"Sea Dog, Jackhammer ETA eight minutes."

"Sea Dog copies."

The sensor's eyes shifted back to the gate. The cops had climbed back into the truck. A second later, the truck began to pull away, kicking up a wake of dust behind. The two remaining guards watched for a moment, then turned and began running toward the building.

———

Richter glanced at the door then back at the Mexican president. "I think there are more outside," he hissed. "Cover me."

Magaña nodded as Richter dashed to the corner of the room next to the scalding tank. The tank didn't offer much cover, but he had a clear view of the door. And with the Mexican president by the chiller, it created a crossfire, a kill zone. Crouching by the tank, he nodded at Magaña, then trained his weapon on the door.

He didn't have to wait long before the door burst open again. One man, apparently seeing the bodies, jerked to the right, toward Richter, while the second dropped low, crouching by the wash station. Richter trained his sights on the first and squeezed off a shot. As he adjusted his aim for a second shot, there was a staccato roar as Magaña, his rifle set to automatic, took down both men.

———

"We have two more Tangos entering the building."

"Copy, Sea Dog. We see 'em." There was a pause, then, "Sea Dog, pull off Target Four. Hold for orders."

"Sea Dog copies. Off Target Four." The sensor glanced back at the police truck. It bounced along the dirt road, a dust plume trailing in its wake. "Sea Dog holding."

"Jackhammer ETA six minutes."

He glanced back at the building and saw the clusters of white blobs scattered around the room. Most were still; only two blobs seemed to ebb and ooze as they moved across the room.

———

Lying still, Pablo Guerrero opened his eyes and saw the American kneeling by Alberto. Even in the dim light, he could see that Alberto was dead, his lifeless eyes staring vacantly at nothing. President Magaña—a puppet of los gringos—was holding a rifle while the American searched Alberto's pockets. *Hijo de Puta!* Guerrero swore silently as he glanced at the floor around him, searching for the cattle prod or a gun, something, anything. They had killed his daughter! His Carolina! They should be on their knees begging for his mercy! But he had underestimated them, and now all he saw around him were the bodies of his men. He reached behind him, blindly searching. Then the American stood, and he saw the cattle prod on the floor next to Alberto. The American turned his head, and Guerrero lay still again. The American spoke—said something that he couldn't hear—and the Puppet answered. Whatever the American had said hadn't been directed at him. He slid his hand behind him again and felt something at the edge of his reach. As his fingertips slid over the surface he could feel the cold metal of the gun.

———

Richter stared at Guerrero for a second. The man was coming to. He glanced back at the cattle prod but decided against it. They couldn't carry an unconscious man, and there was no way they were leaving Guerrero here. He was responsible for too many deaths, too much suffering not only in Mexico but in the U.S. as well. If they left him here, he would only continue to wage his war of terror against the Mexican people until the country collapsed. And even though Fogel was in custody, Guerrero had already demonstrated that the border meant nothing to him and that American blood could be spilled just as easily as Mexican. If they left him here, it was only a matter of time before there was another attack. With the possibility that Guerrero might have access to cesium, it was a risk he couldn't take. He turned to Magaña.

"We need to tie him up." He lifted his injured arm slightly. "You'll need to do it."

Magaña nodded, then slung the rifle over his shoulder. Richter moved to the side so he could watch the door and Guerrero at the same time. As the Mexican President picked up a section of rope from the floor, Guerrero sprang.

CHAPTER SIXTY-NINE

Richter glanced at the door, then, sensing movement, spun his head in time to see Guerrero lunging for the gun. Richter stepped forward and shoved the still-bent Mexican president, sending him sprawling across the floor. He spun and brought his own weapon up as Guerrero rolled over. Richter centered his sights on Guerrero's head then, at the last second, shifted his aim. There was a flash of orange flame from Guerrero's gun, and Richter staggered as something slammed into his hip, a white-hot flash of pain shooting down his leg. He squeezed the trigger, stumbled, then adjusted his aim and squeezed once more.

———

What were they doing? The sensor wondered as he stared at the police truck. The truck had stopped. Then the reverse lights flickered on and the truck began to back up. A moment later, it turned and began to drive back down the dirt road toward the slaughterhouse.

"Target Four has turned around," he radioed. "The police are coming back."

"Roger, Sea Dog. I need a solution on Target Four again. Target Four is priority."

"Target Four is sparkle. Target Four is priority.

"Copy Sea Dog. Engage on my command."

"Copy, Jackhammer. Sea Dog holding. Waiting for your command."

He glanced at the pilot. The pilot nodded. They were ready.

———

Richter glanced down at his leg. He touched his hip and, with a sudden intake of breath, yanked his hand away. He took a deep breath, then gingerly felt his hip again. The wound seemed to be bleeding freely but it appeared that the bullet had only grazed him. Despite that, the pain was intense. He wiped his bloody hand on his chest.

President Magaña slowly lifted himself off the floor, and Richter could see that his chin was scraped raw and he was bleeding from a cut over his eye. Magaña wiped the blood from his eyes then picked up his gun. He looked up at Richter and nodded, signaling that he was okay. Richter turned back to Guerrero. Hands clamped over his knee, the cartel boss was writhing in agony on the floor.

"We need to get out of here now," Richter said. "Cover me," he added then nodded toward Guerrero. "I'll get him."

———

"Jackhammer ETA three minutes," the sensor heard in his earphones.

"Copy," the sensor said as he watched the police truck crest a small rise. The truck slowed and he could see two men in back leaning over the cab with their weapons trained forward. The other two were squatted by the sides, their weapons trained through the rails.

———

Limping, Richter dragged a screaming Guerrero across the floor. As Magaña led the way, he struggled around the bodies and stopped by the door. He peered through the small glass window. There was a short hallway that led to the foyer. On one side were two doors—offices, Richter guessed—and on the other, a third door with the same small window as the one he was peering through. That led, he assumed, to the cutting room. Straight ahead, there was a set of glass doors that led to a foyer. Outside, he reasoned, was a parking lot. HeHe leaned to the side for a better view when he saw it: a body lying on the floor just on the other side of the door. He stared for a second. The figure was hooded, and the hands were bound together from behind.

"Watch him," Richter said, gesturing toward Guerrero. "I'll be back in a second."

He stepped into the hallway. With one eye on the doors that opened to the foyer, he bent down cautiously and checked the pulse of the man on the floor. The man was still alive. But who he was and why the cartel guards had brought him here was anyone's guess. With one hand he began tugging on the hood. The hooded man seemed to understand what he was trying to do and lifted his head.

Richter pulled the hood off and stared down into the grinning face of Terry Fogel.

————

"LZ Whiskey in sight!" the crew chief shouted above the engine noise.

The lieutenant glanced around the cabin, at the hard faces of his men, locked and loaded, ready to earn their pay. He braced himself as the helicopter shuddered, then glanced up at the crew chief. The crew chief stared back then nodded once. No words needed, the message was clear. *Good hunting.*

————

Richter stood in the foyer and glanced out the outside door. The foyer was recessed; the building jutting out on both sides, an overhang creating a short, covered walkway outside. Straight ahead, in the narrow sliver of the parking lot lit by floodlights, sat a battered pickup truck and, next to it, a white SUV. The vehicles were parked in front of a chain-link fence that stretched out of sight on both sides. He pressed a button on the key fob he had taken from one of Guerrero's men and heard a chirp as the taillights on the SUV flashed. Holding his gun ready, he waited for more cartel guards to come running. When none came, he propped both the inner and outer doors open, then returned to the hallway where Magaña was guarding both Guerrero and Fogel. Guerrero, who had been moan-

ing loudly, was now quiet, and Richter realized that he had passed
out from the pain. Fogel was quiet too, but his eyes, Richter noticed, took in everything. He stared down at Fogel.

"Get up," he ordered.

Fogel grinned. "Ah, now. That's a little difficult, what with my
hands behind my back." He made no effort to hide the singsong lilt
of his Belfast accent.

Richter pointed his gun at the Irish terrorist. "Get up," he ordered again.

Fogel stared back for a second then rolled onto his belly. He
pulled his knees below him and a second later he was standing.

"Wasn't as difficult as I thought." He grinned.

Richter ignored the taunt and slipped the hood back over Fogel's
head.

While President Magaña stood watch in the foyer, Richter led
Fogel out to the covered walkway. He scanned the parking lot and,
satisfied that it was empty, led Fogel over to the SUV. Moments
later, after he had Fogel strapped into the backseat, he glanced back
at the building, at the Mexican president standing in the foyer,
and at the forty yards of asphalt and ten yards of covered walkway
that separated them. A long way to drag an unconscious man, he
thought. He climbed into the front seat of the SUV.

Ten seconds later, he pulled the SUV in front of the covered
walkway and left it idling as he went to get Guerrero.

———

The sensor saw the man exit the building, leading the hooded prisoner to the SUV. He felt the hairs on the back of his neck stand up,
but the angle was wrong and he couldn't see the man's face. *Could
it be him?*

He glanced back at the other screen and watched the truck as it
crested a small hill, now only one hundred yards from the slaughterhouse. Unexpectedly, the truck slowed then stopped and the men in
the back hopped out. The truck began to move again, the four cops
jogging behind.

The sensor's eyes shot back to the first screen. The SUV pulled up to the covered walkway and the man climbed out. He was below the canopy before the sensor could get a good look at his face.

His eyes shot back to the second screen. Suddenly the truck began to accelerate toward the gate.

———

"Sea Dog. Engage Target Four now."

The sensor glanced over at the pilot; the pilot's thumb moved over the switch on his control stick.

"Fox One," the pilot called as he pressed the button.

As the Hellfire missile released from the pylon, its rocket ignited, and it streaked away from the Reaper toward the truck five miles away.

———

Richter reached down and grabbed Guerrero by the arms. With a hiss of breath, he tried to ignore the pain in his own arm and hip as he dragged Guerrero to the foyer, leaving a bloody trail in the hallway. His own blood or Guerrero's, he could no longer tell the difference. Magaña stepped out of the way as Richter dragged the still unconscious Guerrero through the foyer out to the walkway. Richter paused to catch his breath when he heard Magaña cough. It was an odd sound, and the hairs rose on the back of Richter's neck. The Mexican President coughed again, his bloody spit splattering on the glass doors. Richter dropped Guerrero, hurried over and grabbed Magaña by the elbow.

"Are you okay?"

"I think I bit my tongue," Magaña said, his voice thick.

Richter studied him for a second.

Suddenly, the Mexican President slumped against the door. In the dim light of the walkway, Richter noticed the blood on Magaña's lips, seeping out of his mouth, running down his chin. It was frothy and bright red. *Oh Shit!* He slipped his hand inside the Mexican President's suit coat, sliding it over his chest. Below his arm, he found the sticky wet spot. The bullet that had grazed his hip must have hit Magaña, he realized. The president gasped, began to wheeze then his eyes rolled into the back of his head and he slumped forward into Richter's arms.

Forgetting Guerrero, Richter dragged a now unconscious Magaña out to the light of the parking lot next to the idling SUV. He gently laid him on the ground. Magaña was struggling to breathe. Richter suspected the bullet had punctured his lung. He glanced up at the SUV, wondering if there was a first aid kit when he heard the growl of another engine. He turned and saw the lights of the truck racing toward the gate.

———

The sensor spotted the two men, one dragging the other into the parking lot. The injured man's eyes were closed. He zoomed into the man's face. *Oh, shit!* he thought as he instinctively reached for the joystick, moving the laser target out into the field, knowing as he did so that it was too late.

Fuck!

———

Ignoring the truck, Richter turned back to Magaña. The president's breath came in short wheezes. He slid his hand up the president's neck, finding a weak pulse. Then he slid his hand back to the blood-soaked area below Magaña's arm. *Damn*, he cursed. He had to stop the bleeding, now! He stood, hoping he would find something he could use in the SUV, when he was suddenly slammed from behind as a bright flash illuminated the night.

CHAPTER SEVENTY

"Ten seconds!" the crew chief shouted.

The lieutenant stood and signaled his men. Moments later, the Knighthawk suddenly pulled up and the lieutenant saw the building pass directly below them as the helicopter settled into a hover over the parking lot. As two ropes dropped from the helicopter, he glanced down. In fractions of a second, his eyes took in the lot, the burning police truck, the smashed gate, the building, and the two men lying in the parking lot next to the SUV.

"Go! Go! Go!" the crew chief yelled.

One by one, the SEALs began to fast rope out the door. Four men from his helicopter would secure the perimeter while the other four—himself included—would breach the front door. Six SEALs from the second helicopter would fast rope into the truck lot on the other side and breach the doors on the loading dock. Then the second helicopter would deploy two more SEALs to the roof.

"Seven!" the crew chief yelled.

The lieutenant reached out and grabbed the rope.

"Eight!" the crew chief yelled again, clapping the lieutenant's shoulder as the lieutenant stepped out of the chopper.

————

Richter opened his eyes and squinted up at the face above him. He tried to sit, but a hand gently pushed him back down.

"Easy, sir," the man said. "You're safe now."

Confused, Richter stared at the man's face.

The man smiled. "I'm just getting an IV set up. I'll give you something for the pain in a minute."

Richter shook his head. "No," he said, his voice hoarse. "Where are the others?" he asked.

The corpsman glanced over his shoulder, shouted something.

"Where is the president?" Richter asked.

The corpsman stared at him, and Richter tried to read the man's eyes. Suddenly, he felt himself being lifted, and they were moving. The corpsman jogged alongside, holding the IV bag aloft. He heard the *whop whop whop* of the chopper and closed his eyes as the dust swirled over him. Suddenly, he felt a wave wash over him and knew right away that it wasn't the downdraft of the rotors. He opened his mouth to curse at the corpsman but no sound came out. He felt another wave and then his body was sinking. *Goddamn it!* He tried to fight it but he began to fall, spiraling down, into the blackness.

———

He woke again sometime later and realized they were airborne. In the dim red light of the chopper, he turned his head, searching. Magaña lay on the litter next to him. Even in the dim red light, Richter could see the ashen face, the vacant stare. A soldier wiped the blood off the Mexican President's cheek then gently closed his eyes.

Richter stared at the body, too dazed to feel anything. He heard a voice in his ear and turned.

"I'm sorry, sir. He didn't make it."

Confused, Richter stared at the new face.

"I'm Lieutenant Stolarz, sir." the SEAL shouted.

Richter nodded as the lieutenant filled in some of the blanks. The Mexican President had been shot. He was dead by the time the SEALs had found him. His brain too foggy to process the news, Richter shook his head.

"We'll be landing in five minutes," Stolarz told him.

Richter wanted to ask where, when the lieutenant frowned.

"Sir?" he shouted. "The six bodies inside?"

It took Richter a moment before he realized what the lieutenant meant.

"Cartel strongmen," he said softly, his words slurred. He nodded toward Magaña. "We took them out."

The lieutenant stared at him for a moment then shook his head. "Hot damn, sir!"

The chopper jerked once, shuddered, then suddenly dropped. Richter felt woozy. A moment later the chopper settled. He turned to the lieutenant.

"Guerrero?"

Lieutenant Stolarz grinned. "You bagged yourself a big one, sir!" He gestured toward the front of the cabin, and Richter craned his neck to see. A now conscious Guerrero was being tended by another corpsman.

"Where's the other one?"

"Sir?"

"There was one more," Richter insisted.

Lt. Stolarz shook his head. "No, sir. Just you three."

There was a sudden change in pitch and Richter felt a shudder and then a sinking feeling again as the helicopter began to descend.

CHAPTER SEVENTY-ONE

"How's the arm?" the president asked as he sat.

Richter held it up, opening and closing his fist several times. "Almost back to normal," he responded. He had torn the ligaments in his shoulder, but thankfully that hadn't required surgery. Although it still twinged now and then, over the last six weeks he had regained full range of motion, or mostly anyway. His hip too had healed; the bullet that had grazed it had done little damage. President Magaña, unfortunately, hadn't been so lucky.

President Kendall smiled. "I'm glad to hear it." After a moment, the smile vanished. They shared a look. "We were lucky," he said. "Damn lucky."

Richter nodded. "We were, sir." But, he thought, although Guerrero was in custody, the threat hadn't gone away. Terry Fogel had disappeared. Review of the video captured by the drone told part of the story. In the chaos that followed the missile strike, a figure could be seen climbing out of the SUV and scrambling along the side of the building where he disappeared. Despite the handcuffs, Fogel had somehow made it out of the SUV and then had avoided not only drawing the drone crew's attention but detection by the Navy SEAL Team as well. A massive international manhunt was underway, but where he was now was anyone's guess.

On a positive note, Richter reminded himself, the FBI had painstakingly traced Fogel's movements over the few months before the bombing, identifying several accomplices in the process. Two weeks earlier, they had arrested a handful of men. Questioning had led agents to a self-storage locker near Buffalo where two canisters of cesium had been discovered.

Pablo Guerrero was in Guantanamo. While the Mexican government planned to try him in absentia for the massacre in Mexico City, he continued to sit in solitary confinement, staring vacantly at the wall. He too, refused to talk, enhanced interrogation techniques having little effect on him. He began to lose weight, absently picking at his food, eating little and pushing the rest away. Doctors had finally concluded that he had lost the will to live. The interrogations had stopped; he was put on a suicide watch, and doctors kept a cautious eye on him while intelligence agents and law enforcement officials decided what to do. Meanwhile, he had been indicted in federal court in Manhattan on numerous charges related to the attack on New York. However, as far as both governments were concerned, he wouldn't be leaving Guantanamo for a long time.

The cleanup in New York City continued. Testing showed that little cesium had escaped the confines of the station and the tunnels. However, the inside of Grand Central Terminal and the train and subway tunnels were still highly radioactive. The debate on what to do with the terminal raged on. While many pushed for closing the station permanently, ultimately knocking it down and hauling the contaminated rubble away—a task that would take years—Metro-North had resumed a limited service. Trains now dropped passengers off at 125th Street and the city had adjusted its bus routes to handle the volume. Further, a separate bus service had been established to transport commuters from the northern suburbs to Penn Station. The exodus that everyone had predicted hadn't materialized. Life for New Yorkers, by and large, continued with many insisting that they would never leave. The large shrouds draped over Grand Central and the crews in radiation suits streaming in and out were a grim reminder of the risk. So were the radiation pagers. They had suddenly become as ubiquitous as cell phones for the many residents and commuters who refused to abandon the city.

Despite President Alameda's initial protest, he had continued efforts to shut down the cartels. Privately, he asked President Kendall to expand Operation Night Stalker, agreeing to place the names of thirty-seven narco-traffickers on a kill list. Various factions tried to seize control of the drug routes, but with Guerrero out of power and with an increase in drone strikes the trade had splintered. The choke hold the cartels had held on Mexican society began to show signs of slipping, although the fight was far from over.

Alameda had established a special commission to determine what to do with the vast tracks of cartel property that had been seized. Proposals were being made for sections of arable land south of Ciudad Juarez. If approved, the program would divide and award the land to the indigenous population in an experiment to try and compensate the families that had been torn apart by the violence over the years. The government would then use funds from seized cartel bank accounts to begin constructing housing and to provide the seed money needed to the new farming communities. If the experiment worked, it would be expanded to other sites around the country.

After an elaborate state funeral, Magaña had been buried in his home state of Michoacán. Neither Richter nor President Kendall had attended due to security concerns. Maybe in a few months, Richter thought, he would make the trip, meet with Magaña's family and tell them what really happened. He would tell Magaña's children how much he admired their father.

Wendy Tillman's body, along with those of the slain Secret Service agents had been returned home. Richter had attended each funeral. Tillman's had been a private event in a suburb of Boston. It had been her childhood home, something Richter had only learned after her death. When he met her family, he realized how little he had known of the woman who had given her life protecting him. Tillman's death was a stark reminder of how fragile life was.

The president's voice interrupted his thoughts.

"I've given this a lot of thought." President Kendall paused a moment. "I'm going to appoint Jessica Williams as National Security Advisor."

"I think that's a wise choice, sir." Richter responded. He had told the president a week earlier that he would not object if someone else was given the job. He was, after all, only serving in an acting capacity.

The president smiled, then leaned forward. His face became serious. "I'm hoping you'll stick around, though."

Richter was silent a moment. He had been expecting this. "What are you thinking, sir?"

"How does Special Assistant to the President sound?"

Richter frowned, momentarily confused.

"You would be my advisor," the president explained then chuckled. "The constitution was silent as to what departments and functions make up the executive branch. That was left for the president to decide, so I have a lot of latitude here." He smiled again then became serious. "As I think you know, finding someone who can me give unbiased advice, someone who can put the country first and not their own ambitions, is a rare thing in Washington."

Richter was silent for a moment. "I would have to speak to Patty first, sir."

The president nodded. "You would. But as I said, I have a lot of latitude here. I'm sure that I could find something important, challenging, and meaningful for someone with Patty's skills and credentials. Something at the State Department perhaps. Or on the congressional staff of someone we know and trust. Or even here."

Richter nodded.

"And if not," the president continued, "Georgetown University is close by." He chuckled. "I think I might also have some pull there too."

Richter nodded again. "I'll need some time to think about it, sir."

"I'm sure you will." David Kendall smiled again.

He paused and Richter could see the question in his raised eyebrows.

"So, Puerto Rico's nice I hear."

Richter grinned. Why was he surprised?

CHAPTER SEVENTY-TWO

Richter sat by the side of the pool, his feet dangling in the cool water.

"Aren't you coming in?" Patty asked with a smile.

"I thought I would just sit here and admire you," he responded with a grin.

She splashed him, and he held his hands up in mock protest.

"Okay! Okay! I'm coming."

He pushed himself off the side into the water, and a second later she was in his arms. They swam and played in the water for some time, oblivious to the people around them. Patty flung her arms around his shoulders and kissed him.

"Come on!" she said. "It's five o'clock somewhere."

He grinned. It was only noon, but Alan Jackson and Jimmy Buffet had just finished telling everyone that the bar was open. As Richter and Patty swam over to the pool bar, Buster Poindexter's voice came over the speakers next, telling the crowd by the pool that he was *feelin' hot, hot, hot*. Taking stools in the shade, they ordered piña coladas then spent the next hour sipping their drinks and talking. Patty's face was animated as she told him a story about her childhood, her first kiss at an eighth grade dance. She laughed, telling him that it had been a disaster. She had waited the whole evening for the boy to kiss her. Then when he finally got up the nerve, the lights had come on; the boy had turned beet red when they found themselves in the middle of the dance floor with everyone watching.

"Now it's your turn," Patty said as she stroked his leg below the water. It was her idea that they trade stories of their past. "I'll even give you some time to think about it," she said as she pushed herself off the stool.

"Where are you going?" he asked.

She leaned over and kissed him. "To the ladies' room," she whispered. She turned, hesitated, then turned back and kissed him again. "And stay away from those girls," she warned, gesturing toward the three coeds in bikinis at the end of the bar.

"Who me?" he shrugged sheepishly. The young ladies had been glancing down the bar at him. He hadn't realized that Patty had noticed too.

"Yes you." Patty shot him a warning look then laughed as she made her way to the stairs.

He smiled back. The three women, he noticed out of the corner of his eye, watched Patty as she walked up the tiled pathway. A handful of men in lounge chairs glanced up as well. He was one lucky man, he told himself.

He sighed and took another sip. It was their second day at the small resort in Puerto Rico. They planned to stay a week, swimming and walking along the beaches, shopping, touring the old fort and the old town—doing all of the things that tourists do. Then in the evenings, they would have dinner in Old San Juan followed by dancing, perhaps, or maybe a show.

He twirled the straw in his glass. Sitting there, in the pool with a tropical drink in his hand, the events in Mexico now seemed a long time ago. But the scars were just beginning to heal, he knew as he subconsciously flexed his shoulder. Both inside and out.

Next week, when they returned, he and Patty had an appointment at the White House, an opportunity to see exactly what President Kendall had in mind. Surprisingly, Patty had agreed to the meeting, was looking forward to it, in fact. Then there was Pat Monahan, who had made several overtures, wanting to know if he would consider coming back to the FBI. And on top of that, there was the phone call from the Secretary of Homeland Security that he had yet to return. The word must have gotten out and, he thought, it was reassuring to have options. Still, he wondered. Would he and Patty be happy in Washington?

He spotted Patty walking back down the path. That was the question, wasn't it? Would he and Patty be happy in Washington? He wasn't sure. But sitting there with a piña colada in hand, with the warm tropical breezes blowing in off the ocean, the smell of sun-tan lotion and the sounds of a steel drum band in the air and Patty coming down the path to the pool, he decided that it was something that he could worry about later. Right now, he had more important things on his mind. He lifted his drink in salute and Patty smiled back.

For a preview of *The Devil's Due*,
L.D. Beyer's historic thriller, read on....

The Devil's Due

County Limerick, Ireland
December 1920

It was such an odd thought for a man about to die, but, still, it filled my head. Will I hear the gun? Will I feel the bullet? I stared at the floor of the barn, the dirt soaked with my own blood. The earth was cold against my cheek and I could hear the pitter-patter of rain on the roof. God pissin' on us again. Only in Ireland. The lights of the oil lamps danced a waltz across the wall and, in the flickering light, I saw a pair of boots, then trousers. Nothing more, but I knew it was Billy. One of my eyes was already swollen shut and I couldn't lift my head from the dirt to see the rest of him. I didn't have to; those were Billy's boots.

"Fuckin' traitor!"

The boot slammed into my ribs, and I heard myself cry out. I coughed, spit out more blood, and tried to catch my breath, but the boot came again. Through one eye, I watched the feet, the legs, dancing with the light, then the flash of Billy's boot striking me in the chest, the stomach, the arms. I heard the thuds, felt my body jump, felt each jolt like lightning, sending agonizing bolts of pain coursing through my body. Unseen hands began to pull me down into the darkness. Yet still I wondered. Will I hear the gun? Will I feel it? Probably not, I thought. A bright flash then, what? Nothing,

I guess. Blackness? I sighed and waited for the bullet, wondering how I would know when it finally came.

There would be no Jesus waiting for me on the other side; that was for sure. No Mary, no saints, no choir of angels. Good Irish Catholic lad that I was, I had done enough in my short life to know that heaven wasn't in the cards. Not for me, anyway. My head exploded in a flash of colors as Billy's boot slammed into my temple. Probably just the blackness, I decided. Maybe that wasn't so bad.

It was strange, but I realized that I wasn't afraid anymore. Not of death, certainly. Billy had beaten that out of me. I wasn't afraid of hell either. Despite all that I had done—and what happened two days ago was sure to seal my fate—I wasn't sure I believed in the Church's view of hell. Seven hundred years of oppression under the British was hell enough. Eternal damnation, I suspected, was in the here and now, in the pains and tragedies of everyday life. And, surely, I was in pain. Billy had seen to that. Pain and regret were all I felt now.

I suppose any man about to die has regrets, and I had my share. A sudden sadness overwhelmed me when I realized that I would never see Kathleen again. My Kathleen.

I don't know how long I laid there with Billy kicking me, cursing me, calling me a spy, a traitor. It didn't matter what I said; he didn't believe me. At some point I stopped feeling the kicks, stopped feeling the pain, and surrendered to the blackness. Maybe I was already dead and didn't know it.

Then from the darkness, I felt a hand on my face, surprisingly gentle, brushing the hair out of my eyes. Kathleen? Then a hiss.

"Oh Jesus, Frankie! What has he done to you?"

Liam?

Hands grabbed me below the arms and lifted me up, my own hands and feet still bound to the chair. I screamed and coughed up more blood, my body wracked with spasms. Surely I had a few broken ribs thanks to Billy's boot. I squinted through the tears and there was Liam, his own eyes wet. What was he doing here? Had they sent him—my closest friend—to put the bullet in me?

My head hung limp, then I felt Liam's gentle hands on my chin. Through one eye, I watched as he dipped the cloth in the pail and began to wipe my face. I gasped when he got to my nose. Liam pulled the cloth away, stared at it for a second, his face a grimace. The cloth was dark red; stained by my own blood. With a disgusted look, Liam dropped it in the pail.

"Do you want some water, Frankie?"

Not waiting for an answer, he held the cup to my cracked and swollen lips. I coughed again and most of the water ran down my neck to join the blood on my shirt. The little I drank tasted of copper.

"Jesus, Liam," I hissed. "Is it a bath you're giving me or a drink?"

Liam just shook his head.

"I thought you were one of us, Frankie."

I coughed again and squinted through the pain. "I am, Liam." I coughed once more, my voice hoarse. "I am."

He shook his head again, and I could see the pain in his eyes.

"That's not what they're saying, Frankie. Three of our boys dead…" His voice trailed off, his eyes telling me what he couldn't say. How could you do it, Frankie?

"And now the British have our names," he continued choking on the words. He sighed and wiped his eyes. "They'll hunt us down. Is that what you want?" His eyes pleaded with me, and I knew what he wanted to say but didn't. Do you want to see me with a bullet in my head too, Frankie?

"Liam…" I coughed again—a spasm—bright, hot lights of pain slicing through me.

He shook his head sadly. "I thought you were one of us, Frankie." There was a hurt in his voice that matched my own pain. How could you betray me? his eyes seemed to ask. He sighed, dipped the cloth in the pail, then wiped my nose again. "I thought you were one of us…"

"Liam…"

He leaned close and whispered in my ear. "For the love of God, Frankie! He's going to kill you anyway. You know that. Why don't you tell him what he wants?" He sniffed then turned away and wiped his eyes. "I can't watch this anymore."

"I didn't do it, Liam."

He stared at me for a moment then leaned close again. "Ah, Jesus, Frankie. Don't you see? It doesn't matter. You know that. If they suspect you're an informant, you're an informant."

He was right, but still I protested.

"I swear on my father's grave, I didn't do it, Liam."

"But you're the only one still alive?"

A small doubt, but his eyes, like his words, told me it was hopeless. If Liam didn't believe me, Billy and the others surely wouldn't. And why should they? It was supposed to be a simple operation. But something had gone wrong—terribly wrong—and now here I was, waiting for the bullet. Better that it would be coming from one of my own than from the fuckin' British. For some reason, that made me feel better.

"I know, Liam," I wheezed. "I know. But I didn't do it."

Liam shook his head, unsure what to do.

"Did you write your letter?" he finally asked, choking on the words.

My letter. My last chance to speak to Kathleen, to tell her in my own words what had happened. Billy hadn't given me the chance, though.

"Just tell Kathleen I love her." I looked up into my friend's eyes. "You'll do that for me won't you, Liam?"

He nodded slowly. "Aye." He paused, his eyes telling me he expected more. "And your mam?"

My mam. What could I say to a woman I hadn't spoken to in three years. Would she even care?

Suddenly, there were shouts from outside, and I flinched at the sharp crack of a rifle. This was followed by two more, then shouting again. I stared up at Liam, unsure what it meant. Before I could ask, the clatter of a machine gun filled the air.

"Oh, Jesus!" Liam screamed. "It's the Tans!"

A fear I never knew gripped me, and I forgot about the pain of Billy's boot. The Black and Tans! For the last year, the scourge of the British army, wearing their mismatched uniforms, had sacked and looted our towns and terrorized our people. Ex-servicemen, soldiers who had seen time on the Western front—and many who had seen the inside of a British jail—they had been sent to supplement the ranks of the Peelers, the Royal Irish Constabulary. These were war-hardened men, more than one who had been languishing in prison for one crime or another. And now, Britain had cleaned out their jails and sent their criminals to be our police. In April, they had gone on a rampage in Limerick; in December, they'd burnt the city of Cork.

"Liam!" I pleaded.

Before he could answer, bullets tore through the windows of the barn, chipping stone, ripping into the wood. The cows and sheep screeched in a panic, slamming into the cart and threatening to finish what Billy had started. Then one of the oil lamps was hit, and seconds later the hay was on fire. Liam slammed into me, and I howled in pain when I landed back on the blood-soaked dirt. He was screaming as he frantically clawed at the ropes that bound my hands. The fire raged as chips and splinters flew. Soon the sparks hit the ceiling and the thatch began to smolder, the sheep and cows shrieking all the while.

"Come on, Frankie!" Liam screamed as he struggled to untie me.

I felt his arms pulling, dragging me through the dirt to the cow door in the back. He kicked it open, peeked outside, then pulled me through.

"For fuck's sake, Frankie! I'll not be dragging you the whole way! Get up! Run!"

I struggled to my feet, the emotion and adrenaline masking the pain. I limped after Liam across the field, scrambled over the stone wall, falling once and crying out in pain. But somehow, I got up and kept going. Behind me, the guns went silent, but the screech of the animals, the shouts and the sounds of motorcars carried across the fields. I lost sight of Liam, knowing he'd done his part in setting me free. Now I was on my own.

I kept running, unsure where to go, just wanting to get away. But I couldn't run all night, not with broken ribs and the life nearly beat out of me.

As the sounds died behind me, I stopped for a moment to catch my breath. Hands on my knees, I looked back across the field, expecting to see British soldiers, or worse, Billy. But in the darkness I saw nothing. I turned again then hesitated. Finally, I realized there was only one place I could go.

Copyright © 2016 by L.D. Beyer

Acknowledgements

Writers lament the solitary life, but for most novels, the process of taking the beginnings of an idea that exists only in the author's mind to a completed manuscript and then on to a bound and printed book is a team event. *An Eye For An Eye* would have never been possible without the help and encouragement of many along the way. My thanks goes out to all of you.

For Jennifer Stolarz, my friend and first-round editor extraordinaire. What else can I say but thank you. For Allison and Jeff and for Chuck Mullins, for willingly reading my early drafts. For Pat Galizio, for your never-failing friendship and support. For Andy Yin and Kevin Hoffman, longtime friends, who helped me get the Metro-North scenes right. For Sergeant Bill Leahy, New York State Police, for helping me understand how local, state, and federal officials work together to protect the greatest city in the world from the constant threat of terrorism. For Chris England, Lieutenant FDNY—one of New York City's Bravest—for helping me get the disaster response scenes right.

In addition to the expert advice I received from Bill and Chris, the following sources were extremely helpful to complete the picture.

Report from Engine Company 82 by Dennis Smith and *The Last Man Out: Life on the Edge at Rescue 2 Firehouse* by Tom Downey, highlight the incredible bravery and humility of the men and women who willingly put their lives on the line every day. Thank you to everyone who wears bunker gear and carries the irons.

Securing the City by Christopher Dickey showcases the extraordinary measures the New York City Police Department and city officials take to protect New York from terrorism. Thank you for your tireless efforts to keep us safe.

Killing Pablo by Mark Bowden and *The Cell* by John Miller provide great insight into the war on drugs and the fight against organized crime. For good measure, I also watched several classic movies, including *The French Connection* and *Goodfellas*.

SWAT Teams by Robert Snow helped me better understand Emergency Response and Special Weapons and Tactics.

Last Best Chance, a well-produced documentary by the Nuclear Threat Initiative, paints an all-too-realistic scenario of the threat dirty bombs pose to America.

Once again, the technical guidance I have received has been outstanding, and any errors are mine and mine alone.

For Faith Black Ross, my editor, and for Lindsey Andrews, who did an outstanding job on the cover. Thank you both.

Finally, for Kaitlyn, Kyle, Matthew and Mona, as always, none of this would have been possible without your belief in me.

L.D. BEYER is the author of two novels, both part of the Matthew Richter Thriller Series. His first book, *In Sheep's Clothing*, was published in 2015 and reached the #4 spot on the bestseller list for Political Thrillers on Amazon Kindle.

Beyer spent over twenty-five years in the corporate world, climbing the proverbial corporate ladder. In 2011, after years of extensive travel, too many missed family events, a half dozen relocations—including a three-year stint in Mexico—he realized it was time for a change. He chose to chase his dream of being a writer and to spend more time with his family.

He is an avid reader and, although he primarily reads thrillers, his reading list is somewhat eclectic. You're more likely to find him with his nose in a good book instead of sitting in front of the TV.

Beyer lives in Michigan with his wife and three children. In addition to writing and reading, he enjoys cooking, hiking, biking, working out, and the occasional glass of wine.

If you enjoyed this book, please consider writing a review on Amazon, Goodreads, or the platform of your choice.

To learn more about the author and for the latest information on new releases and events, go to http://ldbeyer.com.

52096159R00211

Made in the USA
Lexington, KY
16 May 2016